Viking Veng

**Book 11 in the
Dragon Heart Series
By
Griff Hosker**

Published by Sword Books Ltd 2015
Copyright © Griff Hosker First Edition
The author has asserted their moral right under the Copyright, Designs and Patents Act, 1988, to be identified as the author of this work.
All Rights reserved. No part of this publication may be reproduced, copied, stored in a retrieval system, or transmitted, in any form or by any means, without the prior written consent of the copyright holder, nor be otherwise circulated in any form of binding or cover other than that in which it is published and without a similar condition being imposed on the subsequent purchaser.
A CIP catalogue record for this title is available from the British Library.

Cover by Design for Writers

Prologue

My daughter Kara and my galdramenn, Aiden, were married in Cyninges-tūn, my stronghold in the Land of the Dragon.. Cyninges-tūn was my home and it was theirs. It was a place where we were safe; protected by the mountains and the Water. Both had seemed destined to end their lives as powerful wizard and volva but the Norns had determined otherwise and now my daughter was carrying Aiden's child. They had lain together and now a grandchild grew within my daughter. My people were both awed and overjoyed by the union. What kind of powerful shaman would come from such a union? The universal opinion was that it would be a girl. Normally such prognostications would come from Kara or Aiden themselves but the chatter in Cyninges-tūn was only filled with suggestions for the name of a girl. Of course we all knew that the child would eventually name herself. I had been born Garth but by deeds I had become Dragonheart. My son had been born Arturus but he had become Wolf Killer. It was our way. How did one know what a tiny pink bundle would become? My recently born son had been called Gruffyd. It had been Brigid, my wife's choice, and I liked the name but when he grew who knew what he would be called. That would be decided by the Norns, the Weird Sisters who spun and plotted the lives of men.

The wedding of the two seemed to galvanise my people. There was purpose in their lives. This was exciting and it was a journey into the unknown. It was different from our normal lives. We had fought off enemies from the north of the old Roman wall and destroyed traitors from within who sought to take what was ours but we were stronger as a result. We had tried to live peacefully and use trade to prosper but that was not meant to be. We had young men who wished to go A-Viking. We would be true to our spirit. We would go raiding. **'The Heart of the Dragon'** would have her figurehead placed at her prow once more; my Ulfheonar would oil their mail and sharpen their swords and the wolves would fall amongst the sheep again.

Chapter 1

We had a full crew as we headed south past the islands of Man and Ynys Môn. We were not raiding the old Roman province of Britannia. We had heard, through those who traded with us from afar, of unrest in the Empire. There had been a time when we had feared the Empire. When Charlemagne ruled he had done so with an iron fist. Since his death, a couple of years earlier, his son Louis the Pious had been Emperor. He was not the strong man his father had been and many neighbours and subjugated people rebelled. He had deposed one of our allies, Seguin I Lupo, in an attempt to establish his authority. It had failed and his authority and grip on the rich Empire were not as strong as they had been.

We had suffered at the hands of Charlemagne. Now we would profit from his son's weakness. The Empire was rich. Its churches were full of treasure and it had long wide rivers up which we could sail. My men were keen for the adventure and, if I am honest, the chance of combat. Our home was secure and we could raid with impunity. Their lusty voices filled the air as they chanted while they rowed.

The storm was wild and the gods did roam
The enemy closed on the Prince's home
Two warriors stood on a lonely tower
Watching, waiting for hour on hour.
The storm came hard and Odin spoke
With a lightning bolt the sword he smote
Ragnar's Spirit burned hot that night
It glowed, a beacon shiny and bright
The two they stood against the foe
They were alone, nowhere to go
They fought in blood on a darkened hill
Dragon Heart and Cnut will save us still
Dragon Heart, Cnut and the Ulfheonar
Dragon Heart, Cnut and the Ulfheonar
The storm was wild and the Gods did roam
The enemy closed on the Prince's home
Two warriors stood on a lonely tower
Watching, waiting for hour on hour.
The storm came hard and Odin spoke
With a lightning bolt the sword he smote
Ragnar's Spirit burned hot that night
It glowed, a beacon shiny and bright
The two they stood against the foe
They were alone, nowhere to go
They fought in blood on a darkened hill

Dragon Heart and Cnut will save us still
Dragon Heart, Cnut and the Ulfheonar
Dragon Heart, Cnut and the Ulfheonar

I stood at the steerboard with my drekar captain, Erik Short Toe and Haaken One Eye, the leader of my Wolf Warriors, the Ulfheonar. Normally Haaken would have led the song and the chant for he had composed it but we had more than enough warriors to row our powerful war ship. We did not have many Ulfheonar these days but we had many young warriors who were keen to sail with us. Back in Úlfarrston my other drekar, **'Red Snake'** and **'Odin's Breath'** were preparing to follow us. We would come back richer and with tales to keep us warm in the winters to come.

"It will be strange not to have Aiden with us, Jarl Dragonheart."

I tapped the chest which was next to Erik our captain. "His charts are within and now that Erik has learned to read Aiden's marks and make marks of his own we will have my galdramenn in spirit. Besides I want him at home when the child is born."

"Aye; the young one will have incredible powers. Do you not fear such a powerful witch in your home?"

"The child comes from my daughter and I do not fear her and from Aiden who is like a son. What should I fear?"

"Remember the witch Angharad; she almost suborned Kara and turned her into a force against you."

I laughed, "I thought Wolf Killer was the one who still harboured such fears. No, my friend, the child will be a force for good. I believe that she will be the spirit of my wife Erika reborn."

Haaken nodded. He had lived with me through all my trials and tribulations. He was the questioning voice which made me examine my actions. He was good for me. I know not what I would do should he fall in battle. Both of us had outlived all those with whom we had first fought. The ones around us, even Snorri and Beorn the Scout were little older than my son, Wolf Killer. We were the grizzled warriors with whom we had first stood in the shield wall. Soon we would look to the younger warriors to take on our mantle. Wolf Killer would now be the protector of my land. He had fine warriors to guard the borders; my jarls: Ketil Windarsson, Sigtrygg Thrandson and Arne Thorkellstad.

Erik pointed to the southern sky; it was clear. "The Gods have given us fine weather. Considering it is so early in the year we are having a fine voyage."

Haaken shook his head, "Do not tempt the Norns, Erik. They have a nasty habit of upsetting well made plans."

"They will do what they will do, Haaken One Eye. You of all people know that you cannot foretell what they have planned for us. When they tire of playing with us we will be discarded. Until then we do what we do." I stretched, "And now I will rest and I will plan what we do when we reach Frankia"

As I lay down and closed my eyes I knew already what I would do. Seguin I Lupo had told me when I had last visited with him, before he had been deposed, that there was a mighty river which the men of Frankia called the Seine. It was like the Ouse, it wound deep into the heart of the rich land of Neustria. We could sail deep within the Empire and attack and raid at will. No nation and no Empire had a fighting ship like the drekar we sailed and all three of my drekar were the fastest afloat. Whilst on the water we had our own stronghold and could fend off all foes. We would use the river as a seax into the heart of the Franks and my Ulfheonar would wield that weapon.

When I awoke we were passing the wild Welsh coast. We had been allies in yesteryear but now they were enemies. My wife Brigid had come from these lands. We knew them well. Once we had passed them then we would have to negotiate the sharp teeth that were the savage coast of Corn Walum. I walked down my drekar. The sleep had refreshed me. The wind was coming from the west and my men rested. I saw those who were awake speaking with my handful of Ulfheonar. I knew that each of them yearned for the mail which my wolf warriors had won. You could see those who had experience for they had helmets and mail shirts. Most had been captured in the last battles with the men of Northumbria and Strathclyde. The new warriors hungered for such prizes. To gain the mail you had to kill the man. That was the first test for my young warriors.

I saw young Rolf Eriksson. He had incurred my wrath by fighting with Olaf Grimsson over a young girl the previous year. However since he had joined my crew he had changed. He had become a good warrior and now he sported a fine helmet, a mail coif over his shoulders and leather armour. Even now he was advising some of the younger warriors. That was how we prospered. We took raw young men and turned them into fighting machines. We were Vikings and we were unstoppable.

We pulled in, as darkness fell, in the islands called Syllingar Insula by the Romans. For Erik and my Ulfheonar they were a magical place. We had been lured into a cave on three occasions and we had met with an ancient witch who had foretold events in our lives. We did not fear her but we respected her. We often stopped at her island home but the only times we saw her were those times she chose to appear. This time was not one of those. The small bay was a safe anchorage and we ate hot food on shore.

"When will Asbjorn and the others arrive?"

"They should be sailing even now. It is young Olaf Grimmson's first voyage without Erik's guiding hand. I suspect that Snorri will watch him carefully and Asbjorn keep him close company."

Snorri was an Ulfheonar but he had been a ship's boy with Erik Short Toe. I had given him command of our newest drekar, **'Red Snake'**, captured from Magnus the Foresworn. They also had Cnut Cnutson on board. He was the only son of Cnut who had been with me when the Gods had touched my sword and made it the most feared weapon in the Viking world. It would be an experienced crew.

Erik laughed, "I would like to bet a silver piece that they reach the river in Frankia within a tide of us! Olaf will be keen to impress and Snorri will not wish to miss any treasure and booty we might find."

I guessed he might be right.

The next day would be the most dangerous part of our voyage. We would be sailing along the coast of Wessex and its king, King Egbert, hated my family. My son had run off with his young wife and, as if that was not enough of an insult, we had bloodied his nose more than once. It had given him an implacable hatred of all Vikings. He waged war on us whenever he could. I was not worried about his ships; we could easily defeat them but I knew that if we landed on his shores then he would move heaven and earth to get us. By the time we had passed Kent I breathed easier. It was dark when we left the coast of Britannia and headed across the water to Frankia. We knew the coast but not well. We had seen the River Seine but never travelled it. We were in uncharted territory and we had no galdramenn with us. We were Viking warriors and when the world was against you then all you could do was fight back and die hard!

We reached the mouth of the estuary before dawn. Even Haaken had to row against the current. Once the wind could hold us against the flow we stopped. Erik kept us in the middle of the enormous estuary. It was like a sea, it was so wide. We prepared our war faces. We had no idea what defences they had but before we could venture upstream we had to make sure our way home was secure. I smeared the red cochineal around my eyes and donned my helmet. One of the ship's boys, Thorir Svensson helped to attach my wolf cloak. Normally Aiden did that for me. These were my preparations for a raid, they were a ritual. We had smelled wood smoke from the northern bank and so, when we were ready Erik took us inshore. Dawn was breaking to the east. Those who lived close by would be opening their gates and be ready to go about their daily lives. They were in for a shock that morning.

The ship's boys raced ashore and tied us to the trees which were along the banks. We used plenty of rope. We did not know how much the river rose and fell with the tide. I left four of the younger warriors with Erik Short Toe to guard the drekar and then I sent Beorn the Scout off north to find a settlement. The Ulfheonar led; it was our right. The rest formed a band behind us. Most of them carried a spear. Some had good swords but most had one they had taken from a dead warrior. When they returned to Cyninges-tūn the first thing they would do would be to pay Bjorn Bagsecgson to make them a good one. I held Ragnar's Spirit and felt its power race through my body. I was ready.

When we reached the top of the bank we saw that there was another, smaller branch of the river. Across, on top of the other bank, lay the palisades of a small settlement. I saw the fishing boats drawn up on the small beach below the bank. It explained why they had not built on the other side. This would be easier for them to launch their boats. The river was narrow and looked shallow but I did not want to risk mailed men. Beorn The Scout awaited me. "It is but thirty paces across, Jarl Dragonheart."

I nodded, "Rolf Eriksson."

The young warrior eagerly ran towards me. "Yes, Jarl?"
"See if the river can be forded."
"Aye, Jarl."

He was about to run straight into the river. "Take off your helmet and coif in case you have to swim."

I could see he was reluctant to lay down his treasures but he complied and then he stepped into the water. I had chosen him because he was not the tallest of warriors. He only came to my shoulder. If he could ford it then we all could. He reached half way successfully. The water was just above his knees but, as he neared the other bank it came first to his waist and then to his chest. I feared we would not be able to ford and then he began to rise as the water became shallower and he stood on the other bank waving.

I was the jarl and I led my men across to Rolf. I handed him his coif and his helmet. "You have done well. Rolf Eriksson. I will not forget this."

Beorn overtook me and ran, with my Ulfheonar, towards the palisade. It was still dark but growing lighter moment by moment. I drew my sword and waved my men forward. There had been a time I would have scouted carefully but I now knew that surprise was a better weapon. No one could have seen our drekar approach and they would have no idea that Vikings were about. We headed up the bank toward the wooden walls. They had no sentries upon the wall but they had a shallow ditch which ringed it. It was not a defensive ditch but one to drain off water when it rained. I joined Beorn in the dead ground below the gate. He pointed behind me at the rising sun. He whispered, "The two guards left the gate not long ago. They will be going to open it."

I went back to the rest of my men. "Erik Wolf Claw, the Ulfheonar will secure the gate. Once it is open then bring the rest in."

Erik had failed the test to be an Ulfheonar but he was a good warrior. He stood a little prouder, "I will not let you down, Jarl Dragonheart."

Leaving him to organise the warriors I led the Ulfheonar to Beorn. With Snorri missing there were now just nine of us. It would be enough. I doubted that there would be warriors within and if there were then they were not very good ones for they had not kept a full watch. I knew that my warriors who remained at Cyninges-tūn would not relax their guard until dawn had fully broken and the gates been opened.

We moved forward. There was a bridge across the shallow drainage ditch. With no one on the walls we moved over the bridge and stood waiting for the gates to open. I stood with Haaken on one side and Olaf Leather Neck on the other. We were a formidable threesome. I knew that we would terrify them. Haaken wore an open helmet and had long since deigned to wear a patch. His empty eye socket terrified enemies. Olaf Leather Neck had the broadest shoulders and thickest neck of any man I had ever known. Added to that he had no front teeth. Unless they were made of stone we would have the advantage over the gate men once we burst in.

I heard voices approach. Had Aiden been with us he would have translated their words. As it was I just knew they were approaching the gate. I heard two voices. Behind us the sun's rays were now spreading west. I hefted my shield a little higher. I was in the middle and I would be the first one inside the walls. I held my sword slightly behind me. I heard the bar removed. I needed no words from my oathsworn. They had followed me often enough. When I heard the bar being rested against the walls I barged forward with my shield. In two strides I was inside. A sentry had been knocked to the ground. I skewered him with my sword. The other two sentries lay butchered by Haaken and Olaf and none had made a sound. We raced into the heart of the huts. Already people were emerging but it was not because of us. They had neither seen nor heard our entry but when they looked up from their tasks they did scream. They saw nine mailed warriors racing towards them. The women and children ran while the men looked for weapons. We fell upon them. Ragnar's Spirit spilled much Frankish blood that day.

When Erik Wolf Claw led the rest of my men to race through the oppidum it was all over. The women realised the futility of fleeing and they gathered their children around them like mother hens with their chicks. The old women wrung their hands and the old men glared hatred at us.

"Erik Wolf Claw secure the gates."

I took off my helmet. I was sweating already. I shook my head. It was a sign that I was getting old. In times past I would have barely noticed my exertions. Haaken said, "There will be no saga here, Jarl Dragonheart. My wife and the women of Cyninges-tūn could have captured this."

"I know, Haaken One Eye, but we now have a base. When our drekar arrive we can sail up the river and we can raid with impunity. No one can cut us off from the sea. I am happy. We will let the new men take what treasures they can find. Have some animals slaughtered. I am hungry."

I turned and saw Rolf Eriksson. "Here Rolf, help me off with my cloak."

He unfastened the wolf skin. "That was easy, Jarl."

"It will not always be so. The Allfather smiled on us today. We will make a sacrifice to him in thanks."

I walked to a bucket and doused myself in it. I agreed with Erik; it had been easy but it was always the same. We could achieve surprise when we raided somewhere for the first time but our victims would learn and it would become harder. When my other drekar arrived we would strike hard and fast before they had time to organise. Louis the Pious was not his father but there would be warlords who had fought alongside Charlemagne. They would know how to deal with Vikings. It was a pity that we did not speak their language. It would have been useful to find out more about which of their towns were worth sacking.

I sent a messenger back to Erik. He and his men could come around the headland and shelter in this smaller tributary. It would make the drekar safer and we could feed all that way. Already my men had butchered a cow and two sheep. They were being skinned as the fires were prepared. I waved over Olaf, "Olaf Leather Neck, organise guards for the villagers. We will take back as slaves those who seem worth the trouble."

"And the others?"

"For now we keep them. There must be a lord here."

"Perhaps we have killed him already."

"Then examine the bodies. He will have some seal around his neck or a ring upon his finger. See if anyone can speak our language."

By the time Erik and his men had brought my drekar around there was the smell of cooking meat. Olaf returned with a slave. "I did not find a lord but I found this slave. He is Norse and was captured as a child when Charlemagne's men captured a drekar. The crew were all killed save him. He had seen but six summers when first he came."

"What is your name, boy?"

"I am Hrolf son of Gerloc."

"How many summers do you have?"

"Twelve or thirteen, my lord, I am not certain."

I nodded. I liked him. He was not afraid of me and stood proudly. "You are now free. When we leave you can come with us if you wish or we can drop you closer to your home."

"I know not where my home is. I will stay with you if you will allow. You look like a warrior. I wish to be a warrior." He turned and pointed an accusing finger at the families. "They treated me as a piece of dirt. If I had been a warrior then they would not have done so. Will you make me a warrior?"

"Aye I will. But first we will feed you up." In truth he looked like bones covered by thin skin. "Now tell me who is lord here? Did we kill him?"

He shook his head. "He left three days ago with his oathsworn. He has six of them. They rode horses. These are horse people. I know not where he went."

"What is his name?"

He looked sad, "He is called lord. I tend the pigs, Jarl. They rarely speak to me."

"Then you do not know of any large towns around here?"

"I know that there is one. It is a very big town and is three days from here down the river. It has a stone wall built by the Romans. I have heard men speak of this."

"Good. Any churches of the White Christ?"

"There are many and they are along the river."

I ruffled his hair. "You have done well." I waved over Rollo Thin Skin. "Find our new crew man some better clothes. Take them from the villagers if you have to and then feed him. His is now one of us." I should have heard the Weird Sisters spinning then but I did not. I could not know how tightly woven our threads would be. Our coming was not an accident. It was meant to be, it was *wyrd*.

I waved over Haaken and Beorn the Scout. "There is a large town three days east of us but I know not what lies between. The captive told me of churches along the river but they could be beyond the bend of the river close to the large town. Beorn, take three warriors and scout along the banks of the river." I shaded my eyes and looked up at the sky. "Be back by noon. You and the others will need the rest and the food should be ready by then."

"Aye Jarl." He trotted off.

"Haaken, you and I will see if we can make this burgh a little easier to defend."

"If they come we run, do we not?"

"If we have filled the bellies of the drekar then we run. If not we stay and make them pay." He gave me a quizzical look. I bent down at the pile of captured weapons. I picked one of the short swords up and bent it across my knee. "If we fear men with weapons such as this then we ought to become farmers."

"You are right."

I realised, as we went around that this had been a Roman fort. They had, however, used the stones on the gate. I saw fragments of Roman words and even I recognised that they were upside down. They had made this oppidum on the site of a fort which had existed before. I could see the foundations of some of the buildings. We had been in enough of them to recognise the layout. Although they had used the foundations the buildings were made of wood. Where was the rest of the stone? A platform ran along the top of the ramparts and they had two gates; one at either end. We climbed the stairs and looked out from the northern gate. I could see farms in the distance. I would send men out in the afternoon and evening to eliminate them. We did not want word spreading yet. Glancing down into the ditch I saw that it had rubbish in it; bits of bone and broken pots. They had not maintained it. I would set our new slaves to clearing it.

As we walked back to the river side I saw the fishing boats drawn up, still, on the beach. We could tow them back and use them to transport the slaves back to our home. We descended the steps. "Have the villagers clear the rubbish from the ditch. It will keep them occupied and stop them thinking of escape. If they are exhausted they will be less likely to run. I will speak with Erik Short Toe."

Erik had secured the drekar in the small tributary. "It is a little shallow, Jarl."

"I know but you shall not be here long. Step the mast. Tomorrow we row up the main river and see what we can raid."

"What about the other drekar? They are not here yet."

I smiled, "Do you doubt that they will come when they said?"

He nodded, "You are right. They will be here by evening at the latest."

"We will leave half a crew here and the rest will be crammed aboard my drekar and we will row up the river."

"Aye." He turned to his ships boys. "Right my lads, let us get the sail stowed and then the mast on the mast fish!"

I sat before the roasting meat and joined my Ulfheonar. Finni the Dreamer brought me over a horn of something. I sniffed it, "Cider, Jarl. It is drinkable and that is all! This is a poor village. I thought the Empire was rich."

"It is. When Beorn returns we will have better targets."

I had just been brought the liver of the cow we had cooked when Beorn the Scout returned. He took off his helmet and cloak and slumped down beside us. Finni gave him some cider. He drank and wrinkled his brow. Finni smiled, "Not much reward for a morning's work eh?"

Beorn pointed east. "There are two monasteries downstream. The first is about five miles away and is built of fine stone. Roman stone." I now knew there the stone from the fort had gone. "The other is across the river on the southern bank. It too is built of stone but it has a wall around it and a tower. The one on this side has many monks. I am surprised you did not hear the bell tolling."

"I thought I heard something but my ears are not as sharp as yours Beorn. Are there warriors by the tower?"

"Aye. I saw no mail but they have sentries. We saw men on horses. They looked to be nobles hunting."

"Good. You have done well, now eat." The cow's liver was hot and sweet. My men knew I was fond of it. As I ate it, the pink juices running down my fingers, I began to formulate a plan. I would take *'Heart'* and attack the fortified monastery. I would send the rest of my men across country to attack the other monastery. Once they were eliminated then we would be safer; for a while at least.

Chapter 2

"The drekar are here!"

We had built a signal fire on the headland between us and the Seine. It had been a beacon for my captains. The two captains edged their drekar towards us. The women and the children had cleared the ditch. They were exhausted and that would make them less likely to attempt to flee. When the sixty warriors tramped from our drekar I saw all hope leave their eyes. They might have risked escaping one ship's crew but three made escape impossible. After Hrolf had eaten I had asked him more about the warriors in this part of Frankia. I discovered that they had many armed men but few warriors. He was Norse and knew the difference. He also told me that their nobles fought on horseback. That did not worry me. We had fought horsemen before and we always won.

"A good voyage Asbjorn the Strong?"

"Aye Jarl Dragonheart. You need not fear for Olaf. He is a good captain. He is not as reckless as one might expect from one so young."

"He had Snorri watching him! Come we will talk while we eat. Now that you are here we can strike."

Eystein and Asbjorn had been Ulfheonar while Snorri still was. They sat with my elite warriors. As they ate and drank the rough cider I told them what we had learned. "We leave when it is dark. You will lead your crew to the monastery down the river. I will go on my drekar with my crew and that of the **'Red Snake'**. The monks always rise early. We should attack while it is dark. But remember they will be awake!"

"From what you say Jarl, the monastery you attack is well defended and has walls."

I nodded, "And the prize will be richer. I will have twice the number of men you will have. We leave your captains and ten men to watch the captives and the drekar. You will be back first for you have a shorter journey. We will have to fight the river."

"And this other town; the big one three days down the river; what of that?"

"We take two drekar and row down the river to explore this land. I will decide if the town is worth taking when we are closer."

"Good. I will select the men who are to stay."

My Ulfheonar took the opportunity to rest and to sleep after we had sharpened our weapons and oiled our mail. The sea could destroy mail if it was not kept well oiled. I waved over Rollo Thin Skin. "When we go on the drekar tomorrow bring Hrolf the captive with us. His language skills may be of use."

"Aye Jarl. He has been badly treated. He has burn marks on his feet and he has been whipped. His back looks like one of Aiden's charts."

"He is one of us now. Care for him Rollo. Find him a seax. A Viking, no matter how young, needs a weapon. How old would you say he is? He thinks he has seen twelve or thirteen summers. But he looks young and thinner."

"Aye I thought him to be just ten summers old. He needs fattening up. He only ate what the pigs did not." He shook his head. "He eats constantly. I fear he will be ill before the night is out."

I went down to my drekar before it was dark. I needed to make sure that Erik Short Toe understood what we would be doing. He was looking at the charts which Aiden had made. He had a piece of charcoal and was amending them. "Aiden can tell me off when we return home, Jarl, but if I do not make the marks I will forget."

"He will not become angry. He is soon to be a father. That will mellow him. Besides knowledge is like gold to our galdramenn."

He nodded, "Aye."

"We will be heavily crewed. I will leave six men on board when we disembark. I want the drekar turned around and ready to leave in case we are pursued. We will leave before dawn in any case. We have taken enough chances already. If what Hrolf says is true then this town three days away is a port. There may be ships using it. We can take them if we happen upon them."

My sleep had been fruitful. I had realised that the river was like a giant fish trap. The only exit was the mouth and if we put our ships there we could capture more ships and cargo than by raiding. We would first see what riches the two monasteries held and then become fishermen.

We rowed down the river in silence with no chants. With three and four men to an oar we were overcrowded but we were fast. Beorn stood with Snorri at the bow. Half way down the drekar Haaken was ready to repeat any signals as we slipped silently down the Seine. The bank to the south of us looked quiet and I saw few dwellings. The banks which led to the higher ground were gentle. They were not cliffs; they could be scaled. Once again it was the wood smoke which alerted us to the presence of a town. The smell came down stream towards us. Beorn waved us to the right and the south bank. There was a bend in the river and then I saw, silhouetted in the dark up on the high ground, the walls of a monastery complete with walls and tower. Across the river I heard the tolling of the bell which summoned the monks to prayers. It was echoed from the monastery close to us.

Erik knew when to turn towards shore even without the instructions from Beorn. There was a wooden jetty there and a small boat tied up to it. That might prove useful. I slipped over the side as the ship's boys tied us up and headed up the path. My Ulfheonar had not rowed and they were already armed and mailed. While the rest prepared themselves I waved off Snorri and Beorn. They would find a way up the slope to the gates. I waited until the ship had been emptied and then Erik Short Toe began the laborious task of turning it.

I raised my sword and pointed up the hill. We began to march up the well worn path. There were stones beneath my feet. I suspected this had been built by the Romans. I saw pinpricks of light from the buildings above us. I wondered if they had sentries. The night was as black as the inside of a cave and I doubted that they would have seen anything. There was no reason for them to be suspicious. We moved quickly. Beorn appeared from the shadows and mimed to me that there was a gate and it was guarded. I signalled for my men to wait while I went with my Ulfheonar to inspect the defences.

We moved confidently for we wore black cloaks and our mail was black. We would not be seen. Beorn and Snorri had their new bows with them. They had bought them from a trader. He had acquired them from the far north of the world, from the Saami people who live close to the ice at the top of the world. They were smaller and far more powerful than any bow we had. They both knocked an arrow as we headed to the gate. There was a shallow ditch and a wooden rampart atop a stone wall. The gate looked solid enough and there were two towers. We saw this from forty paces away. The ditch was bridged by a narrow wooden walkway. I saw two sentries. They moved from the gate to the end of the wall where there appeared to be a small shelter. We watched them until we had established the pattern.

I waved Snorri to one end and Beorn to the other. They would fell the sentries and silently kill them. Vermund Thorirson went to fetch the rest of the war band. I led the rest across the wooden walkway and we waited by the gate. I did not wait for Snorri and Beorn to return. They would kill any guards who patrolled. If the sentries made a noise when they fell then was *wyrd*. We did not worry about that. Finni and Olaf Leather Neck stood with their backs to the wall; they held a shield before them. Olaf had a long two handed Danish axe hanging from his back. That would be his weapon of choice. Ulf Olafsson waited with his back to the wall and when Vermund returned with the men he joined him.

Slinging my shield over my back and sheathing my sword I stood on the shield. My two warriors raised it to head level and then pushed up. Vermund and Ulf did the same with Haaken. I could just grasp the wooden stakes above me. My two Ulfheonar gave one final push and I pulled myself over the top of the wall. I quickly looked down the ramparts and saw that the sentries were both dead; each had an arrow in his throat. I went to the stairs, sword drawn and descended to the inner yard. In the distance I could see the glow of candles in the monastery and I could smell bread baking at the western wall. The monastery of the White Christ was coming to life.

Reaching the gate I began to lift the bar holding the gate. Haaken joined me. We laid it to the ground and then Haaken pointed up. There was a second one. It would have been a hard one to break down. When we had removed the second one we pulled the gates open. My men flooded in.

I led one group of warriors towards the church of the monastery. We could see the light glowing from the doorway. Haaken led a second group left while Olaf took more to the right. We did not make a noise. We had told our men to be silent until the alarm was given. I could hear chanting in the church. I pulled my shield tighter around me and did not slow down as I hit the door hard. It crashed open and a collective wail went up. What they shouted I did not know but they began to flee. I ran straight down the middle of the candlelit church. I could see that the candlesticks were all made of metal. In the dark I could not tell what type but it mattered not. If it was gold then we would be rich beyond our wildest dreams but even bronze or copper was valuable.

Outside I could hear the shouts of alarm and the ring of metal on metal. Battle was joined. Suddenly a sword stabbed at my right side. I barely had time to sweep Ragnar's Spirit down. It clanged down on to the sword and sparks flew. I brought the side of my shield across and it hit the warrior in the side of the head. I saw that he had a mail shirt which came below his waist. This was a noble. My shield knocked him to the ground. Before he could rise I stabbed him in the throat and he bled his life away. I went directly out of the rear door. I turned and saw that I had six warriors with me. That would be enough.

Once we left the church we entered a world of black night. I saw the monks fleeing. I guessed that there was a gate on the other side of the settlement and they were heading for it. We began to overtake them. I saw that Rollo Thin Skin was racing ahead of me. He was followed by the young captive, Hrolf, who wielded his seax. He was a Viking. Rollo had no armour yet. He pulled back his arm and hurled his spear. I heard something crack as it entered the back of the monk who fell screaming and writhing on the floor. There were guards at this side of the walls and the two of them ran towards us in an attempt to protect their priests.

I did not want my young warriors to die needlessly. "Behind me and watch my back!" The two guards had spears and oval shields. I did not stop but swung my sword overhand at the man to my right as I punched my shield at the one to my left. As my sword struck and then shattered his helmet and skull I felt his spear slide across my mail. But for the high quality mail I would have had a spear in me. As it was the sentry was knocked to the ground where he lay dying. Hrolf leapt on him and dragged his seax across his throat. I did not break stride. With Rollo at my side we ran towards the two priests trying to open the gate.

"Just knock them out! They are valuable!"

I brought the flat of my sword across the back of the head of one of them while Rollo used the shaft of his spear to lay out the other.

"You have done well. Rollo, guard this door and let no one leave!"

"Aye Jarl."

I pointed my sword at Hrolf, "Today you became a man. Take the sword of the man you slew. It is now yours!"

I ran to the side of the settlement where Olaf had led our men. I could see flames and hear a great clamour. I knew the new warriors would be busy taking the treasure that they found. My Ulfheonar would be securing the town. It was the difference between my oathsworn and the rest. As I raced around a corner of the church I saw horses. There were stables and some of the nobles must have reached their horses. They were charging Olaf Leather Neck and his men in an attempt to reach the gate.

Olaf had men around him who wore no armour. I caught sight, from the corner of my eye, Beorn and Snorri as they raced to help Olaf and the six men he led. The four horsemen had spears as they charged. I raised my sword and roared as I ran to their aid. Olaf Leather Neck was a doughty warrior. He swung his long two handed axe as the horsemen charged. The two young warriors next to Olaf fell to spears which threw them to the ground but Olaf's axe bit into the neck of the first horse. It severed it in one blow and the horseman fell to the ground. Olaf was not a novice. He ignored the stunned man, leaving him to the young warriors around him. Instead he swung his axe at the next man. He missed the horse's head but hacked through the noble's leg and into the side of the horse. The last noble had to stop his horse to prevent it from falling. There were dead animals before him. I swung my sword hard into the rump of the horse. It bit deeply and the horse fell backwards. The noble was pinned beneath it and I swung my sword to take his head. We had fought horsemen before. A dead horse made a horsemen helpless.

As Olaf was pulling his axe from the dead horse a warrior ran towards his unprotected back with his spear ready to kill my Ulfheonar. Rolf Eriksson raced between them. He smashed the spear in two and then backhanded the spearman with his sword. Olaf nodded his thanks and retrieved his axe. The last two nobles who tried to flee on their mounts were slain by Snorri and Beorn with their arrows.

I ran to Olaf, "We should name you Olaf the Mighty! I have never seen such blows. Two horses with two strikes!"

He looked sadly at the two young men who had fallen next to him. "I would that they had lived. They were fearless and stayed by my side. They will be in Valhalla."

"Truly!"

Olaf turned to Rolf and said, "You have saved my life young Rolf." He took his Danish war axe. He had captured it when he had slain its owner two winters before. "Take this as payment for my life."

"I cannot take your axe!"

I smiled, "Do not insult Olaf, Rolf. Take it."

He did so. It was right that Olaf should pay for his life. It pleased the Gods and ensured that others would do the same in the future. Olaf would capture another fine weapon soon enough.

"Olaf, have your men search for treasure. Have the dead horses butchered. We will eat well tomorrow. Meet me at the main gate."

I was confident that we had won. The nobles would not have fled had they thought that we could be defeated. As I walked through the streets I saw many dead. Not all were warriors. In the dark my men would have killed first and asked questions later. Haaken and my other Ulfheonar had already gathered the captured monks and the riches from the church. I saw three Holy Books. Those along with the metal from the church had made the raid profitable already. The weapons the nobles had had were also a boon. And the coins and food we would take back would also make my men rich.

"Haaken, have everything gathered here. I will see Erik Short Toe. We can use the men who guarded it to begin loading. I would head downstream as soon as we can."

"It was a good haul. If all of the men hereabouts are as poor as this we could conquer it in a matter of months."

I shook my head. "If you wish to stay and conquer this land then do so but I intend to go back to the land which Olaf the Toothless and Prince Butar chose for us."

"Aye you are right. But we have no worthy subject for a saga."

"Speak with Olaf Leather Neck and you may have one. Great deeds were done this night."

In the event the sun had broken by the time we were ready to return to our camp. We were so laden that I had to send forty warriors along the southern river bank on foot for our ship was overcrowded. When they reached the coast Erik would ferry them across. Snorri and Beorn led them. They would use the opportunity to scout out that side of the river. I saw Asbjorn and Eystein as they drove their captives and treasure along the northern bank. We had succeeded. We would now have enough food to last some time. What we needed was a knarr to transport it back to our home.

When we reached the camp and had unloaded the captives and the animals I saw that we had a problem. We needed a pen to contain them all. I set the monks to building a wooden fence under the supervision of Haaken. We built a tower for the guards who would watch over our valuable human treasure. More animals were slaughtered and, along with the hunks of horsemeat we had taken, we ate well.

I took off my armour and went to the river to wash. I watched Erik ferry Snorri and his men across. "Is there aught worth raiding yonder?"

Snorri shook his head. "A few farms but that is all and the weapons these warriors use are poor."

"Perhaps the Emperor or the King of the Franks keeps the better warriors close to hand. Remember the Emperor of the Romans in the East? His bodyguards were the better armed warriors."

"Aye you may be right."

"Erik, you had better erect your mast again. Tomorrow we sail up river." I returned up the hill. I waved over Asbjorn. "Have your drekar and *'Red Snake'* moored in the middle of the river. Use a half crew. We can use the fishing boats to change them. I want no ships in or out of the river. We charge a heavy price for any ship which wishes to use this river now. We own it. Tomorrow we take *'Odin's Breath'* and *'Heart of the Dragon'* to spy out this mighty city upriver."

"We are all rich men already. The monastery had metal candlesticks and plates as well as a chest of gold."

"There is more yet to be had fear not. We make the most of this raid for in the future they will protect against the likes of us."

Young Hrolf wandered over as Asbjorn left. He held up a helmet which was too big for him and his short sword. "I am a warrior now, Jarl."

I laughed, "Listen to Rollo and you will be."

He nodded seriously. "And one day, Jarl, all of this land will be mine and I shall make these people bow the knee to me." Many people would have ;laughed at such a bold statement but there was something about this young Viking that made me take him seriously. He reminded me of myself. Taken as a slave but destined for greater things. Perhaps the Norns had put him in my way. Was I a thread in someone else's web?

We gathered all the treasure together and sorted it into chests. Although it was my raid and I had the right to claim it all that was not my way. I had four chests and we divided the treasure into equal amounts. One was for me, one for the crew of my drekar, one for Asbjorn's and one for the **'Red Snake'**. When we had sold the slaves and the Holy Books we would divide all that way too. When we returned home then each man would be given his share once the leaders and the captains had taken their share. It would spread throughout our people and we would all be richer. I cast my eye over the treasure. I always hoped for a link to my past. I sought blue stones and the symbol of the wolf. Sadly there were none.

That night Haaken sang one of his songs. The younger warriors yearned to be named in one of his sagas.

The Saxon King had a mighty home
Protected by rock, sea and foam
Safe he thought from all his foes
But the Dragonheart would bring new woes
Ulfheonar never forget
Ulfheonar never forgive
Ulfheonar fight to the death
The snake had fled and was hiding there
Safe he thought in the Saxon lair
With heart of dragon and veins of ice
Dragonheart knew nine would suffice
Ulfheonar never forget
Ulfheonar never forgive
Ulfheonar fight to the death
Below the sand they sought the cave
The rumour from the wizard brave
Beneath the sea without a light
The nine all waited through the night
Ulfheonar never forget
Ulfheonar never forgive
Ulfheonar fight to the death
When night fell they climbed the stair
Invisible to the Saxons there
In the tower the traitors lurked
Dragonheart had a plan which worked
Ulfheonar never forget
Ulfheonar never forgive
Ulfheonar fight to the death
With Odin's blade the legend fought

Magnus' tricks they came to nought
With sword held high and a mighty thrust
Dragonheart sent Magnus to an end that was just
Ulfheonar never forget
Ulfheonar never forgive
Ulfheonar fight to the death
Ulfheonar never forget

After he had finished and been applauded, he sat with Olaf Leather Neck and Rolf Eriksson. They told him their tale. He would begin composing a new song. Rolf would be immortalised. When he died and went to Valhalla then others would know of his courage. Hlif, the girl he and Olaf had fought over, was now a distant memory. When he returned she would hear the song and wonder if she should have taken him when she had the chance. Perhaps her father would be happier with her settling for a farmer.

With **'Red Snake'** fully crewed and waiting in the estuary entrance we took the other two drekar and headed up stream. We had left enough guards to cow the captives; if danger threatened then **'Red Snake'** would come to their aid. As we headed up the river I could see why it might take three days to travel overland. The river was wide and had enormous loops. Apart from the two monasteries we saw little which looked as though it might reward a raid. There were farms and if we found nought else we would take what little they had.

"Jarl Dragonheart, on the river bank, look!"

Karl Karlsson, the ship's boy who was seated on the top of the mast, pointed to the north. I saw riders watching us. We had been seen. From the scale armour I took at least two of them to be nobles, They rode parallel to us. The wind was with us and the men were taking advantage of the rest. I did not like the idea of us being shadowed.

"Haaken, have the men on the oars. Let us exercise these Franks and see how determined they are."

My men enjoyed a challenge and soon the oars were cutting through the water. Asbjorn saw what we did and, he too, copied us. I smiled as I saw the riders urging their horses to match our pace. It was an impossible challenge. When we came to the larger bends in the river they had to travel further than we did and soon we left them behind. We were almost at the walled town we had heard was the main settlement in the area when we encountered the Frankish ships. There were four of them.

Erik shouted, "Down sail!"

I shouted, "Oars in and prepare for battle!"

We were both longer and lower in the water than the four ships but they had an aft castle in which archers would wait. We had not expected a river battle but we were prepared for one.

"Snorri, archers!" I pointed to the aft castle of the nearest ship which was making directly for us. It was only later I deduced that they must have been heading down the river to engage with us and our encounter was just *wyrd*. Perhaps the Norns thought we had had it too easy.

I donned my helmet and picked up my shield. The Franks had made a grave error of judgement. They outnumbered us but they did not have the skills for a sea battle. We did. Snorri and his archers could loose an arrow further than any other archer I knew and soon they were releasing a rain of death upon the castle of the nearest ship. When it had been cleared Snorri switched to the next target.

"Erik, put us next to the first ship Snorri and his archers hit."

"Aye Jarl."

I shouted to my crew, "Men of Cyninges-tūn let us see what treasure they have aboard these apologies for ships." Their roar should have warned the Franks what was about to be unleashed upon them. "Snorri, attack the other ship!" While Snorri and his archers kept one ship busy we would board the other.

Olaf Leather Neck had the grappling hook ready. He hurled it. One of the Franks tried to grab it but missed and it bit through his hand and into the wood. I heard him screaming. He was pinned and could not move as Olaf and a dozen men pulled us closer together. The side of the Frankish ship canted over with their efforts and the weight of men on their deck. It meant the two decks were the same height. I jumped up onto the strake and grabbed the rigging with my shielded left hand. I held my sword in my right. Spears were thrown at me but the shield I held before me deflected them all. When the gap was less than two paces I leapt across the water to land on the Frankish deck. I swung my sword sideways and felt it bite into the arm of the man who was racing to gain the glory of killing a Viking Jarl.

I punched with my left hand at the three warriors who advanced towards me. I brought my sword over my head as I pushed at the three of them. It smashed through the shoulder of the middle warrior and he fell screaming to his death in an ever widening pool of blood. I was no longer alone as my Ulfheonar joined me. There were just six of us on the deck of the Frankish ship but that did not daunt us. We charged the men before us. With our mighty shields and superior swords we could both attack and defend better than our opponents. Our mail meant that any blows which we did not deflect did not harm us.

We began to harvest the Franks. Our swords cracked on theirs but we were stronger and our enemies were forced to take a step back. On the moving deck of the ship that could lead to disaster. As the man I fought struggled to keep his feet I punched with the metal boss of my shield. His had none. My blow made him fall and as he fell backwards I lunged forward to rip open his gut. By now even our new warriors had joined the fray and numbers were levelled. Although they did not enjoy mail and good helmets they were well trained and ferocious warriors. The Franks leapt into the water to escape the wrath of the Viking warriors.

Erik's voice came to me, "Jarl! We are in danger!" I saw that the Frank had boarded my drekar.

"Cnut Cnutson, hold the ship." I pointed my sword at those around him. "You six help him!"

As we raced back to our own ship I knew that Cnut would be able to do as I had asked. He had served with Erik for two years. He was a fine sailor. Our deck was now lower than the Franks. I stood on the side of the Frank's ship and launched myself like a bird to the deck below. I crashed atop four men who had surrounded Einar the Red. I heard the spine of one of the Franks snap as my mailed body hit him. I became a whirling killer as I laid about me with sword and shield. The two of us slew the remaining three.

Einar hefted his shield around and followed me into the fray. Erik and his crew were beleaguered at the steering board. Our sudden appearance took the Franks by surprise and we charged their unprotected backs. With the Ulfheonar next to us we made a great slaughter. The survivors tried to clamber back aboard their own ship but its higher sides made it hard for them and we cut them down as they did so. The Frankish ship disentangled itself and headed back up stream to the Frankish stronghold. It drifted like a ghost ship for its warriors lay dead upon the deck of my vessel or their corpses floated down the river towards the sea. The fishes would feast upon their flesh.

I ran to Erik. "Have you losses?"

He pointed to the two dead ships' boys. "They died protecting me."

"Then they will be in Valhalla." I looked across to *'Odin's Breath'*. Asbjorn had also managed to capture a Frank. "Erik turn us around. Signal the others. We will return to the mouth of the estuary."

I had thought to scout out the stronghold but they would be ready for us. In my mind I formulated a plan. If we fled down the river they would think they had hurt us. I would lure them to us the next day by using *'Red Snake'* as bait. We had two more ships now and could actually begin to sail our cargo to the port of Lundenwic and sell them there. Once more the gods smiled on us. I remembered that I owed them a Blót. I would remedy that when we reached our camp.

The current was with us and my men rested. Haaken stood by me. "We could have attacked the town."

I shook my head and pointed to the sky. "We did not have surprise upon our side. Our warriors are spread out in four ships. It would have been difficult to coordinate the attack. I believe I see the web of the Norns and the hands of the gods in all of this. We have had a victory now. And we know that the Franks know we are loose in their land. We eat, we rest, tomorrow we set a trap and, if all goes well, we may yet sack their town." I looked back up the river. This had been meant to be. My plan had been a good one but the Weird Sisters had other plans for me and my war band.

Chapter 3

We left the two drekar at the mouth of the estuary and used the two captured Frankish vessels to ferry our men to the camp.

On the way downstream the crews of the captured ships had stripped the bodies and flung them in the river. Cnut Cnutson looked proud of himself as he ferried me to shore. "Thank you for your trust, Jarl Dragonheart."

"You have earned it." I nodded to all the young men who had been with Cnut. "Each of you have."

We set sentries and we ate. I summoned my captains and Ulfheonar so that I could explain my plan. "We will send ***Red Snake*** upstream tomorrow morning with a full crew. I will be aboard with Snorri and Beorn. I will take my banner. We will sail close to the walls of the town. I intend to make as though we are going to attack it. It may be that they will be defeated easily but I doubt it. It is more likely that they will force us back to our ship. We will then sail slowly back downstream for I believe that they will pursue us this time. I will draw them here where we will have a wall of vessels. We will destroy them. It is when their ships are destroyed that we will attack, over land and destroy their town."

"It is a risk."

"Life is a risk, Olaf Leather Neck. However I shall make a Blót this night in the river. I would have the gods on our side against these soldiers of the White Christ. I will ask for volunteers for our crew but I will choose from the volunteers."

I preferred to sacrifice a horse. They were the animals the Franks favoured but there were none. The noble who had ruled this coast had taken them. I chose, instead, a ram. He was a fine animal and the gods would appreciate the gesture. I led him down to the river and invoked the help of Odin and the other gods before I sacrificed him. He did not struggle. He was happy to be given the opportunity of living with the gods and his body was taken out to sea. It was all good.

I had more than enough volunteers. I chose forty. Olaf Grimsson was proud that I had chosen his drekar. He and Bolli the shipwright had spent long hours repairing the drekar so that it was now a fine vessel. Smaller than the others it was very manoeuvrable and I had chosen it because it could turn easily in a narrow river. This was not a narrow river but we needed speed to make a surprise attack.

We left in the middle of the night. Snorri and Beorn acted as ship's boys guiding us safely through the dark. We had the mast on the mast fish. I wanted us to be invisible. As we were small and had a double crew we moved quickly through the dark water of this Frankish river. There was no drag from the mast and we reached the town before dawn. The thin grey in the east told us that it was not long before dawn but it was a good time. Olaf Grimsson swung the drekar around. It was a moonless night and there were clouds. I had Olaf Grimsson land us some six hundred paces north of the settlement which squatted on a piece of high ground above the river. As I led my warriors up the slope he and his crew drifted down to the middle of the river where they would wait until needed.

Snorri and Beorn ran silently up the cobbled surface which led from the river. The dark stone walls rose ahead of us. They were not high walls but they had towers at each corner; Roman towers. We had ten archers with us. Each archer also had his shield and a sword but first they would eliminate any sentries who stood on the walls. Snorri ghosted next to me. I held up my hand and my column of warriors halted. He spoke quietly, "They have lifted the bridge over the ditch."

I nodded. It would cause a problem but not a major one. I had no intention of storming the town. I had but forty men with me. I wanted to bloody the nose of the Emperor's count, the man who ruled this land in his name. I wanted him angry. An angry leader made mistakes. As we neared the stronghold I saw that the houses had spread between the walls of the castle and the river. There were dwellings and there were warehouses. I knew from my visit to Seguin I Lupo that wine was traded here.

Beorn and Snorri waited at the edge of the settlement. I waved them to the walls. They would buy us some time. I had not been certain that we would find warehouses but I had hoped. The Blót had been a good one and the gods had rewarded us. It was up to us now to seize this opportunity to become rich. As my archers went to the walls I waved my sword to spread the men out in a thin line. I led them forward.

They had a town watch. Two sentries armed with spears appeared from the shadows when my men and I descended like wolves. I led and all that they saw in the dark of night was a black mailed giant. I swung my sword and hacked one of them across the neck. The blow was so powerful that it bit down to the bone. Before his companion could cry out a warning he had been speared by Arne Fleet Foot. They were the last silent deaths. A cry from the walls behind us told me that a sentry had died noisily. Those in the houses were slow to waken. The first that most knew was when my men burst in and slew the men.

Now that the alarm was given there was no need for silence and I roared, "Dragonheart!" The cry was taken up and I heard screams of terror as my men began to butcher the men. I led a handful down to the river and the warehouses. The sky was becoming lighter. I reached the river as my men slew those who guarded the wine warehouse. "Olaf Grimsson! Ho!"

"We come!"

While we had been heading up the slope my drekar captain had raised the mast. We would not use the sail but I knew without looking that my wolf banner would be flying from its top. He would bring the drekar to the jetty. I saw that there were some ships there but most looked to be small river vessels. The larger ones were missing. "Rollo Thin Skin; we will take two of these smaller ships. Load them with wine from the warehouse and destroy the rest."

"Aye Jarl."

"Send a messenger to me when all is done. I want the Frankish ships towed. We have not enough men to crew them."

As I ran back up the hill I shouted to my men to begin loading the ships. I reached Snorri and Beorn. They were sheltering, with their men, behind two small huts. The occupants lay dead. They were guards. Snorri pointed to a body lying close by. "Sven Carlsson is dead. He died well."

"That is all that a warrior can ask." I looked to the east. Dawn was coming. "We keep their heads down. I will announce myself soon." I knew that my name was known. All had heard the story of the Viking with the sword touched by the gods. They knew that my reach was long. I had been in the heart of Din Guardi in the land of Northumbria and killed a well protected enemy in the heart of that fortress. They knew I had taken a king's wife for my son. They knew my name. I wanted it to be the lure which drew them into my trap.

My men were making it hard for any to stand on the walls of this huge town. I could hear the clamour from within. They knew they were being attacked but all that they could see was shadows. They knew that Vikings were on their river and had seen two drekar the previous day. They would be wary. They could not possibly know that I had but one small drekar. It would only be when dawn broke and they saw the single, small drekar in the river, flying my banner, that they would know our numbers and then they would wreak their vengeance upon us.

Whoever commanded the walls finally began to think. They brought up shields behind which to shelter. Snorri chuckled, "A little late for some of their men, Jarl."

"Aye he must have been asleep. They will soon see our drekar. Be ready. I want the archers back on the drekar as soon as there is danger. The three of us will be the last to board."

I was not being reckless. I was counting on my armour and the skill of my two Ulfheonar. The alleys leading to the river were narrow and it would be hard to flank us. I doubted that mailed warriors would be the first after us. It would be those who were fleet of foot and without armour who would recklessly charge us.

As soon as the gates opened, when light made the river clearly visible, I shouted, "Back to the drekar!"

My archers hurried back to the safety of the drekar. The three of us stood shoulder to shoulder and began to walk backwards. The bridge over the ditch was lowered and a horde of Franks rushed towards us. By then we were in the middle of the huts. Most of them made for us but some spread left and right to go down side ways in this jumble of buildings.

The ones facing us ran at us. I took the spear which was thrust at me on my shield and, dropping my right arm a little brought my sword up into the chest of the warrior. I ripped it to the side and exposed his ribs. I thrust forward as the next spear came over my head and stabbed the next warrior in the throat.

With dead Franks on the ground before us the three of us stepped back and made our way down to the river. There was a barrier of bodies between us and the others and we easily made the river. Those who had run down the sides of the warehouses and huts now tried to attack our flanks. They were stopped in their tracks by the arrows from my drekar.

"Come, Jarl Dragonheart. We are ready to sail!" I could hear the urgency in Olaf's voice. He did not wish to be the one who lost Dragonheart!

Just then I heard hooves as a mailed warrior galloped down through the huts from the direction of the castle. He was mailed with a fine helmet and held a long spear before him. He came recklessly towards me. He hunted glory. He would kill this Viking. If he expected me to flee he did not know us. We angled our shields to form a solid barrier and held our swords above them. The horse slithered and tried to stop. The spear shattered on our shields and Snorri despatched the horse with one blow from his sword. The warrior fell from its dying back and I took his head. Slipping my shield behind my back I took the helmet from it, throwing it on the drekar and held the skull by its hair. "Get the body on board. The armour is good." I held the head up and shouted to the Franks, "I am Jarl Dragonheart! Fear me Franks!" I hurled the head towards the advancing Franks.

They would not understand the words but they would the gesture. As I turned stones and arrows thudded into my shield. I walked to my drekar. I stepped on board and Olaf took us, with the current, into the middle of the river.

Olaf was letting the current take us away from the missiles which rained upon us. The shields of my men formed an impenetrable barrier and we were safe.

I took my helmet off. "Strip the mail from the body and throw it overboard while they can still see us. I would anger them." The warrior had been young and had a good suit of armour. I guessed he was a young noble. The manner of his death would anger his people and our treatment would aggravate the situation. The body was dumped unceremoniously over the side. I saw warriors shaking their swords at us.

Snorri said, "Has the plan failed Jarl? There were no ships to pursue us."

"They must have more ships than the ones we tow. There were two we did not destroy yesterday; where are they? They will have them moored somewhere else. We will let them think we have been taken in by their deception. They may know my name but they do not know me."

The boats we towed were heavily laden with barrels. They made our progress slow. More barrels lay on our deck and we were low in the water. We would not be travelling quickly. We had oars and could move swiftly if we had to but I was content with the pace. I looked up and saw my banner fluttering at the top of the mast. They would now know who I was. There was just one wolf warrior with such a standard.

Ketil Ketilson was the ship's boy at the masthead. As we turned one of the loops in the river he shouted, "Jarl. There are Frankish ships. They follow. I can see their masts."

"How many?"

"It is hard to tell but I count at least five masts."

"Good." Turning to Snorri I said, "Have the archers gather at the stern. We will discourage them. Beorn, have the men prepare their oars. I would not risk tempting the Norns too much."

"Aye, Jarl."

I picked up the jug of cider and drank. It was not beer but it refreshed me. We had turned the next loop in the river when we saw them. They had full sail and were in an arrow formation. I turned to Olaf, "How far to the mouth?"

He knew what I meant by the question, "They will catch us before we reach it."

"Beorn, run out the oars but just use one man to an oar." The *'Red Snake'* was a threttanessa. We would just need twenty six men to row. We would still have fourteen and my Ulfheonar to fight. "I want to keep us within their sight."

I was counting on the fact that there was a bend at the mouth of the river which would prevent them from seeing my ships. My four ships would not have a sail hoisted. By the time the Franks saw them they would struggle to turn and, I hoped, they would entangle themselves in each other's rigging. They closed with us and we upped the beat and gained on them. We were tantalizingly close to them. They would assume that our men were tiring and, once we reached the open sea, they could use the wind and surround us.

A voice from the prow shouted, "I see our drekar!

"Ready to ship the oars! Olaf I want you to put us between our two drekar. Have two of your ship's boys climb the ropes to the small Frankish ships and then cut them. They will not drift far."

He nodded and shouted to his crew. His ship's boys knew how to steer and they could beach them if they had to.

I saw that we had less than half a mile to go. "Ship oars!" With oars shipped my men grabbed their weapons. The Frankish vessels seemed to race down the river towards us. Had I timed it right? Would we make the safety of our line before they caught us.

Snorri shouted, "Release!" and a small shower of arrows flew towards the leading ship. Two Franks fell into the foam at the ship's prow. On the other Frankish ships shields were raised and their vision became limited.

My captains had left a gap for us to use. As we sailed through the boys cut the ropes of the boats we towed and Olaf threw the steering board over. Erik Short Toe threw a line from the stern of *'Heart of the Dragon'* which Beorn caught and tied while Asbjorn threw one from the bow of *'Odin's Breath'* for Snorri to catch. With men pulling hard our progress towards the sea was arrested and we formed a solid wall of wood.

I ran to the landward side and, donning my helmet held my shield before me. I saw the Frankish ships as they tried to lower their sails and turn at the same time. I guessed they did not trust the bows of their ships enough to ram us. Had our positions been reversed we would have rammed. Our ships were well made and a single piece of oak formed the keel and the kjerringa. As the Frankish crews fought the river, the wind, the waves and their sails archers on all of our drekar and captured prizes loosed arrows at them. I saw men pitched overboard as they were pierced by arrows. The leading ship could not turn and her hull banged and cracked sideways into mine.

I slung my shield across my back and began to climb the wooden walls of the ship. The crew were so busy trying to sort themselves out that I was almost at the topmost strake before someone tried to spear me. It was a clumsy attempt. I held on to the strake with my right hand and pulled hard on the spear. He did not let go and he was pulled over the side. I heard the crack as his neck broke upon my deck. I pulled myself over the side of the Frank. There were warriors at the stern of the ship. Four of them had mail and wore the round helmets favoured by the Franks. They ran towards me. I drew Ragnar's Spirit and slashed before me to buy myself time to swing my shield around. The edge caught one of the blades but it still caught on my byrnie. There was force behind the deflected blow.

These Franks were not used to fighting on board a ship. I spread my legs wide and stood facing them. I saw Haaken leading my warriors over the stern of this Frankish ship while behind me Snorri and Beorn flanked me. Fighting on a ship was not the combat of movement. You stood still and you took the blows. If you moved then you fell. If you fell then you died. The Franks ran at us and that was their mistake. One slipped and Beorn brought his sword across his face. With no nasal his blade bit into the cheek and head of the Frank. I took a blow on my shield and then slid my sword forward. I was face to face with the Frank. His breath reeked of garlic. As my sword bit into his scale armour I head butted him. I had a full face helmet and I heard his nose break. I pushed with my shield and felt him step backwards. I stabbed again, hard. I did not break his links but the blow winded him and he doubled up. I punched with my shield into his face. Unconscious he fell back and I skewered him to the deck.

Haaken and his men had cleared the area around the steering board. A second Frank had come to the aid of this leader and Franks were preparing to board us. Shouting, "Ulfheonar!" I led my wolf warriors across the deck to meet these new attackers. They too forgot that we were on a moving deck and they moved too quickly. Nor did they wear armour. When I slashed across in a wide arc I was rewarded with spurting blood and ripped guts. Two men fell. I held my shield to take the axe blow which came from the Frank standing on the side of the other ship. I swung my sword across his legs and sliced through one and into the second. He fell screaming between the two hulls.

Before we could board the second Frank the steersman managed to turn the steering board and move away from us. The crew raced up the lines to try to lower the sail again. They had had enough. Olaf picked up a spear and hurled it into the back of the nearest seaman. He plunged to the deck. By the time the sails were lowered it had cost them a quarter of their crew. While my men despatched the Frankish wounded I watched the two survivors head back, slowly, upstream. We now had three more Frankish ships. More importantly we had the river. None could enter or leave without our permission.

With **'Red Snake'** in the middle we tied the three ships we had captured from shore to shore. It was not a solid barrier but with thick ropes slung between all of the vessels it was an effective barrier. The two end ships were secured to the land. After all was secure I was ferried ashore by Erik. My men all beat their shields and chanted, "Dragonheart! Dragonheart! Dragonheart!" Over and over. I would be foresworn if I did not say that I enjoyed their adulation. I was a warrior and we had tricked and vanquished our enemies. I had seen few of our own men die. It had been a great victory.

As I passed the pen containing the animals and the captives I saw that they were all cowed and fearful. I daresay they had seen their ships and thought we would be defeated. Instead they were now even further from safety than they had been.

As we stripped the ships of the treasure we realised that we had beaten well armed and armoured men. These had set out to destroy our war band and they had failed. After I had stripped my armour I went with my Ulfheonar to the river where I had made the Blót. We took off our kyrtles and walked into the river to immerse ourselves completely. It was our way of thanking the gods for rewarding us with victory and we cleaned the blood, sweat and dirt from our bodies.

"And now, Ulfheonar, we will feast and we will enjoy our victory. Haaken will sing us a song!"

After the saga we sat around the fire eating the slaughtered animals and enjoying some of the wine we had taken. While most of my men wrestled and diced away some of their treasure I sat and talked with Haaken, Asbjorn and Eystein.

Haaken raised his horn, "Hail Jarl Dragonheart! Now you are a galdramenn as well as the mightiest warrior."

"I am no galdramenn."

"Then your plans succeeded mightily. What do we do next?"

"Tomorrow we send bands out to raid the farms hereabouts and then we sail, the following day, to take this Frankish stronghold."

"What if the King of the Franks brings his army here?"

"Then, Eystein, we fight them but I do not think they will come. The Empire is large and it would take time to gather such an army."

"You are not worried?"

I laughed, "Why should I worry? I have seen nothing here which makes me think we might lose."

Despite the heavy night of drinking my men were up early. I divided my men into four bands of fifteen and sent them out to the north of the river to raid and to plunder. The rest I retained with the Ulfheonar. We sharpened swords and we prepared for war. The tides meant that we would leave our stronghold mid morning the following day and sail towards the Frankish castle. We would surround it and then plan our attack. It would be a night time attack. Our presence during the day and our martial and fierce appearance would put fear into the hearts of the defenders. We had discovered that our arms and armour could win a battle for us before we had even started.

The bands came back driving animals and carts. The captives were tied behind them. I saw that some of the Franks had defended themselves for some of my men bore wounds but none had died.

I was up well before dawn to prepare for the day. I ate well from the cold cooked carcass of the slaughtered cow. I drank well and then I prepared my war face. My Ulfheonar joined me and not long after dawn we were ready. We would just use the two larger drekar. My warriors were all prepared to embark on the ships when suddenly one of the sentries shouted, "Jarl Dragonheart! There is a Frankish army! They are heading this way."

Had Eystein predicted this? It made no matter. We would meet them and defeat them. Luckily we were all close to our camp preparing to depart. "Form three battle lines!"

I led my men back to the fort and then to the land before it. We arrayed ourselves in three long ranks. They outnumbered us but we had reserves on our ships. I saw that there were twenty nobles on horses and the rest were a mixture of spearmen and farmers. It was not the army of the King. However they did outnumber us.

The enemy arrayed themselves before us. If they thought to daunt us with their numbers then they failed. My men began banging their shields and chanting my name. Some of the younger ones left the line to bare their rear at the Franks. "Do they come to fight, Jarl?"

"I think, Haaken, that they came to make us flee. They must have had spies watching us to gauge numbers and they brought enough to outnumber us."

I watched as four of the mailed horsemen gathered to speak. I did not recognised the banners but I suspected that they belonged to the ruler of this land. The four of them eventually detached themselves from the others. One of them rode to fetch a slave who was being held by mailed men. They approached to just beyond their own bow range. Snorri and Beorn could easily hit them. They took off their helmets, a sure sign that they wished to speak.

"Asbjorn take charge. Haaken, come with me and let us see what these Franks wish."

I took off my helmet and we walked towards them. I saw that the slave was an old Viking. I recognised the tattoos he had upon his face. He came from the land of the Norse, the land of snow and ice.

The older of the mounted men, the one with the greybeard spoke. The Viking nodded, "This is Grimoald son of Pepin the Great, Mayor of Neustria."

I nodded, "Mayor?"

"Like a Jarl or a prince."

"Tell him that I am Jarl Dragonheart of Cyninges-tūn. Ask him does he come to fight or to talk. We are happy to do either."

I saw the ghost of a smile on his face as he translated. I could see that this Grimoald did not like my answer. His voice was angry when he spoke. The Norseman's voice was calm in contrast. "He says you are a brigand and a bandit and he wishes you to leave this land." He glanced around and then added, "You slew his son yesterday. He is not happy."

"Tell him that when we have taken enough of the riches from this land we shall leave for we have slaves to sell. Priests fetch a high price."

When that was translated I saw that it had struck a nerve. He spoke again and the slave said, "My master says he must speak apart."

"Tell him he has until the sun is at its height and then we let our blades do the talking."

After the words had been spoken I received a black look for my pains. Haaken asked, "What goes on here?"

"I suspect we have a high ranking priest amongst our captives. We may become rich men here without fighting."

"That does not make for a good saga, Jarl."

"No but it makes for rich men and allows to us to raid again this year."

They were away for some time and the discussion was heated. Eventually they returned and it was a red faced and angry Grimoald who spat out his words. The slave was smiling when he spoke them. "The Mayor wishes you gone and his people returned. What will it cost for you to leave and for the captives, all of them, to be returned?"

I tried to work out what we could sell the captives for. He had not mentioned the Holy Books and we would slaughter the animals before we left. "Five thousand Imperial gold coins."

It was an outrageous amount. I expected them to say no but when the offer was made the younger noble next to Grimoald nodded and spoke to the Mayor. He appeared to have more power than the older man. The slave turned with the message. "They agree."

"And we want you as well."

His face showed that he had hoped for that. "But they may say no."

"Then we will fight. You are Norse and we will not leave you here with these Franks."

He nodded and translated. Again there was a discussion and then the younger man took out his sword and slashed the slave down his cheek, taking out his eye in the process. Haaken's hand went to his sword and I said, "Bide your time, Haaken."

The slave put his hand to his face to stop the bleeding. He glared hatred from his one eye at the noble and said, "He agrees but he has marked me so that all the world will know that I was the slave of a Frank."

"Tell him to have the gold here by noon the morrow. If not I will hang his monks one by one." I stared at the younger noble as I did so.

In answer they nodded and rode away. I took out a cloth and held it to the slave's face. "Come we will get you healed. What is your name?"

"Hermund the Unlucky."

"How long have you lived with them?"

"Ten summers."

"Now you are free. We will take you back with us." I turned to Haaken, "Have the men begin to load the Frankish ships with the Holy Books, the wine and the other treasures. They shall have their captives and nothing else."

"Aye Jarl."

I led Hermund to the pen where the priests waited. I noticed that the eldest of them, a priest with a white beard was seated on a log. The rest squatted on the floor. He was the important one. I said to Hermund, "Tell them that I command that they heal you and then tell them what I told the Mayor."

He did so and my suspicions were confirmed when the white bearded priest gave orders. I now knew who the important priest was. I made sure they did a good job on Hermund's eye. I knew how they should heal for Aiden was a great healer. They did a good job. He stood. "What is his name?" I pointed at the bearded priest.

"He is Bishop Thuderic of Julpille."

I nodded. "Come let us get you some better clothes and food." I saw Rollo Thin Skin and Hrolf as I entered our camp. "Hrolf. Here is another countryman. Get him food and clothes. He is one of us now. He is Hermund One Eye."

He looked at me, "One Eye?"

"Well you are no longer unlucky for you are a rich man. You are one of my men and that means you share in my bounty."

The afternoon was filled with the sound of animals being prepared for the voyage; some would be eaten and the smaller ones taken with us. Some carcasses were salted but we soon ran out of salt. We would eat well on the voyage home. The next day the captives were closely guarded. I had Hermund bring a burning torch and I spoke quietly to Haaken and gave him instructions. I sought out Hrolf. "Come with us. I have a task for you."

We waited before the walls and watched the sun climb into the sky. I had Bishop Thuderic tethered to Hrolf and on his knees. My sword was out. "Hermund, tell him that if they are late he dies."

When the words were translated the Bishop looked up at me with pure hatred in his eyes. I smiled. The followers of the White Christ feared their priests but not I. Just before noon I saw the Franks. Four men carried the chest. They laid it before them. I waved four of my men forward. They were led by Snorri. He reached them and opened the lid. He waved and nodded. I shouted, "Count it!"

The Franks did not understand my words but when he began to take each piece out they began shouting. I said to Hermund, "Go and tell them that when we have counted half of the money then the women and children will be released and when it is all there then he can have the priests. Return here when you have delivered my message."

He did so and I heard the raised voices. He came back and he was grinning. It was his first smile since he had been scarred and lost his eye. "They are not happy Jarl Dragonheart."

"Good I am not here to make Franks happy." When Snorri raised his hand I said, "Release the women and children. Hermund, tell them to go."

They ran as though they feared I would change my mind. The younger noble rode over along with a second. They had the same design on their shield; silver stars on a purple background. Hermund rejoined me and he scowled his hatred at the noble. The Frank appeared oblivious to the hate. He spoke to Hermund, "He says he will remember you, Jarl Dragonheart."

I nodded. "Tell him I will remember his face too."

"He said he is Lord Charles of Rheims and he is close to the King."

I laughed, "Tell him I have pissed on kings before now and I have yet to see one I respected!"

I knew I had angered him.

Snorri raised his hand and began to come back. I said to Hrolf, "Translate this word for word as I say it."

"Aye Jarl Dragonheart." I nodded to Haaken who took the burning brand from Hrolf.

"I believe, in your Holy Book of the White Christ it is written *'an eye for an eye and a tooth for a tooth'*?" He nodded. "Then know this, Frank, a Viking never forgets and a Viking's vengeance is terrible to behold. If I see you again you will die. Haaken!" Haaken plunged the burning brand into the right eye of Bishop Thuderic. The bishop screamed and there was a hiss and the smell of burning flesh. "An eye for an eye! I never said you would have them unharmed did I?"

Charles of Rheims drew his sword and I drew mine. I said, "We can fight here, now, Charles of Rheims but if we do then every one of these priests dies. Speak! Give me an answer. Do we fight? " My men had their seaxes at the throats of the priests in an instant. This was one of those moments upon which lives were changed.

Hrolf gabbled his translation as Snorri and the gold was taken to safety.

Charles of Rheims sheathed his sword and said something before turning and galloping off.

Hermund said, "He swore that he would have revenge for this act. From this day forth all Vikings will be burned alive. This is war."

The priests took the Bishop and headed for the safety of the Frankish lines.

Haaken laughed, "Then life becomes interesting once more! We have another enemy who seeks our lives!"

We had the time to load the ships secure and to ensure that we could tow the smaller boats too. We used them for the goods we had captured. I prayed that we would have safe winds to take us home. It would make a perfect end to an almost perfect raid.

Chapter 4

It was a veritable fleet of ships which sailed into the river at Úlfarrston. We had had more room on board but we had been forced to travel at the pace of the slow Frankish ships. The men who captained them for me were not impressed by their handling. We would use them for spares and for firewood when we were done. By the time we reached our friends Hermund's wound was less angry. Aiden and Kara would be able to do something for him, of that I had no doubt. He and Hrolf had become popular with all of the men on my drekar. Hrolf, in particular, was seen as a future warrior. He constantly harangued Haaken and the others for stories of my life and my adventures.

We had never returned with as much treasure or as few losses as that one voyage. We had been away for some time but there were men who would now be able to afford a full mail byrnie, a new sword and a helmet as good as mine. Others would buy animals and begin their own farms while there were some who would use this as the opportunity to marry. My only worry was those who had stayed at home would be a little jealous. Wolf Killer would not be among them. He would have a third of my treasure and Kara and Aiden another third. I had enough for my needs. I shared with my family.

Coen ap Pasgen, the headman of Úlfarrston, could not believe the treasure as it was brought ashore. We did not have enough carts to carry it all. I pointed to the captured vessels. "When the Frankish ships have been emptied and Bolli the shipwright has taken all that he needs then use the wood to make carts."

"But they are seaworthy ships, Jarl Dragonheart."

Erik Short Toe, who had stepped ashore with us spat into the water. "I would not sail on the Water with those let alone the sea. I feared they would capsize each league we took closer to home. Make them carts, headman, that is all they are fit for."

Coen shook his head still. "We have merchants now who sail with knarr which are full of weed. And worm. They would pay for such ships."

I smiled, "If they wish to buy them then you have permission to sell them. We will share the profits."

My Ulfheonar organised and guarded the treasure. I rode ahead to my home with just Haaken for company. It was one of the rare privileges I enjoyed. Others served me. My land looked welcoming as we emerged from the forest and looked on the Water with Old Olaf smiling down. It had been a good raid and we had not been away too long but it was good to be home. That side of being a Viking always felt alien to me. Perhaps that was the old people, my mother's folk. This had been their land and it was part of me.

Grim the fisherman, Olaf's father, saw us as we emerged from the forest and he sailed north to tell the people that we were home. Although it would take many hours for my warriors to reach Cyninges-tūn, wives and mothers would begin to prepare food for their Vikings.

"Are you worried about this Frank, Lord Charles of Rheims, Jarl?"

I shook my head, "He lives an ocean away and we have seen their ships. If he sailed here he would need to be a braver man than I take him for. But if he chose to come and seek vengeance then we would defeat him. They have no heart for fighting; we saw that. If they had then they would have attacked us the moment that they saw us outside their settlement. They outnumbered us but they were afraid to take us on. As soon as they waited to speak, then I knew."

"Perhaps they feared for their families."

"And that is what I mean. If my family was threatened it would not stop me fighting but if anything happened to them then my revenge would be terrible. It would be the same for you. The vengeance of a Viking is a terrible thing to behold.

"Aye but I am not jarl. I follow you and I serve you. I would not have that decision to make. You do."

We rode the last few miles in silence. He was right; he was always right. He knew me better than any man alive and we had stood side by side since we were little more than children. I knew not what I would do without him. His words made me think and reflect.

Those who lived along the edge of the Water and the feet of the Old Man came to greet us as we passed. Many had sons and husbands who fought alongside us. They did not ask after their warriors, they showed their respect by honouring me.

"The Allfather watches over you, Jarl."

"You have had a great victory, Jarl Dragonheart?"

"The wolf returns; we will all prosper."

My people believed that their well being and that of the land depended upon me. Only good could result from my return. They believed that the crops would be greater, the animals more fertile and the Water be filled with fish. They also knew that we rarely came back from a raid empty handed and that meant they too would benefit from our success.

Haaken left me a mile or two from my hall. He had his own hall up in the woods on the foothills of the Old Man. There his family awaited him. His wife Unn would be happy to see her hero return. I had a mile to travel lone and I saw Cyninges-tūn growing larger as I drew close to its wooden walls. It gave me comfort to see the solid walls and ditches. They made us safe from attack. We had not suffered one since the wolf winter many years ago but we were vigilant.

Brigid and Gruffyd waited at the gates for me. Of Aiden and Kara there was no sign. I was worried, briefly, and then I realised that if anything bad had happened then the people we had passed would have told us. It was more likely that Kara wanted Brigid to enjoy the welcome without the distraction of my two spirit guides. I smiled as I approached my family. Gruffyd was standing, albeit unsteadily. He was growing. A Viking warrior saw his children growing by stages. He would be away and when he returned it would be as though his child was a different being.

I dismounted. The pony wandered to the Water to drink. He would not stray far. Gruffyd held out his hand and I swept him up. His little arms wrapped around my head. He smelled clean and I felt dirty. "You have grown my little warrior and yet it has been less than a moon since I last saw you."

I put my left arm around Brigid who hugged me, "He began to walk four days since. He was determined that he would not be carried."

"Quite right too." I wandered down to the Water and placed him on the back of the pony. "Hold on to the mane." I put his hands into the pony's mane and led him by the reins back to Brigid.

"Be careful! He might fall!"

"And he will learn not to do so a second time. He is a Viking, my wife, he must learn to take knocks and blows. It will make him harder."

"But he is a child."

"There is no such thing as a Viking child; there are only Vikings who have yet to spill blood."

She shook her head. "Why did I marry a Viking and live among such people?"

I laughed, "Because you wanted a real man and not someone who would allow you to be mistreated."

She hugged me as we walked, "You are right. I forget those dark times but some of your ways are still a mystery to me."

"And that means you will never have a dull life will you?" I was in a good mood. I enjoyed the banter.

The gate was thronged with my people. They too called out their greetings. I waved a hand behind me, "Your men folk return. We have had a good raid. We have gold, Holy Books and meat which we must eat for it was not salted. Tonight we feast!"

They all cheered. Had we not had success I would have told them. They knew that I was never foresworn. They had the truth from me; no matter how unpalatable. I turned to Brigid. "Where are Kara and Aiden?"

"In the house of women. She is close to her time. Macha and Deidra are with them. Kara was convinced that your granddaughter awaited your return to enter this world."

I heard the scepticism in her voice, "And you do not?"

"I am still a Christian. How can I believe that?"

I nodded. "There will come a time." I handed her the reins of the pony. "I will see my daughter and then I must use the steam hut. I need cleansing."

"I sent Uhtric to light it when Grim brought the news of your return. I will come with you." She gave me a wry smile, "I would like to cleanse you too."

I kissed her, "I believe that is how Gruffyd came into the world."

"And perhaps he needs a sister eh?"

Scanlan, the headman, greeted me as I headed towards my daughter's hall. "We have much iron which needs trading, Jarl Dragonheart."

"Good but make sure that Bjorn has the first choice of the iron. Many warriors will be buying new weapons from him!"

"It was a good raid then?"

"It was."

"That is why more people are coming to our land to settle. We have had many visits from merchants too. Our home is growing."

"Then we must make a sacrifice to the gods, Scanlan. It does not do to take them for granted."

"Aye Jarl."

I strode into the house of women. My daughter provided a refuge for those women whose husbands had died or chose to live with other women or wished to be a volva. Deidra and Macha who had been servants of the White Christ lived there and ran it. Aiden was the only man, apart from me, who was allowed in.

Aiden came to greet me. "Jarl Dragonheart, Kara said you would come this day and she was right."

"Is the child born yet?"

"No but it is coming soon. The women know such things."

Even though they had been captured many years ago and we had treated them well, Deidra and Macha were always a little apprehensive around me. The fact that I was here and the birthing was so close also made them uncomfortable. The Norse women saw it as natural. The followers of the White Christ did not. Kara was lying on a pile of skins. They were sheepskins topped by the skin of a wolf. I was a wolf warrior and the skin would give my grandchild the protection of the wolf.

"You will have a granddaughter soon, father."

"Good." I kissed her on the forehead. She looked radiant. I saw in her face my dead wife, Erika.

"Mother is here with us too. She is happy."

That was the trouble with having a volva for a daughter; she read your thoughts. "I will go and be cleansed then I shall return."

She nodded, "And when you do I will be cleaned and ready with our child suckling in my arms."

I turned to leave. I saw that Aiden was torn between his wife and the desire to speak with me. "Stay with Kara. My news will wait. A few hours will not change it."

When I returned to Kara and Aiden I felt like a new man. I had been cleansed and Brigid had combed and oiled my beard and hair. I had learned to enjoy such pleasures in Miklagård. I had left the warrior in the steam hut and now I was Jarl Dragonheart ruler of the land of the waters, Cyninges-tūn. We left Gruffyd with Uhtric and went to see Kara. My daughter had been right and my granddaughter suckled at her breast. Brigid shook her head, "How did you know?"

Kara frowned, "I am a volva. I know my own body. I knew."

I saw that Aiden looked proud. I clasped his hand. "The babe is well?"

He laughed, "How would it be otherwise. She has healthy lungs and eats well."

"Have you named her yet?"

"We will dream it tonight. The spirits will tell us."

The baby had finished suckling and Kara held her out to me. "Meet your grandfather, child."

I picked up the baby whose eyes had closed. She had that smell which all babies have. I closed my eyes and sniffed. I could smell Wolf Killer, Gruffyd and Kara when they had been born. I held her close. Her tiny fingers wriggled into my beard. I put my mouth close to her ear and said softly, so that only she would hear, "I swear that I will guard you and your parents with my life. I am Jarl Dragonheart and you are descended from the ancient ones of this land. One day you will grow into the most powerful woman in this land. I am no wizard but I can see that. You are part of me and part of this land." I kissed her and handed her back to Kara. Kara nodded and I saw tears in her eyes.

Brigid took my arm. "Come husband, let us go. They need to be alone with their child and the people have a feast prepared for you."

The old warrior hall in Cyninges-tūn was now used by my people for feasting. Most warriors had their own farms and homes. As I entered they all cheered. None of my Ulfheonar were there. They would be with their families but all those, like Rolf Eriksson who had been on the raid, were. Karl One Hand who had been an Ulfheonar was now the warrior who watched my home when I was absent. He stood aside from his seat at the end of the table and greeted me, "Hail Jarl Dragonheart! Until we have the songs sung by Haaken, tell us of the great deeds that you performed in Frankia."

I waved them to their seats and then said, "Instead of my words hear the stories from a new Viking; a warrior who will fight alongside us. Come, Hrolf son of Gerloc, warrior of Neustria and tell your new family your story and how the Norns wove it into my story and Hermund One Eye will fill in any gaps. I would eat and drink for I have missed Thorbjorg the ale wife's beer!"

Thorbjorg swelled with pride at my praise. Hrolf began to tell his story, haltingly at first but growing in confidence when my people hung on his every word. Hermund helped him out a couple of times. I smiled for it was obvious that Hrolf had never had such attention before. I could see him growing and becoming a Viking once more. He and Hermund had been close on the voyage home for they had much in common. Hermund had taken the young slave under his wing. Even as I listened to them I was planning for their future. I leaned closer to Brigid. "I would have these two live in my hall."

She laughed and kissed my cheek, "For a Viking you have the softest of hearts. Dragonheart indeed! They should have named you lamb's heart! But I love you for it. You did the same for me and I will be eternally grateful. Of course they shall live in our hall. It is *wyrd*."

It was my turn to laugh, "We are changing you then. You now believe in *wyrd*!"

"Let us just say I see events occurring which my beliefs cannot explain!"

The evening degenerated into a beer fuelled celebration of our life by the Water, beneath our mountain. I waved over Hermund and Hrolf. The young Viking was still glowing from the attention. "Until you are ready for your own home my wife and I would like you to live with us and my son in my hall. What say you?"

I thought that Hrolf would burst into tears of joy. He seemed incapable of speech. Hermund smiled and spoke for them both, "We have both spent many years with a yoke around our necks and slept with swine. We do not deserve this honour but we would not show you disrespect by refusing. We will sleep in your hall and serve you as best we can although what you need in a one eyed slave and an unproven youth I know not."

"You have both proved yourself and look around. I do not discard those who serve me because they are not whole. Haaken lost an eye and is the mightiest of the Ulfheonar. Karl One Hand was Karl Word Master until he lost a limb fighting for me. If you are one of my people then I protect you unto death."

Unprompted, they both knelt. "We swear to be your men, Jarl."

"You are happy to be oathsworn?"

"We are."

I took out Ragnar's Spirit. "Then swear on the sword which was touched by the gods."

I saw the awe in their eyes as they laid their hands on the blade and intoned their oath. Their words were so quiet as to be almost inaudible but it mattered not; the Allfather heard them and they were binding. They were my men until they died.

I always enjoyed my first day home from a raid. I got to walk and talk among my people. As usual, my first visit was to Bjorn Bagsecgson my blacksmith. He was like Thor himself beating out metal in his smithy by the Water. He stopped as I approached. Grinning he pointed to the pile of metal in the corner. "It was a good raid Jarl."

"Aye it was and the Allfather protected us, we lost but a handful of men."

"These candlesticks from the churches of the White Christ; do you wish to use them or melt them down?"

"We need no plates nor candlesticks. I doubt that we will get the value we should from selling them. Use them. I would have a golden wolf made for my son and each of my grandchildren." He nodded. "I know that Aiden normally makes such things but it is his child and I would like to surprise him."

"My grandson, Bjorn Bjornson, has worked with Aiden. If you would give him the opportunity I am certain that he would do a fine job."

"Good. Make it so and I would have two short swords made for Hrolf and Hermund, the two captives we rescued."

"That is generous, Jarl, they were thralls."

"But for them, Bjorn, we would not have had the success we did. Remember that I too was a slave once."

He laughed, "Aye I remember. You and Old Ragnar up in the mountains fighting snow and wolves. You were so scrawny in those days we were convinced that a strong wind would blow you over. You have grown."

"Aye I learned much from old Ragnar. It was he gave me my first bow and my first sword. I continue as he would have done. " I pointed to the pile of metal. "You will have many orders for swords."

He smiled, "And I have smiths who will make those. I chose whom I smith for. Your swords will be done first. Do you have any ideas about the design?"

"A wolf's head pommel springs to mind."

"And length?"

"Hrolf is small and Hermund is to live in my home. They need them only for protection. When Hrolf grows we will see about a warrior's blade."

"Aye, I could do that."

As I left my smith I looked at the Old Man of Cyninges-tūn. In the morning he always seemed to smile. Perhaps it was the sun's rays from the east which did that. It was another reason I walked the eastern shore in the morning.

My Ulfheonar arrived at noon so that we could divide the treasure. The last of it arrived from Úlfarrston in the mid morning. The other warriors who had fought with us were there to receive their share. I saw Hrolf and Hermund hanging back. When I had divided it up I called them over. There were two gold pieces in the chest. "Here is your treasure." I also handed them a shield, a sword belt and a helmet. The shields were not as good as ours, they were Frankish, but they would do for a while.

"Thank you lord," Hrolf proffered his short seax. "And I have a sword already!"

"That is not a sword for a Viking. Bjorn the Smith will have your swords ready before too long. A warrior who fights for me has only the best."

Bjorn's grandson worked hard and he worked quickly. It took him but two days to make them. His father already had the mould we had used to make the ones for my Ulfheonar. It was just a case of melting down the gold and casting them. I think he was keen to impress me. When he showed me the first one I was impressed. He had even found a fragment of the blue stone for each of the wolves' eyes. "They will be ready on the morrow, Jarl when I have polished and fitted the thong."

I handed him one of the gold pieces I had been paid by the Franks.

He shook his head, "It is too much I cannot accept such a fortune."

"I have underpaid you for this wolf will protect my son and my grandchildren. Take it or I will be insulted."

My son arrived four days after the feast. He came with his son and his wife, Elfrida with her new child. I had not seen them since the birth of Elfrida's daughter, Erika. I hugged him when he dismounted, "Thank you for watching over my land while we raided. There is treasure for you in my hall."

He nodded. "We did little to earn it. There were no raids and no incomers. We had peace."

I embraced Elfrida, "And how does my granddaughter fare?"

"She is healthy, Jarl."

"And she has a cousin now with whom to play. Kara gave birth to a daughter too."

Elfrida and Kara got on well. They were like sisters and she was pleased. "What is the child's name?"

I shrugged, "They have not dreamed it. When a volva and galdramenn get together it is a world of the spirits they inhabit. They will tell us in due course. All I know is she has the right number of everything and she looks healthy."

Brigid shook her head, "Ask him if the babe smiled at him!"

"She did!"

Brigid and Elfrida laughed, "It was wind but my husband always thinks that all babies smile at him."

We all went to my hall where Kara and Aiden waited with their new child. After Elfrida had said how beautiful she was and Kara had said the same about Erika I asked. "Do we have a name yet or do we still say her and she?"

Kara looked at Aiden; he said, "We dreamed and we had the same dream. A she wolf came down from Olaf's mountain and the bairn suckled. We both saw her grow strong and powerful. She became a dragon."

I nodded, "She has a heart like her grandfather and the spirit of the wolf. What is her name then?"

"Ylva, female wolf."

I took out the four golden wolves and placed them around the necks of my son and grandchildren. Tears filled Kara's eyes, "*Wyrd*!"

All of the family nodded and said, as one, "*Wyrd*."

Chapter 5

The early summer was a time for hunting. It made us all into better warriors and produced better animals for inevitably we killed the weaker beasts. But warriors can only hunt for so long and then they yearn for the chance to hunt men. My young men wished to go raiding again. Success breeds confidence. I was loath to spend a long time away from my family. I urged my men to raid without me but all wished to be led by me. I was seen as the good luck charm. Wolf Killer was the one who persuaded me. "My warriors wish to join with you. My drekar, *'The Wild Boar'* is restless too. She needs to feel the ocean beneath her keel."

I spoke with Brigid. She laughed, "A Viking asking a woman if he ought to raid? It is true the old ways run strong in you. Your people need the raids. It keeps them strong and we will be safe enough if you do not take all your warriors."

It was true; we were protected by the mountains. Úlfarrston guarded the south, Thorkell's Stad the north and Cyninges-tūn sat like a jewel in the centre of a crown of mountains. When Aiden managed to tear himself away from his daughter he visited with me and we discussed what we might do and where we might raid. Aiden frequently visited with Siggi and the other knarr captains who plied the seas trading for us. They were his spies. They returned with goods we could not get elsewhere and information. It was snippets. There would be a piece here and a piece there. The result was that Aiden's mind was filled with pictures of the world and, in particular, Britannia. When you added his skills and his mind he was a formidable weapon.

"It seems to me that Mercia is ripe for a raid."

"Is not King Coenwulf in the process of conquering Dyfed?"

"He is Jarl and that is a good reason to attack him. He has recently captured Rhufuniog from the men of Gwynedd. They will be vulnerable to a raid from the north and King Coenwulf is busy in the far south of the land."

The area was well known to us. We had frequently raided there. The Welsh churches in that area were richly endowed and there was a monastery at St. Asaph. What Aiden said made sense. Although there would be Mercian warriors there their attention would be on the west and not their own lands to the east. We knew the rivers well. The Maeresea and the Dee were easy rivers for us to navigate. We had taken Caerlleon before now. It was also less than half a day's voyage from Úlfarrston. Perhaps Sigtrygg would join us. He had been Ulfheonar and his warriors would also be restless. Once more my galdramenn had provided a solution.

"And would you sail with us or does my granddaughter demand your presence here?"

I spoke the words in jest and he had the good grace to nod, "You are right. I should come with you. Who knows what treasures you and your warriors might overlook."

"The Holy Books we found in Frankia were not overlooked were they?"

"No Jarl and we should sell them as soon as we can. The priests of the White Christ look after them better than we do."

I was decided and I sent messages to my jarls that any warriors who wished to come raiding should gather at Úlfarrston by the end of the next moon. I would choose those who would come then. I gave the same choice to my Ulfheonar. They were all happy to come with us. When I was talking with them I noticed that Hermund did not look happy. "What is the problem Hermund?"

"I feel, Jarl Dragonheart, that I should raid with you but I fear I cannot."

"You think you should come because I rescued you?"

"Aye Jarl."

"Then stay here. My family needs protection and you now have a sword. I will have more than enough warriors who wish to raid. I will not think any less of you for staying behind. My wife needs protection. That is your task."

"Thank you Jarl." The relief on his face touched me. Not every Norseman was a warrior.

Hrolf said, "But I would come with you Jarl."

"It will be dangerous. My men cannot watch over someone because they are young."

He nodded defiantly, "Aiden told me that you went on raids when you were little older than me."

"That is true."

"Then I shall go for I would be you when I am older."

"Very well. But you look after yourself."

Sigtrygg wished to raid and so we would take four ships. I would leave *'Red Snake'* at Úlfarrston. Her presence in the river would make others think we were all at home. The warriors who gathered were too many for me to take. Those who were older I left behind. Those without a helmet and a shield I left behind. Eventually we had four fully crewed drekar. As we were travelling so close to home I took Siggi and his knarr. We would be able to protect him and we could bring back greater quantities of slaves and treasure.

I decided we would leave at noon and that way we could be ready to raid their towns and monasteries by dawn. Other knarr left that morning for our iron was in great demand as was our timber. As we were about to set sail we saw a ship approaching. Sails could mean danger and so we waited. When the knarr came to a rest in the harbour I breathed a sigh of relief. It was a trader from Hibernia. The captain had heard of our raid in Frankia and chose to profit from it. He brought fine clothes and fabrics from far away. They were the sort of things we could not get other than by trade. As most ports were now closed to us it was a sign that we were being sought out.

We left before he had the opportunity to trade with us but those who remained would soon reward the captain's enterprise with gold. I also knew it would be the start of an avalanche of such traders.

Hrolf would not be a passenger and I set him to work with the crew of the *'Heart of the Dragon'*. To be fair to him he did not shirk from the work and leapt up the sail and the rigging with the other boys. He showed no fear. He had confided in Rollo Thin Hair that he thought he had been reborn when I had freed him. His life began that day on the Seine.

Aiden had already planned where we would raid. Nantwich had great quantities of salt as well as vast granaries. Some of the meat we had taken in Frankia had spoiled. Had we had more salt we could have preserved it. There might be no wheat or corn but there would be oats and barley. Both were valuable. He also thought that there was a monastery close by the burgh. It would not be our only raid but it would be our first one. By attacking deep in Mercian land we would draw his horsemen there and that would allow us to raid along the Clwyd Valley where we knew there were riches to be had.

We reached the Maeresea before dark. It was a sparsely populated land. The first time we had raided we had captured my steward, Scanlan and his family. In the years since we had taken most of those who live in this land as slaves. The Mercians had not settled it and Caerlleon was their northern outpost. We would avoid that. After we had disembarked we moored the drekar in the middle of the river. We left enough guards to repel any enemies. Then we headed south east twenty miles to Nantwich. It took most of the night but Snorri and Beorn were familiar with the paths and Aiden had his maps and charts with us.

We had avoided the settlements along the way. It was dark of night and there was no moon. We were a black shadow moving across a black land. We only had a handful of Ulfheonar but my men all affected darkened clothes and armour. Some of our enemies called us the Black Vikings or the army of the dead. We were not offended by the title. Snorri, Beorn and the other scouts reached us as we saw the faint first light of dawn.

"Nantwich is a mile along the road. They have sentries."

We knew the layout of the burgh. I sent Wolf Killer to the east, Sigtrygg to the south, Asbjorn to the west and we took the north. No one would escape and each of the four gates would be assaulted at the same time. They would not know what hit them. As the crew of *'Heart of the Dragon'* ran along the old Roman road I felt my years. I was not as fit as I had once been. However I could still keep up with them I was just not as fast as I had once been. There was a dark shadow ahead and I knew that it was Nantwich. It rose from the plain along the bend of the river. The river would not be a barrier for us; it was Asbjorn and his men who would have to ford it. We halted while men adjusted their shields and their armour.

I waved Hrolf over. "Your task is to stay with the galdramenn and guard him."

"Am I not to attack with you, Jarl Dragonheart?"

"You are to do as your Jarl orders and nothing more!"

"Yes Jarl."

I knew that Aiden would watch over him. Aiden and he had much in common.

I led my men towards the burgh. Built by Coenwulf it was a copy of the Roman forts. With four gates and a pair of towers guarding each gate they were well made. However the Saxons had not worked out how to make their ditches as deadly as the Romans. There would be no traps and the far bank could be climbed without difficulty. We did not run. Ours was the shortest route. The others would have to run to reach their gates and enable us to assault at the same time. Beorn the Scout and Snorri did run. They strung their bows and ran to the side of the ditch. I might worry about the warriors on the other gates failing to make a clean kill but not my two archers. No matter how many men were on the gate they would die and die silently.

As we approached the gates I waved. Olaf, Ulf, Finni and Vermund ran towards Beorn and Snorri. Even as we approached I heard the two arrows as they sped towards the doomed sentries. Before they had fallen to the ground my four Ulfheonar held their shields ready for us to leap upon them. This time it would not be me who would leap it would be Rollo Thin Skin and Erik Wolf Claw. I went with Haaken and the rest of my band to the gate. I heard a shout from the southern gate. The alarm was given. I did not worry; it was inevitable and we would soon have control of this northern gate.

I held my shield tightly and felt that of Haaken nestling on my right arm. Rollo Thin Skin and Erik Wolf Claw swung open the gate and we ran in. There were shafts of light as people emerged from their huts to see the danger. We were already racing towards them through the packed walkways of the burgh. It was only the north to south and east to west ways which were straight. The others were cluttered alleys and paths. I yelled, "Spread out!"

Haaken and I worked as a pair. We slew two Saxons before they even knew we were there. A blacksmith came from his forge roaring and swinging his hammer. Haaken took the blow on his shield and I slashed the smith across his middle. It was when we neared the warrior hall in the centre that we saw organisation. An eorledman was organising a shield wall. I shouted, "Ulfheonar, to me!"

Haaken and I kept moving resolutely forward towards the twenty warriors. Even as we approached I could see, from the light spilling out of the hall, that half wore mail and had full helmets. They locked shields to form a double row with their backs to the hall. Olaf Leather Neck appeared at my left with Finni to his left. Vermund stood next to Haaken and Ulf on his right. Two arrows thudded into the two warriors on the extreme left of the shield wall and I knew where Snorri and Beorn were.

We were a natural wedge and I did not break stride. I chose the man I would strike. He was in the front rank. He had a full face helmet and a mail coif but his shield was made only of wood. There was neither boss nor iron strengtheners. That was his weakness. His spear jabbed towards my face and I easily turned it with my shield. My sword was held behind me and he was now weaponless. Those around him had stabbed at Olaf and Haaken. Their spears were also redundant. They relied on their locked shields and double line of men. I stabbed forwards at the junction of their shields. I wriggled the sword as it met resistance and I pushed hard. I am a big man and with my mail I am heavy. Behind me I felt the weight of the bodies of my other warriors and the Saxon line began to move.

I pushed again with my sword. I found myself face to face with the warrior who cursed me in Saxon. "You will rot in hell pagan!"

I head butted him as I replied, "I am a Viking and I will be in Valhalla drinking, Saxon!" As he recoiled his foot slipped a little and my blade finally found something soft. I pushed hard. I felt warm blood pouring down my blade and on to my hand. I pushed harder. I watched the light go from his eyes and he fell. There was a gap and I stepped into it and punched the next warrior with the boss of my shield. I had room to swing and I brought my blade overhand to smash down on his helmet. It did not break the metal but it stunned him and he too fell to the ground. I stamped across his throat as I turned to stab into the side of the next warrior. A shield wall only works when it is a solid wall. As soon as it is broken it becomes a liability for it is rigid. My Ulfheonar spread down the line slaying the Saxon warriors.

When they all lay slain, dawn had broken and the burgh was ours. Wolf Killer and the other jarls joined me at the warrior hall. "We have secured the gates! It is a great victory Jarl Dragonheart!"

"Aye, Wolf Killer, it is. Have carts collected and begin to collect the booty."

I took off my helmet and put my shield around my back. I held Ragnar's Spirit in my hand. We moved back towards the gate. I saw Erik Wolf Claw and he was cradling Sven Thorirson. Sven was wounded. I knelt down and saw that he had been gutted. His left hand cradled his entrails. Sven had been on many raids with me. He opened his eyes. "Jarl Dragonheart, my life hangs by a thread. Soon I will be in Valhalla. Honour me by cutting the thread. Odin himself will welcome a warrior slain by Ragnar's Spirit. I was ever your man. I have been privileged to fight alongside you."

"And I have been honoured to be served by you. I will care for your family as though they were my own. I will see you in Valhalla." I plunged Ragnar's Spirit into his heart and with a sigh he died. "Have his tokens and his sword taken back for his son." Karl nodded. They had been friends.

Aiden and Hrolf entered the gates soon after we began burning the bodies of our dead. If we had buried them then they would have been despoiled by the Saxons. Their heads would have been placed on spears and their manhoods placed in their mouths. It would not hurt the dead but we would not afford them that satisfaction. The mail from the dead warriors we had slain was distributed. Everything of value was put on carts and the few horses we found were attached. We chose only the captives who would be of use to us. There were boys who would work in our mines and girls and women who would be of service in our homes. The rest we left. They would tell others no doubt of our presence in Mercia but by then we would have reached our ships. We headed north and west.

Aiden had been disappointed in the finds. The church had no Holy Books worth taking and there were no maps or writings. The Eorl of Nantwich had not been a literate man. Hrolf tagged along behind Aiden. He listened as we spoke. "We have a great deal of salt and barley now, Jarl."

"Aye, I shall send it back with Siggi and the knarr. The captives can be taken too. The animals we captured we will eat."

"We leave for the Clwyd?"

"First we rest and then we head to the Clwyd. I will send Wolf Killer in his drekar to wait off the mouth of the river. I would have you go with him. That way we attack from two directions. If they flee they will head into our fish trap."

When Hrolf became a great warrior and leader, many years later, it was the education he had listening to us speak which gave him a knowledge that could not be bought.

It was a slower journey back for we had carts but we were not bothered by our enemies. I saw horsemen watching us but we were too great a host to attack. Caerlleon was many miles away. Even if they sent warriors we would have reached our drekar before they could intervene. We loaded the knarr as soon as we reached the Maeresea and those who had wounds were sent with Siggi to guard the prisoners. There were wails and tears as the captives saw their fate. They would not be rescued. They were to be taken to our homeland and there they would end their days.

I sat and ate with Aiden, my jarls and my captains. "We sail tomorrow for the mouth of the Dee. Aiden will go with Wolf Killer. The rest of us will land and head across country to the head of the Clwyd Valley. The drekar will go to the mouth of the Clwyd. We will sweep down the valley and Wolf Killer will land and head up the valley. St. Asaph is close to the mouth of the river. Wolf Killer will capture and hold it." He nodded. "I have no doubt that they will have a watch tower and they will see the drekar. They will assume that we land a large force and will flee up the valley."

Sigtrygg laughed, "And they will run into our arms."

I nodded. "I hope so but if not we destroy all hope when we appear at their monastery."

Asbjorn was a thoughtful warrior. "Who will we fight? Are these Saxons or the men of Gwynedd?"

"A good question. Coenwulf and his Mercians have captured this land but I do not think those whom he defeated will see us as saviours. We fight everyone." A Viking had no friends.

We left at dawn to sail around the piece of land which separated the two rivers. I knew that we would be seen and our movements reported to the Mercian garrisons but I knew what they did not. I knew where we were going. The tide was in and that was a relief. We disembarked three of the drekar leaving a skeleton crew on board. Even though it was high tide the mud of the estuary still sucked at us as we headed to the dunes. Thanks to Aiden's Roman maps we knew that it was no more than ten Roman miles to St. Asaph but we would have to go fifteen miles to get up the Clwyd valley and in position. We did not use the roads but ran across the fields, through the woods and down the greenways. I wanted us to be as hidden as we could be.

After two hours of hard running we reached the Clwyd. Here it was narrow, less than twenty paces from bank to bank and fordable. We drank while we gathered ourselves. Snorri and Beorn leapt off like hares. As we rested we heard from the west the sound of a tolling bell. It did not sound like an alarm bell but one summoning the monks of the White Christ to some prayers. They seemed to do it both day and night. Satisfied that we were close we crossed the river. There was another river, the Elwy, about a mile ahead. I had seen it once. Snorri and Beorn would tell us exactly how close it was.

I split us into our war bands with mine in the middle. We were the largest and we had the Ulfheonar. We moved more slowly now for we had obviously formed the trap and the drekar had not been seen. Snorri and Beorn returned. "The river is half a mile to the west of us and the monastery just two miles north of us."

"Good. Asbjorn, take the right. Sigtrygg the left."

We spread out in a long loose line. We were not trying to be a shield wall but a line of hunters waiting for the game to come to us. Hopefully the human prey would come to us. When I heard the alarm bell I could tell the difference. It was strident and accompanied by shouts which we could hear. We could not see the monastery. The ground was undulating. We could, however, hear the monks and those who had fled the monastery as they ran towards us. We stopped and held our shields before us. The first ten ran into our blades. The cries of the dying arrested the others and they turned and ran back to the monastery.

"Erik Wolf Claw, take four men and search the monks for treasure. They have crosses around their necks. Often they are made of silver or gold."

We moved towards the monastery. After half a mile it came into view. It had a low wall around it; it was meant to keep out animals and not Vikings. As we approached I saw the monks fleeing north and west. My drekar were there. I remembered that the King of this land had had a palace at Rhuddlan. Perhaps the Mercians had defended it. It made no difference we would sack the monastery.

We climbed the slope and I shouted, "Only kill the priests if they fight. They are worth gold to us." I knew that the Danes and some Norse killed them out of hand. It was a waste. They were literate slaves and could be sold in the slave market. The monastery was not just a church. There were many buildings and houses. My men began to flood through them gathering anything of value. The animals were being herded together and the ones who had been slain were stripped of anything of value. I went with Haaken to the church.

Some of my men were carrying out the fine linen, curtains and candlesticks. I sought other treasures. We did not have Aiden with us but he would have told me where to search if he had been with us; beneath the altar. It was their most holy place. Often they buried their saints there. The relics from such saints were worth gold too. I did not understand it myself but we had profited from such sales before.

Men moved the wooden rails which surrounded the altar and lifted the carpet. The red woven carpet was also worth taking. Beneath it we found what I had sought; a trapdoor. It was not obvious. You had to know what you sought but there was a line around the stone which showed where it had been lifted and replaced. I laid down my shield and took out my seax and ran it around the edge. Once the accumulated dirt had been removed I nodded to Haaken. He placed his seax on the opposite side of the stone to me and we both began to prise it up. At first I thought it would not move and we would break our blades but it began to rise, as though spirited up and we pushed down harder. As soon as we could we slipped our hands beneath it and lifted. There was a rush of cold and musty air.

I grabbed one of the burning brands and held it in the hole. This one was deeper than most of the Roman ones we had discovered. I saw that there were steps leading down. I took off my helmet and placed it on my shield. Taking the torch I descended. It was not high enough to stand but it was extensive. I saw pillars supporting the floor of the church above me. There was a stone tomb. I only recognised a couple of the letters but I guessed that it was the tomb of the saint after whom the monastery was named. If we found nothing else then I would desecrate it but it took time to open such tombs.

As I swept the torch around I saw the treasure we sought. There were boxes and chests. Some were small but one was large. "Haaken, get down here. We have treasure."

Between the two of us we were able to manhandle the large chest to the entrance and lift it out. The smaller ones we managed a little easier. I left the saint to his rest. His bones would not be disturbed; at least not this time. I slung my shield on my back once we reached the church. I shouted for my men to return. We gave them the boxes to carry. "Snorri, are there any horses?"

"No, Jarl. The monks fled with them. They have gone to the fort just down river."

"Then we carry what we have. Let those without mail carry the boxes."

"Do you not wish to see their contents?"

"No, Haaken, that can wait. They would not have hidden them if they contained nothing of value. It will be better if Aiden is there when we examine them."

"Aye Jarl Dragonheart."

"Any sign of our drekar?"

"No Jarl but the fort is on a piece of high ground and blocks the view of the river. They would struggle to come this far."

Had I brought the small drekar, **'Red Snake'** then we would have managed it. Perhaps I had made an error of judgement.

I led my warriors down the river towards the distant fort. Asbjorn took his men to the right and crossed the river. I went along the northern bank while Sigtrygg stayed on the south bank. We found discarded objects as we went. There were fine garments and tapestries. They had managed to get them thus far and then fear of capture made them hurry. We gathered all that had been dropped.

Then I saw the mast of a drekar. I knew that it would be my son's. I hoped that the Saxons had no machines of war or they could damage the drekar. We needed all four of them. We began to climb up towards the wooden wall which encircled the hill fort. "Have the treasure taken to my son's drekar." I had no idea how many men were within the walls of this burgh but I doubted that they would be able to defend it for long. I had enough men with me to do as we had at Nantwich and attack all four sides at once. We also had time on our side. If the garrison at Caerlleon had been summoned they would have gone to Nantwich first. We had a whole day before any help would reach this valley. We would make them sweat and then attack at night.

As I crested the rise arrows headed in my direction. I brought my shield around but not before one had struck my helmet. I heard a cheer from behind the walls. I raised my sword and my men yelled, "Dragonheart!" It was an answer to the defenders. It would take more than an arrow to kill me.

We formed a shield wall. My Ulfheonar were the front rank with the others behind us. I peered over my shield to view the gate and the walls. There was a ditch running around the outside of the wall and a bridge across it. They would have archers in the two gate towers. It would have to be my Ulfheonar who attacked. We had mail. I turned, "Archers, clear the towers and the walls. Snorri, organise them."

Sigtrygg brought his men from across the river to join us. "A sturdy burgh."

"Aye, have your archers join Snorri. When Asbjorn and his men reach us we will see if we can clear the walls."

Soon we had the archers from our three bands releasing shower after shower of arrows. The Saxons were poor archers and they did no damage to us. Our shields were as solid a defence as the walls behind which they sheltered. In contrast they were not armoured and the archers decimated the walls. I saw men pitch to their deaths before us and others who fell into the burgh.

Suddenly the gates opened and ten horsemen galloped towards us followed by a host of spearmen. They would outnumber us until Wolf Killer brought his men from the drekar. With our archers sheltering behind us we had but forty warriors to face them. "Lock shields!" We had fought horsemen before. They were not as fearsome as many believed. Lacking the stirrups they used in the east they could be easily pulled from their saddles. The danger lay in the hooves of the horses. They were the killers.

As I expected the horsemen did not charge our wall of shields but tried to get around the rear of our lines. The spearmen ran at us with their weapons held before them like a hedgehog. The secret was to watch the spear and use a sword to break the shaft. It was then a useless piece of wood. The ones who made the mistake of attacking the Ulfheonar paid a heavy price. I watched Haaken contemptuously smash the ash shaft of the spear before bringing his sword around to take the warrior's head. I knocked a spear head up with my shield and then eviscerated the warrior with my sword. Inevitably the combat broke into small groups. I led my Ulfheonar forward. The gates were open and the Saxons before us fled.

"Come we can take this burgh!"

We began to run up the hill. Suddenly I heard, "Jarl Dragonheart! Beware!"

I turned in time to see two of the horsemen who had survived galloping towards me. I braced myself. Rolf Eriksson, who had shouted the warning raced over to attack the horsemen. He had the long Danish axe given to him by Olaf. He swung it at the leading horse and it bit deep into the beast's chest. The rider was flung over the dying animal's head and landed at my feet. As the second horsemen tried to swerve out of the way Rolf raised his axe high over his head and brought it down on the horseman. It chopped through his thigh and into the horse. The rider fell screaming to the ground and took the horse with him. As I slew the Mercian at my feet Rolf took the head of the other rider and then ended the horse's suffering by taking its head.

He stood panting, the lust of battle in his eyes. Olaf laughed, "I can see you were made for that weapon. You are Rolf Eriksson no more from this day forth you are Rolf Horse Killer!"

It was just the spur my men needed, "On!"

We raced to the gates which the last men inside were trying to close. We hurled ourselves at the gates and they sprang open. Haaken and Ulf slew the two men who had tried to close them. We were inside their fort and they had no chance. We were killers and we had the roar of battle coursing through our veins. We fell upon the sheep within the fold and every warrior was slaughtered.

The captives were subdued and kept in the church which lay within the fort. We stripped it of all its riches. The monks were cowed. There were no women at all. I guessed that the garrison were the warriors who had captured the fort from the men of Gwynedd. We had a fine collection of mail and swords. There were Holy Books, linens and tapestries. We ate well. Rollo's kill had provided the meat. We ate horse. With our ships sheltered beneath the walls we brought Wolf Killer's crew into the fort. I doubted that there were any Saxon warriors close by but it did not do to take chances.

Aiden explored the church and found some Roman writings and other parchments from the time of the Warlord. He sat poring over them while Haaken began composing his song about Rolf Horse Killer. The young warrior now had the mail shirt from the warrior he had killed as well as his sword. He was a rich man. More than that, however, he now had a reputation and he would be immortalised in a saga.. I saw Hrolf looking enviously at him. He was a hero and Hrolf was a friend of the hero. Such things are important.

"Tomorrow, my son, I want you to take a war band and scour the valley. See what else we can find. Sigtrygg you will go with Snorri and Beorn to the coast I would know where the nearest Saxons are. I cannot believe these are the only warriors left."

"Do we not return home?"

"Not yet, Asbjorn. There is still much to be harvested. We will leave this land a wasteland before we return to Cyninges-tūn. This will be our last raid of the year. We might as well make it a fruitful one. There are many farms and they will have both animals and grain."

Aiden came to speak with me when the others began to drink and celebrate our victory. "Jarl, your ancestor built this as a hill fort. I found carvings on the floor of one of the rooms. It was being used to store food but I think it was like the Roman Praetorium we found close to the Wall."

"*Wyrd*."

"You are right Jarl. The Norns threads spread through time, do they not?"

"Did you find any treasure?"

"A few coins but nothing much. I think the chests you sent to the drekar will be more interesting. I had them stored in the hold. They have locks and as we found no keys it will take time to unlock them."

"I could smash them open you know."

"It will not hurt to wait."

My war bands spent the next day exploring the two ends of the valleys. We garnered much grain and animals. The people fled at my men's approach and so we had no slaves. Sigtrygg found a watch tower. They slew the Saxons there but found no others. If the Welsh chose they would be able to reconquer their home. We divided the mail, weapons and coins amongst the four crews. Sigtrygg would sail directly home but the rest of us would sail to Hibernia and sell the slaves to Hakon the Bald in Dyflin. Whilst not a friend or even someone I would care to share secrets with he was an ally and was keen to trade. He was useful in his own way. He would never raid. His men did not raid. He just controlled Dyflin and taxed the whores and the merchants. He was not a real Viking but he was Norse. He might, however, be able to broker the sale of the Holy Books. He would take a share of the profits but it would save us the job. We headed for Dyflin.

We had not been there since we had sought Magnus the Foresworn. Hakon had been helpful. We had paid him for his help but he had been useful, nonetheless.

He had grown fatter since our last visit. But he was pleased to see us. "I have missed not only your trades, my friend but also the tales of your adventures. You are the last true Norseman. You fear no man. Tell me what you have been up to and where you acquired these monks."

"You will buy them?"

"Of course. There is a lucrative market for such men of learning. Why I might even sell them back to the Mercians." He sent for his moneyer and we were given a small chest of silver. "Who know, King Egbert of Wessex might pay good gold for such as these."

"We also have some fine Holy Books but those we took from Frankia."

"I heard that you had upset Louis the Pious. His cousin Charles of Rheims has sworn to hunt you down and kill you."

"The seas between us are too wide for me to worry about that and he has poor skills with weapons. I fear him not."

"Whom do you fear?"

"No man save myself. If I were my enemy I would be afraid."

He laughed, "As would I. You are like a terrier. You care not the size of the beast. Once you sink your teeth in you do not let go. I am glad that you are my friend."

"It is the only way to keep your lands and people safe."

"Will you stay?"

"No, for I have two new granddaughters I am keen to see and their fathers are desperate to see their wives. I will send the Holy Books and you can sell them."

"For a commission."

"Of course. A quarter of their value?"

"A half."

"Because you helped me in the business with the Foresworn I will say a third but no more."

He shook my hand, "Then it is done."

As we left my son said, "How do you know he will not cheat you, father?"

"Because he knows I am Dragonheart and he fears me. Besides we help him more than he helps us. He will be keen to remain friends with us. He will not cheat me."

Chapter 6

Although it was a short voyage home the winds were against us. We discovered that was the work of the Norns and we did not reach Coen ap Pasgen's port until the middle of the night. The tide was wrong for a landing and we waited in the estuary until the tide turned at dawn. It soured, somewhat, the successful raid. We had hoped to be home earlier. Each warrior was keen to tell his family of our successful raid. We unloaded the ships and used the newly made carts to transport them home. As we docked I saw knarr leaving to trade. The channel was a busy one these days. Each time we left or arrived there would be some knarr or other leaving.

"Siggi, we shall send you the Holy Books. Hakon the Bald has promised to sell them for us."

"Aye Jarl and we have much iron to sell too. Should I take a cargo of that as well?"

I nodded, "We have few others who will pay a fair price."

We set off up the road to our home. It was early and I did not expect a reception. We were half way along the road by the Water when Karl One Hand galloped up to greet us. "Jarl, there has been a raid. Danes came through Wolf Killer's valley and slew many of his. They destroyed Windar's mere. Windar is dead along with most of his warriors."

The Norns had been busy. I saw that the tides had been the work of the weird sisters. They delayed our return. "When was this?"

"The news arrived late last night. Two shepherd boys witnessed it from the fells. They brought the news directly to us. I suppose it might have been two days since, perhaps less."

"Does Ketil now about his father?"

He shook his head. "I was going to ride there this morning with that news and then Grim spied your return."

I turned to Wolf Killer. "At least your wife and children were safe here in my hall."

His face was grim, "Aye, father but my men's families were not here. They will have been taken."

I had decisions to make. "Snorri, get back to Úlfarrston. I need Sigtrygg and his men. Have them meet us at Elfridaby."

"Aye Jarl."

"Wolf Killer, take your men to Elfridaby and find out the extent of the hurt we have suffered. I will follow with my men." He turned. I put my hand on his arm, "Wait for me. That is my command!"

"Aye Jarl."

"Karl One Arm, ride to Ketil and tell him the news. Have the men from Ulf's Water meet us at Windar's Mere. We go to war."

By the time we reached Cyninges-tūn Aiden and I had formulated our strategy. We could not take all of our men. We needed to defend my home. Perhaps this was more than a raid or perhaps a lure to drag us away from our home. We had used such strategies ourselves before now. We would leave Arne at Thorkell's Stad and ten warriors to help Karl One Arm. The rest would come with us. "I want you to stay and help Karl."

"But..."

"I will need warriors and not wizards, Aiden. I will rest easier if you are at home."

Poor Elfrida was distraught when we arrived. Kara and Brigid were offering comfort. "They were my people and they have been taken!"

"Fear not Elfrida. We will follow them. They will not escape my vengeance."

"But they could go anywhere."

"No matter where they go we will follow." I meant what I said. I was angry. Danes were Vikings too. They would learn just how terrible my vengeance would be.

We saddled all the horses that we had. If it came down to it I would use the horses to enable the Ulfheonar alone to follow them. We were better warriors than any axe wielding Dane. We were the wolf warriors! Kara and Brigid came over to me, Brigid stroked my face. "Take care my husband."

Kara said, "Aye, father, for if these Danes are clever enough and strong enough to sweep up a valley and destroy all who live there then they will be formidable foes."

"Fear not; I am angry but I will use my head and my mind."

I sent my men who were on foot down the Water under the command of Erik Wolf Claw. I saw tearful goodbyes as men and their families were torn apart again. I led my Ulfheonar and six other mounted warriors towards Windar's Mere.

When we reached it Ulla and the men from Ulf's Water awaited me. They had had a shorter journey and they had begun to bring order to the devastation left by the Danes. I saw that the Danes had taken the heads of every one of the men. Their heads were now on the tops of spears. Windar looked bloated on his spear. "We knew nothing of this Jarl. We smelled smoke but we thought they were feasting. There has not been a raid in this valley for many years. We did not think this was happening. We should have kept closer contact."

I shook my head. "This is the work of the Norns. It was *wyrd*. Take down the heads and see if you can find the bodies. It would not do to have Ketil see his father thus."

I wandered around the burned and wrecked homes. All of the old, both men and women, lay dead. I saw men who had lived with Prince Butar on Man; men who had come with us from Norway and now lay butchered. Only the younger women had been taken. I knew why they had taken them. The dogs lay dead but the other animals had been taken. That gave me hope. It would slow them down. We had a chance to catch them. Even as I viewed the carnage my mind was looking across the land. They had to have come from the south and east. Any other route would have made them pass close by one of my Stad. That suggested the land around the Ouse, Jorvik, as the Danes now called it. Eanred's weakness had made them bold.

Ketil rode in alone with a lathered horse which was close to falling. He threw himself from its back and ran to me. "Where is my father?"

Ulf and his men had not found the bodies. I presumed they lay in the Mere. It was another insult and a way of hurting us. I pointed to the row of heads. Ketil dropped to his knees and bowed his head. "He was a good father but he was no warrior." He remained silent and then rose with a face like black steel. "Where are they Jarl Dragonheart?"

I pointed to the south east. "They have gone yonder. The rest of my men are meeting at Elfridaby. They suffered the same fate."

He looked at me, his own pain forgotten, "Wolf Killer and Elfrida?"

"They are safe. Elfrida is in my home and Wolf Killer waits for us."

"Then let us ride."

"Your horse is too tired and we need your men. Ulf can watch your stronghold but we need to wait for your warriors." I pointed to the heads. "And these need to be buried. We owe them that."

He nodded. We made a barrow where the warrior hall had been. The bodies of the old were laid within as were the heads of those who had fought. We covered them with earth. After we had invoked the gods to ease their passage into the Otherworld I said. "When we have punished these Danes we will rebuild Windar's mere but we will not desecrate where they lie. We will build a new Stad and this one will be stronger and better."

Ketil's band had hurried. They saw the barrow and their faces became as grim as their jarl's. We marched south. Even though they had travelled far Ketil and his men were determined not to slow us down and we reached the camp which Wolf Killer had made soon after dark. Sigtrygg and Asbjorn were there with the rest of my warriors. This was not the joyous camp we had had at St. Asaph, this was a brooding camp filled with the dark thoughts of those who seek revenge.

I sat with my jarls. Wolf Killer spoke. "My scouts found their trail. They are heading south and east back to the land of Northumbria. They took only girls, boys and young women. All else were slaughtered."

"Perhaps some of those who live in the remote parts live still."

He nodded, "Perhaps."

"We will follow them tomorrow. I will send Beorn and Snorri ahead on horses. They will catch them. The animals they have taken will slow them down. We will catch them."

When all else had retired, exhausted, I sat with Wolf Killer and Haaken. Haaken had watched Wolf Killer growing up and knew him as well as I did. "You are troubled, my son."

"Aye. It is the timing of the raid. Did they know I had left my people unattended? Did they know I raided?"

Haaken shook his head, "They are Danes. They have travelled from the other side of this land. You would have had word of a large war band in our land. They came after we had left for Wales."

He had not thought of that and he looked up at me with knowledge in his eyes. "Then they thought to find me!"

"Aye, my son. I see the hand of Egbert in all of this. He has not forgotten what you did. Wessex is grown powerful but it is still a march too far for him to punish you personally. Danes are mercenaries without honour. They fight for gold."

"Then we must end this. We must fight Egbert!"

"Did you not hear my words, my son? King Egbert is too powerful at the moment. When we knew him he was growing in power. There is now a fight between him and Coenwulf to see who rules this land. Egbert will win. We will have revenge but unless you wish your son growing up without a father we take revenge on those who did this first and then plan Egbert's punishment. The hand that paid them is beyond our grasp, at the moment. We will pay back Wessex and we will hurt King Egbert for his part in this raid but I fear he will not let us get within a sword's length of him. He knows our skill. Sleep now, Wolf Killer. Tomorrow we hunt these Danes and show them how our people, the people of the wolf, wreak revenge. We will take on Wessex when the time is right and not before."

I stayed awake a little while longer with Haaken. We were older and could survive with less sleep. "I believe you are right about Egbert but do you fully comprehend the implications of taking him on?"

"It is not as though he has forgotten us. If we take the war to him it will not change the way he feels. The alternative is to sit here and wait for his mercenaries to raid and to kill. We will hurt him so badly that he will shy away from any further action for fear of us. Aiden read, when we were in Miklagård, of an insect called the locust. It spreads across a land and devours all in its path. It comes in plagues. When it has passed over the land is dead. We will do that to Egbert. We will tear the heart from his land."

We were a large band but, despite that, we moved quickly and with purpose. We retained the horses but we walked beside them. I did not want the other warriors to have to watch the Ulfheonar ahead of them having an easy time. We found the first body just ten Roman miles from Elfridaby. It was a girl of thirteen summers. The blood show what had occurred and how she had died. She was not one of Wolf Killer's people and Ketil buried her for he knew her family. They had been his father's folk. We found two more in the next few miles. The Danes seemed to be flaunting us; daring us to stop them. It made us more determined than ever and the band moved as fast as though they all rode horses.

A weary pair of scouts rode in before dusk, "We have found them Jarl. They are in a small village in the valley of the Aire. From their fires there are a hundred Danes. They have killed the men who lived there too."

Wolf Killer snapped, "They are Saxons! I care not!"

"Use your head, my son. It shows that they have not come with the permission of Eanred or they would have left his people alone. It tells us that they are more likely to have come from Egbert." I turned back to Beorn. "Is it close enough to reach this night?"

He shook his head. "It is not an easy way. We could reach it in two hours during daylight."

"But could my Ulfheonar reach there by dawn, if we rode horses?"

Beorn smiled, "Aye Jarl but we would need to change our horses."

"We will find you new horses but Snorri, you stay with Wolf Killer and Ketil; show how to find this place and we will ride now."

"What will you do, father?"

"We will attract the attention of these Danes and stop them from leaving. Get there as soon as you can and approach in battle formation. We will attack them immediately that we see them. If the Allfather has forsaken us then we will have a glorious death but I believe we will defeat them!"

It was a pathetically small number of men I led to tackle this war band but sometimes incredible odds meant nothing. It was what was in your heart which counted. I had been told, when I was young, that I had the heart of a dragon. It was now time to put that to the test. Beorn was right about the road, it was a twisting route we took. The horses were relatively fresh and we made good time. We smelled the smoke and saw the glow of their fires long before we reached them. Beorn the Scout took us in a long loop to get to the other side of the settlement in the Aire valley. We found the old Roman Road. Dismounting I looked around for a place to defend. There was a small knoll. It rose just three paces above the surrounding land and was topped by a solitary, windblown tree. That would do.

"Hobble the horses and let them graze. We will use this as our last defence. Beorn, come with me and Haaken. We will explore the camp."

We left our shields on the knoll and Olaf and the others began to make it easier to defend. They cut down scrubby branches and twisted bramble vines to make a natural looking barrier before us. Ulf and Finni began to dig ankle breakers in the ground which the Danes would have to cross if they found us. We knew how to defend. I drew my seax as we headed towards the settlement. Even though it was late in the night there were still Danes drinking while others pleasured themselves with the captives. We crawled along to the edge of their camp; we constantly looked for sentries. There were none. They were either confident or reckless but, whatever the reason, there were no sentries. We crawled closer; I needed to hear their voices for who knew what knowledge we might gain.

There were three men at the edge of the camp. One slept while the other two spoke. "Harald Iron Shirt should have gone further into the land of the Dragonheart. We slew all that we met. It was easy. I like not this running with our tails between our legs."

"Sven you are a fool. Firstly the Dragonheart wields the sword which was touched by the gods. Would you face him in battle?" I saw and heard nothing but I guessed that Sven shook his head. "Nor would I. Besides we have been well paid. Had the man who stole Egbert's wife been there then we would have succeeded. Our Jarl can recruit more men. We took gold from the two settlements. We are richer and we lost few men. Harald Iron Shirt is a good leader. Besides the information we had was good. We knew that the Dragonheart would not be there. It made our task easier. This is a good raid. We will be rich."

"I do not like running!"

"And the running has made me tired so I will join Einar here and sleep."

I had heard enough and we could have left then but I wanted our enemies to fear us. I motioned to the other two and they followed me as we crept towards the three Danes. As one we jumped on the three warriors. I held my hand over the mouth of one while I slit his throat with my seax. I heard only the death sighs of the others. Taking a sword from one of the dead men I took his head and, finding his spear I jammed it on the top. The others copied me and we crawled backwards with our grisly trophies until we were beyond sight of the camp. We placed the spears in the ground next to the road and returned to the knoll. We went around the side to avoid the traps which were there.

"They are led by Harald Iron Shirt and Egbert paid them to kill my son. Have any of you heard of him?"

They shook their heads.

Haaken said, "They have more men to call upon and this Harald seems a careful jarl. From what they said, Jarl, he is trying to avoid you."

"Then he is in for a shock on the morrow."

Dawn was not far away. We could see the camp when the sun came up behind us. We were seated behind our wall of thorns and traps. We would not be seen until I chose to make us appear, as though by magic. Wolf Killer would be up before dawn; well before dawn. I had no doubt that he would have had the men on the road before the first rays had burned away the dew. The Danes appeared in no hurry to move. I saw men going to the river to collect water and to relieve themselves. I heard screams as some of the captives were hurt; I knew not why but the Danes were a cruel people. They would keep their captives in a state of perpetual terror. We were different. We took away the prospect of escape but did not treat them badly. Slaves were valuable to us. We would either sell them or use them to work. Why damage our own goods?

It was when they spied the three heads that uproar spread throughout the camp. The dead Danes were visible to us while we were hunkered down and invisible. I saw warriors run to the dead men. The crowd parted and I saw Harald Iron Shirt for the first time. He did not wear mail but had the lamellar armour I had seen in Miklagård. He stared around. He seemed to look directly at us but we kept still for I knew that it was an illusion. With darkened mail, cloaks and faces he would see shadows that was all. Snorri had his bow strung and ready. Harald Iron shirt shouted orders. The Danes were sent left and right to search the sides of the road. Then Harald Iron Shirt shouted another order and his men began to herd the captives and animals. They were ready to move.

When three Danes began to walk along the road I nodded to Snorri. He sent an arrow into one of them and even as they were looking around for the bowman he had sent another into a second Dane. The third turned and ran, shouting the alarm. An arrow felled him.

This time they knew where the danger lay; to the east. They could not see us but the six dead Danes were testament to our position. The Danish Jarl had to use a third of his men to guard his captives. They were too valuable to leave. He formed up the other fifty or so warriors and made a wedge. He stood behind the three warriors who were the tip of the arrow. I saw that few wore mail. The majority had a helmet.

I said quietly, "When they are a hundred paces from us we stand. Snorri use your bow to kill any who is foolish enough to show you flesh."

We had learned that timing and a fierce disposition could win a battle or give you an advantage at the very least. They were advancing and looking for enemies they could not see. That made them wary and a little afraid. When a warrior could see an enemy he was less of a threat. When he was hidden then he was an unknown quantity.

I stood and, raising my sword shouted, "I am Jarl Dragonheart of Cyninges-tūn and I am here to punish you!"

Even as my words hung in the air the Ulfheonar stood behind me and, banging their shields, chanted, "Ulfheonar!" over and over.

The wedge stopped. The warrior to the right of the man at the front turned to speak with Harald Iron Shirt. Snorri's arrow plunged into his exposed neck and he fell to the ground. A second arrow hit the next warrior and the shields all rose as one.

I knew that Wolf Killer and my men were hurrying towards us and I needed to buy some time. I yelled, "Harald Iron Shirt, come and face me as a man. Stand before your Danes and fight me!"

I knew I had stunned them. I knew his name. There was magic in that and I had challenged him. Would he face me?

"Why should I fear a handful of men dressed in the skins of dead animals! Charge!"

It was a mistake. Although his men ran at us there would be no heart in them. Their leader had refused the offer of battle and the chance to show his courage. Even if he survived one of his men would challenge him. Harald Iron Shirt was as good as dead. Snorri's bow snapped three times and three men fell in the one hundred paces that they ran towards us. They reached the tangle of branches, bramble vines and traps. They ploughed on, those at the front propelled by those behind. The front three all found the ankle breakers. The holes were as deep as a man's arm. I heard the sound of two legs breaking. The force of warriors behind trampled over the wounded men and more fell. The wedge was in disarray. I saw Harald Iron Shirt fall and then struggle to his feet. Snorri had but a dozen arrows left but he used them all well.

Three men leapt on the backs of the fallen, thereby avoiding the traps and threw themselves at us. I held Ragnar's Spirit before me and impaled one. My warriors all wore mail, it gave us an advantage. When eight men were slain Harald Iron Shirt yelled, "Fall back and form a line!"

He knew he would lose more men so long as he kept up a frontal attack. He had to use superior numbers, he had to surround us. Even as they moved back Snorri used the last of his arrows and then, laying his precious bow down he took up his shield.

"They will try to surround us. Be ready to fight back to back."

Haaken laughed, "Better to attack them Jarl Dragonheart. This Harald has lost much honour already."

He was correct. The Dane had spread his men out in a long line to completely encircle us. We could attack him. "Haaken is right! On my command we charge them."

Finni laughed, "This will make a glorious tale, Haaken!"

"Aye if we live!"

Olaf snorted, "Then we tell the tale in Valhalla and even Odin will listen!"

The Danes came steadily. I waited until they were just twenty paces from us and spread out. The ones at the extreme ends of the line were hurrying to close with us and attack our unguarded backs. It made the ring thinner.

"Now!"

Using the dead Danes we launched ourselves towards the advancing line of warriors. I brought my sword hard across the neck of one warrior while punching at Harald Iron Shirt with my shield. It was understood that it would be me who fought their jarl. Both sets of warriors realised that but as the Dane reeled back I could see fear in his eyes. He swung his sword at me. He liked to fight in the traditional Danish manner. He would batter my shield arm and hope to break my arm or bend my sword. He would do neither. I did not swing at his shield I half lifted my arm and, as his shield came up thrust the blade upwards towards the metal plates. They were secured to each other by wire. My sword ripped through one of them and scored a cut on his side. I stepped forward as he recoiled and put my weight into my shield. His blow was weak, for he was falling back and my body absorbed it. I half lifted my sword again and he brought his shield across his body to block the blow to his weakened armour. I swing Ragnar's Spirit across his shoulder and bent a metal plate while cutting through a wire.

I knew that my Ulfheonar were close by me and they had slain their opponents. They protected my back and sides. Ahead of me I heard a roar as Wolf Killer brought the rest of my men to attack the Danes guarding the captives. I saw Harald Iron Shirt's eyes as they flickered in fear at the sound. I grinned, "You are the one who is now outnumbered. Be ready to die."

He brought his sword around again in a wide sweep intended to take my head but the weakened armour got in his way. His armour looked good but it was not. The hit barely registered with me. I stabbed forward and this time the weakened plates gave way and my sword entered his side. He sank to his knees. His sword fell to the ground. He had no strength left to hold it. He glared up at me. "Finish it. Give me the warrior's death."

I shook my head, "It was my son's people and Ketil's father that you killed. They can make that decision." After slicing through his hamstrings I kicked away his sword and joined my men as we hacked our way through the Dane's oathsworn. They did not fight hard. There were few of us but they quickly ran towards the east. My men advanced and butchered from the west. Wolf Killer and his men had vengeance in their hearts. In the daylight we could see that some of Wolf Killer's men had been taken as captives. Some of his warriors had seen their daughters dead on the journey to this valley. They were in no mood for mercy. I swung my sword across the back of the fleeing Dane I had caught and cut through to his spine. He fell twitching to the ground.

Those of our warriors who had no armour ran after the Danes. I waved over some of them. "Take our hobbled ponies. They are in a dell yonder."

The young warriors eagerly took up our offer. The galloping hooves promised death to the Danes.

Ketil and Wolf Killer were both covered in spattered blood when they reached me. I took off my helmet. Both men dropped to their knees. "Thank you for the courage of you and your Ulfheonar, we are indebted to you."

"These men were not warriors. They were carrion! Their leader lives still. I leave his fate to you two."

I followed them to Harald Iron Shirt. The wound still bled. He would not be moving anywhere soon. Ketil was angry and he smashed the Dane across the face with his fist. "Kill me and send me to Odin!"

"The Allfather would not welcome you even with a sword!" Wolf Killer could be ruthless. "Give him the blood eagle!"

"No!"

"I will do it! It is vengeance for my dead father! He should have died in peace not slaughtered by those such as you."

With his armour stripped and discarded Ketil tore his clothes baring the Dane's back. He took his seax and ripped open the flesh down to his spine. He peeled back the flesh revealing the ribs. Harald screamed the whole time. He did not take his punishment with stoicism. It seemed to make Ketil more determined than ever to carry out the ceremony. He broke each rib in turn and pulled them out to form the wings. Harald passed out with the pain but Ketil did not falter. Finally he tore out the lungs leaving them flapping like the wings of an eagle. It was then that Harald died. None of his Danes lived to see his death but we left his body as a reminder to all of the price for hurting my people.

As I headed down to the others I saw Hrolf watching with his mouth wide open. In his hand he held a bloody seax. He had killed. He walked with me. "That is a terrible death, Jarl Dragonheart. How could anyone bear such pain?"

"He did not bear pain, Hrolf. I have seen this done before and the warrior never uttered a sound. Those who suffer in silence go to Valhalla. Harald Iron Shirt will not. He is a nithing. He had the chance to fight me. Had he done so he might have died with a sword in his hand. He chose to let his men fight for him."

"He knew that he would die."

"We all die Hrolf; it is the manner which is important but today was not my day to die and I am born again,"

Chapter 7

The captives were still in shock. They were relieved to be rescued but they had suffered at the hands of the Danes. Many of the women and girls wept uncontrollably. We remained in the small, now deserted settlement. Our men returned from the hunt bringing with them the weapons, arm rings and treasure they had taken from the dead Danes. Much of the treasure had been taken from Windar's Mere in the first place. We had been lucky to recover it. My jarls joined the Ulfheonar and we sat around the fire to talk and to plan.

"I doubt not that there will be Danes who will return from whence Iron Shirt came and they will tell what we did. Some may even come and seek his body but I do not think they will risk our wrath again. However, Wolf Killer, you need to watch your borders even more."

He shook his head. "It is too far from your home, father. When I first chose to live there I was arrogant. I thought to outdo you and create somewhere as fine as Cyninges-tūn. I was wrong. I freely admit it now here in front of your warriors."

"It shows that you have grown into a fine man, my son, that you can admit to that. I do not call it arrogance. It is the process of growing up. You would live in Cyninges-tūn?"

"No Jarl, with your permission I would settle the land at the head of Windar's Mere. It is good land and I can protect the way to Cyninges-tūn." He looked at Ketil "But if you wished to rule where your father did then I would understand."

"No, Wolf Killer. This is *wyrd*. I would find the memories too painful and besides I like Brougham."

I nodded. "Good then that is settled and we now need to decide what to do about Egbert."

Sigtrygg said, "He is a powerful king. He rules most of the land of the Angles."

I laughed, "You must think me arrogant as my son once thought himself, Sigtrygg. We cannot defeat King Egbert but we can punish him."

I could see that they were intrigued. Asbjorn leaned forward, "Punish the King of Wessex; how?"

"Egbert attacks others. He rules Kent and he has captured Corn Walum. He has defeated the men of Dyfed and he has repulsed Coenwulf and his Mercians. We attack him. We raid his heartland, the place he feels safe and secure and we will let him know the price he pays for this blood feud. I will invite those like Hakon the Bald and Thorfinn Blue Scar to join us on this raid. They will gain much treasure and the extra numbers will show King Egbert that we are serious."

Haaken advised caution, "Remember when we allied with Sihtric Silkbeard and Ragnar Hairy Breeches. That did not end well."

"And this time I make them swear to follow my orders. If they do not then they do not come."

Haaken seemed happiest of all. "I think this is a good thing Jarl Dragonheart. It does not do to run from our enemies. Egbert especially."

"We did not run."

I looked at Wolf Killer, "We did my son but we had but two boat's crews and we were in Lundenwic. Only a fool would have stayed but Haaken is right. You face up to your enemies. You either defeat them or go to meet Odin. It is as simple as that."

I glanced around at the faces. Some, especially the Ulfheonar were nodding. Some of the others had doubt etched on their faces.

"I will not order any jarl to follow me. My son and I will go but each warrior makes his own decision. It will take me some time to seek out allies who may wish to raid with us."

Haaken rubbed his hands together, "It is said that the churches of Wessex are filled with gold!"

"I doubt that but they are richly endowed."

Snorri said, quietly, "Aiden will know such things. He has his maps and his writing."

I was tired and I lay down to sleep. Just before I slipped off into a deep sleep I wondered about the chests which we had recovered from St. Asaph,. What had Aiden found in those? What twists and turns had the Norns laid in store for me?

We returned to the land around Elfridaby slowly. The captives had suffered enough and there was no need to hurry. Some of Wolf Killer's men stubbornly chose to live in the land they had farmed. He brought the rest of his men to Cyninges-tūn. There were things he needed if he was to build a new town. We headed through the dale of Grize. As we passed through those fly infested woods I saw to my great relief that Finn, his son Sven and Thora, Sven's wife had all survived unharmed. I was happy. In fact it brightened and lightened my mood. Thora had lost her first husband, Gray, when outlaws had come to my land. She had saved my life and she was a symbol of hope. I returned to Cyninges-tūn with more optimism than when I had left. Ketil left us to head north to his home. He wished to raid but he had no drekar and he needed to protect his land.

The women of Cyninges-tūn had word from Grim the Fisherman that we were heading back up the Water and they were waiting at the gates to greet us. We had been away for a short time but they knew we were chasing Danes. They felt for the captives and when they saw them returned there was great celebration. I allowed the other families and Wolf Killer to go ahead of me. Brigid would understand. I went to my hall where she waited with Gruffyd and my servants.

"You saved the captives. I am glad."

"Some died. They were young girls."

"I will pray for their souls."

Even though they were not Christian Brigid still believed that they had a soul and that her prayers would help them. It was kind but it was a wasted gesture. Kara and Aiden came to visit with me when they had seen to the wounds and hurts of those who had returned with us.

"I have spoken with Wolf Killer. He tells me you intend to raid King Egbert."

There was no judgement in Aiden's voice. He had a mind which could think things through well. "If we do not he will send more men to do us harm and the next time we may not be so lucky."

He nodded, "I think it is a good idea, Jarl Dragonheart, so long as you choose the right place."

I smiled ,"And, of course, you can tell me the best place."

He laughed, "Aye, I believe I can."

"Tell me, did you examine those chests we brought back?"

"Not yet Jarl. They are here in your hall. I had thought to do so when you are present."

"Then when we have supped we will do so. It will be a diversion after the last few days."

A brief silence descended upon the hall. Kara said quietly. "Ketil performed the blood eagle."

"Aye daughter. He had much anger in him. I did not think that Wolf Killer would have done so alone but Ketil... it was his father."

"I will speak with him when he comes for the raid. I have potions which will help him to sleep and to clear his mind." My daughter was even more powerful than Aiden. Her skills and knowledge were legend.

Aiden had Uhtric bring the chests to us. It was tempting to open the largest one first but the smallest of the three looked the most intriguing for it was delicately carved and had, upon the lid, a dragon. A Viking couldn't ignore such signs. Aiden patiently worked his picks into the lock until it rustily groaned open. There was a heavy, musty smell within. The box appeared filled with wood shavings. I felt slightly disappointed. Then I removed the shavings. I found a dagger in a sheath and a ring. There was nothing else. I had seen daggers before but the ring intrigued me. I held it to the light of the candle. It was a signet ring and had the image of a mounted man on a rearing horse. I handed it to Kara. She closed her eyes. "This belong to an ancestor or yours. It speaks to me." Opening her eyes she handed it to me. "Put it on your finger."

I took the ring and slipped it on my forefinger. It fitted perfectly, "*Wyrd*."

"Aye father. You must wear it and use it."

"But mine is the sign of the wolf."

Aiden said, "I believe it was also the sign of your ancestor. My wife is right. You should wear it. You need not use it; you do not write but its power will protect you."

My attention returned to the dagger. The sheath was decorated in the same rich fashion as the sword we had found but when I took out the blade it was not rusty. The wood chips had, somehow, protected it. The blade was much slimmer than a seax and had a sharp point. The pommel was plain save for a single small blue stone. I handed the blade and sheath to Aiden. "This is the blade the ancient Roman soldiers used. It is called a pugeo and I saw them in Miklagård."

I nodded, "It would be a good blade to use. Its tip would find its way through chinks in mail."

"Aye."

We put the dagger to one side and Aiden opened the second chest. This one had felt heavier. When it sprang open there were no wood chips but it was filled with coins. Most were of silver but I saw the glitter of gold amongst them. Aiden and I picked some up to examine them. Some were marked on one side with the same image as my signet ring. Aiden held up one golden one and turned it over in his fingers. "This one has the mark of Rome upon it. I wonder why these two chests were placed in the monastery."

I went back to the smaller chest and rubbed away some of the dirt and detritus on the top. I could see something. "Uhtric fetch a cloth and some water." When he returned I rubbed the side of the wooden chest with the water. It revealed the carved horseman on the rearing horse. I repeated it with the second chest and it was there also.

Aiden went to the lock of the other chest. "Then this may contain more clues to your ancestor."

"Hold, let me clean the top." I used the dampened cloth to clean the top. This time there was no rearing horseman but a cross. "This did not belong to the warlord."

"But we shall open it anyway."

It proved the hardest to open and when it was opened, like the first one it was covered in a layer of wood shavings. Aiden cleared them away and his face showed that he had found the greatest treasure of all; writings.

Brigid could not keep the disappointment out of her voice. "No gold? I thought it would be a suit of golden armour at the very least."

Kara smiled and put her hand on my wife's arm, "This is greater treasure. This is knowledge. Knowledge gives us all more power than any suit of armour."

Aiden took them out one by one and laid them on the table. He unrolled them as he did so and organised them. When he had the parchments on the table they filled it. He pointed to a large number on one side. "These are maps, charts and lists. The others are writings. I have much reading. Could I take them to my hall, Jarl? I will need to study them."

"Of course."

I took the pugeo again and took it from its sheath. It looked as though it had been used but yesterday rather than many years ago. Kara and Aiden carefully studied the rich haul of documents. I knew that they could not resist. Kara gave a little squeal of joy. "The lists are lists of herbs and how they can help cure ailments. I know some but there are others here that I have not seen. There are even drawings of what the herbs and plants look like."

I laid the dagger down and went to look at them. I recognised them. "I have seen these before." I pointed to one.

It was rare that I could surprise Kara but I did. "I have never seen such plants and I wander the land looking for new ones constantly. Where did you see it? In the east?"

I shook my head, "No, we have seen these," I jabbed my finger at another four, "and these at every Roman fort we have visited. They are a normally growing wild in a small walled area. I only remember because I once slept there and I noticed their fragrance."

"Then I will take my women to the Roman fort close to Windar's Mere. We will bring them here. This will help our people live long and healthy lives. This is *wyrd*."

Just then Aiden laid down the parchment he was reading and poured himself a horn of ale. "These were written by the priests of the monastery. Most talk of the saint, Asaph who founded it but there are many references to someone they call the Warlord of Rheged and, at other times, in different hands, the Dux Britannicus. It is your ancestor." He picked up one parchment. "Here the priest says that the Warlord was the most Christian pagan that he knows. He says he is more Christian than many priests and yet he is pagan."

Brigid came and stroked my hair, "And that is like someone else that I know. I find this strange, husband. Does the blood course through the centuries? Are the dead reborn?"

"We are all tied by threads to the past and to the future. There are threads which bind us together. There is a plan to all this. We are human and we do not see it but the Norns and the Gods, they do."

The two of them left with the parchments leaving Brigid and I to reflect on the night. "They are right, husband, the gold is not as valuable a treasure as the others. You have learned about yourself."

I shook my head, "I have learned what I might be not what I am. Would my ancestor, the warlord, have allowed the blood eagle?"

"Perhaps. If you had stopped Ketil would he have been unhappy? Would he have resented you?"

"He may have done but a good leader does not heed such things. He does what is best not what is popular. Besides Harald Iron Shirt deserved the death. He had neither honour nor courage."

"And that is where we differ for we are taught to forgive our enemies."

"Yet they are still punished for murder. They are hanged." She nodded. "Then the result is still the same, death. Harald would have been dead no matter what. It is only the manner which upsets you."

I awoke energised. The previous night had made me more determined than ever to punish King Egbert and send a message to the world that no one was too big to be punished by Jarl Dragonheart.. Before I began to plan this great raid I visited with Aiden. "All of these parchments," I swept my hand around them. I suspected he had been poring over them all night, "are important. I would have you record our deeds. The stories Haaken tells and sings can be passed on but he only records the glorious things. I would have the future know how we lived. It is what the monks do. Macha and Deidra can help you."

"That is good, Jarl and Macha and Deidra will be happy to help me. I have spoken with them. They miss the work they did when they lived in the Christian House of Women."

"Good." I turned to leave.

"Jarl, I have found how the Warlord died. It is written here."

I was more than interested in this. If our lives were somehow entwined through time then this could have a bearing on me.

"The Warlord was betrayed by his nephew. He was poisoned and then slain when he was helpless. His son became warlord and killed the murderer. Then he too was betrayed by his second in command. He vanished beyond Wyddfa."

"And this wizard, the one whose tomb we found..."

" Myrddyn."

Aye. What happened to him?"

"He vanished. He just disappeared. The new warlord kept seeking him but he disappeared from this world."

"And we found his tomb. Who laid him there?"

"I know not. The more we discover the less we know. There is still much to learn. I would visit Wyddfa again."

"That would be too dangerous."

Kara had been listening. "My father is right. The Weird Sisters will decide what we ought to know."

I bowed to the two of them. They knew the spirits better than I did.

Even though we had been successful in our pursuit of the Danish war band we had still lost warriors. There were homes with men who would never return. I went around each one giving them their share of the coins we had reaped as our reward. It would not bring back their men folk but it might allow them to buy animals. Our people were fine cheese makers. We would survive.

Wolf Killer took his men off to the Mere to begin to build their new home. We had all learned lessons from the places we had built and we had learned from each other. He left Elfrida and his family to be protected at Cyninges-tūn. I had given the rest of my jarls and warriors a month to decide if they would raid with me. Five days after our return I went with my Ulfheonar and some of the single men down to Úlfarrston. I told Brigid that we might be away for half a month. She understood. She was with child once more and Kara and Elfrida would be better for her than me.

When we reached Úlfarrston I warned my other captains that we would be raiding in a month or so. Olaf Grimsson was honoured that I chose **'Red Snake'** to visit Dyflin and Ljoðhús. I had brought with me two swords which had been made by Bjorn Bagsecgson. They would be gifts for the two jarl. We were lightly crewed. I just had twenty men with me. We were not going to war, we were going to make allies. As we left I saw a knarr leave as another arrived. So much trade; we were prospering.

Dyflin was the shorter of the two voyages. We left at dawn and reached it by dusk. This time we would accept Hakon the Bald's hospitality. I made it clear to my Ulfheonar that they were to stay relatively sober and keep their ears open. Aiden had taught me that all knowledge was valuable; even gossip. Olaf had brought some goods to trade. We always had an excess of fine worked metal. Bjorn's smiths made excellent tools for ship building. Olaf could build up his supply of gold and silver.

Hakon the Bald appeared more than happy to see me and even more delighted that we would stay the night. I had already primed Haaken to sing a song of our adventures. Such sagas encouraged young warriors to join a venture. "Come, Jarl Dragonheart, we will drink some of the fine wine you brought from Vasconia."

"Before we do and before I am in my cups I would speak with you on a delicate matter."

He might appear rotund and jolly but Hakon had a sharp and cunning mind. "You intrigue me. Come we will walk along the river bank it is restful there."

Dyflin was a bustling town. It was a mixture of Úlfarrston and Cyninges-tūn. There were Hibernians and Norse, cheek by jowl. The accents and the language was varied. It felt quite exotic. Hakon found a quiet spot beneath a tree. He dismissed the two boys who were fishing there. "Now then Jarl, what is this about? Do you seek revenge on the Danes who raided your land?"

I shook my head, "They are dead or fled. We destroyed them."

"Did you lose many men? I heard that Harald Iron Shirt is a cunning warrior."

I was immediately suspicious. How did he know who it was? I had not spoken his name. I kept my face expressionless. "He was a coward and without honour. Ketil Windarsson gave him the blood eagle."

He nodded, "And that is only right for such a coward. What do you wish of me then?" I saw cunning in his eyes. He knew more than he was saying.

"Do you know who put him up to this?"

Affecting an innocent look which did not fool me he shook his head. "You have many enemies, Jarl Dragonheart, but I would have thought that this Harald operated for his own gain."

"Had he done so he would have taken more than he did. He attacked but two settlements.. It is no matter. No the reason I come to you is that I am going to raid. The Saxon lands proved a rich source of treasure I would go with more drekar next time. I wondered if you had any young men who might wish to join my venture."

"Mercia?"

"Perhaps. We have yet to decide. If any wish to come with me then they will be told after we sail."

"You are a careful man. But warriors like to know the dangers before they sail."

"Then I do not want such warriors. Those who sail with me must expect to sail beyond the western sea."

"I see. I will ask then."

I took the sword from my belt. "As a gift for your support in this matter I have had a sword made for you." All of Bjorn's swords were well made. I had paid for two particularly fine specimens. It was not just a generous gesture, others would see the blade and they would wish to buy them from Bjorn. He was now the richest man in my land.

"A generous gift. I will do as you ask and encourage my young men to see such an adventure."

As we walked back I could see his cunning mind at work. There would be dissatisfied young men in his land. If they came with me he would be rid of them. He would be more secure and he would have put me in his debt. I understood the way his mind worked. It was why I had not mentioned Egbert or Wessex. I suspected that he knew something of the matter.

That evening Haaken was in fine form. He sang the saga of the death of Magnus the Foresworn.

Brave men fight for a Jarl who is strong
Whose sword is sharp and reach is long
They row and fight for honour and glory
When they do not then their end is gory
Ragnar's Spirit the legend blade
Ragnar's Spirit by Odin made
With a heart as black as Hel's domain
Magnus Foresworn brought death and pain
He killed the weak and ran away
Hiding deep in Din Guardi
Ragnar's Spirit the legend blade
Ragnar's Spirit by Odin made
Standing high atop a rocky mound
The castle was built on perfect ground
With no way in save through the gate
The killer hid from his well earned fate
Ragnar's Spirit the legend blade
Ragnar's Spirit by Odin made
Dragonheart led with light of blue
Ten Ulfheonar brave and true
Beneath the sea and black of night
They sought their way to the castle's light
Ragnar's Spirit the legend blade
Ragnar's Spirit by Odin made
When the sea surged high and lapped the feet
A boon of Odin they did entreat
When the waters fell and the door they found
They entered the castle and made not a sound
Ragnar's Spirit the legend blade
Ragnar's Spirit by Odin made
Up to the tower remote and cold
They went well armed with hearts so bold
The traitor fled, he tried to run
To the east and the rising sun
Ragnar's Spirit the legend blade
Ragnar's Spirit by Odin made
Ragnar's Spirit flashed in the night
Bringing death bloody and bright
The traitor fell to the rocks below
He tumbled long and he tumbled slow

The warriors fought King Eanred's men
Taking Saxon god with them
Odin moved the sea and sand
To help the noble wolf warrior band
They rode away with heads held high
And praised great Odin in the sky
Ragnar's Spirit the legend blade
Ragnar's Spirit by Odin made
Ragnar's Spirit the legend blade
Ragnar's Spirit by Odin made

The men of Dyflin banged their tables and demanded three more recitals. I saw Hakon the Bald give a nod of approval as he stood and said, "A fine saga and worthy of the great Haaken One Eye. Jarl Dragonheart looks for a crew to join him on a raid of the Saxon shores. I will provide the drekar, who will join the crew?"

The story had worked and we had a goodly crew. Gunnstein Berserk-Killer was the one they chose as captain. Despite his dramatic title he was a relatively young man but I liked him straight away. He had honest eyes and his handshake was firm.

"I will lead a crew and we will follow you for a raid." Hakon nodded and went to fetch more ale. Gunnstein then added quietly, "I grow tired of living off whores and Hibernians. I am a warrior and I would take heads of my own. Where do we raid?"

"Bring your drekar to Úlfarrston by the end of the month and we will have decided by then."

Like me he was not drunk and he smiled, "It is good that you keep your counsel. Jarl Hakon welcomes many guests here in Dyflin and I would not drink with some of them!"

Enigmatically he left it at that.

The next morning as we headed north Snorri said, "I did as you asked, Jarl, and I listened. King Egbert sent emissaries to Hakon last year. It seems he asked Hakon to poison you. Hakon said he would think about it."

I was under no illusions. If Hakon had thought he could have killed me and not suffered for it he would have done so but I still inspired a little fear in him. "You did well and I am glad that I did not reveal all to him."

I sat next to Haaken who was rowing. "It was a good saga although, as I recall it did not happen exactly the way you said."

"It is the licence of the singer and the composer. It worked did it not?"

"Aye. Repeat it again at Ljoðhús and we may have another crew."

Thorfinn Blue Scar was the jarl at Ljoðhús. He was the opposite of Hakon the Bald. For a start he was trustworthy and secondly he was a warrior. I had fought alongside him. I could happily tell him of our enemy.

As we entered the bay I noticed that there was but one drekar moored. We tied up to the jetty and Thorfinn himself came to greet us. "My friend! What brings you here?"

I took the sword I had for him. It was better than the one I had given Hakon,. This one had a dragon etched onto the blade and the pommel stone was a blue stone. It was not the same as mine but a deeper blue. "Here is a present for you."

He took it and ran his fingers along the etched dragon. This is a fine sword." His eyes narrowed suspiciously, "What do I have to do to earn this prize?"

I laughed, "It is yours to keep and we will sail back to our own home now if you wish."

"No, my friend, stay the night and tell me what you really came for."

Once inside I told him of the attack by Harald Iron Shirt. "I know of him. He is a hired sword who leads a band of brigands to do the work of the highest bidder. He fought alongside Alpín mac Echdach. Had I found him I, too, would have given him the blood eagle. The world is better off without him."

"Aye."

"And you want to find the man who paid him?"

Something in his voice told me that he knew who it was. "You have an idea who it was?"

"Three months since a ship came from Wessex. King Egbert let it be known that he would make an ally of anyone who brought him the head of your son and return to him his wife, Elfrida."

"You told him no."

"Of course. Like you I am never foresworn."

"Then I can tell you that I intend to pay back this Egbert and I will lead a raid on his land. I would, with your permission, offer the chance of glory to any of your young men who wish to go A-Viking."

He nodded, "Most of my drekar are away raiding the Irish. But my youngest son has a drekar. When would you want them?"

"We sail at the end of the month."

"Almost winter eh? A clever strategy. My drekar will be returned by then. If my son and his crew wish to join you then they will be ready by the end of the month. But for tonight we will fete and feast you. I would hear more of your voyages and your raids. Every trader who visits us tell us something new. Sometimes they are exaggerated so much they are hard to believe."

"Then I will tell you the true version and after you shall hear Haaken's version." He laughed.

It was a good feast. We got on better with these brethren who lived on the exposed island where life was hard and the warriors harder still. I met his son, Gunnar Thorfinnson. He agreed to join our raid even before he heard Haaken's song. I saw a little of Wolf Killer in him for he lived in the shadow of a famous father and was keen to make a name for himself. Haaken's sagas, he sang two of them, were received even more rapturously than in Dyflin. He positively glowed with the adulation or perhaps that was the ale.

As we boarded our drekar the next morning Gunnar promised to come to Úlfarrston at the end of the month in his father's drekar, *'Raven Wing'*. We had our warriors. Now I needed Aiden to choose the target.

Chapter 8

Half a month seems a long time but not when you are preparing to raid. My jarls told me who would be joining my raid. Ketil took the drekar of Sigtrygg for my southern jarl had the early winter sickness. He coughed constantly and both Kara and Aiden advised that he stay in his hall. They gave him potions to heal him. It meant his ship, *'Crow'* was crewed by two war bands. Wolf Killer and Asbjorn both offered to come too. Eystein the Rock sailed with Olaf on *'Red Snake'*. We double crewed where we could. With ship's boys we would have almost four hundred men. It would be the largest raid I had ever led. I had to make sure we got things right.

Aiden and I pored over the maps and charts. The new one we had found in St. Asaph gave us added information. We knew from traders and gossip that King Egbert was in the far west of his kingdom subjugating the land of Corn Walum. That mean that his heartland, around Wintan-ceastre, would be undefended. There were nunneries and monasteries close by. We counted on the fact that he would keep part of his treasury there too. We would need to capture the port of Hamwic but from what Aiden had discovered it was not likely to be well defended.

"Will you travel with us, Aiden, or do you intend to stay here with your family? It is your decision."

"I will come with you for I am keen to see what I can discover. It is the centre of Wessex and there may be knowledge for me there."

"Good. My warriors always prefer a galdramenn with them."

I was only taking a hundred or so of my own men and so we were able to leave thirty warriors to guard our home. Bjorn and his smith were also doughty fighters. My home would be safe. Arne's numbers, at Thorkell's Stad, had also grown. He and his men did not wish to raid. We had a ready force should someone like Harald Iron Shirt return.

We left just as the harvest was being gathered. It would be a good time to strike Wessex; with the King away most of his men would be working in their fields. With luck we would have a grain harvest too. Siggi and Coen Ap Pasgen's captain, Raibeart, accompanied us as we set sail. I anticipated great rewards and they would bring back more than we could carry in our drekar. The one problem with taking the knarr was their speed. We had to stop twice on the way south. We knew many deserted beaches and landing sites. As we had so many ships and warriors we were not worried. Perhaps this was the way we needed to raid in future. I could not envisage a danger to us. Once we left the safety of the sea then there would be danger but with our drekar close by we were safe.

The last leg of the journey took us close by the cave of the witch. Aiden sensed her presence but the Norns allowed us to travel east without incident. We did not travel as fast as we might have done. I wanted to land at night and take Hamwic without alerting the countryside. I knew that we were observed but as we had never raided Wessex before I gambled on the fact that they would think we were heading for Frankia. Our raids there were well known. There was a Frankish price on our heads!

Aiden had the maps and Erik was the best captain. Under furled sails we rowed up the channel between the island of Vectis and the mainland. The sun had set behind us and we had a ship's boy in the bows watching for the tell tale white foam that would mark breakers. There were two rivers, the Test and the Itchen. We knew that Hamwic lay on the Itchen. Our plan was to sail up the Test and cross over the narrow neck of land and attack the port from the landward side. We saw no fishing ships as we rowed up the channel. It was wide and there appeared to be no danger from either fort or warship. We went in one long line. That had been my decision; if we struck any hidden danger then only one drekar would be damaged. The gods were with us and we struck neither hidden reef nor rock.

We used hand signals and the oars were lifted from the water so that Erik could lay us alongside the muddy bank. I felt the keel as it grounded. That was not a problem. Once we had disembarked she would ride higher in the water anyway. As soon as the keel touched Snorri and Beorn the Scout led ten of our young warriors to leap ashore and spread out in a thin line. They would warn us of any danger. I followed with the Ulfheonar. The mud tried to suck us down. The tide was on its way out. We struggled to the grassy bank and I waited for the others to join us. With so many drekar it would take some time to land all of our men.

As soon as Asbjorn and his men joined me I led us all towards the distant port. We could smell the wood smoke and see the slight glow from the huts and halls. Snorri and Beorn took off with their young scouts close by. They all had bows and if there were any guards or sentries then they would die. It was scrubby ground we crossed. From the cow pats and sheep droppings it was used, during the day, for grazing. That told me that there would be animal pens close by. We could use those for cover. We had travelled but five hundred paces when I began to make out the wooden palisade. To our left I heard the sound of animals. They were the animal pens. I waved Asbjorn and his men to the left. They could use the animals to mask any noise and movement. I went for the gate.

Snorri and Beorn rose like wraiths beside me. They pointed to the gates and drew their fingers across their throats. The sentries were dead. From the lack of noise on the other side of the palisade I guessed that it was the part which would be busy during the day; the workshops and warehouses. I drew my sword and ran to the gate. While my young scouts clambered over the low palisade we prepared to launch ourselves into the heart of the Saxon settlement.

Ketil and his men appeared behind me. We now had at least three crews ready to fight. The people of Hamwic had no idea what was about to descend upon them. The gates opened silently and we entered. We made not a sound. I wanted to be as far in as I could get before we were noticed. If we could reach the Itchen side of the town then we could stop anyone escaping and giving the alarm. It was my eager young scouts who gave us away. They were so eager to impress me that they burst out of the narrow alley and were seen by some men who were by the fire in the heart of the town, talking. My young warriors released arrows but the shout still went up. "Vikings!"

There was no longer any need for secrecy or quiet and the Ulfheonar howled like wolves as we fell upon the Saxons. I had been right, most of the warriors were with the King but there were still enough to make a defence. Bagsecg Rolfsson had raced too far ahead and he was hacked in two by a warrior who led six others. None had mail but they handled their weapons like seasoned veterans.

"On me!"

My Ulfheonar flanked me and we ran at them as they tried to allow time for their families to flee. We hit them at speed and they stood still. The blow from the sword struck my shield but the sheer weight of me and my armour drove my sword deep within the leader's body, I felt my sword scrape his spine and he died. I lowered my sword and allowed his body to slip from it. My other, younger warriors, had heeded the death of Bagsecg and they moved together. They reached the gates and shut them. Hamwic was ours. By the time dawn had broken we had slain all of the men and gathered the women and children in the centre of the settlement.

"Ketil, take your men and bring around the drekar. This harbour is a better one in which to wait."

Asbjorn, begin to gather the grain, animals and treasure. We will send it back to Úlfarrston."

Gunnar Thorfinnson asked, "Do we not divide it now?"

"We will gather it at Úlfarrston. That is close enough to all our homes. You and your father will get your share. I am Jarl Dragonheart; trust to my word."

He bowed his head a little, "Sorry Jarl. This is the first raid where I have served another Jarl."

"We will divide the captives here and you may use your share as servants while we are here."

Gunnstein Berserk-Killer smiled, "Then we raid more? Good. I thought that this was it and my sword has only tasted blood once."

"As soon as the knarr is loaded then we leave for Wintan-ceastre. I would strike there before word is out that there are Vikings in the heart of Wessex."

Gunnar Thorfinnson said, "But surely we contained them all."

Olaf Leather Neck snorted, "Some will have escaped. The boys who secured the gate found it open. The men of Wessex will be drawn here."

"Aye, I want five men from each boat to stay here and guard the drekar and the town. Erik Short Toe, my captain will command."

Snorri and Beorn were sent to find horses. Aiden took out his maps. "There should be a Roman Road running north. It is twelve Roman miles to Wintan-ceastre."

"We can be there before noon?"

Aiden smiled, "You and the Ulfheonar can but I fear that the ones who are like me may struggle."

"It will be a good test of the warriors we lead." Snorri and Beorn the Scout rode up. "Take the road north and scout out Wintan-ceastre. It should not take you long. One reports back to me. We will be on the road. The other can remain to watch the town."

"Aye Jarl."

We ate while the captives were divided and set to work. I addressed the men who were the guards. "You must hold Hamwic and the drekar for us. We are nothing without our ships. Those whose swords have yet to drink will soon have the chance." They banged their shields.

With the prospect of more treasure and battle everyone ate quickly and I led the column north along the Roman road. We went at a fast pace. I had found a horse for Aiden. He rode with us. My men did not mind and the new warriors had heard of the power of this galdramenn. They watched him warily. I had given Gunnar Gunnarson the honour of carrying my banner. He had shown himself to be a doughty warrior when we had fought the men of Strathclyde. It lay easily across his shoulder as we headed north. It would be the only banner we fought beneath. We wanted King Egbert to get the message; do not anger the wolf with the heart of a dragon.

The thin sun was climbing, albeit slowly, when Beorn the Scout found us. "We have seen the town. They know not that we are here for the gates are open." He swung his arm around. "I have seen a monastery and a nunnery just a mile or two from the main road."

I halted the column. This was too good an opportunity to miss. "Asbjorn, take your men and find the monastery which lies yonder." I pointed in the direction Beorn had indicated. "Aiden go with them. Gunnar Thorfinnson, take your band to the nunnery. Beorn lead them there, Aiden will show you how to find their secret treasures." I went close to the son of Blue Scar. "Make sure your men do not hurt the women. They are more valuable if they are left untouched. Beorn here has been raiding these many years. Heed his advice."

"Aye, Jarl."

"Take whatever you find back to Hamwic."

My slightly depleted band continued north. I was gambling again. When word got out then every church of the White Christ would hide their treasures. Every man who could bear arms would gather to fight us. They would raise the fyrd. Although not warriors they would be fighting for their land and their families. They would die hard! I wanted to have Wintan-ceastre securely in my hands before that happened. I intended to use it as a base to ravage Egbert's homeland.

It was only after our raid that they began to make Wintan-ceastre into a well defended burgh. Before that morning Egbert and the men of Wessex had thought that their town was safe. My men waited in the woods a mile and a half from the walls and I headed, with Haaken and Wolf Killer to my scout. When we reached Snorri I saw that the Saxons had built a wall running around it and a ditch but they only had towers at the main gates. It showed they were complacent. Speed was of the essence. We would be seen when we were a mile away. Once we reached that point it would be a race to see if we could reach the gates in time.

"What do you suggest Wolf Killer?"

"Most of Gunnstein Berserk-Killer's men have no armour. They should be fast. If we send them to run and reach the gates they might get there before they are closed."

"Good, then you take your men now and go around the walls to the northern gate. Secure them."

"Aye, Jarl."

My son had been an Ulfheonar. He knew how to use cover. In addition he and his men were keen to wreak revenge on the man who had ordered the slaying of their families. Their blood lust had not been slated by the slaughter of the Danes.

"Gunnstein, when we head towards the town I want you and your men to run and try to reach them before they are closed. It will be a hard task. If you do not reach them then have your men with bows clear the gates. It will take them some time to organise a defence."

"Aye Jarl. I am honoured that you give me this chance for glory. I will not let you down."

"You will learn that it is not others that you need worry about. You will do well if you do not let yourself down."

With the men from Dyflin leading we headed up the road. We moved at double speed. It was but a mile and half. The closer we came to the town the more I could see its extent. I saw the high buildings within. I saw that the town itself covered a large area. It was no Lundenwic but it was becoming one. Hope rose when I saw Gunnstein and his men just five hundred paces from the gates. They were still open. Did they have no sentries?

"Hurry! We may catch them with their breeks down!"

Gunnstein was just a hundred paces from the gates when they began to close. I saw a mailed figure with two others run across the ditch. It seemed impossible that they would make the gates but I saw that the gates did not close completely. The men of Dyflin ran to their leader's aid.

"Come, let us show the men from Dyflin that the warriors of Jarl Dragonheart do not let down their comrades!"

We ran and we ran hard. I could see that the gap in the gates was narrow. It looked to be no wider than two warriors. Gunnstein's men were suffering casualties as those on the walls hurled rocks, spears and released arrows at them.

I shouted as I ran, "Archers support those at the gates! Run!" Snorri kicked his horse hard in the flanks and led the archers to the wall. As soon as he reached the ditch my scout leapt from his horse and began to release arrows. He was deadly. He did not miss. The rest arrived piecemeal but gradually they began to wear down those on the walls.

We, too, arrived little by little. Olaf and Finni were the first there and they roughly shouldered aside those without armour. I kept my eye on the gates. They were not closing. Olaf and Finni reached Gunnstein. I saw Olaf's sword as it was raised high and then descended. The gates moved apart a little. Ulf joined the four at the gate and then Haaken and I added our weight to Olaf, Ulf and Finni's backs. It was like a dam bursting. Our added weight broke the backs of the defenders and the gates sprang open. We flooded in. The gates were breached.

Ahead of me I saw a Saxon leader organising a hurried shield wall to face us. I did not give him any time. We leapt towards them roaring our war cry, the howl of the wolf. It was daylight now and our red eyes and blackened armour were terrifying. As we ran towards the waiting warriors I saw fear in their eyes. I headed for the leader. I heard him exhorting his men to great deeds against the pagans. I brought my sword from high above my shoulder and put all of my strength in it. It struck his shield and I heard a crack as his forearm broke. He gritted his teeth and jabbed at me with his sword. I raised my shield to take it and then struck him hard in the face with it. He reeled back. I brought my sword sideways across his head. The blade bit into the helmet and knocked him to the ground. I was about to end his life when the warrior next to him stabbed at me with his spear. It rode over the links of my mail and stuck in the side of my byrnie. I twisted and hit him in the face with the pommel of my sword, he screamed as the crosspiece went into his eye. He made the mistake of lifting both hands to his face and I stabbed him a second time in the middle, ending his life.

With their leader down the Saxons ran. "After them!" Hrolf appeared behind me. He was a game youth and even though he had no armour he was always up with the leaders and those who were in the thickest part of the fray. "Keep your sword at the throat of this one. I think he is an eorl." I lifted up the chain he wore around his neck. It had the symbol of Wessex upon it; a cross with a bird in each corner. "He may be useful."

"Aye Jarl. He will not move save by your command!"

I hefted my shield up and ran after Haaken and the others. The warriors we had fought were running as fast as they could for the northern gate. I saw women and children cowering in huts and buildings. This was not supposed to happen to them. They lived in Wessex, in the most powerful kingdom in the land, they were supposed to be safe. Suddenly the warriors stopped running and turned to face us. I saw why for I could see the northern gates were open and Wolf Killer and his men were charging.

We did not break stride. We ran at the Saxons knowing that our mail and our shields would protect us and we were fighting men who were already defeated. They had run from us once because they were afraid of being killed and now they had no choice. That was the difference between us, my men cared not if they died for if they did then they would go to Valhalla. The heaven of the White Christ must have a less attractive proposition to the Saxons. I swung my sword over my head. The young warrior held up his sword to block it but his sword was short and badly made. Hitting it close to the hilt Ragnar's Spirit shattered the sword in two and continued to bite into his neck. He fell to the ground. Even as I pulled my sword back I saw that they had all been overwhelmed and killed.

All around my warriors banged their shields and chanted my name. I was less excited. These had been poor excuses for warriors. Anyone with any skill would be with Egbert. These were the reluctant heroes. I sheathed my sword, slung my shield around my back and took off my helmet. The air felt cool and refreshing but the air was filled with the smell of blood and death.

I turned to walk back to Hrolf and the Eorl. When I reached them I saw a well dressed woman kneeling and cowering before Hrolf. Her face was marked where she had been struck. Hrolf said, "This woman tried to assist the warrior. I did not understand her words and so I hit her." He said it without apology. Nor did he need one. He had done exactly as I had asked.

"You have done well. You may sheathe your weapon now I do not think we will be in any more danger, at least not for a while." I turned to the woman. "This is your man?"

"He is my husband, Eorledman Centwine and I am his wife Lady Aethelfled." She pointed an accusing finger at Hrolf, "That boy hit me when I tried to help my husband!"

"That boy is a warrior and was obeying orders. Your husband should be dead by rights. He would be if that warrior had not tried to help him." I pointed to the dead and blinded warrior.

"That was our son Ceanwealh."

"He died well with a sword in his hand."

She seemed to realise that I was speaking to her in Saxon and speaking it well. "Are you a Saxon?"

"I had a Saxon father but I am a Viking."

"A pagan!"

She spoke the words as though she was insulting me. "Of course!"

"What will happen to us?"

"The town is mine and all within it. I will sell you."

Her hand went to her mouth, "You cannot! We are Christians!"

I laughed, "Then worship a god who will protect you next time."

Her husband began to come to. She looked at me and I nodded, "Hrolf, find a water skin."

I wondered what he had thought of our conversation for he spoke no Saxon. "Aye Jarl."

The Eorl opened his eyes and saw me and then his wife. She said, "Ceanwealh is dead, he tried to save you. He did save you."

Her husband looked distraught. "I would he had saved himself for then it would be me who was slain. Is that not right Viking!"

I think he said the words not expecting me to understand them for he looked surprised when I answered him. "I have just told your wife that we will sell you."

That truly shocked him. "Sell us!"

Hrolf returned with a skin and I handed it to the woman,. She poured some into his mouth and then on to the hem of her dress. She began to wipe the blood away from her husband's wound. He shook his head, "I am fine. Do not sell us Viking. I have money. I can pay more than you would get for selling me."

I laughed, "We will take all the money that is here, Eorl, I can sell you and have your money."

He shook his head, "My money is not here it is in my hall and that is not in Wintan-ceastre."

This was a way to make even more money. The Franks had done this. Perhaps it was the religion of the White Christ which allowed them to pay ransom. We would never do such a thing. I turned to Hrolf, "Continue to guard them. I will send some help."

He snorted, "I need no help for one Saxon and his bitch!"

Smiling to myself at his youthful arrogance I sought Wolf Killer and Ketil. I found them as they finished off the last of the warriors. Wolf Killer looked happy. "If they are all as easy as this perhaps we ought to conquer Wessex."

"It would not be as easy for King Egbert would have better warriors. Besides our home is better. Have the captives and the captured goods sent to Hamwic." They nodded. "And then we will send out scouts to find what other treasures we have." I spied Rolf Horsekiller and Thorir the Slow. They had with them a string of horses. "Where do you go with these?"

"They make good eating!"

"They make better mounts. Take them to Hrolf. He is with a pair of captives. Wait with them and keep the horses safe. There is other food for us to eat."

They went off happily and I went in search of Haaken and my Ulfheonar. They had found some ale which they had broached. Having been the ones who faced the greatest danger they would allow the others to do the menial tasks while they enjoyed the rewards. I took the proffered horn and raised it to them. Snorri, I have a task for you, Finni and Ulf." They looked attentively at me. "We have an Eorl who says he will pay us rather than selling him as a slave."

Olaf said, "So we get his money and then sell him anyway?"

"No, Olaf, if I give him my word then I will keep it. We use this as a way of making coin and exploring the land. When you escort him for the money beware of tricks and traps but, more importantly, see where else we might strike."

"We do not go home yet?"

"No, Vermund. We have not yet begun to pay back Egbert. And there is little need. We have seen naught yet which suggests danger. We keep a good watch. There are horses. We can send scouts out to give us early warning of warriors. If Asbjorn and Gunnar Thorfinnson have had as successful a day then we will have much to send back to our home."

I returned to the disconsolate looking pair of Saxons. "These three men will ride with you to fetch the gold for you and your wife's freedom. When you return then we will let you go."

"My wife stays here?"

"Of course she does. We all know how treacherous Saxons are! I would not trust one as far as I could throw one."

I could see that part of his plan had vanished with my words. "And how much do I pay?"

I smiled, "All that you have."

"But that is wrong! I refuse!"

"Then you shall both be sold." His shoulders drooped in resignation, "You should have fought with Egbert rather than offering to stay and defend this town." His darted look of hate showed that I has guessed correctly. He had taken what he believed was the safest course of action. "You are an Eorl. You will take more from those who work your land and you will become rich again. You will have your lives."

"You swear that we will live?"

"I am Jarl Dragonheart and I am never foresworn."

He recoiled, "I did not know that it was you!" He seemed to see our wolf cloaks for the first time.

"Then you can tell King Egbert, when he returns, that this is the price he and his people will pay each time he tries to hurt me or mine. There is nowhere he can hide from my vengeance."

He shook his head ruefully, "We advised him against this course of action. Elfrida means nothing to him. It was his pride which was hurt, that is all."

"And you have paid the price." I waved to Hrolf, "You can let him go." He nodded. "Snorri, take care. This one may be treacherous."

As they rode off I waved Gunnar and my banner over. "Guard this woman with your life."

"Aye Jarl. I am sorry that I could not keep up." He shook his head, "I made the mistake of fighting when I should have followed."

"You are a warrior. My banner entered with my warriors and the Saxons know who I am. That is enough."

Chapter 9

We ate well from the supplies in the town and we slept well in comfortable beds. The Saxons were soft. The warriors who had taken the supplies to Hamwic returned at dusk. The two raids on the monastery and nunnery had yielded huge amounts of slaves, books and gold. It was all going well. I sat reflecting in the warrior hall of the Saxons. Haaken came over to speak with me. "For someone who has just had another great victory you have a face which looks like a man who has lost his favourite sword."

"It is the Norns."

"The Norns?"

"Things have gone too well. The last time they went well, in Frankia, Windar's Mere and Elfridaby were ravaged. This went too well. What have the Weird Sisters planned for us now?"

"Then let us leave. When the ransom is received we head back to Hamwic and sail home."

He made it sound so simple. "But will that be enough for the men we lead?"

"They follow wherever you lead and they are grateful for the treasure they accumulate. They talk of you as lucky."

"And that is a mistake. The Norns do not like such arrogance."

"But it is not your arrogance; there is no one more humble than you." He emptied his horn of ale and pulled a face. The Saxons could not brew beer to save their lives. "What is the worst that could happen?"

"King Egbert catches us."

"And we fight him. When we fought for him at Lundenwic did you see anything to make you afraid?"

I found myself stroking the blue pommel stone. It gave me comfort. It was a connection to the warlord and my past. "Of course not. If they do come then they will have marched from Corn Walum and that is hundreds of miles but..."

"Do not begin to doubt yourself. This land is rich and if we are to teach King Egbert a lesson then we make him and his people hurt."

He was right. "You have convinced me. See if the men can find any wine. Surely the men of Wessex who have coin cannot suffer this piss!"

Hrolf was hovering nearby and Haaken waved him over. "Young Hrolf, find us some wine and I will put you in a saga."

He grinned, "I would rather have a helmet and sword!"

I laughed, "You have served me well. That is a deal. Find us the wine and I will have Bjorn Bagsecgson make you both."

He disappeared and returned in an amazingly short time. He had an amphora of wine. I recognised the seal, it was Vasconian wine.

Haaken frowned, "You knew where this was before we asked you."

"Of course!"

"Do not be critical of someone with initiative, Haaken. If you had been a slave as I was then you would know that you take the chances which come your way.

You have done well Hrolf but do not be so reckless when next we fight. I would not have you lose your life before we make you into a mighty warrior."

We sent scouts out the next morning and they scoured the land close to the town. My men on the walls kept a close watch for Snorri and the Eorl. At noon Aiden, Asbjorn and Gunnar arrived.

"We have filled all the knarr and sent them back to Úlfarrston." Aiden hesitated, "I sent **'Red Snake'** with them as an escort. It seemed prudent not to risk her alone."

"You did well, Aiden. It is what I would have ordered."

Gunnar Thorfinnson was almost bursting, "We have riches beyond belief. The slaves alone are worth a fortune!"

Gunnstein Berserk-Killer nodded, "And there is no opposition. I can see why you are so successful, Jarl Dragonheart. It is not just your sword but your mind too."

"Well my mind is working on how we get to keep our gold and our lives. I will rest easier when our scouts bring us news and when Snorri and my Ulfheonar return with the ransom. I did not trust that eorl!"

The scouts returned an hour before dusk. The news they brought was mixed. The first scouts reported many farms and churches within a few miles of us. It seemed we could continue to raid. However the last scout brought less welcome news. He had travelled the furthest. "Jarl Dragonheart there is a town some twenty or so miles north east of us. There are many men making their way there. They are raising the fyrd."

"Do you think they would be ready to march this day?"

"I doubt it Jarl. I saw lines of men marching to join them."

"Good. Send for the prisoner."

The Lady Aethelfled arrived. I could see that my men had looked after her and she looked a little more defiant than when her husband had left. "Has my husband returned?"

"Not yet. How far to your home?"

"It would take almost a day to get there."

"Then you should know he has not. There is a village twenty or so miles north east of us."

"Ferneberga."

"Probably. Does it have an Eorl?"

A self satisfied smile filled her face, "The Eorl Beothild; he is a mighty warrior and a cousin of the King! He will come and swat you like a fly. God will punish you, pagan and Eorl Beothild will be the weapon he uses!"

I smiled, "That may be. Take her away." When she had gone I said. "They will come to fight us. If they leave at dawn they will expect to be here by the middle of the afternoon. They will march on foot. We will also leave here at dawn and meet them on the way. We will choose a ground I like. They will expect us to sit behind these walls and await our fate." I turned to Asbjorn and Gunnar Thorfinnson. "Leave a small garrison at Hamwic and return here with your men."

Gunnstein Berserk-Killer came over to speak with me after my men had left. The Ulfheonar sharpened their swords and drank. "You and you your men seem remarkably calm about this. There is an army coming to fight us and you are choosing to meet them on their own ground without knowing their numbers."

I nodded, "My men have done this before as have I. We do not meet them on ground which they have chosen. We choose where to attack them and that is the difference. As to the quality of the warriors... I have not fought with you or Gunnar but the rest I know. They stand when I say stand. They charge when I say charge. They obey orders and they only retreat when I order them to do so. In addition Saxons are the worst archers I have ever seen. The only archers who can compare to our men are the Welsh. Without seeing the battlefield I know that my archers will cause more death before the men of Wessex reach us than they have seen in a lifetime. When we charge, and we will, we will hit them with our mailed men in the centre of a line of steel. No matter how many warriors they have they will have more who are not, the fyrd. The fyrd are fine and good when all goes well but when you hit them hard they remember the cow at home which needs milking or they think of their family. They are Christians and they fear to die."

He nodded. "I see. What you say makes sense. The trouble is I have followed a leader like Hakon the Bald who never takes risks. He connives and uses treachery amongst his enemies to keep control. We rarely have to battle in Dyflin. The Hibernians are always too pleased to fight amongst themselves."

"Do not misunderstand me. When King Egbert returns it will be a different matter. We will be fighting the best which Wessex has to offer and they will have great numbers. With the King present the fyrd will fight harder but this Eorledman does not frighten me."

Despite my confident words I worried about Snorri and the ransom. The Eorl Centwine had headed north. Snorri could be beyond help behind enemy lines. I wanted my Ulfheonar safe more than I wanted the ransom.

Leaving Aiden to command the small garrison I led two hundred and twenty warriors north east. We left at dawn. I had Beorn and ten scouts riding ponies ahead of us to find somewhere where we could surprise and then fight our Saxon foes. I had forty archers in one body and they were led by Finni. I would have preferred Snorri but he was still missing. He was in Saxon lands and I was worried.

Beorn and his scouts met us five miles down the Roman Road. "Two miles ahead, Jarl, the road passes through a forest. The trees close to the road are spindly but the enemy will only see us when they are five hundred paces from us."

"Good then we will use that."

When we reached it I was pleased. We had passed nothing better. "Finni, I want the archers behind me and the Ulfheonar. Wolf Killer, you will have your men in the woods to the right. Gunnstein, you will be with him. Asbjorn, will be to the left, Gunnar, have your men support him. The rest will be behind us but I wish to show just my men to the enemy. Let the rest remain hidden."

While they took their positions I spoke with my jarls. "We make them bleed and I will retreat through the woods. When Gunnar Gunnarson signals with my banner then you fall on their flanks."

"You take a great risk, Father."

"We are the best armed, armoured and trained warriors. We can retreat together."

"But there are just six of you!"

"With archers behind but the six of us will fill the Roman Road." I pointed to the ditches. "We have time to make ankle breakers there. They will rush to flank us and they will fall."

The men set to work with a will. My Ulfheonar became the experts directing the work. We knew our business. It was the business of death. They dug pits the depth of a leg and covered them with vegetation. I sent Beorn to keep watch on the enemy. Wolf Killer came to speak with me. "This is a risk we do not need to take."

"You mean I do not need to take?"

He smiled and nodded, "There are three women at home who will make my life a misery if I fail to bring you back alive."

There was a spider's web in the tree next to me, "And there are three women who weave and plot; it is they who will decide if I am to live or to die. I could sit behind my walls and die of poisoned meat because the Weird Sisters have tired of me. This is good, Wolf Killer, and I do not believe that this is my day to die." He nodded. "I have given you the place which is the most crucial. We need this fyrd surrounding and destroying. When they are attacked in the rear and the flanks they will panic. It is in the nature of farmers to do so. Our retreat will make them think they have victory and your attack will snatch it away from them. Without hope they will not stand."

It was noon when Beorn rode in. "They are less than two miles away. They will reach us soon."

"Good. Put your horse behind the archers and join us. Gunnar, my standard!"

Leaving the archers and the rest of my men on the road out of sight I led my handful of men and my banner out into the open and we marched to a spot two hundred and fifty paces from the edge of the woods. We all wore our shields across our backs and our swords were sheathed. I turned to inspect the woods. I knew where my men waited and I could detect their presence but I knew that the Saxons would not think that two hundred men awaited them.

"Remember they know not the Ulfheonar nor how we fight. Those who fled and reported us will say that there is a war band of Vikings raiding. They will see our cloaks and our black armour. At best they have heard of some warriors who think that they can become wolves but they are Christian. They will dismiss the idea. When they see us turn and run they will take us for scouts or a vanguard and they will run after us. We lead them to the very edge of the wood where we turn and fight. The men who will shelter behind us have no armour and the Saxons will think that we are weaker than we are. We fall back in one solid line."

Haaken laughed, "I think that we can do that, Jarl Dragonheart. We just have to make sure that Olaf Leather Neck here does not try to kill them on his own."

Olaf chuckled, "I will leave some for you, Haaken One Eye, that way you may mention me in a saga."

"Gunnar, your task is harder. You must stay behind me and hold the standard high. When I shout your name then it is the time to signal the attack."

"Aye Jarl."

"Jarl!"

I turned as Erik spoke. The Saxons were coming. They were an untidy sprawl spreading out long both sides of the Roman Road. They were led by five men on horses. They were mailed horsemen. I spied some shields and helmets in the mass of men but it was hard to estimate either numbers or quality. What I did know was that there appeared little order. They halted and I saw the horsemen hold conference."

I nodded, "The mounted ones are the nobles and the leaders. We kill them and the heart will go from the rest. When they come we wait until I shout run and then we pretend we are the Welsh and we run!"

We watched as they neared us. We waited. They spied us and spoke for a few moments. Then I saw a horseman raise his sword and they began to come towards us. They walked and then, when they saw us standing and not running, they began to run. "Now!"

We turned and we ran. I could hear the hooves and the feet on the cobbles behind us. Their shouts, cheers and jeers filled the air. As we neared the woods I saw that my jarls had successfully hidden their men. I shouted, "Archers stand. Men of Cyninges-tūn stand behind the Ulfheonar. Today is your day." The moment we reached the very edge we turned to face them. I slid my shield around as did the others. The six of us filled the road. There was no gap and the only way around us was through the trap filled drainage ditch. Glancing down I could see no sign of the ankle breakers but I knew that they were there; cunningly hidden beneath the vegetation.

"Archers, release!"

I heard Erik Wolf Claw as he took charge of the men from Cyninges-tūn. The arrows, all forty of them rose high in the air and plunged down on to the Saxons. They struck them when they were a hundred paces from us. The mailed men were not hurt but the horses were and those without armour were struck. More arrows followed. The wounded horses bucked and reared. Their flailing hooves smashed skulls to pulp and shattered bones. We had achieved more already than I could have hoped.

The leader, I took him to be Eorl Beothild, did not panic. He rose and, after slitting the throat of his dying horse began to organise his men into a shield wall. I heard his voice as he shouted, "Form a line. Kill the horses who are injured. Edgar, take men into the woods and outflank them!"

All the time he was speaking his men were dying. The arrows rained down. Men hid beneath any shelter they could get. Most had small shields which were of no use at all.

"Forward!"

They came at us in a wedge. We had locked shields and swords held across the top of them. The wedge began to spread into the sides of the road, into the ditch. The ankle breakers were in the shady part of the forest. They would see their chance to outflank us. The Eorl Beothild was not in the front rank. He and three others were four men back. The five at the front were mailed and I saw battle rings around their arms. They held spears and their helmets were well made.

I waited until the leader was close to me and when he jabbed his spear at my head I did not bring my shield up. I had no need to. Our shields were locked and we had a barrier of wood and iron before us. Instead I moved my head away from the spear thrust, it glanced along the side of my helmet and then I rammed my sword into his open mouth as he roared his triumph. I twisted as I pulled it out and he fell. Two more men fell to my Ulfheonar.

"Fall back!"

We took a step back as they adjusted their front. Two men came at us. This time they were warier. They tried to hit me in the face with their spears. They could see my mouth and they aimed at my throat. I had a coil of mail around it but they would not be able to see that. Olaf and Haaken's swords darted forward as I used Ragnar's Spirit to deflect the two spears. I broke the head on one spear as both men were stabbed by my oathsworn. Both dropped to their knees. They were wounded only but their pride would keep them in the battle and would kill them.

"Fall back!"

My archers were still releasing arrows and men's attention was on the skies and not on their feet. Some at the side were eager to escape the misery of the arrows and they left the wedge to outflank us. I heard their shouts as they found the ankle breakers and the traps. The point of the wedge had now disappeared. There were six men facing us and they filled the road. The next time they surged forward we would be equally matched. I saw that Eorl Beothild was in the second rank.

"Fall back!"

They had not reached us when we fell back. The step took them by surprise and Eorl Beothild must have thought that we were fleeing his wrath for he shouted, "At them!" They charged.

"Brace!" We all put one leg behind us and leaned forward as the Saxon ran at us. Had we been in the open they would have pushed us back but the ditch and the hidden traps caused confusion as men fell into those trying to push. The traps did not kill but they hurt the enemy. The front rank struck us. Some of these had swords. We kept our shields locked and they took most of the hits. The rest were taken on our swords. I saw the look of surprise on the warrior before me as his sword bent when he hit Ragnar's Spirit. I head butted him and brought my sword down on the side of his head. Although we were too close for a good strike I stunned him and I felt him slip to the ground.

"Fall back!"

We had now fallen back some ten paces into the woods. Another five and I could signal the attack. One of those with a good byrnie and sword stepped into the gap created by the last fallen warrior. He was young and eager to get to me. He shouted, "Come, let us show these Norsemen that the men of Wessex have guts!"

As he swung his sword at me I shouted, "And you will spill them here whelp of Wessex! You fight the Wolf Warriors!"

I had his attention, "And you fall back like women. Stand and fight!"

Next to me Olaf had more space and be brought his sword high above his head to smash into the helmet of the warrior next to the arrogant young man. Olaf's mighty sword split the helmet and the young man was spattered with blood, brains and bone. Distracted by the blow the young warrior's eyes flickered to the side and I stabbed forward. Being young he had quick reactions and his sword came up to block but he had no mail mittens and my blade sliced across his knuckles. Two fingers were hacked from his hand and he stumbled.

"Fall back!"

Each time we fell back we left a line of dead or wounded men and the Saxons had to slow as they approached us and clambered over the bodies. I gambled that we had moved back far enough and as the Saxon line lurched forward I shouted, "Gunnar!"

Even I was taken aback by the roar from a hundred and twenty Vikings who roared their war cries and charged the flanks of the Saxons.

"Men of Cyninges-tūn, now is your time!" We unlocked our shields and ran at the stunned Saxons. The maimed Saxon looked up in horror as Haaken swept his sword towards him, his head hit Eorl Beothild who looked stunned by the sudden reversal in fortunes. I took advantage of his hesitation and distraction I swung Ragnar's Spirit towards his left shoulder. He hurriedly tried to get his shield up. He might have been as Lady Aethelfled had said, a mighty warrior who had fought many battles but his reactions were slow. It slowed the strike of my blade, it did not stop it. It bit into his shoulder breaking the mail. As I drew back the sword I saw that its edge was bloody. He knew he was hurt and he desperately struck at my head with his long sword. I had quick reactions and my shield blocked it.

The handful of mailed men who stood near their Eorl were fighting hard against my Ulfheonar but elsewhere the battle was going our way as my men hacked and slashed their way through the demoralised fyrd of Wessex. With little armour and poor weapons they were no match for Wolf Killer, Asbjorn and their battle hardened veterans. Erik Wolf Claw was leading the archers around the flanks of the enemy to cut off their retreat.

I feinted at the Eorl's weakened shoulder. As I had expected he tried to raise his shield to counter it. The effort cost him dear. I stabbed forward with Ragnar's Spirit and he managed to bring down the edge of the shield and he blocked it. I realised that the bone across his shoulder had been broken. Not only was he bleeding; the jagged ends of the bones were grating together. He was a brave man as he stoically endured the pain.

"Surrender and I will give you the warrior's death!"

"I am a Christian and I will send you to hell, pagan!" He launched himself at me with his sword. He put every ounce of strength left to him into the strike. All of his years of experience struck where he thought he would do the most damage. It was a mighty blow and my shield shivered but it cost him dear. Before he could even withdraw his sword I had darted forward with my blade and put my entire weight and strength behind the strike. My sword had a sharp tip. It tore through the mail links and entered his leather byrnie. I pushed harder and the leather suddenly gave way. I felt warm fluids flood over my hand and I twisted as I stabbed. I heard a grunt from him. Our faces were almost touching and I saw a tendril of blood begin to seep from his mouth. I thought he was smiling and then I realised he was dead. I pushed the body from my sword.

Around me my Ulfheonar stood with bloodied swords and the bodies of the vanquished lay around us. The battle ahead had moved on and the Roman Road was strangely quiet. There were just the moans of the wounded and dying punctuated by the panting of my warriors. We were too tired to pursue. That would be left to the archers and the warriors of Wolf Killer and the other jarls.

Olaf was tending to Erik who had taken a savage cut to his face. "The women love a scar. You could have a blue one like Thorfinn."

Erik snorted, "I will just have a scar. I am ugly enough without making it blue!"

I saw that Gunnar had also been wounded albeit slightly. Had I fought alongside any other warriors then it would not have gone as well as it had.

I took off my helmet. One or two of my warriors from Cyninges-tūn were going around ending the pain of our badly wounded warriors and despatching the Saxon wounded. There were many of our men who would survive if we could get them back to Aiden who would heal them.

"Gunnar, gather the wounded who can be healed and take them back to Wintan-ceastre. Tell Aiden we have won a great victory. We need food and medicine. We will start back when my son and the other jarls return."

Haaken pointed his sword at the men around the Eorl. "They fought well. Had there been more like that we might not have had such an easy victory."

I looked down at the body of Audun Red Hair. He was but seventeen summers old. For him it was not easy. "And when word reaches Egbert he will bring many more warriors like this and they will be fresh from the slaughter of the men of King Mark."

"How soon do you think he will be here?"

"Even if a rider had left yesterday when word reached Eorl Beothild it would still take three days to reach King Egbert. We have at least seven days to empty this land."

"You will sail before he returns?"

"Perhaps. We came here to punish King Egbert and not to die."

Olaf Leather Neck shook his head, "It does not do to run from our enemies. It becomes a bad habit."

I reflected on those words.

Chapter 10

It was almost dark when we warily reached our destination. Men were laden down with the treasure they had captured. To many of the poorer warriors this was a byrnie, a helmet, a sword but all had some coins and many had the arm rings they had taken from the more experienced Saxons. Our warriors had pursued them for some miles. I doubted that they would be in any position to fight for Egbert for some time to come. Some of the crops which still lay in the fields would lie there until they rotted.

I was relieved to see Snorri and my other two Ulfheonar when we reached Wintan-ceastre. He looked worried as we entered the gates. "We were worried, Jarl. We should have been at your side and not acting as nursemaids for this puling, whining Saxon." I noticed the Eorl and his wife were sulkily sitting together and the Eorl had blackened eyes. Snorri saw my examination and said, "He annoyed me and I shut him up. Had you not given your word I would have ended his life."

"Was there much treasure?"

"Aye, two chests of it. He offered us a small one but Ulf has a nose for gold. We found it all...eventually. We took a little longer to return as we had to dig up five large pots which contained his treasure."

I stared at the Eorl, "I should have you executed out of hand, the both of you! I said I wanted all that you had!"

He cowered, almost hiding behind his wife, "You gave your word!"

"Aye and unlike you I keep it." I pointed to the gate, "Leave now before I forget my promise."

"Leave? But there may be brigands out there! We will leave in the morning."

I laughed, "If there are brigands they are Saxon and you are an Eorl. You leave now or I sell you."

They stood and hurriedly headed for the gate. I neither saw nor heard of them again. I walked with Snorri to the fire which was burning, My men were roasting the ox we had slaughtered. "Did you learn much?"

He nodded, "They have few fortified burghs. There are many halls and farms. The Eorl lives at somewhere called Werham. There is an old fort close by. I am guessing that if we raided they would retreat there. It looks ancient with space for their animals. It could be defended and we would lose many men trying to take it."

"It seems to me that we have more than enough. We will raid for the next couple of days and hopefully our knarr will have returned by then."

I felt very dirty, bloody and in need of my sweat hut on the Water. The Saxons did not appear to be keen on being clean. I sought Hrolf, he was always close to hand. He seemed keen to impress. "Hrolf I need water to bathe."

"Aye Jarl. There is a well by the church. I will haul the buckets for you."

I followed him to the Saxon church. It had already been stripped of everything which was of value. My warriors were seeking out the empty houses which they would use to sleep. Animals were already butchered and the smell of cooking meat permeated the air. Were it not for the lack of decent beer my men would think they were in a perfect world.

I stripped naked as Hrolf pulled up bucket after bucket of water. I doused myself in its icy grip. I felt alive. Wolf Killer approached and he joined me. "The Saxons need to take a lesson from those in the east and build bath houses. At least we are close to the healing waters at home."

"This will do."

"It was a good victory today, Jarl."

"Aye my son. It went better than we could have hoped."

"Egbert will not be so gullible. He knows how we fight. This Eorl did not give you enough respect."

"Perhaps it was the quality of the men he led. Less than half were warriors."

Hrolf said, "When I am a jarl I will lead the best of warriors."

Wolf Killer laughed, "You have some years to go young Hrolf."

"The men say that you and your father were jarls before you had seen twenty summers."

It was my turn to laugh, "He is right, my son. Besides, it is good to have dreams and ambitions."

"You are right Jarl Dragonheart and one day I shall return to Neustria and conquer it. I shall have a land such as yours."

Wolf Killer towelled himself dry with his wolf cloak. "You would not wish to be jarl of Cyninges-tūn?"

"That will be yours when the Dragonheart is gone and I would not fight fellow Vikings. The Jarl did not fight Vikings to take it did he?"

Wolf Killer shook his head, "You are too wise for one so young."

"When you are a slave you grow wise or you die. Is that not right Hrolf son of Gerloc?"

He grinned, "It is Jarl."

I handed him my sword and a silver penny, "Here sharpen my blade. We have not finished harvesting Saxons yet."

"I need no coins to sharpen this magical sword."

"Nonetheless I will pay you. Every man is worth his price. You are not my oathsworn and I pay all others."

"I am your oathsworn, Jarl Dragonheart, Hermund and I both swore."

"I realised you were too young to make such a promise. I do not hold you to it. Do not make such hasty decisions. If it is meant that you go to Neustria then you need to be your own man or serve a jarl who wishes to carve out a new home. I am content with Cyninges-tūn. I will fight to keep it but I will not fight to take another's Cyninges-tūn."

"But I may follow you?"

"I am honoured that you do."

"Then it is well."

I left, the next day, with the bulk of my men for Hamwic. Gunnar Thorfinnson remained at Wintan-ceastre with Gunnstein. The two of them would raid the surrounding area. I intended to use my drekar to raid to the west and to the east.

We would strike from the sea. If we left in the dark of night we could use surprise as dawn broke. We carted all of the treasure, grain, animals and slaves we had captured, back to Hamwic. If danger threatened then we could send our gains back by knarr. It would not do to have lost what we had gained.

I rode with Aiden as we headed the few miles south. "We have gained treasure, grain and weapons. Have you gained knowledge?"

He nodded, "The monastery had many books which have valuable information for me. Some wrote of the time of the Romans. I now know where more of the Roman Roads were built. Others gave cures for some ailments. There was one parchment which told how to alleviate brain fever by drilling a hole and allowing the bad vapours to leave the head."

"That sounds a little hard to believe."

"We have both seen men who have survived savage cuts to their head with parts of the skull missing. It seems it is what is within the skull which is more important. However I believe that part of our success has been that we protect our men's heads with helmets. When I return home I have ideas about helmets which will afford better protection."

"The monks wrote about that?"

"No Jarl but they have things written by Romans. I do not think the monks had read them. They were dusty and buried beneath well read pieces about the White Christ. They have much knowledge that they are not using." He shook his head. "They study their religion too much. We just follow our ways and live good lives. They seem to hold the rituals in higher esteem than the purpose."

"That is too deep an idea for me. Just so long as our people benefit and are happy then I am satisfied."

We used two ships to raid; our biggest ones. I headed east with **'Heart of the Dragon'**. We used warriors from Cyninges-tūn. Wolf Killer took **'Wild Boar'** and Ketil's men to augment his own and they went west. We left enough in Hamwic to protect it and our supplies. Aiden remained poring over his books. He had identified two targets for us. There was a port to the east with a good harbour. It was not far down the coast. Wolf Killer's target was a huge port. I was more interested in it as an anchorage but we knew from the books that it was used to land cargos. There were warehouses.

I sent Asbjorn over land at dark of night. We rowed with stepped mast to the east. Thanks to Aiden we knew the precise position of the town and port. Erik slowed the drekar down and allowed the tide to take us close to it. The burghers of the town, Aiden said it was called Portesmūða, must have heard there were Vikings close by for they had put a thick hawser across the harbour to stop ships entering at night. It reminded me of the Golden Horn in Miklagård. Had it been made of metal then it might have stumped us. As it was we soon sawed through it with our blades and entered the harbour.

There were many cargo ships; they were Saxon versions of the knarr. More importantly there was no palisade. They obviously felt secure. As we sculled towards the ships I began to think that we would have another easy time of it. That was until the shout went up. They had a town watch and we had been seen.

We were less than a hundred paces from the jetty when the shout went up. We had enough way to drift in and my warriors shipped their oars and grabbed their shields. A few arrows and spears clattered off the side but only one man was hit. I stood at the prow. My hand touched the dragon's head. It brought us luck.

As soon as we touched I leapt ashore with Haaken and Olaf by my side. A moment later Snorri and Beorn jumped from the stern. I ran directly at the town guard who were rushing to push us back into the sea. I did not break stride as I swung my sword sideways to hack into the thigh of the bowman. I cut through to the bone and he fell to the cobbles blood gushing from the wound. The effect was to start a panic back to the houses where the townspeople were arming themselves to repel the raiders from the sea. I heard a distant shout and knew that Asbjorn and his men had arrived. My Ulfheonar and the men of Cyninges-tūn, led by Erik Wolf Claw despatched the thin line of poorly armed warriors and then the rest threw themselves to the ground pleading for mercy.

"Let them live!"

Olaf Leather Neck shook his head, "We need no more slaves. We have sent enough to the market and they will fetch a lower price."

I smiled, although in the dark no one saw it, "I have a better idea. We will use the method we tried with the Eorl."

Haaken was curious, "What is that?"

"We let them buy their freedom. It will save us time and effort searching for it. I lived in such a village and these people will find devious places in which to hide their gold and silver. Gather them all."

Dawn was breaking by the time the population of Portesmūða had been assembled. My men made them drop to their knees. I had silence imposed and then I began. "I could have all of your heads taken. I could have your women raped. I have conquered you and you are mine to do with as I wish."

A greybeard said, "Spare us, Viking. I beg of you."

"Then should I sell you in the markets of Dyflin?"

A woman wailed, "Better to kill us than give us to those pagans."

I let them all wail and weep before I shouted, "Silence!" It became quiet save for an occasional whimper. "Or you could buy your freedom."

The greybeard said, "Buy?"

"You all have money hidden away. Give me the money you have and I will let you live and not sell you to the men of Dyflin."

He snorted, "You will take our gold and kill us anyway."

Snorri smacked him about the head. I said, unsheathing my sword, "This is Ragnar's Spirit, the sword touched by the gods. I swear by this sword that if you give me your coin then you shall live. I am Jarl Dragonheart and I am never foresworn."

I saw the greybeard look at some of the others. He nodded and said, "I have heard your name. They say you are a wolf but an honest wolf. We would live."

My warriors watched them as they went to their homes and brought out their coins. We took them, every one. I kept my word. Even those who had but two silver pennies were allowed to live and to remain free. We took their animals and their grain and we sailed back to Hamwic.

As we sailed in to the Itchen I thought about sailing home. The thought was fleeting but I should have heeded it. I might have come up with excuses that we waited the drekar or we had not been defeated but in my heart I knew that we should have sailed and we did not.

My other jarls had equal success. Gunnar and Gunnstein sent cartloads of captured grain, animals, weapons and treasure. My son returned with fine mail and slaves. Yet we still waited for the knarr. Five days later the knarr had not arrived and the weather was worsening. I summoned my jarls from Wintan-ceastre. When they arrived, a day later, laden with booty I said, "We leave two day's hence even if our knarr have not arrived."

Aiden nodded but said nothing. Haaken spoke for all of my jarls. "We should stay. We have not yet milked this Saxon cow dry."

"None the less we go for I have decided."

I was Jarl Dragonheart and my word was law. We prepared to leave. The Norns must have heard my words or perhaps the gods decided that we had enjoyed enough good fortune for before we could leave King Egbert and his army arrived. I had withdrawn my men to Hamwic and Wintan-ceastre, our sentry, had been emptied. Our attention was to the south and west. We sought the sails of Siggi and his knarr. It was the sentries from the gates at the north who sounded the alarm.

"Saxons!"

As soon as I heard the words I knew that I had delayed too long. The drekar were not ready for sea. We had loaded nothing. I went to the jetty and, cupping my hands, shouted, "Erik prepare the drekar for sea."

"Aye Jarl, but the tide is not yet right! We need another two hours."

That decided me. We might not have two hours. I ran to the northern gate. Aiden, the Ulfheonar and my jarls joined me. Sven pointed north west. "There Jarl Dragonheart, emerging from the trees."

I followed his finger. I could see emerging from the trees a mile to the north west, Saxons. Gunnstein Berserk-Killer said, "It may be a group of scouts. This does not mean it is the Saxon army. We should ride out and capture them before they can send word."

Wolf Killer shook his head. "These are Saxons. They are not afraid of us seeing them. See more men emerge from the trees and some are mailed. This is an army." He looked at me. "Egbert."

"Aye. Aiden have all your books, papers and treasure secured on the drekar. Have the coins spread equally amongst them."

"What of the grain, tapestries, cloths and animals?"

"Leave them. If we have to we will tip them in the river." He hurried off. He had a quick mind and he had seen the same as I had. "Prepare to fight." I pointed to the north east. There was a small headland. From the wall of Hamwic to the river was only six hundred paces. "I want every archer in here with the gates barred. The rest of us will form line twixt here and the river."

Gunnar Thorfinnson said, "But we will be trapped if we are defeated."

Asbjorn was quietly spoken but I could hear the derision in his voice, "Dragonheart is never defeated."

"Thank you Asbjorn but I hope that we can be taken off from the river. We cannot be outflanked there and we can hold them until the tide rises and our ships can come to take us off. The archers can protect us. When we are embarked then they will fire the walls and we embark them at the jetty. Snorri you command the archers. Have the men use the captured Saxon spears. Make a barrier of them before us and each man holds one. It will stop them charging too recklessly at us." I was aware that we were close to the river. Our ally could become our enemy if we were forced backwards.

In the time it had taken me to speak more men had emerged and I saw the blue banner of Wessex with the cross and four birds. A second banner emerged that of the dragon. It too signified Egbert. The Saxons were gathering on the hill and organising their ranks. We had no time to waste. "Hurry!"

I ran to don my mail and my helmet. Hrolf ran to me. "Here Jarl Dragonheart! Your sword." He held up his hand and there was a scar across the palm. "It bit me! I am touched by the gods too!"

I smiled at his enthusiasm, "That is a rare wound, Hrolf. Those whom Ragnar's Spirit touches normally die. You may be right. The gods must have marked you down for something special."

I sheathed my sword and heard the words which gave me a kind of hope. "Knarr approaching!"

I ran to the jetty and saw, a mile and half down the channel, the three knarr approaching. It would take an hour for them to reach us. We could not leave now. "Aiden have the knarr loaded as soon as they dock."

"Aye Jarl."

I turned and saw Erik and his crew fitting the mast. "Erik I want the drekar to pick us up from the other side of the headland. Come as soon as you can. Have *'Red Snake'* here to wait for Snorri and his archers."

"Aye Jarl." He grinned, "The Weird Sisters eh?"

"*Wyrd.*"

"Truly *wyrd*!"

As I reached my shield I saw my standard. "Hrolf, today you shall carry my standard!"

I saw joy on his face. "Thank you Jarl Dragonheart!"

"Listen for my commands. When I tell you to withdraw you must wave the standard towards the sea until I tell you to stop."

"I will be behind you, Jarl. I will hear."

There was a reason for my choice. I needed every warrior who could wield a sword if I was to extract us from this trap. I now knew that I was meant to fight Egbert but I wanted us to return home. I did not want three widows waiting in Cyninges-tūn for husbands and fathers who had died here in Wessex. We had done all that I had hoped. We had ravaged Egbert's heartland and we had sent him a message. We had had success in battle and we had great treasure.

I hurried out of the gate. Snorri and his archers were already stacking the wood they would use to bar the gates and to fire the walls. "*'Red Snake'* will be at the jetty for you. Stay safe."

He grinned, he was still the young Viking who had once crewed my drekar, "Aye Jarl. We will guard this flank. If we are not on the drekar it is because we died doing our duty."

My Ulfheonar were already organising the men of Cyninges-tūn who would fight in the centre. I had not decided that, Haaken and my oathsworn had. I saw Wolf Killer's men on the right and Asbjorn's on the left. Gunnar and Gunnstein were not my men and my jarls would protect the Dragonheart.

Olaf pointed towards the woods. It was higher than the river and we could see Egbert organising his men. They were forming lines and readjusting their front for our defensive position. Had we had time we would have made the ground before us a death trap but we would have to rely on nature. We were on drier ground for there was much sand. The wind had made low dunes and that gave us solid footing. Between us and the Saxons was a low lying piece of ground. In places it was marshy. It would prevent them from picking up too much speed when they charged. I saw horses with the men of Wessex. They would not worry my men but our allies might not have fought them.

I stepped to the front of my men who were organising their lines. "If they charge with horses stand firm. Pull their lances and they will fall from them." I pointed to Rolf Horse Killer who stood with his two handed axe. "Young Rolf here slew two and today his axe will eat more horseflesh. Do not fear them. Make them fear you!"

They all gave a cheer and began banging their shields. I saw Rolf swell with pride. He had been mentioned before battle. Odin would hear his name and, if he fell, be ready to welcome him knowing him to be a hero already.

As I walked back to my men I heard the gates of the town slam ominously shut. Then there was the sound of hammering as Snorri made sure that the gates would not be breached. We were now reliant on Erik and the drekar reaching us and, more importantly, getting us off. If we did then warriors would have to sacrifice themselves for their friends. I had seen, on Man, the men of Harold One Eye as they had prevented us from closing with that snake. They had bled their lives away but saved their jarl. I looked along the ranks of men. I knew the Ulfheonar would make that sacrifice. How many others would choose that most glorious of deaths?

"How many can your one eye see, Haaken?"

"More than enough. This will be a battle worthy of a saga for they outnumber us."

"Aye and they have just marched the length of Corn Walum and Wessex to reach us. They must have marched since dawn and they think we are trapped. The odds are more even than you think."

The Saxons began advancing down the hill. I recognised King Egbert. He rode a jet black horse that was much larger than those the Saxons normally used. He was trying to make a statement to his men and, I suspect, us. It would not work. We rode a horse to get to a battle not to impress our enemies. When they were just beyond bowshot they stopped.

"What do they intend do you think?" Olaf Leather Neck hated precursors to battle. He expected the enemy to charge and then fight.

Haaken said, "They may wish to talk."

My oldest friend was right. King Egbert and three of his men rode towards us; they had taken off their helmets and their hands were held before them with an open palm.

"Haaken, Wolf Killer, let us go and see what King Egbert wishes to say."

I was happy for the delay. It gave Aiden more time to load the knarr and Erik Short Toe more time to reach us. I would talk all day if needs be.

We halted thirty paces apart. There was mistrust on both sides. We took off our helmets. The air felt cool. It was good. King Egbert's face was angry. He glared at Wolf Killer. An accusing finger jabbed out, "Wife stealer!"

I saw Wolf Killer begin to colour. I raised my hand, "If you are here to insult us then turn and fetch your men. We will fight! You asked for this truce not us. We have grown used to hewing Saxons. The eorls you left were not very good." I pointed to the walls of Hamwic. We had placed the heads of the dead leaders there.

The warrior next to King Egbert glared at me. "I am Ethelbert the brother of Eorl Beothild. I will have your heart for this."

I gestured behind me to my banner held proudly by Hrolf. "I will not be hiding. Come get me when the fighting starts. I will not run and I will gladly send you to your brother." I turned my gaze back to King Egbert, "Was this your only purpose in speaking? You wished merely to insult us and allow us to smell your horse's piss?" His horse had opened his legs and was urinating. The steam rose. Haaken and Wolf Killer smiled. The horse had squatted slightly and it was hard for Egbert to maintain his dignity in the face of such a basic need.

"I came here with an offer. If you and your men surrender Wolf Killer and yourself to me for judgement then the rest of your men may go free."

I nodded, "That seems reasonable. I will ask them." I turned, "King Egbert says that he will allow you all to go free with all of your treasure if your surrender my son and myself to his judgement. What say you?"

Their answer was to begin banging their shields and chanting, "Dragonheart!" over and over again.

I smiled. "I am sorry. We would be happy to come with you for I am certain that Saxon justice is fair. After all Elfrida chose to go with my son rather than bear the weight of an ox but my men have spoken. Unlike you I am no king. My men follow me because they choose not because their duty is owed."

"Then today you will all die!"

"That may be but when we sail away to my home remember this, King Egbert, the king who hires others to die for him, that if any more hired killers come to my land to do harm to my people then we will return and we will not leave. We will conquer Wessex and slaughter every Saxon that lives here. We are not Danes. We are Norse. We do not forgive and we do not forget. We are Vikings and if you hurt us then you risk Viking vengeance. I speak here plainly before you and your lords so that there will be no misunderstanding."

My voice had become gradually louder and my words echoed across to his army. They seemed to hang in the air.

"Then know this, Viking whelp; I will send no more killers to your land for all of you and your band of pagan brigands will die here this day and we will build a wall with your skulls as a permanent reminder to others that death is all that they will take from this land of Wessex."

He jerked his horse's head around and headed back to his men. As I approached Olaf Leather Neck he asked, "We fight?"

I nodded, "We fight."

"Good then I have not sharpened my sword in vain."

I made my way back through the thicket of planted spears and stood in the front rank. Our two rows of men looked too inadequate to face the horse who began to descend towards us but then I remembered, they were merely Saxons, we were Vikings!

Chapter 11

Their plan became clear as soon as they moved. They had their horsemen on their left and their heavily armed and mailed men in the centre. They would be the housecarls of the king. They would have been ordered to get to me. I saw that they were led by Eorl Ethelred and he had, behind him, the dragon war banner.

I shouted, "They come for me and Wolf Killer! That means the rest of you will have poorer warriors facing you. We hold and you slaughter!"

Once again the cheer was reassuring. I glanced to my left and saw the walls of Hamwic bristling with archers. Our left flank would be secure. I hoped that Gunnstein Berserk-Killer and his men from Dyflin would weather the storm of the horsemen. The heart of my line had the experienced warriors in the front rank. Even those in the second rank had fought many times. We would hold and we would be the rock upon which the Saxons would break.

As I had expected King Egbert and his banner of Wessex remained close to the trees. He was not committing his entire army. He had at least a third in reserve. If we showed weakness or we faltered then they would fall upon us and exploit it. The Saxons who advanced kept a tight line with shields held before them. As soon as they were in range Snorri and his archers sent arrow after arrow into their ranks. Those with mail largely survived but their shields were on the wrong arm and many with armour found their sword arm struck by arrows. They began to edge and bunch towards the centre.

I hear Eorl Ethelred shout, "Hold your line!" Those around him heeded his command but the ones behind began to drift to their left. The horsemen on the left flank suffered. They had no room to manoeuvre. When the housecarls were fifty paces from us the Eorl ordered the charge and they ran at us. I presumed they had seen the spears planted in the ground and chosen to ignore them. It was a mistake. The cohesion of the line was destroyed as men dodged the bristling spears. I glanced to my right as I saw the leader of the horsemen decide to charge Gunnstein. They were the first to strike our line and I watched in admiration as the men from Dyflin held their nerve. The horses refused to strike the men and, as they reared and bucked their riders fell to the ground to be butchered. Others were pulled bodily from the backs of their horses and hacked to pieces.

Then my attention was drawn once more to Eorl Ethelred. He was keen for revenge and he and his oathsworn decided to eliminate the spears by hacking at them with their swords. It meant they had to hold their spears in their shield hands and when my men in the second rank hurled Saxon spears and javelins they could not protect themselves. Eight warriors fell. Others replaced them but I saw that they were not the Eorl's oathsworn; they were not housecarls.

The Eorl, however, had now carved a path towards us. He came with his men tightly bunched around him. He held his spear overhand. I saw that he had a good shield. Not as well made as mine but better than those we had encountered up to now. He also had a mail coif under his open face helmet. It paid to notice minor details such as that. I had no doubt that he would be weighing me up but I had a slight advantage. I was cold and he was hot. I could goad him and make him act rashly. I heard the battle raging on our flanks but I had to concentrate on the man before me. One false move could give him the edge.

"Ready to join your brother? He lasted but two blows. Tell me you are a worthy opponent!"

My barbs struck home and he shouted, "I will do more than that I will take your head and piss in your empty skull!"

I shook my head and laughed, "And I took you for a Christian!"

He jabbed angrily with his spear at my head at the same time as the two men next to him tried to stab me in the gut. I had to do two things at once. I brought my shield across as I smashed down on the shaft of his spear. The tip of the spear came into the corner of my eyepiece before I managed to hack the shaft in two. I felt a prick as it caught my skin. A little more to the left and I would be like Haaken, one eyed!

He threw the broken spear away and reached for his sword. I had little space in which to move and so I brought my sword to clatter into the side of his helmet. At the same time I pushed with my shield. Olaf Leather neck had taken the head of one of the men next to him while Ulf Olafsson was smashing the second spearman's weapon in two. I had put my left foot behind me to allow me to attack with my shield before the fight had begun. Moving your legs and your feet could bring an advantage to two evenly matched warriors. My blow had stunned him a little and he was slow to draw his sword. I stepped forward on my right leg and brought my left knee hard into his groin. I connected and I forced him to step back. I smashed his face with the boss of my shield. He had no nasal and his nose broke. Blood sprayed everywhere. I had suffered such a blow and knew that your eyes watered. I shifted slightly to my right and brought my sword across his neck. He tried to block with his shield the sensed movement but my move had fooled him. The blade tore through his mail coif and came away bloody.

My Ulfheonar had not been idle. As I had stepped forward they had carved a clear path on each side of me and now formed a wedge. Haaken was to my right and Olaf Leather Neck to my left. The men who had swarmed to help the Eorl were not his oathsworn but they were brave men. Had they locked shields and come at us together it might have been different but Haaken, Olaf, Ulf and Finni were able to deal with each individual as they tried for glory. I narrowed my eyes. If I could kill this Eorl then it would dishearten the rest.

I now had my left leg before my right and I lowered my right leg a little. Holding my shield high I stabbed upwards, springing forward as I did so. He blocked the blow but with my weight behind it he found himself forced back. I brought my sword back and raised it. Stepping forward again I swung my sword at his weakened coif. His blow to my middle was easily blocked by my shield. His shield took my blow but my shifting weight meant he was forced back again and his right arm flailed as he tried to keep his balance. I was tiring but I brought my sword overarm again and brought it down at his neck. He too was tiring. His shield barely blocked the blow and he staggered again.

I used my shield as I stepped forward and hit him with the boss. My whole line, although smaller than the Saxon's, was moving forward. We were like five wedges as each boat's crew fought for their jarl. I had to end this before I became too tired and we were overextended. I punched again with my shield; this time at his shield. The edge of my shield hit his bloodied and damaged nose. It also pulled up the Eorl's shield. I seized my opportunity. I rammed my sword beneath his byrnie and eviscerated him. I twisted as the contents of his stomach fell along my blade.

He fell at my feet. I brought my sword's edge across his neck and severed his head. I held it high and yelled, "Ragnar's Spirit!"

Erik Wolf Claw took advantage of the shock it created. He leapt forward and stabbed the standard bearer in the neck before grabbing the standard and dragging it back towards the river. The Saxons before me recoiled at the sight of the gory trophy. The Eorl's oathsworn all lay dead and their dragon banner was taken. I had the chance to look down the line. The Saxon horse had been defeated. Snorri and Gunnar, along with Ketil had cleared our left flank. When I looked to the trees I saw King Egbert organising his men for a second attack. His eorls were rallying those who had fled.

I turned to look to the river. Erik and the drekar were fast approaching. It was time to take what we had and leave. "Snorri! Fire the town!" I saw him wave his acknowledgment. I shouted to my men. "Get the wounded aboard the drekar. If you want treasure now is the time to take it. We leave!"

I realised I still held the head of the Eorl and I threw it away. I turned to Hrolf. He was spattered with blood but I think that was Saxon blood. "Take the treasure from the Eorl, Hrolf!"

"Aye Jarl Dragonheart."

I saw Olaf on his knees. "What is it Olaf? Are you wounded?"

He shook his head, "No Jarl but Haaken took a blow to the head. He is breathing but he is unconscious."

I suddenly saw that it was Haaken lying beneath Olaf. "Get him to Aiden!" If aught happened to Haaken I would never forgive myself. He was my rock. Always on my right I knew that I was safe in battle so long as he was there.

I saw the Saxons as they advanced towards us. They had many more left than we did. Smoke began to billow from my left as Snorri fired the town. Soon it was as though a fog had descended upon the battlefield. My remaining Ulfheonar formed a protective wall around me and Hrolf. We backed towards *'The Heart of the Dragon'*. Already my men were being pulled aboard the drekar. When I felt the river lapping around my ankles I stopped. I would be the last to board.

"Hrolf, get my banner aboard."

"Aye Jarl." He struggled to do so for he was laden with the Eorl's mail and sword. I saw Cnut Cnutson helping him aboard. It had not been long since he had been a young warrior like Hrolf. He would remember what it was like to be the young one on a raid.

It took time to board the drekar, Erik had brought her in bow forward and the was the highest part of the drekar. The thick smoke from the burning town of

Hamwic was now so thick that I could barely see my hand before my face. There was just Olaf left in the shallows with me when three warriors suddenly hurled themselves at us from the murk of the mist. Luckily for the two of us we had not dropped our guard and our shields were still held high. Their spears struck my shield. I slashed my sword horizontally and had the satisfaction of feeling it strike flesh. Olaf Leather Neck brought his sword from high over his head and smashed the skull of one warrior to a pulp. I saw shadows in the smoke. I lunged forward and my sword tore into the stomach of one of them at the same time as Olaf finished off the last one.

We waded further into the water. Spears were hurled from the prow of my ship as the hands of the Ulfheonar hauled us aboard. My men were at the oars and we backed out into the river. Had the Saxons used bows which were any good then they might have made life difficult for us. As it was we had all the time in the world. I saw the flames licking high into the sky as Hamwic burned. The men of Wessex would know the consequences of attacking the family of Jarl Dragonheart of Cyninges-tūn.

I went to the stern where Aiden was tending to Haaken. "How is he?"

"The blow was to the side of the face where he has his good eye. The wound looks close to it." He pointed to a long scar which ran down the side of Haaken's face from the corner of his good eye.

"You think he may be blind?"

He nodded, "There is a possibility. But when I took off the helmet I found a depression in the skull on that side too."

I shook my head. "I am confused."

"When I read books in the libraries of Miklagård I read that the part of the head which is responsible for the eye is the side opposite to the eye." My confusion must have shown. Aiden shrugged. "I know it makes no sense to me either. We will know more when he awakes. He breathes and it is regular."

I took off my helmet. "Do we know how many we lost?"

Aiden's hand went to my eye. "You are wounded!"

"A scratch. It will heal itself."

Aiden shook his head. "If anything is left in a wound it can become bad and poison the whole body. Turn your head to the light." My Ulfheonar had gathered around Aiden. "Give me room!"

He used some vinegar to clean the wound. It stung but I had borne worse. "Give me your new Roman knife." I handed him my pugeo and he poured vinegar on it. "Finni hold his head and do not let him move."

I saw the tip of the dagger coming directly for my eye.

"Look up to the sky Jarl." I did so and saw just grey flecked clouds. I felt a really sharp pain and then the trickle of blood down my cheek. "It is done." I looked down and saw a pool of blood in the palm of his hand. He let it drain away and what was left was the tiniest piece of metal I had ever seen. "It is the tip of the spear head. The very end. Had we left it then your head would be poisoned and you might be in as bad a way as Haaken here. Hold still while I sew up the wound." He washed it again with vinegar. It hurt but I kept silent.

Then he sewed it. I knew that he would take his time and use very small stitches. Kara would critically examine his work when we were back in Cyninges-tūn.

By the time he had finished we were close to the channel leading to the sea. The waves looked a little choppy. I saw Hrolf. He had been close by the whole time I had been seen to by Aiden. "Come young Hrolf and show me the treasure we took from the Eorl."

"He had fine mail and a good sword. He had a golden cross and he had this bag."

He took out a leather purse which bulged. "Have you looked inside yet?"

"No Jarl Dragonheart."

"Then let us do so for soon this weather will worsen."

He handed me the bag and I emptied the contents into my palm. There were six large golden coins and six jewels. The largest was a red one the size of my thumb. "A fine haul; we are rich warriors."

"We Jarl?"

"You carried my banner and you stood by me. Of course some of this is yours. We will share it out at Úlfarrston with the rest of the booty."

Erik Short Toe pointed to the black storm clouds above. "It seems the Norns may have something to say about that. I think we have a storm coming, Jarl Dragonheart."

"Secure Haaken. Aiden watch him." I looked astern. We were the last of the drekar. "Do your best, Erik."

"Aye Jarl. Tie everything down. Thorir and Cnut take in a reef or two on the sail. I would not risk our stick."

I had endured this before. The wind was a wild one from the north east. It came from our homeland, the land of the Norse. It was Ragnar's wind. Sometimes the old man did not know his own strength! We would not need the oars and my men hunkered down where they could. We rigged a cloak over two chests and placed Haaken within. I sat the Aiden with him. Hrolf clung on to the chest for dear life. He had little experience of ships. Most of his life had been ashore in Neustria.

Day turned to night as we were tossed and turned by waves and wind. The waves grew larger and larger as the day became darker.

"Captain, I have lost sight of the other ships!"

"Do not worry Thorir, they have good captains and we have only to worry about us."

We lost sight of the shore and the sun. We knew of the passage of time for Aiden kept turning the hour glass but we had only the hope that the wind had not changed direction. We were heading west. That was all that we knew. By the sand in the hourglass we knew we had been at sea for eight hours when disaster struck or perhaps the Norns were bored. The sail tore. We had a spare but it was below deck. Erik shouted, "Every man to his oar!"

I took Haaken's place. Only Aiden and Haaken were spared the oars and we rowed. We rowed to keep us into the waves and with the wind. If we had not then we might have turned sideways on and broached. We rowed. Dark day became night and still we rowed. My muscles ached. I felt as I had when I had been Hrolf's age and gone to sea for the first time. The flesh on my hands was red raw from the salt and the oars. And still we rowed. The storm showed no sign of abating. Then we heard. "Land Ho! Rocks and surf ahead!"

The Weird Sisters must have become bored with us. We were going to be wrecked at the edge of the world.

"Back water!"

We reversed our oars as Erik tried to stop us running aground on these sharp teeth. I felt us turn and, as we did so I felt the ship heel alarmingly. Then there was the dreaded sound of something scraping our hull. We were thrown up in the air and then the bow plunged into the sea. Water flooded down the length of the drekar. When we settled we were all sat in water. It came half up the chests upon which we sat and yet the sea was suddenly calm. We had stopped. The wind still blew but not as ferociously.

"Bail her quickly! We may be holed."

We used everything we could to empty the water out. My back and arms burned with the exertion. It seemed to take forever but, eventually there was just a puddle running the length of the drekar.

"Captain, I see a beach and a light!"

I stood and walked to the stern. Erik and I looked at Aiden, "Well?"

He closed his eyes. When he opened them he smiled. "It is the witch. She has summoned you again, Jarl Dragonheart."

I nodded. It was *wyrd*.

Erik said, "Let us get the drekar on the beach and we can see the damage in daylight."

The crew rowed with a will to get her on land. Any land was all that they craved. It was when the older warriors and the Ulfheonar began to have worried looks on their faces that the new crew members asked questions. Normally Haaken would have answered them but he lay unconscious still hovering between life and death, this world and the Otherworld. It was left to Olaf Leather Neck to tell them.

"There is a witch in these islands and she called our drekar here. She will speak with the Jarl and Aiden." He shook himself, like a dog trying to dry its fur. "But I will not venture into her den. I will stay above ground and hope that they are returned to us."

Aiden took me to one side. "We should take Haaken ashore and build a fire and shelter for him."

Perhaps it was because we were on the island but I knew what he would do. "You are going to cut his skull open."

"Aye Jarl. We were meant to come here to save Haaken. It might be that the witch knows the answer. I will ask her but she summoned us. I felt something when the storm was at its height. I said nothing for I knew that we would be safe." He pointed ashore. "That light tells me that I am right."

I looked up and saw a light on the land. "Aye, Olaf, get Haaken ashore. Light a fire and rig up a shelter."

He looked at me. Olaf feared nothing but I saw terror in his eyes. "You will descend to her cave?"

I smiled, "I am Jarl Dragonheart, it is *wyrd*!"

"Aye Jarl and it is times like this that I am glad that I just follow you. I would not change places with you for all the gold in Rome."

"We are each given a thread by the Weird Sisters and we follow it."

A small voice sounded besides me. It was Hrolf. "Jarl I would come with you."

He had surprised me, "You would come and visit with a witch. You would go into the bowels of the earth and leave this world behind?"

I looked to Aiden, he closed his eyes as Hrolf spoke. "I heard a voice in my head. It told me to descend. I am terrified but the voice was that of my father. He died when I was captured. I must go where I fear to go. Please may I come?" Aiden opened his eyes and nodded. He had spoken with the spirits.

"Aye Hrolf. You have courage I will say that."

We clambered over the side. Erik was not so afraid that he did not securely tether his ship to the shore. The fire was lit and the shelter rigged but every eye was on the three of us as we headed up the rocks to the light glowing from the earth. I had been here many times and yet each time was like the first. It frightened me. Only Aiden was not afraid. For him he was returning home to the world of the spirits.

I had not changed after the battle; I was bloody, sweaty and dirty, I still wore my mail and had my sword strapped to my side. I entered the cave first. I was Jarl. Hrolf held on to my cloak, as though it would protect him and Aiden followed behind. I heard singing. We descended to the cave where a fire burned and a pot bubbled. The witch was the same one I had seen each time I had visited. She did not look up but she said, "Another who is not afraid of an old woman. Welcome Hrolf son of Gerloc."

I had kept on walking but I felt my cloak being tugged. "Fear not Hrolf. You will not be harmed so long as your heart is pure and your mind clear."

The witch looked up at me. This time she looked younger than she had before. "You grow in wisdom each time you visit, descendant of the warlord. Your new bride must be good for you. Your two new babes testify to that."

"But I just have a son!"

She cackled, it was not a pleasant sound, "And now you have a daughter or you will soon have. You should heed the words of Brigid. She may not be a warrior nor a volva but she has a good mind. Use it. Her words are wise." She waved a hand, "Sit and eat. You must be tired after fighting the Saxons and the sea." She began to ladle the broth into wooden bowls. "The Allfather is pleased with you, Jarl Dragonheart. The followers of the White Christ fear you more than any other man."

She handed us the bowls of broth. I knew that there would be a potion in the steaming liquid and I wondered if I should warn Hrolf. I decided to taste it first. I held the spoon of steaming grey broth to my lips. It was too hot to drink and I laid the bowl down on the rock before me.

"Are we here for you to guide us?"

"Perhaps. You are becoming wiser."

"Is Hrolf supposed to be here. He believes he is."

"Then if he believes so it must be true. He is meant to be here." A cunning look came in her eyes. "Before I guide you there should be payment."

I looked at Aiden. There was normally no payment involved. I was suspicious.

She smiled and suddenly looked ten years younger. "You have a red stone you took from the Saxon. It is a pretty thing and I would have it."

Hrolf jumped up, "We do not have it! It is still on the drekar."

She frowned at him and I waved him to his seat. "Do not try to lie to the volva, Hrolf. She knows your mind."

As I took out the jewel he asked, "How does she know we have the precious stone?"

I handed it to her. "She reads our minds and speaks with the spirits. There are no secrets in here."

"Wise, wise, wise. How you have grown. Perhaps the spirits should have sent the Welsh girl to you sooner." She played with the stone in her hands and, holding it to the firelight shone its light in the cave. The dark cave suddenly became alive with shimmering red lights which danced and sparkled. Hrolf's mouth dropped open. The witch put down the stone and put her hand on Hrolf's. "You should eat the broth if you wish to learn what you will become." She looked at me. "You have saved this child and he has a line which stretches into the future. His family will be remembered long after you are dead, Jarl Dragonheart but they will not know that they would have been nothing without the Viking slave who changed the world. Your time with him is coming to an end."

I picked up my bowl and began to eat. "Eat Hrolf." He had been waiting for me to begin and he spooned the broth into his mouth. It was grey in colour but it had a pleasant taste. I tasted the sea and shellfish. There was something else, something aromatic. I could not quite place the taste. I emptied the bowl and laid it down. I began to feel incredibly sleepy. My eyes became heavy and I wished to sleep. I found a patch of sand and I laid down. I would rest for a moment and then ask the witch what was on my mind. Was our war with Egbert over? Who were our enemies? Was there a spy in my land? I only got as far as the third question in my head when I began to fall into the hole in the cave which had just opened before me.

I found myself in the cave beneath Din Guardi, the one the Saxons called Bebbanburgh. I knew the way out of this trap and I headed for the door which led to the kitchens. The door opened and I waded through the bodies of dead Northumbrians. Ascending the stairs I began to creep past the King's chamber but I heard a shout and many guards rushed out at me. I had no sword and I ran to the tower where I had thrown Magnus to his death. This time the steps seemed to go on forever. They went up and up, ever climbing. Hands grabbed at my feet and no matter how hard I ran I could not escape. Eventually I burst through the door but there was no tower, there was nothing and I began to fall.

The rocks below loomed up at me like the savage teeth on a shark. I braced myself and found myself flying. I knew not how but I heard Erika's voice in my ear. "Beware the face that smiles with the eyes that do not." I opened my mouth to speak but no words emerged. Who was this enemy? Was it one of my own men?

I saw that we were flying over the sea. I saw a sea battle beneath me. It was Gunnar Thorfinnson and his drekar was surrounded by Vikings who swarmed across his deck and then it was gone. I saw the three legs of Man flying from the drekar. I saw Dyflin in the distance. It grew closer and closer to me. The walls of the town were in front of me and I braced myself for we would crash into them but we did not. The walls disappeared and I saw that we were in the chamber of Hakon the Bald. It was empty and I found my feet were now on the ground. I wandered his chamber. His cloak, trimmed with fine fur lay on the bed. He had a sword laid upon the bed too and it was tipped with a red stone. It was a twin of the stone I had given to the volva. I went to the table and there were golden coins on them. Each one was embossed with a cross and four small birds. They had come from Wessex! In the corner of the room I saw a shield; upon it were the three legs of Man.

The door burst open and many guards surrounded me. I tried to fly but I could not. Erika had forsaken me. I was grabbed and dragged down a narrow corridor. I heard growling and howling. There was a pit before me and in it were ten hungry wolves. I was hurled into the pit. As I fell I saw the laughing face of Hakon the Bald. The red eyes of the wolves waited for me and their hungry mouths opened to devour me. As my head entered the mouth of the largest I felt no pain. I just saw a large black hole opening before me and then a light, a red light. I headed for the light and it grew brighter. I rushed towards it and, as I leapt out saw that I had claws and my arms were covered in fur. Hakon the Bald cowered before me as I leapt, with the rest of the pack, to devour him. Before my teeth sank into his flesh there was a blinding light and then darkness.

I slowly opened my eyes. The cave was dark but there was a dim light coming from the entrance. The fire was long cold and there was no sign of the witch. Aiden sat watching me and Hrolf slept yet. He smiled and handed me a skin of water. I drank. It felt cool and refreshing. He said, "We should get the boy to the surface."

We carried Hrolf, who was heavier than he looked, up the passage to the cave entrance. The light almost blinded me for the sun was bright. It was cold but the sun was shining. We laid Hrolf on the rocks and I shaded my eyes. I could see my men on the beach. They had a fire going and there were men in the water working on the drekar.

"You saw?"

"I saw you both."

"Hrolf dreamed too?"

"You heard her words before you dreamed. The Norns have used you to save Hrolf and shape him into the man he will become. His people are destined for greatness."

"But not mine?"

"Your greatness will die with you. You will be remembered but as a legend only. Your sword and your deeds will live on in the stories men tell."

I felt as though the air had been sucked from me. "You dreamed this?"

"Kara and I dreamed this when our daughter was born." He smiled, "It is better this way. Our family is safe in the land watched over by Olaf the Toothless and the Water. When you go to the Otherworld the world will forget that our people exist. When the rest of the land is in turmoil they will live and grow in peace. For generations to come it will be as though Cyninges-tūn is hidden from the world. The spirits will hide it from the gaze of men."

I nodded. What else did I expect? I was a tool of the gods and the Norns. In many ways this was better. Old Ragnar who had brought me up and made me the man I had become was remembered by few. Had I not named my sword Ragnar's Spirit he would not be known at all. Aiden was correct. This was better.

"And what of Hrolf? What is his destiny?"

"He will leave us soon and follow another. It is not because you are a bad leader but he needs to wander for a while and you are a rock now. Your heart is in Cyninges-tūn. He will settle his own lands when he has learned how to lead." Aiden smiled, "I was granted a view of the future. His descendants rule the land of Egbert and Eanred; every Saxon king is nothing compared to the fruit of his loins. He must return to Neustria and conquer it but that will be many years hence when he has sailed the seas and learned to be a leader.

"That is good."

"It is meant to be. You came into his life so that he could see what a good leader is like. It is now up to the Norns to shape him into someone who can conquer nations."

It was almost as though he had heard us. He opened his eyes and looked around, startled. "How did I get here? The horses!"

"We carried you here. What is this about horses?"

"I saw me leading many mailed men on horses and we were attacking a shield wall of Saxons who were on a hill. They had axes and they were hewing my men and horses as though they were trees." He shook his head, "That cannot have been me. We do not fight on horses."

I smiled, "Ask Aiden. He dreamed what you dreamed."

"Truly?" Aiden nodded. "What was the dream?"

"It was your future."

"I will lead horsemen?"

"Apparently so. I saw that in my dream too. You had long shields which covered half your body."

"Aye I did! But I could not see you there, Jarl."

"That is because I am not in your future. The Weird Sisters have spun and their threads determine that we part."

"But I owe all to you. I would serve you. I wished to be your oathsworn!"

"I told you once that you had to make that decision when you were older. Now you can see why. Do not give an oath which binds you until you are certain it is the right one. Now come. Gunnar Thorfinnson is in trouble."

"How do you know Jarl Dragonheart?"

"I dreamed as you did. He is being attacked and I think I know where and by whom."

Chapter 12

My men all stood as we approached. Even the Ulfheonar, who had witnessed this before, were curious. I had worked out that we had been there all night. I saw Erik up to his knees in the water. "Any damage?"

He grinned in a mystified sort of way. "There is nothing but I was certain I heard us grind over something. There should be damage."

Aiden said, "The Norns wished us to visit here. They would not harm us."

I pointed to the north, "And now we must leave. Gunnar is in trouble."

Rolf Horse Killer asked, "How do you know, Jarl?"

Olaf Leather Neck said, "He dreamed it. The spirits told us and it will be true. Sharpen your axe boy, you will need it before long."

Aiden looked down at Haaken, "We cannot leave yet. We must attend to Haaken."

"You will cut his skull?"

Aiden looked to Olaf, "Has he stirred?"

"No, galdramenn. We gave him water as you said but he stirred not."

"Then I cut him. Build up the fire and boil water. Olaf I need a thin piece of metal as big as the palm of Hrolf's hand. I want the edges as smooth as you can make them."

Erik Short Toe said, "I have such a piece of metal. There is a hole in the middle will that hurt?"

"A small hole."

"Big enough for a leather thread."

"Then that will do."

"While I heat the knife he needs the side of his head shaving." He pointed to the left side of his head; the side near his empty eye.

"I will do that." He was my friend and my oathsworn. We had stood together in many battles. It was right that it would be me who helped my comrade.

I took my seax and knelt next to my oldest friend. I could not save his life but I could help those that would. I lifted his hair. He was vain and would hate the fact that his hair would be shorn but we had no choice. My seax was so sharp that I used it as a razor. I gently sliced the hair from the side of his head. I handed it to Hrolf. "Keep this safe, Haaken will want it." Then I slowly drew the blade across the depressed section of his skull. With the hair gone the hollow became clear to see.

Aiden said, "That is enough Jarl Dragonheart. You are a good barber!"

"I hope I am a better friend."

As I stood Aiden knelt and took my place. "No Jarl, stay here and hold his head. He sleeps now but he may move. It is *wyrd* that you are the one to help save him. Your friendship began when he lost his eye you are bound through all eternity."

I knelt and held the back of his skull securely. Aiden took my pugeo from the fire and used the tip to cut away a flap of skin around the depression. There was blood but not as much as I had expected. He gently lifted the flap and exposed the bone of Haaken's skull. I could see that it was broken and cracked.

"This is the critical time, Jarl Dragonheart. Now you must keep him still. I must remove the fragments of bone."

I did not envy him his work. He took away the larger pieces first and then used the tip of the blade to pick out the tiny ones. I felt a movement. "Aiden! He moved."

He said quietly, without lifting his head, "Then hold him. Olaf, the metal plate."

Olaf handed him the plate. I saw that it was just slightly bigger than the hole. *Wyrd*! Aiden placed it over the hole and I saw him breathe out. Then he took the bone needles and the animal gut in his right hand. He carefully and gently sewed the flap of skin back in place. I saw that where there had been a depression there was now a bump, albeit small. I felt a movement. "Olaf, hold his arms and stop him moving."

All around us my crew watched in morbid fascination. This was magic of the highest order. Aiden had been inside a man's head and it looked as though he might bring Haaken back from the dead. This was a White Christ miracle!

When he finished he sat back. I saw that he was sweating as though he had been lifting heavy weights all day. I maintained my grip on Haaken's head. "Haaken will owe his life to you, Aiden."

"No, Jarl, he owes his life to the parchments we took from Wessex. They told us how to do this." He looked up at Erik. "Where did you find the metal plate?"

"It was in Hamwic. I think it came from a Saxon ship."

Aiden touched his golden amulet, "*Wyrd*!"

I saw my Ulfheonar do the same. I held my friend's head still. He was not out of danger yet.

"You can release him. He will awake soon enough. Carry him on board while he is still asleep."

My Ulfheonar allowed no one else to carry their brother. They laid him in the centre of the drekar, close to the mast. There the motion would be the most gentle. Once he was aboard I said, "Let us head north. We have another brother to save!"

We took the fish the men had cooked on board the drekar. Erik had fitted the new sail. We would repair the old one when we returned to Cyninges-tūn and keep it as a spare but we would need a new one for the next year. I was starving and I grabbed one of the still warm fish and greedily ate it. I wiped my fingers on the old frayed rope Erik kept by the steering board. It was an old trick Josephus had taught him. Josephus had been a sea captain we had rescued. He had taught Erik all that he knew about sailing, We had named a drekar in his honour. It had been plagued by the worm and sunk but his memory lingered on. I wondered if that was my destiny. A memory of what I had taught others and how my deeds had changed their lives. Josephus had told Erik to hang the pieces of rope so that men's hands were not greasy when they worked the ropes and sails. He said that should we ever run out of food the ropes could be boiled and the grease would make a soup to keep us alive. I did not relish that soup but we did as the old captain had advised; we kept old frayed ropes for a day we hoped would never come.

Erik waited for me to join him, the wind was blustery and he said, "Did your dream show where Gunnar was attacked?"

"I saw the three legs of Man."

"Then it will be the sea close to Ynys Môn." He looked up at the masthead pennant. He grinned, "The Norns must wish us to get there quickly; see how the wind takes us swiftly."

The wind had veered and was now from the south and east. I wondered where the rest of our ships were. Had they waited for us or sought us out? I doubted that Wolf Killer and my other captains would have done that for they would know that I could look after myself. Besides, they, too, might, have been spread over the ocean by the stormy seas.

I could do nothing more and I wandered to the centre of the drekar where Aiden and Hrolf knelt next to Haaken. My Ulfheonar had made a shelter for him to keep the worst of the spray away. I sat on Haaken's sea chest which was by his head. Aiden was dripping water into his mouth. "How is he?"

Hrolf burst out, "I saw his eyes flicker. Aiden is a great wizard is he not, Jarl?"

I smiled, "He is indeed and I am lucky to have him."

"Is it true he was a slave?"

"No, Hrolf, that was me. Aiden here was a hostage."

Aiden nodded, "My father did not want me but the Dragonheart did."

"Your father did not want you?"

Aiden shrugged, "It is better this way. I have a life I love and I live with people who chose me just as they chose the Dragonheart. That is worth more than the red stone we gave to the witch."

"How did she know?" I knew that the question had been in Hrolf's head since we had met the witch.

"She is not of this world. She is of the spirit world." He looked at Hrolf, "She was not a living person, she was a spirit."

Hrolf clutched his hammer of Thor. Olaf had given him one when we had left Neustria. It had been his before he had become Ulfheonar and now had the golden wolf as a charm. "But her hand touched mine!"

"And it was cold? As though she was dead?"

He recoiled as though she had just touched him. We laughed. "I felt the same, Hrolf, the first time I met her."

"You have met her before. Jarl Dragonheart?"

"Many times. One day when I meet her it will be in the Otherworld and I shall be dead."

I saw all of my men clutch at their wolf amulets.

The winds did indeed carry us swiftly north. We passed the mouth of the Sabrina in the middle of the afternoon. We were close to Dyfed and the place where I had found the blue stone. Haaken awoke. "Lie still Haaken."

He did as Aiden had ordered but he opened his eye; the shelter stopped the sun from blinding his good eye. "Where are we? On the '***Heart***'?"

Olaf and the other Ulfheonar knelt around him. I think they were fascinated to see what change the metal plate would make. "Aye, old friend. You were wounded."

He closed his eye again. "I remember a mighty blow and then all went black." He suddenly opened it and said, "I dreamed, Jarl and I saw you and Aiden." He closed his eye and opened it once more, wider this time, "No, that is not right. I dreamed I fell into a dark place. I saw Cnut and Beorn. They were drinking and I asked them to share their ale with me. They said they could not. The ale was Odin's nectar and was for dead heroes. They said I would have to wait and they told me to find you, Jarl. I wandered. I returned to the cave at Din Guardi but it was empty and then," his face and his voice became animated, "and then I fell beneath waves and I was drowning until I saw your hand come beneath the waves and drag me up and then I saw Aiden." His eye flickered to my galdramenn. "You put your hand deep inside my body and then all my pain disappeared and I slept."

I saw that my men clutched their wolves. Olaf Leather Neck said, very quietly, "Aiden took away part of your head and he touched your mind. You have a metal plate in your skull, Haaken Iron Head!"

He put his hand to the bump on his head. "I thought it felt different." His voice betrayed his fear. "Will I die, Aiden?"

"One day, Haaken but not from this blow. You are healed. You will not fight for some time and you will need a new helmet but I am pleased with my work."

"And I owe you a life, Aiden, and another to you, Jarl Dragonheart."

I shook my head, "We are brothers, we owe each other nothing." I nodded towards Olaf, "Do you want the name Olaf Leather Neck has given you?"

"No Jarl. I have been Haaken One Eye too long to lose that name besides there are some who would say I have always had a hard head." We laughed, "Tell me what happened; I can see that I have missed much."

I stood, "Hrolf and Aiden can tell the tale for I believe you will have a good saga and this time you will be the hero of it. I go to speak with Erik."

I had felt a change in the wind. I hurried to the steering board. Erik pointed to the masthead. "The wind changes. It has veered to the south and west. The gods wish us to hurry."

"How far to the coast of Ynys Môn?"

"With this wind we will be there shortly after dusk."

I spoke my thoughts aloud, "Gunnar does not know the waters around Ynys Môn well, he will not take the narrow passage. He will head towards Hibernia. The men of Man will wait close to the Calf."

"You think they planned to attack our ships? It is not an accident?"

"You know that where we are concerned there are no accidents." I suddenly remembered my dream. "Hakon the Bald knew where we were going. I wondered why he sent Gunnstein; he was not oathsworn. He cares not if his ship survives or not. He hopes to benefit from our raid. He would buy a better ship or even take one of ours!"

"You know this for certain, Jarl?"

"No Erik but the spirits have given me enough clues. Besides if we hurry and find naught then we reach home that bit quicker and it will just be my pride which is hurt. It may be that the Norns wish that too. Perhaps I am become too arrogant."

Erik laughed, "You are many things, Jarl Dragonheart, but arrogant is not one of them. They will be there and I hope we are in time." He suddenly stopped. "Perhaps all of our ships are in danger?"

I thought about that. Closing my eyes I listened to the words in my head. I heard nothing. "Aiden."

My galdramenn hurried to me, "Aye Jarl?"

"Is it just Gunnar who is in danger?"

"If we are to believe your dream then I would say aye." He paused. "Sometimes, Jarl, a small stone falls from the top of a mountain. In nine cases out of a hundred it will nestle close to where it falls but at other times it gathers pace and it gathers brothers and it becomes an avalanche which changes the face of the world. When Egbert paid those Danes that was the stone. You decided to wreak vengeance upon King Egbert and that meant we had to take men from Dyflin and Ljoðhús. It may be we serve the Norns and that they want a change. Hakon the Bald and the men of Man may be the ones to suffer the wrath of the Weird Sisters and we are merely tools."

"There Erik, you have your answer." I cupped my hands to shout above the wind. "Prepare for war!"

Hrolf came to help me don my red cochineal. I had not fought in it the last time but this was different. We were ready for this fight and we could prepare properly. I went around the newer warriors such as Rolf Horse Killer. I gave them all the same advice. "If we have to fight at sea them place your feet wide apart and keep your weight low. Feel the drekar. Our ship is well made and she will fight for us. If we have to board another vessel then remember that we may have to fight their drekar too."

"Will we fight the men of Man?"

"I believe so but whoever we fight we will win!"

They all banged their hands on the deck. "Listen for my orders and when I say board do so and when I order back to this ship then you obey me!"

"Aye Jarl!"

Fights at night were rare. Most captains did not wish to sail out of sight of land at night time. Those who lived on Man knew their waters well. When we had lived on Man we had lived on the north and the east. Those who had filled the space we had left chose the south and the west. That was why Erik was making for the channel around the Calf.

We had five men with bows on board our drekar. The rest were with Snorri aboard the *'Red Snake'*. Beorn took them to the bows. They were little enough but they could make the difference. If they could clear the stern then we would have a chance to take any drekar which we met. Although the wind had not abated the proximity of the coast meant that the swells were smaller. As night fell we risked sending Thorir Svensson to the mast in the hope that his young eyes would spy out any other vessels.

I had begun to think the Norns had toyed with us and there was no danger when I heard , "Ships ahead, captain."

"Where away?"

"Due north."

As I passed down the ship to reach the prow I heard Haaken, "Let me fight."

I stopped, "Haaken One Eye you will stay where you are. Aiden, Hrolf, stay with him."

Hrolf said, "Am I not to fight?"

"You are young and you are brave but today you would be a liability. I would not risk a warrior to have to save you. Stay here and hold my banner for me. Let our enemies know whom they fight."

Satisfied he nodded, "Aye Jarl."

I stood on the topmost strakes and leaned against the dragon prow. Peering into the dusk I saw the shapes of three ships. I could see their sails flickering in the dark. They disappeared as a wave came before us and then reappeared. I could hear nothing but the sound of the sea and the crack of our sail and ropes. The wind was now coming from the steerboard quarter. We would be able to choose whom we attacked. I had no doubt that there was a drekar which was being attack by two others and I guessed that they were on each side of **'Raven Wing'**.

We were about half a mile away and we had time to make the right decision. I joined Erik Short Toe, "Which ship do we attack? The one to **'Raven Wing's'** steerboard or the other one? Which one would you choose?"

"The other one, Jarl Dragonheart."

"Then I leave it with you. Olaf, have the men on the steerboard side. Beorn have your archers target the ship on our steerboard."

I donned my helmet and made my way to mid ships. We were now close enough to begin to hear the clang of metal on metal as they battled on Gunnar's ship. **'Raven Wing'** was smaller than the two which attacked her but she was double crewed. The men of Man were not having an easy time of it. Had they attacked a single drekar they would have won by now. If Gunnar was dead I swore that I would have revenge on the men of Man. It was a powerful oath for I made it to myself. I would honour the oath.

The darkness hid us from the drekar. The crew at the stern were too busy keeping the ships close together. I stood, holding the sheet in my left hand with my shield around my back. It might have looked precarious but I had done this since I was Hrolf's age. You never forgot. The first the enemy knew was when we were thirty paces from them and Beorn and his archers cleared the stern of the ship. The noise of the battle on **'Raven Wing'** disguised the noise of dying sailors. As we bumped next to them the jar made those on the far side of the drekar turn around. Thorir Svensson threw a grappling hook as the sail was lowered. We were tied together.

I jumped aboard and was swinging Ragnar's Spirit two handed even as I landed. The warrior who turned at the unexpected noise lived but a heartbeat before my sword bit across his chest and laid him open to his heart. My Ulfheonar led but the men of Cyninges-tūn were not far behind and we flooded across the deck of the drekar. The handful of men they had left aboard their ship were soon despatched and I leapt to the top strake of the Manxman. I saw that Gunnar and his men had paid a heavy prices. There were but twenty of them gathered around the stern and they were beleaguered. Shield to shield they faced their enemy. We had no time to waste. I yelled, "Ragnar's Spirit!" as I leapt aboard Gunnar's drekar. The Ulfheonar were right behind me and I saw the terror on the faces of the men of Man as they turned and saw the red eyed monsters who appeared behind them. My name was known to them; I was their enemy and they knew that I would be merciless.

Time was of the essence and I swung my shield around before hurling myself at the warriors who stood between me and my ally. The warriors who stood before me had no armour and had expected to be victorious. When my sword slashed across the back of the first warrior, spraying the others with his blood it sent a ripple of shock through the others.

I heard Gunnar shout, "It is Jarl Dragonheart! On!"

The combination of the two sets of warriors had an immediate effect. We slashed and hacked through them. Beorn brought the archers over and they began to loose their arrows at those on the drekar tied to the other side of **'Raven Wing'**.

I recognised one warrior who faced me from his shield. He had been a warrior who had followed Jarl Erik. He had been called Audun the Fair. From his armbands I guessed he must be a jarl. I slew the two warriors who stood between us. Audun the Fair looked to escape but the other drekar had cut its grappling lines and was drifting away with the wind. I left my men to slaughter the others and I faced Audun the Fair.

"I see you have not changed your ways. Your Jarl was ever one for the knife in the back and it seems that you are just as treacherous."

"Old man, today you die and I will take your sword from your dead fingers!"

"First kill me and then boast!"

Bracing myself with legs wide apart I brought my sword over hard and high. It smashed into his shield. It was not a blow I would use on land but on a moving drekar it sometimes worked. As the blow hit he tried to adjust his feet and he slipped. He used his right hand to steady himself. I slashed at his arm and severed it. I brought my blade backhanded and ripped across his throat. His body fell at my feet. All around me the survivors were being slain. There was no mercy for those attacked at sea. I might have liked a prisoner to question but the men from Ljoðhús were in no mood for such mercy. They butchered them all.

I saw that Gunnar was wounded. He was lying close to the steering board, "Aiden!" I saw that he had a bad wound to his right arm and a savage cut across his lower jaw. Blood was everywhere.

He looked up at me. His damaged jaws gave him a strange grin. "Thank you Jarl Dragonheart. You came for us."

I took off my helmet and knelt next to him. "I am sorry we came so late."

He had a puzzled look on his face. "Late? How could you know?"

"The spirits warned me and we came as fast as Odin's wind would bring us."

"We owe our lives to you. But they have slain more than half of my crew."

"They died with swords in their hands and they are in Valhalla. We have another drekar. The gods favour you, Gunnar Thorfinnson."

Aiden leapt to his side and began to tend to him. Gunnar winced as Aiden applied vinegar. "The arm is the most dangerous. I must sew it, Jarl."

He nodded, "I will bear it."

To keep his mind off the wound I told him of our experience. He stared at me with wonder on his face. "We only endured a short storm and then the winds died. We lost the other ships and wondered if any had survived."

Aiden nodded his gratitude to me and said, "Jarl I will make the stitches as small as I can but it will take longer."

He laughed and I saw him wince with the effort, "I am going nowhere. Stitch away."

"I will crew this other drekar with my men. Have you enough to crew yours?"

"Thrand Sigurdsson is a fair sailor." He pointed to the ancient warrior next to him. "He should get us home safely enough."

I shook my head, "You will come to Úlfarrston. We have treasure and booty to divide."

By the time we had transferred the crew they had stripped the bodies and thrown them over the side. It was almost dawn. The wind had died and it was a slow and stately progress north. Had we been attacked by any sort of numbers it would have gone ill with us. The gods smiled on us and we saw the welcoming mouth of Úlfarrston by noon. We had made it home.

I was happy to see the other drekar and knarr moored in the estuary. **'Red Snake'** was on the beach and she looked to have suffered severe damage. The others all had the look of ships who have survived a storm. We were not the only ones to suffer.

Chapter 13

From the work being carried out on the other ships it looked as though we were the one which had suffered the least damage. The lost sail had been our most serious hurt. We edged towards the jetty. Aiden had refused to allow Haaken to move and, much to his chagrin, he was forced to be carried ashore on a litter. He showed great strength of character as he faced down the mighty warrior, Haaken One Eye. "When my wife says you may walk then you shall do so. Until then you are carried."

The younger warriors were quite happy to carry him. I went ashore first while they manhandled him to the land. My jarls rushed to greet me, "I thought I had lost my father!"

"No, Wolf Killer; we took a detour to see the witch! Her decision, of course." He and Asbjorn stared at me. They knew the importance of such a visit. "I will tell you all later." I looked at Gunnstein. "I know you will be keen to return to Dyflin but much of what the witch said concerned you. Would you delay your departure and come to Cyninges-tūn with us? Gunnar is wounded and he cannot travel for a couple of days. His crew were attacked."

"I saw the other drekar." Gunnstein looked worried, "It was not the men of Dyflin was it?"

"No, Jarl, it was the men of Man. They attacked him close to the Calf of Man. We will divide our treasure here so that it is safely on the ships before they sail."

"It will do no harm. We only arrived yester eve and your shipwright, Bolli is dealing with *'Red Snake'* first. She barely made it home. It will take a few days longer to make our drekar sea worthy. We would enjoy your hospitality. Asbjorn has been singing the praises of your ale."

And so we divided the treasure. There was so much that I was surprised that any of the drekar and knarr had made it back. The slaves were penned at Úlfarrston. We sold many to Coen, his burgeoning town needed workers, and the rest were kept secure. We would divide those when the drekar sailed. We followed the wounded and the bulk of the men on the long march to Cyninges-tūn.

Our homecoming was heralded, as usual, by Grim the Fisherman and everyone turned out to greet us. As we were further down the road it was my younger warriors who received the greatest accolades. I was pleased. They had done well. King Egbert and the housecarls of Wessex were a formidable foe to have routed. The wounded, being mounted on litter strung between horses and ponies, had reached home first and I knew that Kara and her women would be ministering to their wounds. I daresay Aiden was looking nervously to his wife for her approval. He had worked miracles and I hoped she approved.

Winter had been a chilly suspicion in Wessex, here I could see its icy grip. The ground was hard and the air was sharp. We had campaigned later than normal but it had rewarded us handsomely. Normally, as we rode north, I would talk with Haaken. This time I could not. Wolf Killer had hurried on to see his wife and children and so I rode alone. It was no bad thing for I had much to occupy my mind. Hakon the Bald was the problem with which I wrestled. I believed the witch and the spirits. They had told me he was guilty of treachery. I had to consider what to do about him. Then there was the problem of Man. I had sworn to avenge Gunnar had he died. He had not but I still felt betrayed. The trouble was I had missed speaking with Aiden, Haaken and my daughter. The three of them gave me a perspective which my wife Erika had provided. I was my own man. I would make my own decisions. However Ragnar had taught me to listen to others. I would talk with Gunnar and Gunnstein. I would seek counsel from Aiden, Kara and Haaken and then I would speak with the spirits. Only then would I make up my mind.

When I reached the gates there was just Brigid with my son waiting for me. I saw a small bump which told me that the witch had been right. I had never doubted her for the spirits knew all. I wondered if Brigid had known before I left. Did she know it was a girl? My son recognised me now but, too young to articulate words which made sense, he just giggled and threw his arms around me. I felt dirty as I hugged him. I needed the waters of the Water and my sweat hut. Brigid hugged me and said, "I have sent Uhtric to light the fire in the sweat hut. It will take some time to reach the right heat."

I put my arm around her and, holding Gruffyd in my right arm led her to my hall. "We can talk. I have much to tell you and you, I have no doubt, have things to tell me."

She stopped and stared at me. She held her front. "You know?" I nodded. "How?"

"I saw the bump but I confess that I knew already and I sought confirmation. We landed at the island of the witch and she told me we were to have a daughter."

This time her hand went to the cross about her neck. "Kara said it would be a girl! I doubted her but now..."

We walked to my hall. I did not say that this proved the spirit world was stronger than the world of the White Christ. My wife was clever, she would work it out. There was ale and honeyed oat cakes, still warm from the fire, waiting for me. As I ate them I told her the events which had unfolded many miles hence.

"When Siggi returned with the knarr we were sent word and there was great celebration. Then when you were delayed in your return we worried."

"We were never going to return quickly but I must discover what delayed Siggi and the knarr. It almost cost us dear."

"Do you think that Egbert will forget Elfrida and your son now?"

"He will never forget us but that is different from will he try to hurt us again. We have much to do. I need my hut and your counsel first and then I will speak with the others."

"My counsel? I know nothing."

"True you know nothing of war but you lived in a poisonous world of intrigue and back stabbing. You survived. You may not know war with swords but you know war with words and insinuation."

"That I do."

Uhtric sailed us across the Water and my servants watched over Gruffyd. We stripped off and entered the hut. It was not perfect but the temperature was rising. I added more charcoal to the fire. We walked to the Water and immersed ourselves in its icy grip. We rubbed each other's hair and then went back into the hut. It seemed much hotter already. I sat with my arm around my wife. "Young Hrolf did well."

"Tell me again what the witch said. I was thinking of you when you told me that part. I will comb your hair and beard and trim your hair while you do so." We kept combs and a knife for shaving in the hut. She sharpened the edge and then began to comb my hair.

"He is to serve another lord who will take him raiding and enable him to become lord of Neustria."

"You raided there."

She was right. It had gone from my mind. What did that signify?

Brigid was thinking too. "Perhaps that means that your spirits do not want you to raid so far afield."

I kissed her. "You are right and I was blind not to see it. I cannot help Hrolf and he must seek others who can but why do the spirits want me to stay closer to home? Wessex will be harder to raid now. Egbert will close that door and bar it too."

"There must be other places you could raid. Or perhaps they wish you to stay at home and look after your wife and your daughter." She giggled.

I kissed her again, "Perhaps you are right. We could still raid your former home, Mercia and," my voice hardened at the memory, "those snakes on Man."

I could feel my thoughts taking order. When I had walked up the road I had not known what to do. Having spoken to someone who knew nothing of war I had learned what to do.

We then talked of other things; what we might think of calling the baby, what Gruffyd had done since we had been away. They were inconsequential and yet vital all at the same time. The flap opened and Aiden appeared. "Could I join you, Jarl?"

Part of me resented this intrusion into a private world I was enjoying but I knew that Aiden would not have asked if it were not important. "Aye, it is now hot enough."

He went outside to shed his clothes and then re-entered. Brigid said, "You knew it was a girl too?"

He shook his head, "Not until the witch told us. Kara knew because she was here and the spirits of her mother and Olaf the Toothless spoke with her."

I saw my wife taking that in. I was thinking of Haaken. "And what did my daughter say of your handiwork?"

Aiden laughed, "You are becoming fey too, Jarl. You know why I came here! She has examined both Gunnar and Haaken. They will both heal." He grinned and suddenly looked like the young Irish boy again. "She was impressed with my skill. She looked at Haaken's head and said that he may walk around but he should not risk war until the winter is passed and gone."

Brigid said, "As winter is here already or at least the first frosts have come, you will not fight again." I remained silent. She looked at me. "Surely you will not need to fight again?"

Looking at Aiden I said, "What are your thoughts on Hakon the Bald?"

"We will need to speak with Gunnstein. I trust him but I wonder what he knows. The attack by the men of Man could only have been prompted from two sources, Dyflin and Ljoðhús. Of the two Jarls I trust Blue Scar more and I cannot see him risking his own son's life. Odin would never forgive such an act. The men of Man could not have predicted which of our ships they would catch. We were just lucky that it was Gunnar and not the knarr." Then, almost as an afterthought he added, "Siggi was nearly captured on his return south. That is why he was delayed. It is lucky he is suspicious and knows the waters. He avoided their trap and sailed between the island and Wyddfa."

"A dangerous route."

"Aye but the gods were with him. He managed to evade his pursuers but it added two days to his journey."

"I need to speak to all the others." I turned to Brigid. "Have we food enough to feed the jarls?"

She stood, "Aye but I needs must be at our hall to organise!"

I detected criticism in her tone if not her words. "I am sorry but this is my land and I must make such decisions."

She nodded, "I know but I would have you as my husband and Gruffyd's father at home; at least for a time."

"And I promise that I will be home at Yule and until the first green shoots spring from beneath winter's cloak."

She smiled until Aiden said, "If the Weird Sisters allow!"

The smile changed to a frown, "Then I curse the Weird Sisters!"

I was shocked, "You must recant those words!"

Aiden said, "She is of the White Christ. The Norns ignore such curses but your husband is right, my lady, it does not do to provoke them."

We sailed back to our home and Brigid became a whirlwind. Aiden and Uhtric went to inform the jarls and Kara. I dressed in my robe which I had brought from Miklagård. It was my one piece of luxury. I was not vain enough to wish to impress my young jarls but I knew that it would. I wore it for it made me feel better. I enjoyed the soft smoothness against my skin. I knew that my jarls would have eaten in the warrior hall. It was later than we normally ate already. Brigid, however, managed to find some food which could be cooked quickly and I still had a few amphorae of Vasconian wine. It would suffice. Hospitality was important. There should be food and drink when we talked.

I greeted them when they arrived. It was only when they walked in that I realised how I must have smelled when I had greeted my wife. They smelled of blood, sweat and the sea. I felt slightly guilty about my own appearance. Elfrida had come too. She hugged me and then went to find Brigid. Kara kissed me on my forehead, "I heard the witch approved of your actions, father."

"It appears so."

"And you need this counsel to make a better decision?"

"I do."

"It is good." She lowered her voice, "Aiden and I will listen more than we speak. We will try to read men's minds."

"I trust them all."

"You trust most of them but you have some doubts." I nodded. "We will listen."

This was the first time that three of them had been in my hall. I saw them look at the old sword of my ancestor which I had discovered in the cave close to Wyddfa. This was not the time for that story.

"I have asked you all to remain with me because we were separated by the storm and you do not know what transpired in the cave with the witch." I saw Gunnar and Gunnstein clutch their hammers. It was a natural reaction for a warrior. "What she said concerns all of us to a lesser or greater degree. Aiden and I have spoken of the dream and we have our own interpretation. My daughter will listen now and she will tell us what she thinks. I have fought alongside all of you and I think I know your hearts. I would welcome your views."

Wolf Killer nodded, "Did the dream speak of Egbert? Did the witch mention him?"

I smiled. Like my son I would have liked to have slain Egbert and ended this feud. It was not meant to be. "Be patient my son." I told them of my dream and that of Hrolf. I did not offer my interpretation but I watched Gunnstein.

It was Gunnar who spoke first. He looked drawn for he had two bad wounds but anger burned in his eyes. "I thank you again for coming to our aid, Jarl Dragonheart and I see that the men of Man owe me for my dead warriors."

I nodded and there was silence and then Gunnstein spoke quietly, "You are missing the point, Gunnar Thorfinnson; how did the men of Man know that we would be sailing with laden ships? It is not the raiding season. If we had not come on this raid then my drekar would have been laid up for the winter, having her hull cleaned."

Gunnar was still angry about his own men and he could not see through the fog. He shrugged, "An accident! *Wyrd*!"

Wolf Killer said, "The men of Man are treacherous and they are lazy. In the summer they keep a close watch for traders. We escort our knarr and they have learned to avoid them."

"Then that is a good reason for them not to attack us for we had five drekar!"

Ketil was the youngest of the jarls and had the least experience of sea warfare but he was a clever young man. "When we left to make war on King Egbert I said goodbye to my kin in Brougham. I gave my younger brother the power to rule in my stead for I did not expect to return. The King of Wessex is the most powerful king in the land and we were going to fight him with a handful of warriors. If the men of Man knew what we intended then they would expect us to have lost many men. It would be the perfect time to attack the warriors of Cyninges-tūn. If they could defeat the Jarl Dragonheart then this land would theirs for the taking."

Wolf Killer nodded, "So how did they know?"

Gunnstein looked at the horn of wine before him and then downed it. "I have listened to the words and I have thought of your dream. There is a connection to Wessex and to Man. It is Hakon the Bald. We wondered how King Egbert could have reached Hamwic so quickly. He arrived two days before we expected him. He was warned. In the Dragonheart's dream he saw the red stone such as we found in Wintan-ceastre. There were the coins of Wessex. It is clear to me that Hakon the Bald was connected. I know not how for he did not know where we raided. I only discovered that when I arrived here."

I glanced at Kara and Aiden who both nodded. I said quietly, "And you suspected before the dream was revealed to you. Is that not right, Gunnstein Berserk-Killer?"

Every eye was on the warrior from Dyflin. He kept his head down and then raised it, to look me in the eye. "I am sorry. I apologise to all who lost warriors. I suspected something but I had no proof."

Gunnar slammed the table, "Then you should have told us! I have lost fine warriors, oathsworn!"

I stood, "Keep calm voices. This is not a trial. We try to discover the truth. Peace Gunnar Thorfinnson!" He nodded and I sat.

"I had no evidence just suspicions. Hakon did not like me. He never has. I think he thought me a threat. The men who came with me on the raid were the ones he did not like. The drekar is the oldest and slowest that Hakon owns. Is that enough evidence for you Gunnar Thorfinnson? Would you have expected treachery had you known that? If I had said, before we sailed I think Hakon is trying to get rid of me what would you have said?"

Gunnar had the good grace to laugh at himself, "I would have said you were foolish. I am sorry, Gunnstein Berserk-Killer. I am angry."

"And an angry man makes bad decisions. Gunnstein could only see the significance of Hakon's actions in light of what happened. Looking back is always safer than looking ahead." I gestured to the silent Kara and Aiden. "I am lucky. I have around me those who can see into the future and into men's minds."

They all nodded. Wolf Killer said, "Are we certain, then, that Hakon the Bald betrayed us?"

My son had asked a good question. "Certain? No. We would need confirmation of that."

Gunnar said, "I still wish revenge on the men of Man."

"As do we all but have you enough men? Would not your father wish to join you?" He nodded. "Then that revenge is a dish best served cold. We will join you after the winter and we will raid Man. They will feel our steel."

"And what of Hakon? Do we let that serpent sit and plot?"

"No, Wolf Killer. We find out the truth and then we end the threat."

"You have a plan?"

"First does anyone disagree with my words and Gunnstein's explanation?"

They chorused, "No Jarl."

"Then I do have a plan. I will take a drekar and a handpicked crew and we will return with Gunnstein to Dyflin. It will not seem strange for Hakon is owed a share of the loot."

Gunnar snapped, "But he is treacherous! He should get nothing!"

"And when we uncover his treachery then he will get nothing save a blade. But we must uncover the truth first." I turned to Gunnstein, "Are there others like you in Dyflin or are they all as bad as Hakon?"

"There are some warriors but there are many like Hakon."

Ketil said, "If you take the head then the body may writhe around but it can harm no one."

"You are right, Ketil. From what Gunnstein and my father tell us then this Hakon has eliminated all opposition to himself. Gunnstein is the only leader left. It was a cunning plan to have him killed by Egbert. It saved him the trouble."

"And when he is dead then what?"

I turned to Gunnstein, "Could you rule Dyflin?"

"Aye."

"Then there is your answer, Gunnar." I looked everyone in the eye as my gaze passed around the room. "Unless there are any who do not trust Gunnstein?"

Without hesitation they all said, "We trust him!"

"Then we leave as soon as *'Red Snake'* is repaired."

Wolf Killer said, "*'Red Snake'*? Why?"

"Firstly you will all need to go home and see to your own lands. Secondly I want Hakon to think he has succeeded. When we arrive, after such a delay, it will be a shock. I have no doubt he will paint a face to meet us but that shock may give us an edge. Thirdly I want him to be off his guard. The smaller ship will do that. He will think I have few men with me."

The next day we returned to Úlfarrston and Wolf Killer and Ketil returned home. I made sure that Bolli was working on the damaged drekar and we divided the spoils of war. I bade farewell to Gunnar. "I will attack Man with you when you are ready. Send word to me and the Manx drekar will be repaired. She is half yours, remember that."

"It has been good to sail with you Jarl Dragonheart. You are a different leader from my father and a man may learn much. I know I have." He smiled, "I will be less hasty and less likely to anger. You are right, it clouds the judgement."

Coen watched the drekar head down the channel. I took the time to look around the port. It had grown and I saw many improvements. "It looks like Úlfarrston is thriving. There is much building work."

"That is largely thanks to you and to the likes of Finni over there."

"Finni?"

He pointed to a fat Viking who was ordering the loading of a knarr. I seemed to remember seeing him before. He was always busy loading and unloading his knarr. He seemed to be a hardworking merchant. While he looked overweight the warriors who loaded it looked to be veterans. "He came last year. Many have come in recent years for you have made this land a haven which is safe from pirates and thieves. He came from Hibernia. He said he fled Hakon the Bald and the Irish robbers. He has a knarr and he is very successful. He trades with those that we cannot like the men of Man, Mercia and Wales. He had that warehouse built by the river and you must have passed his hall when you journeyed past the shipyard."

"That is his?"

"Aye."

I had noticed it for it was more like the houses my people built. "And others came too?"

"Many traders came here. None are as successful as Finni Foul-Fart but all do well and the town has fine halls. Come I will introduce you to some of the leading burghers. It makes us all richer for they pay taxes and they ensure that there is work for all."

He was right and I saw an Úlfarrston which had grown in size since his father had died. He had learned well from my old friend.

I spent the evening and night with Coen. Many of the new traders were keen to speak with me. I made polite conversation but they only spoke of trade. I found Finni Foul-Fart more interesting. I had to comment on his name. "Your name sounds like that of a warrior and yet you are a trader."

He was not put out by my direct question, "Aye Jarl. When I was younger I did go A-Viking but it was not for me. I am too small and not strong enough. I prefer to eat rather than fight. I trade. The name? I like to eat and I eat too fast. Or I used to. I am afraid the name has stuck but men know me for an honest trader so I do not mind." I nodded. I liked him. "I would like to thank you for making this such a safe haven. We all profit from the peace it brings."

"Thank you." I was pleased when they all departed. It left just Coen alone with me and I needed to speak with him. We sat together at his table after we had feasted and the others had gone. "I need words with you for I have put you in danger. The peace we all enjoy may be shattered."

"How so?"

"I have made enemies and they will come to seek revenge. The obvious way is through you. I will help in any way you like to defend this town or you can be neutral and not stop our enemies. I would understand."

He shook his head, "When first you came you stopped the raids which took so many of our people. We now thrive. We are rich. My father swore to be your man and I did when I became headman. We do not desert our friends in times of hardship. However it is good that you have told us of this danger. We will use more rock from the Old Man to bolster our walls. We will deepen our ditches and we will buy mail and swords from Bjorn. The men of Úlfarrston will stand by you. We may not be warriors such as you have but we have learned from you and we fight our enemies and yours. Never fear. Besides your captains, Erik, Olaf and the others live close by as does your shipwright. They are strong warriors. We are becoming one people."

"I have another boon to ask. My knarr will now trade only with our brethren to the north. I dare not risk them close to Wessex and Man but your vessels may travel where they will. I would have your captains keep their eyes and ears open for us. Is that too much for me to ask? If so please let me know."

He shook his head. "No it is not and I may have someone who can help you." He waved over a servant. "Fetch my brother."

"Your brother? Pasgen ap Pasgen?"

"No, he is too young. It is my half brother, Raibeart ap Pasgen. He went to Wessex with you in his knarr."

I remembered his half brother. Old Pasgen had taken a Saxon slave to his bed. His wife had understood the arrangement and they got on well. Raibeart was the result of their union. I had not see him since he had been a child. I now remembered that he had captained a knarr for us.

"My brother now captains a knarr. He is keen for adventure. If we had warriors who raided he would have happily led them."

"He could have joined one of my war bands."

Coen shook his head, "My father did not train him as a warrior. My training was rudimentary. We can defend our land but we are not Vikings. He would have been out of place."

"I am not a Viking and I come from the line of a Saxon and the Old people."

"But you were trained from a young age." He shook his head, "You do not fully know how other warriors fear you. It is known that a Viking will fight long after all hope has gone. Your ferocity is legendary. Any who takes on a Viking either has a death wish or overwhelming numbers on his side. Raibeart can use a sword and has a quick mind. He is also very clever. My father taught him to read and he has studied the charts which Aiden made for us." He looked up. "Ah here he comes."

He had changed since I had last seen him. But the blond hair he had had as a child had not changed, as mine had. He looked like a Saxon! I remembered him then. I had noticed someone who looked like a Saxon sailing a knarr.

"Raibeart, Jarl Dragonheart has a request to make of you."

"You wish me to captain one of your drekar and fight for you?"

He could not keep the excitement out of his voice. I shook my head, "Not at the moment but I thank you for your loyalty and it may be that I will take you up on your offer but this is not the season of the drekar. Your brother says that you seek adventure?"

"Aye, I do. I enjoy sailing but I want excitement in my life."

"I have a task for you but it may be dangerous, not only for you but your crew too."

"I chose my crew and they are all of the same mind as I am." He looked animated, "If this involves adventure then I am your man."

I nodded, "I will pay you and your crew for the service."

"You need not. I am happy to do it."

"The gods would not be happy if I were to endanger your lives without reward. I will pay you." He nodded. "I wish you to spy for us. We are enemies with

Wessex, Mercia, Northumbria. We are blind without knowledge. You can sail into their ports and trade. We can provide the goods you trade. Our iron is much sought after. I would have you listen to the gossip in their alehouses and waterfronts. Report back what they are about."

He nodded, "That sounds like something I could do. When do I sail?"

"I will have a cargo sent down to you. As payment you keep half of the profits."

"A quarter, I would not rob you."

"Believe me you will be doing us the favour but if you are happy with that arrangement then a quarter. I should counsel caution. You need to say that the iron comes from somewhere other than my land. Say it is from the land north of here; the land of the Scots. Be vague and only give the origin if they ask. And I would use a nickname. It is know that your father was our ally."

He nodded, "That makes sense."

I pointed to his head, "Raibeart Yellow Hair would seem to be appropriate."

He said, "If I were a Viking but Saxons do not use such names. My mother came from Caestir. I will say I am Raibeart of Caestir."

"Good." I stood and clasped his arm. "And when winter's cloak is shed if you still wish to captain a drekar I may have one for you."

His face lit up, "Then I will be truly in your debt."

The next day I made one more visit to Erik Short Toe and Olaf Grimsson. I needed my two captains to know my plans. I felt happier as I journeyed back to Cyninges-tūn. I did not like dishonesty and I hated not speaking the truth but I had learned that sometimes it was necessary when dealing with a devious foe. Hakon the Bald appeared such a man. After the others had retired Gunnstein Berserk-Killer had remained up talking with me. He was now totally honest about Hakon. I discovered that he had used us. Although he had not robbed us when we had traded he had taken more than his fair share and profited. He had used my name, as an ally, to cow other leaders and to intimidate the Irish, who feared me. I could have lived with that but taking the gold of Wessex and betraying us to the Manx men had meant I needed to do something about it.

Chapter 14

Once back at Cyninges-tūn I sent for my Ulfheonar. We had a deer which Audun Thin Hair had hunted and given to me in thanks for his son's safe return. We would feast in my hall. Haaken and Karl One Hand joined us. Haaken had used the time since returning to compose a saga about our fight at Hamwic and the visit to the witch. Of course, this time, much of it was to do with him. My men did not mind. They enjoyed his songs and his stories. After the first rendition there were suggestions for improvement. He promised he would make them and then gave it to us a second time.

When the table banging had finished I spoke. "And now that we have heard the new song I will tell you of an adventure which may result in another saga from Haaken the One Eye, even though he will not partake in the adventure himself."

"But Jarl..."

Brigid had come in with some freshly made honeyed oat cakes flavoured with some spices we had taken from Wintan-ceastre. She laid them on the table with a bang and wagged a finger at Haaken. "The Lady Kara has ordered that you not raid until the new grass. Your wife will need you to do all those things you have put off when you have been following my husband down rabbit holes and sailing the seas!"

My warriors jeered at Haaken's embarrassment and I shook my head. Women did not give warriors the respect they deserved sometimes.

When the noise had subsided and Brigid had left us Snorri asked, "Where to this time?"

"We believe that Hakon the Bald has betrayed us. I intend to visit with him and end his treachery."

"How?"

"When I have confronted him about his deceit I will challenge him to a fight."

Olaf Leather Neck laughed, "He will not fight you! He is a coward and he is fat!"

"Then he will die and that is where the Ulfheonar come in. I will not land with you. You will land from *'Heart of the Dragon'* in dead of night. You will make your way to Hakon the Bald's stronghold and be ready to overcome the guards there if it becomes necessary."

"Who will you have to guard you then?"

"I have volunteers from the warriors of Cyninges-tūn who showed great skills in Wessex. They are honoured to take the risk."

"Jarl Dragonheart, I crave a boon."

"You can have anything you wish Karl One Hand for you have served me well."

"Haaken One Eye cannot follow you. Let me take his place among the Ulfheonar again. I need not my shield for, from what you say we would be wolves and I would only need my right hand to slit throats." He held up his left stump. "I can still use this if I need to."

I saw from the faces of my other warriors that they had spoken of this already. He was right and there was none better with a seax. I relented, "Very well."

Olaf Leather Neck emptied his horn of ale and said, "Before I get too drunk tell me how will we know when we are to slit throats."

I pointed to the Roman horn hanging on the wall. We had found a pair of them when searching an old Roman fort some years earlier. Aiden said that they were called a buccina. "I will take one of those as a gift for Hakon. If you hear it blown then it will be time to let blood be spilled."

They all nodded and banged their horns on the table. I smiled for none asked how many men we faced. It could have been a thousand and they would not worry. Brigid appeared at the door with her hands on her hips, "I do not mind you eating every morsel of food in my house and drinking all of my ale but I will not have you waking the hall! Keep your noise down!"

These warriors who would face any foe without batting an eyelid all nodded meekly and murmured their apologies. When she had gone Finni asked, "Will Aiden be with us?"

"He will be with me for he can read what Hakon thinks. I will have Rolf Horse Killer be his guard."

Haaken had been quiet for a long time. His near experience had made him more reflective. "You are taking a great risk, Jarl."

I leaned back in my seat. "When I was in the cave and spoke with the witch I realised that my days of raiding far from my home are gone. That is what the witch saw in my future. Hrolf needs a warrior as I was when I was younger. He needs someone who can sail beyond the Pillars of Hercules. That decided, and remember Haaken it is the spirits who have decided this, then I need my land making safe. Our most dangerous enemies are in Man and Hibernia. Gunnstein Berserk-Killer is a good warrior and he will make a good Jarl. He will make sure that Dyflin, at least, does not harbour enemies."

"And Man?"

"Gunnar Thorfinnson and Thorfinn Blue Scar have a score to settle with them. I will sail with them when they punish the men of Man."

"We raid Frankia no more?"

"No. We will make Mercia and the land of Gwynedd fear us and become our granary."

Haaken smiled. Since his injury he did not nod overmuch. "Good for it means less rowing and less time at sea. I grow too old for that!"

It took nine days to repair the drekar and many frosts had come and made the ground hard. Winter furs were brought from chests and more logs were cut to be placed in the winter stores. We could fight our enemies well and that included winter. It was rare for us to fight at this time of year but we had to strike quickly. I did not want the evil of Hakon the Bald to fester over the winter. I would make sure that our homes were well protected and then I would leave. We made our farewells. I took twenty volunteers from the town with me. They knew the risks and they were happy to go into a place which might be as dangerous as a wolf pit. Another twenty went to help the Ulfheonar to row my drekar. They would remain on the boat and bring her down to Dyflin after they had dropped off my oathsworn. Brigid and Kara saw us off.

Brigid hugged me and kissed me. "Promise me that you will come back for your unborn daughter will need a father she can wind around her little finger! She will plague her brother but you she will own."

I smiled, "I will return. That I promise."

Kara warned, "Do not tempt the Norns father."

There was something in her voice which worried me, "You have dreamed?"

She shook her head, "No but I sense danger." She paused. "I have had a dream. It has come to me each night since you went to Wessex. There is a knife in the night. It strikes an unprotected back." She hugged Aiden. "I saw no face just a back so you take care too, husband. Watch for treachery!"

Brigid became frightened, "Then do not go!"

I kissed her again, "Kara's words are a warning which we shall heed. I will wear my armour. I will have eyes in the back of my head."

We mounted our horses and we rode down to Úlfarrston.

We rode in silence. None of us wished this journey but it was necessary. Hrolf had volunteered too. After our shared experience in the cave of the witch I knew that our threads were tightly bound. The Norns did not like men to sever the thread they had so carefully spun. Besides which he reminded me of Wolf Killer when he had been young and travelled with me.

Gunnstein and his men were already aboard their drekar. The loyalty of his men was not in question and they knew exactly what we intended. They had sworn an oath to Gunnstein and they would not be foresworn. The three drekar set sail in the middle of the day. We headed north and west to avoid Man. We rowed for the wind was not as strong as we would have liked. It was good for the men in my drekar came closer together as they rowed. They sang the chant of the birth of my sword on that night on Man long ago to invoke the support of Odin. It would make a good beginning to this journey

The storm was wild and the gods did roam
The enemy closed on the Prince's home
Two warriors stood on a lonely tower
Watching, waiting for hour on hour.
The storm came hard and Odin spoke
With a lightning bolt the sword he smote
Ragnar's Spirit burned hot that night
It glowed, a beacon shiny and bright
The two they stood against the foe
They were alone, nowhere to go
They fought in blood on a darkened hill
Dragon Heart and Cnut will save us still
Dragon Heart, Cnut and the Ulfheonar

Dragon Heart, Cnut and the Ulfheonar

Once we had passed the western coast of my land we separated. Erik and the Ulfheonar would make their way slowly to a cover to the north of Dyflin while Gunnstein and my small drekar, *'Red Snake'*, made directly for Dyflin.

I wondered what Hakon would make of us as we sailed into his stronghold. I had no doubt that the men of Man who had survived would have reported our sea battle but they would not know who had survived. I doubted that he had any spies in my land and he would not know where I was. Aiden had been giving me lessons in how to keep a smiling face when all that I felt was scorn and anger.

I spied the masts of eight drekar as we entered the anchorage. I saw the standard of Man on one of them. That might make things interesting. I guessed that, from the number of drekar, there could be four hundred or so warriors there. How many were Hakon's loyal followers? I had to trust in my men and my plan.

We entered slowly and with no shields displayed. We wore neither war paint nor helmets. Our swords and our seaxes were our only weapons. There were two berths at the far end of the river on the opposite side to the Manxman. That too suited for it meant we would have to be ferried across the river and our two drekar would be safer. Dyflin was a sprawling town and almost as big as Wintanceastre. There were many ferrymen eager to earn coins and my standard, at my stern, signified who we were. I went across first with Aiden, Gunnstein and four of his oathsworn. Aiden carried the buccina. I would keep that gift until later on. I wanted Hakon intrigued by it.

We stood on the wooden jetty while the rest of our men were ferried across. "Jarl, look at the ship from Man."

I looked to where Aiden pointed. The ship with the three legs of Man was preparing for sea. We had frightened them.

"I wonder how Hakon will explain their presence?"

Gunnstein said, "I think it confirms his involvement."

"Aye, you may be right."

Normally Hakon would welcome us but this time he did not. He sent his squint eyed lieutenant, Arne the Twisted. It was not an attractive name and had been given because of the way he had been born. His face had a twisted look. It was said his mother had upset a witch and his birth had been difficult. Gunnstein had told me that his nature now matched his name.

Arne the Twisted gave a half bow, "The Jarl was not expecting you, Jarl Dragonheart."

I gave the practised smile which Aiden had taught me. "I promised that I would return his drekar, his men and his share of the profits."

He looked eagerly across the river. "Shall I have them ferried across, Jarl Dragonheart?"

Shaking my head I said, "Let us wait for daylight. It would not do to have them spill into the river eh?" I laughed as though this was a joke.

"Of course, so you will be staying the night?"

"Unless it is a problem?"

"No, not a problem. If you would like to follow me I will take you to the Jarl."

My new bodyguard followed me closely. They were taking their temporary duties very seriously. I saw Aiden smile.

Hakon the Bald was in his hall and it was filled with warriors. There were not four hundred within, it was more like eighty. The other crews must have been elsewhere but I saw that these were his best warriors. Arne said, "I will go and speak with the Jarl!" He scurried across the hall like a demented crab eager for a meal. As we drew close I saw him pointing and whispering. I had no doubt he was preparing Hakon.

"Jarl Dragonheart and Gunnstein Berserk Killer, Arne the Twisted tells me that you have had a successful raid. Where are your other ships?"

"We suffered storms and we were attacked."

"Attacked!" he feigned shock very well. "Who dared to attack the warrior wielding the sword touched by the gods?" He could not keep the sarcasm from his voice. I might have missed it before but now I was attuned to such nuances.

I was direct in my answer. "The men from Man." I stared at him the smile leaving my face. "Did I not see one of their ships tied to your jetty?"

He feigned an expression of surprise, "So that is why they left so quickly! Had I known I would have detained them. You are an ally and a friend."

"No matter. We shall pay them back! That was not our purpose in coming here."

He looked at the warriors behind me, "Where are the Ulfheonar?"

It was my turn to feign surprise, "I did not think I would need them if I was to visit a friend."

"Of course not but we enjoy Haaken One Eye's stories."

"Haaken was badly wounded in Wessex. He is at home recovering." I spoke the truth. Haaken was back on his farm.

"That is sad. He is a great warrior and bard." He gestured towards the table where he normally sat. "Come, you two shall sit at my right and left hands and I will hear of your glorious adventures."

"And our men?"

He waved a hand towards a long empty table at the far end of the room. "They can sit there." He made it sound casual but I understood why he did it. We would have no protection. If there was treachery then they would not be able to reach us. More importantly Aiden would find it harder to read Hakon's mind. I just smiled, "Aiden, take our men to that table yonder."

Aiden nodded. He would command my men if trouble began. I saw Hrolf try to follow me but Aiden spoke in his ear and he complied.

I watched Hakon's servants carefully as they poured the ale. I made sure that they also topped up Hakon's from the same jug. I did not wish to be poisoned. The servant poured Hakon's and them mine. "So, Jarl did you fight King Egbert?"

"Aye. He brought his army." I noticed that the table of Hakon's oathsworn stopped speaking to listen to us. "He has brave men who follow him. Were Haaken here he would tell the tale far better than I could. King Egbert did not impress me as a leader. He sent men to do his fighting and he remained safe from harm. That is not how I view a leader of warriors."

I knew I had hit a nerve when Hakon coloured. He had not led his men in battle for at least ten years. "Then you defeated him?"

I shook my head, "We were betrayed. He came to fight us earlier than he should. Someone had told him what we were about. He brought his whole army but we killed many of them and we escaped with our lives and much of his treasure."

I noticed Arne the Twisted shifting uncomfortably in his seat. Hakon said, innocently, "How do you know you were betrayed? Perhaps it was the Weird Sisters toying with you."

"No, my friend. When we took Hamwic we were told that the King was in Corn Walum fighting King Mark. Even had someone from Hamwic reached him, and none did, then it would have taken him many more days to reach us than he did. He must have started for Wintan-ceastre the day after we landed. We were betrayed."

"But I thought you trusted all of your men?"

"I know it was not one of my men. All of my drekar were with me. No man could have reached Egbert save by a fast ship. No, we were betrayed by someone closer to home and when I find the traitor I will tear his treacherous heart from his body."

"The world is a sad place when we cannot trust our friends." He shook his head, "Come let us drink and enjoy this evening."

I gave a slight nod to Gunnstein Berserk-Killer. "Jarl Hakon the drekar you loaned us needs repair. There was so much weed on her hull that it slowed down the Jarl's fleet. Perhaps *'Dragon's Breath'* would have been a better drekar to use. She is the fastest drekar in Dyflin. Why, I would bet she could beat any of the Jarl's ships."

He looked into his ale as though seeking the answer. "But surely you would have had to sail at the speed of the knarr you took."

He had tripped himself up, "Who said we took knarr with us?"

He looked at me, startled, "Why you did or Gunnstein."

"No, we did not. How did you know?"

"Someone must have told me."

"Someone who was spying on us?"

"I get many visitors here, who remembers where we hear such things."

"And you are not friends with Man?"

"Of course not."

"Then what was the drekar doing in your port?"

"Jarl Dragonheart, this is my hall and I will not be spoken to like this. I have no idea where I heard about your knarr and the men of Man are not my allies."

I nodded, "Perhaps I was mistaken." I stood and shouted, "Aiden."

Aiden stood and left the table carrying the leather bound gift. Hakon looked worried, "What does you galdramenn bring, Jarl Dragonheart?"

"A gift. It is something we discovered in a Roman fort and I thought it might amuse you."

Aiden placed the horn before me and then whispered in my ear, "The spirits have spoken. He lies but we knew that anyway."

I whispered back to him, "I know. Have the men be ready for my signal."

"I like not whispers at my table, Jarl Dragonheart. They hint at conspiracy and plots."

I smiled, "I apologise but he had information which he knew that I needed."

"Information?"

"He is a galdramenn. He reads minds and he speaks with the spirits."

"Reads minds?"

I ignored him and took out the horn. "See this fine horn. The Romans used it in battle to send orders to their men. Interesting eh?"

"Yes, " he said suspiciously.

"Much as you were sent orders by King Egbert," I smiled as I said it and he was discomfited. He started as though he had been pricked.

"That is a lie!"

Keeping my voice calm I said, "Think of your words before you accuse me of lying." I picked up the horn and stood. "I have not used this much but it makes an interesting sound, listen." I blew it. The noise made some warriors jump. It was loud as I knew it would be. I blew a long strident note. The Romans had designed them well and the sound could carry a long way. I had no doubt it reached my Ulfheonar as they waited beyond the gates.

I laid it down and looked at Hakon the Bald. "I accuse you, Jarl Hakon the Bald, of betraying me and serving King Egbert of Wessex. I accuse you of conspiring with the men of Man to attack not only my men but your own warriors, Gunnstein Berserk-Killer and his men."

There was a chilling silence in the hall. His men had heard me accuse the Jarl of treachery and he had not denied it. He shook his head and his voice was quiet as he spoke. "I did not. It is a lie."

I drew my sword. "I told you before that you do not accuse me of lying but we have a way of settling this." I turned to the room. "I have accused your Jarl of treachery. He says I lie. He is your Jarl but I challenge him to mortal combat. Warrior to warrior. Jarl to Jarl! I would not spill the blood of any others but I want no interference!"

Still Hakon sat, his hands on the table. "I will not spill the blood of a warrior who is deluded." His eyes darted around the room looking for support.

I would not kill a man out of hand. If I slew this Hakon the Bald while his sword lay sheathed, even though he was guilty then I would make enemies of all of his men and Gunnstein would not become jarl. I reached down and tore Hakon's purse from his belt. Laying my sword down I opened the purse and emptied the coins on the table. It was a gamble but one worth taking. I picked one up and held it for all to see.

"A coin from Wessex. A golden coin. A coin which bought this jarl's treachery." I threw it to a warrior on the next table and picked up another. "And a second." I threw it to another table. "And third!" As I threw this to another table I ran the rest of the coins through my fingers. "Each one tells me that this man betrayed me. I offer to fight and he declines. Why do you follow a faithless jarl? Why do you follow a man who sends his own warriors, like Gunnstein Berserk-Killer to their deaths?"

A murmur ran around the room and I saw fear in the face of Hakon the Bald as he sensed the mood change. I saw his eyes flicker behind me as he went for his sword. As I reached for mine I felt a searing pain in my back as Arne the Twisted, who was seated next to me, rammed his seax under my left arm and into my back.

"Treachery!" Gunnstein lunged across me to stab the assassin in the neck. Hakon swung his sword at me but I managed to deflect it. The pain in my back was dull but I could feel the blood trickling down beneath my kyrtle. There was mayhem in the hall. My men, led by Aiden, raced over towards me. Gunnstein's men followed. I punched Hakon the Bald hard in the face with my left hand and he reeled back. I brought Ragnar's Spirit over above my head as he fell. He barely blocked the blow and my blade left a tiny wound on his bald head. His blood dripped down to his nose. He tried to wriggle backwards to evade my attack.

"That is right! Wriggle like the snake that you are but I will end your squirming this night!"

Behind me I heard Aiden give a second and third blast to the horn. It was the signal that I was in danger. Hakon tried to kick my legs from under me as one of his warriors thrust his sword at my unprotected right side. I blocked it and Hakon regained his feet. Suddenly a Danish war axe swung over and took the sword from my attacker. Rolf Horse Killer could maim warriors too.

Hakon took advantage of my distraction and lunged at me. Years of good eating and indolence had dulled and slowed his reflexes. I swept his blade aside and, pulling his carcass towards me I head butted him. I knew that the wound was weakening me. As Hakon reeled back I ended it by bringing my sword horizontally across his neck. His reflexes were not quick enough and my sword took his head cleanly.

There was a moment's silence as his men took in the death of their jarl. He had already eliminated many of the leaders who might have opposed him and there was indecision. I heard two shouts. First Gunnstein shouted, "Jarl Hakon is dead! I claim this hall!"

Then I heard, from the far door the shout, "Ulfheonar!"

Confusion reigned as even Hakon's men began to fight amongst themselves. Those who still saw themselves as Hakon's oathsworn, threw themselves at us. This was not a battlefield. We had neither shield nor helmet. Most men had no armour. The benches and the tables proved as dangerous as traps and pits in a ditch and, even worse, you did not know who were your enemies.

Aiden, Rolf and Hrolf stood behind me to protect my back. I was wounded and it would have been foolish to range far. We would have to endure this attack. If the Weird Sisters wished me dead then they would sever my thread and I would join my comrades in Valhalla. The four of us had our backs to a table. I heard a thump as someone jumped on top of the table. I was about to turn when I heard Aiden say, "It is Erik Wolf Claw!" I felt his hand as he jammed it beneath my mail. "I have a cloth. I will try to staunch the bleeding. You should hide beneath the table!"

"Jarl Dragonheart does not die hiding from his foes! If this is my day to die then I face them on my feet looking them in the eye!" Two warriors ran at me even as I spoke. One stabbed at my eyes with his sword as the second tried to gut me like a fish. A warrior worries about his eyes and I blocked that blow. I saw a seax deflect the second sword down and then Hrolf's new blade ripped open the warrior. I grabbed the first warrior and pulled him close to me. I brought up Ragnar's Spirit and it came out at his neck. "You chose to follow a poor leader my friend but you were brave enough. Go to Valhalla!"

It was a terrifying scene before me. The hall was filled with whirling men and blades. I saw warriors stabbed in the back by those they thought were friends a moment earlier. I could see my Ulfheonar carving a path towards me but there was still an army of enemies between us. "Aiden, sound the horn until I tell you to stop!"

My galdramenn began blowing as though his life depended upon it. Men looked up as the strident notes filled the hall. Many stopped fighting and then so did the others. I shouted, "Stop." When the notes stopped they seemed to eerily echo around the hall. "Stop fighting! You men of Dyflin you are brothers fighting brother! You can follow Hakon the Bald no longer and his assassin lies dead. I order you to follow Gunnstein Berserk-Killer; he is a true leader and worthy to be your jarl!" I raised my sword. "This is the sword touched by the gods! If I speak an untruth then let Odin himself strike me down!"

I raised the sword. It was an effort. I felt my life leaving me but I gritted my teeth. If I fell now then a massacre would ensue. There was silence at first one and then another, men sheathed their swords while others began to bang the tables with their swords and chanted, "Dragonheart!" over and over. I sheathed my sword. Snorri led my Ulfheonar to race to my side.

"You did it Jarl! You defeated the evil that was Hakon."

I nodded and that was an effort. I felt my eyes closing. I felt life leaving me, "Tell my son he is to rule after I am gone. Tell Kara she was right. There was a knife in the night and it has killed me." Then blackness took over and I saw nothing more.

Chapter 15

I dreamed or perhaps it was my journey to the Otherworld I did not know.

I seemed to float. I was not in this world but it did not look like the Otherworld. I heard no sounds and I saw no lights. All was darkness. I felt a cold like the coldest snow and ice. It chilled me to my heart. I had a sudden memory. I knew not where it came from; was this the same as those moments before I was born? Would I emerge like a new born babe in the Otherworld? I remembered I had sheathed my sword. I had not died with a sword in my hand! I would not go to Valhalla! I had no concept of this other place. I had expected to die and join those like Cnut, Prince Butar, and Rolf who had died before me. I would not be with my warriors! I would drift in an empty void. I would not enjoy stories of great battles and I would not see those like Ragnar and Butar.

Then I saw a light and I spied, not my dead wife Erika, but my mother. I had not seen her, even in my dreams, for many years. She was suddenly beside me and she put her hands on my wound. I felt it grow warm and I felt more comfortable. Her head came close to mine and she kissed my cheek and I felt warmth return. She leaned close to my ear and said, "*This is not your time, my son. There is work for you yet. You must make your land safe. Make your land safe.*"

She began to fade and I tried to reach for her but I could not move. I tried to run after her but it was as though I was trapped in cloying mud. Then I saw Kara's face and all went black once more.

I opened my eyes and saw, not Kara, but her husband, Aiden. It was daylight. Where had the night gone? Aiden looked worried. I opened my mouth to speak and croaked rather than spoke. He smiled and poured water into my mouth. "He lives! The Jarl lives!"

I heard a cheer. I tried to rise.

"No Jarl, you were as close to death as any I have seen. You lie there until I say you move. Your warriors have granted me the power to order your life until we return home."

I closed my eyes and when I opened them again I spoke, "What happened?"

"The warriors all decided to support you. They had had enough of Hakon. When he refused to fight you they ended their support for him. Gunnstein is Jarl."

"Good. And have we lost many warriors?"

"Two, Sven from Langdale and Einar Karlsson. They died well."

"That is two too many. I will make amends with their families." I hesitated, "and will I live?"

"You will. Arne the Twisted almost ended you life. He found a place beneath your mail. It was a cunning blow and had he been able to point it down rather than up he would have found out if you truly had the heart of a dragon. As it is you have lost a great deal of blood. I do not want you to move for at least three days while we build up your strength. We need Kara to cast her eye over you."

I lay back and closed my eyes. I must have slept for when I awoke it was dark once more. Hrolf was seated next to me and he was staring at me. "Can I get you anything? Aiden said you needed food and ale to make you stronger. Which would you like?"

"Ale?"

He nodded and poured some from a ladle into a horn. "It is warmed honeyed ale with some spices and herbs. I thought it might be a potion but he told me it was just herbs and spices."

He held it to my lips while his arm supported my head. It was warming and aromatic. The smell alone made me feel better. I drank it all.

"More?"

"Not just yet. Let this begin to work."

He put the horn next to the cauldron containing the beer. "When I saw you fall I thought that my world was ending. You are not supposed to die. You are Dragonheart."

"I am a mortal, Hrolf and I can be killed. Many men have tried."

"But you cannot be killed in combat. I have seen you fight and you are better than any you have faced."

"That is because you have not see me face a warrior who is good enough. Hakon was a weak, fat coward. The Eorls I fought were old men or lazy men. When I face a warrior who is as good as my Ulfheonar then I will be given a test."

"Are there such warriors?"

"Aye, they are out there. I am just lucky that I have not met one lately. I have fought them but then I was younger. Each wound makes me a little weaker." I looked at him. "I will die one day and it will be in combat."

"What the witch said, about me finding another jarl, I do not wish to."

"I thank you for that but it is not your decision. It is the Weird Sisters who decide. Your destiny lies in Neustria. You must find a jarl who seeks riches there. You must learn from him so choose wisely. As you saw from Hakon the Bald there are poor jarls."

"Do I need to decide now?"

"No, we have a winter to endure and to reflect upon the deeds we have done. Come the time of the new grass I will take my ships and I will aid Gunnar Thorfinnson to extract retribution from the men of Man. You will still be with us and there may be a jarl looking for someone like you; a young warrior who is favoured by the gods."

"I am favoured?"

"The witch seemed to think so and the Norns have been kind to you. "There is treasure for you in Cyninges-tūn."

"But I was a slave, I did not expect you to honour your promise."

"I am Jarl Dragonheart and I keep every promise that I make. Besides I, too, was a slave once. We share a past."

Aiden returned, "You are awake. Has he drunk?"

"Aye."

"And eaten?"

"Not yet."

Aiden turned, "Come Ulf and Erik, we must help him to his feet." My two Ulfheonar entered and grinned when they saw me.

"Why?"

"You need to make water. I do not want you standing unaided. When you have made water you will want to eat."

"How do you know?"

"I am galdramenn." He laughed, "And I have read it in the writings of the priests."

He was right and I did manage to eat. Three days after I had been wounded I was helped to my drekar. I refused to be carried but it was harder than I had thought. My legs felt as though they would not support my body.

I sail with Erik Short Toe. Sitting by the steering board I spoke to him about Olaf Grimsson. Snorri joined as we spoke, "What think you of our new captain. Did he sail well?"

"From what I saw he did but Snorri can tell you more. He was aboard with him."

Snorri nodded, "He has an affinity with the drekar and the sea. Captains like Erik and Olaf are rare. He does not panic. When we were damaged in the storm he spoke calmly to the crew and knew how to sail her so that the damage did not worsen. I can think of others who might not have saved her."

Erik nodded, "I have followed him and he knows how to get the most from the sails and the hull. Why the questions, Jarl Dragonheart?"

"We have the drekar we captured from the men of Man. It is larger than the threttanessa. Could he handle it?"

"Easily. He would need a good crew."

"We will get him one."

"And *'Red Snake'*?"

"I have plans for her," I added, enigmatically. I ignored their questioning looks. The Norns were not the only ones who could weave threads. I knew the people whom I led. I would make the best of their abilities.

When we landed Snorri found the most comfortable horse which Coen had in his stable. We rode back to Cyninges-tūn at a snail's pace. None of the men left us. They were determined that we would all arrive back together. We had treasure but not as much as we normally had. The warriors we had slain had yielded arms, armour and gold. Gunnstein Berserk-Killer insisted that I have the coins from Wessex which Hakon had had about him. He called it weregeld, blood money and he would have none of it. The treasure we found in his chambers we shared.

Our delayed return must have worried our families. That and the fact that we rode back north through the first of the winter blizzards. When we were detected riding slowly up the road they met us a mile from our gates. Kara and Brigid were well wrapped in fur cloaks but I was angry. My wife was carrying our child. Before I could express my anger I saw that Brigid was weeping, "You are wounded!"

Aiden said quietly, "Kara is a volva, Jarl. I suspect she dreamed of the danger."

I nodded and instead of a scowl I gave a smile, "And it is nothing. Aiden has healed me. I have lost no limbs and no eyes. There is no metal plate in my head so do not cry!" Brigid began to open her mouth to speak, "And this is not the place to discuss my health or yours. We go to my hall and we will talk there."

Kara followed and she put her arm around Brigid. Before I had met Brigid I had not had this fuss. I was a warrior and we gained wounds. Once in my hall Kara and Brigid set to making me comfortable. They would not allow me to do anything. Kara examined the wound and questioned Aiden to within an inch of his life. "Aiden saved my life. Let him alone!"

Brigid rounded on me, "Saved your life! I thought it was a scratch!"

I knew I should have kept my mouth shut but eventually Kara seemed satisfied. "It is good that you do not raid for the winter. It will heal well."

"Perhaps you should give up raiding."

I was beginning to become cross, "Woman! Know your place. I am Jarl Dragonheart and I will do what I will do!"

A flood of tears ensued and she rushed from the room. Kara wagged her finger at me, "Your wife is carrying your fourth child and yet you seem to know nothing about women. She is upset and she worries about you!"

She left to comfort Brigid. Aiden began to dress me. "They are strange creatures, Jarl. They speak and they move much as we do but they are different in so many ways."

It took a whole moon for me to heal sufficiently to be able to exercise and practise with my sword. Brigid would have made it longer but I was determined to get back to the warrior I was. Time had been I would have healed in a week but age was catching up with me. The first thing I did was to visit Bjorn Bagsecgson. I took with me the small bag of stones I had taken from the Saxon eorl.

"It is good to see you up and about Jarl Dragonheart. We were worried."

"Aye, Bjorn, enemies who face me sword to sword I can deal with, treacherous snakes I cannot."

"I heard. I asked for your byrnie and I had been working on it. I have lengthened and tightened the mail around the upper arms. It will be a snugger fit."

"If it restricts my movement then I want it not."

"It will not. You arm will still have free movement but it should be impossible for a man to get a weapon between the mail and your flesh."

"I thank you. I have a commission for you." Before I could continue Aiden came into the smithy. "This is timely. I would take your advice too, Aiden."

"Aye Jarl. Is it to do with Hrolf?"

I laughed, "Reading minds again eh?"

"No but I know that grow close to him as you grew close to me. He is on your mind. And he will be leaving us soon."

"You have dreamed?"

He nodded, "Aye. He will follow another after we raid Man."

"That is good; it is *wyrd*." I took out the pouch of stones and placed them on the anvil. "I would have a sword made for Hrolf. I know I gave him a short sword but he needs more. He needs a special weapon. The Norns have twisted our threads together. A man's sword which he can keep throughout his life. It will remind him whence he came and where he is bound."

They both nodded their approval of such a gesture.

"You wish the stone in the pommel?"

"I do but which stone?"

Aiden moved the two small red ones to one side. "Not those. They are too much connected with Wessex and the colour will make enemies desire it. I think they are what was termed wizard's stones. They can only be owned by a wizard who can control them."

That left the two green and the smaller one which was a blue so pale it looked like a piece of ice. Aiden picked the three up in turn and rolled them around his hand. He had great skill in the making of jewellery and he knew stones better than any man. He put the green ones down.

"I would choose this one. It is a paler version of your blue stone and it speaks to me. The sword would have a name, Heart of Ice."

Bjorn grinned, "I like that name. It sings to me. I can see the sword already." He frowned. "But how would we fix it in the pommel?"

"I would make the stone have ten sides; one for each of the Ulfheonar. If Bjorn could make the pommel have the same number of sides I could melt one of the Wessex coins to seal it."

"Good. I like that. It is fitting."

Aiden fingered the stone and rolled it around. "Did not Hrolf dream of being a horseman?"

"Aye he dreamed that he led warriors who were mounted."

"I have read of a way of using acid to etch a design on a weapon. I could make a horse on the blade."

Even Bjorn was impressed. "If you could do that then it would be a mighty weapon."

"I would need an old one on which to practise."

Bjorn waved to the corner. There was a pile of Saxon blades there. "I am going to melt them anyway. Practise all that you will."

This was *wyrd*. "I would have it ready to give him at Yule."

Bjorn shrugged, "I can have it ready in a week."

Aiden said, "It will be ready."

"Good then let us keep this our secret eh?"

I left and walked to the Water. I had many secrets now. I knew that I had upset Brigid mightily and I had been looking for a way to make it up to her. Yule was a time when the followers of the White Christ celebrated his birth. There had been a story in their Holy Book about wise men bringing gifts. I was no wise man but I would give gifts. I would give the green stones to my daughter and my wife. The red ones would go to Aiden; I suspect he desired them. Hrolf would have his sword and Olaf the new drekar. I had rewarded my Ulfheonar enough times in the past. We would make this a new tradition. It would be our tradition, the people of Cyninges-tūn.

Before Yule I had a visitor. It had been some months since I had sent him on his mission but Raibeart ap Pasgen had not been idle. He rode, with his brother and Erik, Siggi and Olaf, my three captains. It looked like a delegation. Uhtric took their horses and Brigid welcomed them inside. I smiled, "Quite a conclave! What brings you all here?"

Coen pointed to his brother, "When Raibeart returned he had news for you but it concerned us all. I hope you do not mind our visit."

Brigid said, "It is good to have visitors who do something other than fight!"

I rolled my eyes as she went out to organise food and beds. I waved my arm, Sit, please. "Was it successful? Your voyage I mean."

"It was and it was most interesting too, Jarl Dragonheart. Thank you for this opportunity. It has brought excitement and adventure into my life."

Brigid and Uhtric returned with ale, bread and cheese. She looked a little shamefaced. She came over and whispered, "I am sorry for my outburst. The baby!" She kissed me on the cheek.

"I didn't mind."

After she and Uhtric had gone I poured the ale. "Help yourself to food. We stand not on ceremony here. Tell me your tale when you have eaten."

I could see they were hungry. The journey from the sea is long enough at the best of times but in winter it seemed interminable. For some reason the wind always appeared to come from the north and was frighteningly cold. Men called it a lazy wind. It did not go around you but through you.

"I did as you bade me, Jarl Dragonheart. My crew and I adopted new identities. Our strange accents helped. They could not tell if we were Scots or the old people of this land or Saxons who had lived apart for some time. We could have traded all of the iron in Wessex. There is a great need for iron. Weapons are being made in every kingdom. We made a huge profit. Your share is in the chests we brought." I nodded. The coin was of little interest to me. The information might prove to be invaluable. You were right to keep you knarr here. Wessex has put a price on every Viking ship and on every Viking warrior. Your head is worth a thousand gold pieces, Jarl."

"I am flattered."

"We sailed as far as Jorvik, the place the Saxons call Eoforwic. We used that name there and it appeared to allay suspicion."

"Suspicion?"

"They are wary there of all strangers. Your name and that of your warriors was on the tongue of everyone on the river. When we visited the ale houses it was the sole topic of conversation."

"Should I fear that more Danes will come to claim the reward then?"

Raibeart laughed, "Just the opposite. They fear you. The survivors of their attack are broken men who hide in the bottom of a beer barrel. The blood eagle terrified them. Harald Iron Shirt's death was spoken of in every street."

"But the blood eagle is well known. Others have performed it."

"Not for many years. They think you ordered it and they fear you for it. When we mentioned King Egbert's bounty none fancied the prospect of facing you. It was in Eoforwic that we made the greatest profit. There they make weapons to defend themselves from you."

"You have done well, Raibeart."

"I have not yet finished! We had some fine daggers Bjorn had made and some jewellery made by Aiden, we traded them in Lundenwic. There we heard the King Louis has fortified his towns and his ports. He also fears you and your raids."

"And has he put a price upon my head?"

"Aye Jarl, two thousand gold pieces." He pointed to Erik and Olaf. "And five hundred for each warrior and drekar captain."

"Then we can expect hunters to come for the reward."

"They have few ships, Jarl and the water between us is dangerous. The reward is offered should you venture there again." I nodded, "And finally we called at Man."

"Did you have anything left to trade?"

He shook his head. "We called in to see they had anything we could buy to trade. They did not. They have but two drekar left. You destroyed their best one and took the second best. The two they have left are little bigger than *'Red Snake'*."

"And who rules there now?"

"Jarl Erik Eriksson."

Could it be my nephew; the son of Erika's brother? "And how are their warriors?"

"Shaken and unhappy since you defeated them. They curse the name of Hakon the Bald. They know he died and their one ally is gone. Gunnstein Berserk-Killer has shut Dyflin to them. They will have to raid Wales in winter."

"They told you this?"

"No Jarl Dragonheart, I worked it out. There was little food and naught to trade. They looked enviously at our knarr. We left as soon as we could. We called in at Dyflin and Gunnstein told me that all those who supported Hakon have now left his land. He knows not where they have gone but he has rid his land of them."

We spoke of all the other news he had gathered. When Brigid came in to say goodnight we all retired. "I would have you all come to celebrate Christmas with us here at Cyninges-tūn."

"Christmas, my lady?"

My wife smiled, "Yes, Olaf Grimsson, you call it Yule. My husband is allowing us to celebrate it this year."

There was an air of triumph in her voice. I did not mind her the victory. My life would be much easier as a result. They all gratefully accepted the invitation.

I went to visit Haaken at his farm in the week before Brigid's feast. He had recovered, at least his body appeared healed, but I worried about his mind. Although it had not been spoken I thought that he had died, gone to the Otherworld and returned. I knew from my own wound that I had come close. I felt strong enough to be a warrior again; would my oldest friend?

His wife, Unn, was a lovely girl. Haaken had married her when she was but fourteen summers. They had six children but only one boy. She always seemed to be a little afraid of me, I knew not why. She was flustered when I entered Haaken's hall. "Jarl had I known I would have prepared food I...."

I smiled, "It is a brief visit and I need no food. Some of your fine warmed ale will suffice. It is Haaken I need to see."

When she had scurried off Haaken smiled, "She is like a frightened little mouse at times yet when I am away she is like a she-wolf guarding my bairns."

"That is women the world over. I come to invite you to visit with us over Yule. My wife is holding a feast for her White Christ."

"And you approved?"

"I celebrate Yule."

He laughed, "As practical as ever. We shall be there." He examined me. "I heard you, too, came close to death."

"Aye I did. A seax in the back!"

"I am sorry Jarl I was not there to protect you."

"That was my decision. Each of my Ulfheonar has said the same thing but my plan would only work if I was not protected." I waved my left arm to show that the wound had healed. "It is passed. " I examined him in much the same way he had looked at me. "I am here to ask if you wish to raid with us when we sail after the snow has gone?"

He looked puzzled, "Why should I not?" He tapped the side of his head. "This does not bother me and Bjorn has made a helmet which will afford me more protection."

"We are the oldest and the last of the original Ulfheonar. We have both had warning from Odin that we are not immortal. Do you not wish to see your children grown?"

"Aye I do but I would shrivel and die within if I were left behind. I will not let you down, my oldest friend."

"I know and I do not doubt you but I came here today to tell you that I would understand if you chose to stay behind."

"I will be by your side when you sail."

Unn brought in the ale and I told him the news Raibeart had brought. I smiled when I saw how excited he became. He could not stay at home. It was not in his nature. Haaken would die in battle as would I. Like me he was fascinated by Hrolf's dream and the sword I told him I was having made for Hrolf. "Perhaps we should have Aiden etch a dragon on your blade."

I shook my head, "The gods have touched it. Let us leave it at that."

I left happy in the knowledge that Haaken would fight at my side once more. I would feel safer in battle and if we fell... we fell but we would fall as we had fought all these years, together.

Chapter 16

I think that I was as excited as Brigid when Yule came about. I had my surprises all ready. Our guest had been arriving for some days. Brigid, now quite rotund, had enjoyed organising them. She had grown up a servant, a glorified slave, watching her royal relatives enjoying such rituals. Now she was queen of this land and she could be a generous and a kind hostess. The only guests who were missing were Wolf Killer and his family. I had invited him but he had barely finished his new hall at Windar's Mere. He was keen to make that as strong as possible. I understood. I promised to visit when we had celebrated Yule.

We were in her hands for the day she celebrated the birth of the White Christ, the one they called Jesus. Yule was not a day, it was a time. I allowed Brigid to own the one day. Scanlan and Seara, my headman and his wife had toiled for days preparing the hall and the food. We gathered in my hall and she had had our servants and slaves prepare spiced honeyed cakes filled with dried fruits we had brought back from Vasconia. They were the last of our supplies and she had guarded them jealously, I now saw why. She had had the cured meat of wild boars cooked in duck fat over a hot plate. The smell of the spices and the frying pig filled my hall and we had descended like wolves. Kara and Aiden brought Ylva from their hall and I could see that the two were impressed by the feast. The aroma of fresh bread added to the wave of smells which reached every corner. Brigid's goat butter was well known and we feasted in convivial conversation.

I spied, out of the corner of my eye Hrolf, sitting by the door. He had been surprised to be invited. I was about to join him when I saw Aiden leave Kara and sit beside him. That was good. The three of us shared a bond. We had all grown up without blood families and been taken in and adopted. Aiden would help the young orphan.

When the food had been devoured and the beer heated with a hot iron had been drunk, Brigid clapped her hands. "I would like to thank you all for coming, Most of all I would like to thank my husband, Jarl Dragonheart for I know he has broken with tradition to humour his Christian wife." I gave a mock bow and all laughed. The ale and the wine were working. It is traditional amongst my people to give a gift to others on this day." She saw the look of horror on the faces of the women who had brought nothing. Brigid held up her hands, "I give these gifts to you to remind you of this day. There is no other reason. I will not try to change you. You are people who cling to the old ways and I appreciate what fine people you are to have allowed me to live amongst them." She stepped back and the servants moved amongst them. She had had made bone combs for them all. Uhtric was a fine carver of bone and she had had him making them since the summer. She had planned well. Each one was slightly different and all had either a wolf or a dragon carved on them. Everyone was pleased; even the men.

The hall was filled with my friends talking, not of war but of inconsequential things, combs, hair, food they had never tasted before and a new ritual. I could almost see Haaken preparing to tell one of his sagas. I raised my hands. It was almost as though they had been waiting for me to speak. They stepped back in a circle around me. I smiled, I was Jarl.

I had placed a chest under the table upon which the food had been served. Now that the food had been cleared, save for crumbs, it was empty. I lifted the chest on to the table. I smiled as I saw the looks of concern. Would my shoulder hold? I had worked hard on my arm and my back. I was stronger than ever and besides the chest was not heavy.

I opened it. Turning to the chamber I said, "When my wife told me what she intended I thought it was a good idea." I gestured to Haaken. "Haaken wears about his neck a wolf Aiden made for me. All my Ulfheonar do. It binds them to me. I have bound others here in similar ways. There are some I have not." I went to the box. Aiden had made a gold setting for the green stones and it set them off well. The leather he had used for the thong was the finest doe hide. I took one from the chest and placed it around Brigid's neck. "This will match your eyes." She began to cry. I smiled. That was the baby. I took a second for Kara. "And this, my daughter is for you." She kissed me on the cheek as I gave it to her.

I think they all thought that my generosity was over at that point. Bjorn had had his grandson make a setting for the red stone I would give to Aiden. I had made the thong myself. "Aiden you have saved my life this year as well as that of Haaken. You told me that this stone had power. I give it to you so that you may continue to save the lives of my people."

I could see that he was visibly touched.

"Thank you Jarl. This is a great gift. You cannot know."

"But you do and that is what is important." I returned to the chest and then faced them all. Raibeart and Olaf Grimsson." They stepped forward and looked perplexed. I went to the chest and looked in as though searching for their gift. Then I turned. "Your gifts are too big to fit in this chest. Olaf you are a fine captain and have served me well. Erik Short Toe and Snorri have told me of your skill. I would give you the drekar we captured from the men of Man. She is yours to command. You can name her too. What say you?"

His eyes widened and he dropped to his knee, "Jarl I am not worthy. When I remember how Rolf and I behaved and yet you have rewarded me and helped me."

"I saw the stone and I polished it, that is all."

He touched the chape on the scabbard of Ragnar's Spirit. "I swear to serve you with my new drekar," he looked up at me, "*'The King's Gift'*".

"I am no king."

"You are to us."

I nodded and turned to Raibeart. "I hope that you will continue to sail in the winters and fetch us news from afar but I give to you *'Red Snake'*. She is small but she is a good drekar."

Like the others he was bereft of words.

I think they all thought that I had finished. Aiden knew I had not and I saw him seek out Hrolf and stand hard by him. "I have one gift left. Hrolf, come." He hesitated until Aiden propelled him forward. "You have not been with us for long and you will be leaving us soon but the Norns had intertwined our threads so that you are one of us. You may travel far and we may never see you again but you will be in our hearts. I have a gift in this chest for you. I hope that you will use it to carve out your own land. I doubt not that you will succeed. I have been lucky enough to be favoured by the gods and I believe that you have been chosen as well."

I reached in and brought out the blade. Only Aiden knew what I was about and I was happy with the gasps which hissed around the hall. Aiden and Bjorn had outdone themselves. The blade was slightly shorter than mine and the blade a little narrower. There was a depression running down the middle of both sides of the blade. Bjorn and Aiden had designed it that way to make the blade a little lighter and to enable the blood to run down it. On one side a horse reared along the blade, its mane flowing behind like a dragon's tail. On the other was a small warrior with a wolf cloak. Aiden had confided in me, "He is young. This will remind him whence he came. It is right that you are on the blade."

I handed it to him, "Here, Hrolf son of Gerloc, take Heart of Ice and strike fear into your enemies."

He touched it as though it might burn. He ran his fingers down the highly polished blade and his fingers followed the etched design. Finally his eyes stopped on the stone. "It is the stone from Wessex!"

"Aye, and it is one of the many things which tie us together."

The men gathered around Hrolf to examine, enviously, the sword. It was one of the finest Bjorn had ever made. Kara and Brigid joined me. They both kissed me on the cheek at the same time. Brigid said, "You are a kind man, my husband. All of this was well done."

Kara nodded, "I can think of no other who would have put so much thought into such things. We are not worthy of you, father."

I shook my head, "I do it all for my family. Everything I do, I do for my family and my people."

Brigid hugged me, "And I have given you nothing! Nothing but the sharp edge of my tongue!"

I stroked her bump, "I deserve your tongue and you have given me a daughter. If she is half the woman my other daughter is then I will be happy."

The whole day was one of feasting, drinking and songs. I know not how I got to my bed but I awoke the next morning with a throbbing in my head that made me wonder if Aiden had placed a plate there during the night. Our guest all departed and the hall felt emptier. But it was *wyrd*. We had joined together for the one day and we would be bound together forever.

The next morning the weather descended. Within a few hours our home was sealed from the world by a blanket of white. By the end of the week the hills were filled with the howling of wolves and we endured another wolf winter. The last had resulted in many deaths. This one did not. We had learned our lesson.

As soon as the weather abated sufficiently for us to leave our warm and cosy halls I took my Ulfheonar and we visited those farms which were close to us and then headed for Windar's Mere. Although we had heard wolves we found no tracks. They were not close to us but our vigilance did not stop. When we had visited Wolf Killer, we would hunt the wolves before they could hurt our people.

I was relieved that there were no tracks anywhere near my son's hall and he and his family were well. We stayed the night and told each other how we had celebrated Yule. The next day Wolf Killer headed south and east to see his people and hunt the wolves there while I headed north west to the Grassy Mere. We had cleared them from the Loughrigg and Úlfarrberg but that did not mean they would not return.

Hrolf was with us. He attached himself to my Ulfheonar whenever he could. As we headed close to the farm of Audun Thin Hair I said, "This will be dangerous, Hrolf. We cannot watch you when we hunt."

"I do not need watching. If I am to be a jarl and wield Heart of Ice then I need to be as hard as my blade. Besides I wish to watch the Ulfheonar. They are the greatest Viking warriors and I would copy them when I am jarl."

He knew his own mind. He had a boar spear with him but I hoped he would not need to use it. A wolf, in its lair was a dangerous creature. It was more dangerous than a berserker sometimes. Snorri found the tracks of the wolf pack to the west of the Rye Dale. Lang's Dale had been where they had first appeared and where we had first cleared them. From the tracks they had returned. We had a dilemma for we found them at noon. If we followed them then we might be stuck in the hills overnight but if we left them then there might be a snowfall which would mask them.

"We go on. If we have to spend the night here then so be it."

The only one with us who had not killed a wolf was Hrolf and Olaf and Ulf made sure they flanked him. It looked strange for Hrolf rode a small pony and my two Ulfheonar towered over him. He rode well. My Ulfheonar always rode as though they were a sack of grain which might fall off at any time but not Hrolf. He looked as though he had been born on a horse. Of course growing up in Neustria he had been around horses for they were the horse people. Perhaps that was where the dream came from.

When the trail we followed began to climb among the rocks we found a stunted stand of small trees and tethered our horses. I thought to ask Hrolf to guard them but I knew he would not wish to miss the wolf hunt. We were the wolf warriors and when he left us he would never experience again the skill of such warriors.

"Hrolf, stay behind me and keep your boar spear in both hands."
"Aye Jarl."

I could hear the fear in his voice. It made his actions even braver for a man who was afraid and still went into danger was a truly brave man. When he grew to lead then men would follow him.

We had done this many times. Beorn and Snorri were on the two flanks with strung bows and knocked arrows. Haaken, Olaf and I were in the middle. We were well wrapped against the cold and the wind but it would also act as a barrier should the wolves attack us. The problem was that it restricted our movement. We wore no helmets but had fur hats upon our heads. They kept us warm but muted the sounds. We went half a mile and the tracks kept swinging from side to side as though the pack was seeking any predators either before or behind. As we climbed the pack's trail the smell of wolf grew. I knew that we must be close to their lair for their spoor was everywhere. This was their territory. When they went into single file we became wary. No sound would be made from now on. It would be hand signals only.

We took to placing our feet before us. If we were to attack or be attacked then we needed a firm footing. This would be my first opportunity to test my left arm and shoulder. Although the seax had entered my back Aiden had told me that my left arm might be affected. So far it did not. A sudden snow flurry filled our faces as we closed with the rocky wall to our left. It made visibility poor. I was about to order us to retire when there was a black shadow which launched itself at Olaf Leather Neck. Two bowstrings twanged as Snorri and Beorn loosed their missiles. Olaf's spear missed and the wolf lunged at him its flank pierced by two arrows. Finni was next to Olaf. He speared the wolf in the side at the same time as I fixed mine behind its skull. Even as it died a young wolf leapt at Finni. It bowled him down the slope its teeth trying to tear his throat out.

Hrolf was the only one who was close and he bravely thrust his spear into the side of the wolf. It hurt it but did not stop it. The young animal turned its gaze towards Hrolf, A smaller piece of meat and a danger to the wolf it advanced to end the threat. I drew my sword and began to move to help Hrolf. My feet struggled in the snow, "Take out your sword!"

At that moment the rest of the pack attacked my men. Hrolf and I would be alone. The snow seemed to drag me back and slow down time. The wolf leapt when I was but three paces from them. Hrolf stood his ground and swung Heart of Ice towards the flying animal. The blade hacked across the shoulder of the wolf biting deep to the bone but it was not dead. If fell upon Hrolf who had the wind knocked from him. I raised Ragnar's Spirit and as the wolf's teeth began to descend to Hrolf's throat I brought my blade down across its neck. I could not use a full swing for fear of severing the wolf's head and hitting Hrolf. I felt the hot blood spray me and, when my blade struck bone I pulled back and then sawed forward. The wolf lay still. It was dead.

I pulled the carcass from the youth who stared up at me, his face bathed in the wolf's blood. "You live?"

He grinned, "I live! Is the wolf dead?"

"It is." I turned and made my way back to Finni. He had struck the back of his head as he had fallen and I saw that the snow had a pool of his blood. I put my ear to his mouth. He breathed. He was alive but he would not last long. I looked up at my hunters. It had not been a large pack and three dead wolves lay before us. The rest ran.

"Finni is hurt. We must get him to shelter. Olaf, How are you?"

"Embarrassed. I will make amends and carry Finni. He saved me."

I looked up and saw the sun setting to the west. We had taken longer than we should to find the wolves. We would have to spend the night up here. "Snorri, find shelter. The wolf's lair should be close!"

I hoped that they would have left but if not then we would kill them. I suspected it was just the pregnant females and the leader of the pack who were still alive. "Hrolf, stay close to me!"

"But my wolf!"

"Your wolf is going nowhere. It is dead!"

The wolves had found a cave and it would provide us shelter. The wolf's den smelled foetid but there was no growling. Already Snorri was gathering the twigs and fur which the wolves had used to make a nest. He crawled around in the dark gathering them. Gradually our eyes became accustomed to the dark but we would need light for Finni and warmth else we would die of the cold. We needed something dry to start a fire. The others were gathering fuel. Snorri took out his precious flint. He was our fire starter. I left the cave and found Hrolf. "Come young horseman. Let us fetch the animals."

We made our way back to the horses. It was a long walk and we were chilled to the bone by the time we reached them. The snow had been driven half way up their withers. The two of us managed to tie them into two groups and we led them through the snow. When we came to the dead wolves the horses refused to go further and I was stumped as to what to do. Hrolf spoke to his pony and blew into its nostrils. He began to sing. He sang one of Haaken's songs. Remarkably the horses calmed, "Sing, Jarl, sing." I joined him and, slowly at first, the animals moved up through the corpses to the relative shelter of the wall of rock above the cave. There were no obliging trees and so we hobbled them. As the wind had been blowing the snow was a little thinner and Hrolf swept an area clear so that the horses could graze on the thin grass which remained. He took off his helmet and began to pile some of the cleared snow into it. "They need to drink. I am fine, Jarl. Go into the cave."

I shook my head, "Thank you for the orders but I have much to do." I took out my seax and returned to the wolves. I ripped open their stomachs. It was still warm within. My blue hands became much warmer as I butchered the hearts, liver and kidneys from the beasts. They would cook quickly and give us sustenance which would keep us alive. The young wolf I dragged back to the cave. Hrolf look curiously at me. He had finished collecting the snow. It would now have to melt. I handed him the hearts, liver and kidneys. "Take these inside and give them to Snorri. He will know what to do."

The other Ulfheonar had returned with their wood. I took out my sword and hacked off the wolf's head. I then used my seax to skin it as quickly as I could. I had noticed that Hrolf was becoming blue already. The skin of the wolf might keep him alive. My cold hands meant it took me longer than I had hoped. When I entered the cave it was glowing with firelight. Haaken and Erik were examining Finni.

"He has a thick skull and the bleeding has stopped. We have turned him on his side as Aiden taught us and moistened his lips with water."

"Good." I threw the skin to Hrolf, "Here cover yourself with this."

"It is bloody and it stinks!"

They laughed, "And it will keep you warm," snorted Olaf. "Do as the Jarl tells you!"

He did so and then grinned, "Does this mean I am Ulfheonar?"

"A wolf cloak does not make an Ulfheonar, young Hrolf, but it is a start." Olaf's eyes twinkled in the firelight. This was a softer side to my hard warrior.

The young wolf's heart was the smallest and when the outside began to blacken I took it off the stick we were using to cook it. "Here Hrolf, you must eat the heart of the wolf you killed. You will gain his spirit."

He nodded and began to examine it.

"Just eat it and do not look at it!"

"Yes Olaf." His teeth sank in and blood spurted but he ate it all.

My warriors cheered. "Now you are a man! Now you are a warrior!"

We kept the fire burning but we had little wood and it did not keep us that warm. It did allow us to inspect the wolves' home. There were bones everywhere but other than that it was clean. We threw the bones on to the fire too. They would burn and give off a little heat, if not light. When the snow had melted in his helmet Hrolf watered the horses and then began the process again. I could see the Norns at work in his actions. He was a horseman. I heard him shout just before he returned,

"What is it?"

"Foxes trying to take my wolf! I have brought it closer to the entrance."

Olaf snorted, "Then watch for rats!"

Finni came to in the middle of the night. We were all relieved. Head injuries could be dangerous as Haaken had discovered. Haaken used what little light there was to examine the wound. "I doubt you will need a plate," he sniffed, "there is just one Ulfheonar with an iron head."

Snorri laughed, "Some would say you did not need a plate planting to make you that!"

When dawn broke the fire had been dead for some time and we left to return to our home. Our families would be worried. We draped the carcasses of the wolves over our horses. The skins would be cleaned and used as replacements by the warriors who had killed the animals. Hrolf had his. Mine would replace this, my second one. The snow had stopped and been replaced by a biting wind which cut to the very core. Hrolf was grateful for his new cloak.

Snorri counselled him. "It must be treated when we return to the jarl's hall. Piss is good but seek the advice of Aiden and you will need to scrape it until all trace of the wolf is gone!"

He took it all in and, I noticed, rode a little prouder. He remembered the words my men had spoken, he was a man and he was a warrior. He was growing up.

It took almost half a day to return to our home. I knew that Brigid would be worried. Kara and Aiden, however, would have known that I was safe. When I was in danger they sensed it. The warmth of the horses and pony warmed up the wolves' carcasses and they began to smell. We would need to skin them quickly and then cook the meat before they attracted other carrion. As we neared the gates I noticed that Hrolf was edging his pony forward. Normally the Jarl entered first. "Would you like to lead us in, Hrolf?"

His face gave me the answer before he spoke, "I have killed a wolf! Yes Jarl!"

"Then you may have the honour."

As he trotted in Haaken said, "He did not kill it Jarl Dragonheart, you did."

"I know but do I need the glory?"

"No and to be honest he did well. He is just a little older than you were when you killed your first wolf."

"And I was excited too. This is part of his education. It will, hopefully, make a better warrior of him."

Chapter 17

We were visited, a month and a half after Yule, by Raibeart. He had taken his knarr for another spying mission. The iron we sent with him would also fetch a higher price. This time he had not sailed to Northumbria. He went to other ports, closer to home where he could sell our iron and gather information. He rode, with his lieutenant, Garth of Úlfarrston. They were both animated. They had with them a pony and it had two chests. "Silver, Jarl Dragonheart. The price of iron is higher than ever. Your raids have made every king and warlord desperate for more weapons. If we were to take swords we could make an even greater profit."

I shook my head, as I led them indoors, it was wet and it was cold. My warm fire beckoned. "Our swords are for us. Bjorn can make ploughshares for you to trade but not swords."

He nodded, "We also found great news. The men of Wessex have finally cowed King Mark and he is a vassal king. We heard that King Egbert is now turning his attention to Mercia."

That suited me. If he attacked Mercia he could not attack me. More importantly it would leave the back door to Mercia open and we could raid with impunity. "Good that is excellent news. And Man?"

"They have had a bad winter. The snows we had visited them. Some warriors left to find new homes. We passed one of his drekar heading south."

"Where does their jarl live these days?"

"Balley Chashtal, the place where Old Olaf lived."

"And is it fortified?"

"There is a wall around it but it is made of wood."

"And how many drekar remain?"

"One but there are many warriors on the island still. The Jarl holds his Tynewald there once at each new moon. All of his warriors come."

"Good. And will you sail again before you take over the *'Red Snake'*?"

He grinned, "Aye Jarl. If Wessex attacks Mercia then we can profit by selling iron to the Mercians. Who knows, we may make a profit from selling information."

"Be careful you do not get caught. I would not lose my spy."

"Do not worry Jarl we play a good part."

After they had gone I walked along the Water with Aiden. "Do I advise Thorfinn to attack sooner or later, Aiden?"

"I would send a message now, Jarl. You have the chance to rid us of all the warriors on Man. If Raibeart is right and they gather each new moon then that would be a good chance to get them all. They will drink and they will quarrel."

What he said made sense and I sent Snorri to Úlfarrston. Gunnar Thorfinnson had bought some swords from Bjorn and they were ready. When Siggi carried them Snorri could take my message. After he had gone I wrapped up and wandered Cyninges-tūn. The young warriors who had come with me were now men of substance, they were rich. The men who had daughters of an age to marry invited them to their homes in the hope that they would take an unmarried one from them. However when I walked among the halls and huts the young warriors sought me out. Their question was always the same, 'Will I be on your next raid, Jarl?'

I did not give answers. I would decide when the men from Ljoðhús let me know when they would raid. If they chose not to raid Man then I would. It was a risk but I had sworn an oath to myself and I would keep it.

I saw Hrolf with Rolf Horse Killer. There were just a few years between them and they were close. I saw that Hrolf had finally finished his wolf cloak. He was asking Rolf about the fastenings. I heard the end of the conversation. They were so engrossed in the examination of the cloak that they jumped when I spoke.

"If we had had the foresight, Hrolf, you could have saved some of the wolf's bones and carved them into two clasps for your cloak. However you still have coins do you not?"

"Aye Jarl. You gave me my share."

"Then if you are to be a warrior you should look like one. You may need to go to Bjorn Bagsecgson and pay one of his smiths to make one."

He looked at my cloak. He seemed to see the wolf clasps I had had made. "I would like those!"

"These are not cheap but a warrior never objects to such expense. And you will need a good sheath for your sword. You do not want it blunting."

His face fell. He had not thought of that.

Rolf said, "You need not pay someone for that, Hrolf. We can make one. You just need a sheepskin and some wood."

Hrolf grinned. I said, "Well what are you waiting for? I will not take a warrior raiding who does not have a scabbard."

They disappeared. Aiden had come along quietly and he said, "I thought you were not telling your warriors yet?"

"You of all people should know that Hrolf will leave us soon and he is part of this circle. If we raid then he must be with us."

"Aye, it is *wyrd*."

Snorri and Siggi returned far quicker than I would have hoped. Snorri wasted no time in giving me his news. "Jarl Thorfinn Blue Scar will be here within days. He and his warriors have spent the winter preparing for this. They were just waiting for news from us." I looked at Snorri with a question written on my face. "I know Jarl, why could they have not sent scouts out as we did to ascertain the defences?" He shrugged. "They come."

"How many drekar?"

"They bring three. One is a threttanessa. "

"You have done well. How went the trade?"

"Siggi has taken his payment. I sent Bjorn his share and yours is on the horses outside."

"Good. Tell my Ulfheonar we ride to Úlfarrston." I needed to tell the warriors whom I had decided I would take with me but I knew that I needed to speak with Brigid first. She was organising the new clothes the women in Kara's hall had made for the baby. She had had a chest made and she was laying them inside.

"I leave for a raid."

Her back was to me but I saw it stiffen. I could hear, in her voice, that she was fighting tears. "How long will you be away?"

"It could be seven days but it may be less."

She turned, having controlled herself. Kara had taught her how to breathe to calm herself. The smile was back. "You do not go alone?"

I held her close to me, "No, my wife, Thorfinn brings three drekar. I may have nothing to do. I might be able to stand back and watch others fight."

She pushed me away and laughed, "Thank you for the joke, husband. You have made me smile." She shook her head. "The one thing you will never do is to stand back and watch while others fight. You will be in the heart of the fight. That much I know."

The choice of crew was an easy one. Some I might have chosen were now in the Otherworld. Two were now settled into families and farms. It was the young ones I chose; the ones like Rolf Horse Killer, Cnut Cnutson and Einar the Reckless. I took Erik Wolf Claw for he led them well; although he had never become Ulfheonar he had all the qualities that a wolf warrior needed. I chose but thirty. We would have a crew of just forty for **'Heart of the Dragon'**. It would be enough. The voyage was short and four drekar would be more than enough. I did not need Aiden, or, at least, I hoped that I would not need Aiden. I needed no insight into the minds of men. We needed to teach the men of Man that they might raid others and they might attack the ships which plied their waters but they did not attack the ships of Jarl Dragonheart or his allies. Egbert and Hakon had learned that the hard way and now it was the turn of my nephew.

Haaken and I rode ponies while the rest of the crew marched. This would be Haaken's first fight since his injury. I would not insult him by mentioning it again but I did comment on his new helmet. "Bjorn has done a good job with the helmet. I like the face."

Bjorn had cast eyebrows and a realistic looking forehead on the metal piece which covered the eyes on the new helmet. It continued cunningly around to a pair of ear shaped pieces of metal. It protected the sides of Haaken's skull with extra metal.

"Aye I am pleased. It is not as heavy as you would think. If I were to criticise it then I would say it makes my head look slightly bigger than it used to."

I heard Olaf snort behind us, "You have always had a big head! I think Bjorn has made one the perfect size for you!"

My men laughed. It was a good start. They were in the mood to banter and that boded well. The insults continued to be traded all the way to Úlfarrston. There was no sign of Thorfinn but Erik had my drekar tied to the stone and wooden jetty. Each winter Coen ap Pasgen improved the port a little more. We now had tree stumps embedded into the jetty to facilitate our tying up. I saw Finni Foul-Fart as he waved away his knarr. He turned to me, "Another season to be making profits." He gestured towards my drekar. "And you too will be away soon I am guessing."

"Aye, time and tide, Finni, they wait for no man,."

Haaken took charge of the loading of the boat. The chests were placed where the men would row, that was now the job of Olaf Leather Neck. Food had to be stored below the deck as well as spare weapons and spears. I went to speak with Coen. As I neared the walls I saw that he had heeded my words before last year's harvest. He had a new stone tower. It was too high to be climbed using shields and I saw that eight men could man its top. It guarded the south east corner of his walls.

He strode to greet me and saw my gaze. "We will build a second at the southwest corner. My men feel safer fighting behind stone and they are good archers. When I spoke with Snorri he showed me the bow he had from the Saami. We would buy some."

"They are expensive and hard to obtain but I will send Siggi to their land when the ice around their coast has melted." The Saami lived so far away that the only time we could trade was when the sun burned over their land without setting; midsummer.

He nodded and led me to his hall. "You take no knarr?"

"Anything we take we bring back on my drekar. I do not expect this to reward us much. You brother told us that they had had a hard winter. If Thorfinn wishes slaves then he can take them. I would not have any from Man. They may be our enemies now but many of their fathers fought shoulder to shoulder with me and with Haaken."

"Your nephew rules there now." He made it sound like a question. I knew what he inferred.

"There is no blood which links us. My wife's brother betrayed me. His wife was a bitch and although I have not seen him since he was a child I remember Erik Eriksson as a cruel little bully. He used to tease and torture Wolf Killer before my son learned to bloody his nose. I am just surprised that the men of Man follow him."

"He is not a good leader. He knows not how to trade and he likes to live too well." He shrugged, "I have never met him but Raibeart is a good judge of character. He has traded many times with him."

We stayed the knight in Coen's hall and saw the masts of the three drekar as they sailed up the channel the following morning. We bade farewell, boarded our drekar and rowed out to meet them. We stopped within hailing distance of Jarl Thorfinn Blue Scar's drekar. He had put on a little weight since I had last seen him. He cupped his hands and shouted, "Hail, Jarl Dragonheart. Thank you for coming to the aid of my son and his crew. I owe you a life."

"He was sailing with me, you owe me nothing."

"Your warrior said that they were on the south of the island."

"Aye. We know the island well. We will sail around the north western coast and approach across the island. The defences are poor and you should be able to attack the front. We will surround them."

I saw him nod. "My youngest son, Eystein Thorfinnson captains the threttanessa. You would honour me by taking him with you. Gunnar learned much I would have my youngest learn the same lessons."

I did not, in truth, wish to take him but I could not refuse. "Aye, Jarl, tell him to follow me close. We attack at dawn!"

"We attack at dawn!"

Erik turned the steering board and we headed west. Olaf said, disparagingly, "We are tied to a baby again! When do we get to fight alongside warriors like us?"

Haaken looked at him and shook his head, "Because there are no warriors like us! Your whole head must be a plate! Every warrior we fight alongside learns from us!"

Olaf nodded, not upset in the least by the insult. "Aye you may be right. It is a burden laid upon us by the gods!"

We soon had to row. I stood at the stern and saw that Eystein Thorfinnson had heeded his father's orders and was a boat's length from us. When it became dark I would have to have Thorir Svensson keep a close watch upon him. It would not do to have a dragon's prow up our backside before we had even landed. I had already chosen our landing site. South of the Jarl Erik's old hall there was a small uninhabited bay with a sandy beach. It could accommodate two drekar. More importantly, Balley Chashtal lay just five miles from it and the land was flat. We could run it and be there quickly and unobserved. Had the bay been bigger then all four drekar could have used it. This would have to suffice.

Snorri left his oar and watched at the prow. He had grown up on the island and knew it well. Erik lowered the sail and we edged into the bay using oars only. The ship's boys leapt ashore and tethered us to the land. I waved the other drekar next to us. Eystein Thorfinnson came in gingerly. He did not wish to damage his drekar nor did he wish to make a fool of himself whilst I watched. I could understand.

I jumped into the chill waters with my shield around my back. Snorri had already sprinted, ahead with Beorn the Scout to make sure that no wandering shepherd had spotted us. I worked out that we would arrive either just before or just after dawn. I had suggested to Thorfinn that he arrive at the same time. A simultaneous attack was always demoralising for defenders. When everyone was ashore I waved my Ulfheonar, Erik Wolf Claw and Eystein Thorfinnson to my side.

"There is a rough road ahead; when we reach it then we move in a column of fours. It will be quicker that way."

Eystein said somewhat disparagingly, "This should be easy. Your spy said that they had had a bad winter and many had left. This will not be worthy of a great warrior like you Jarl Dragonheart."

I saw my men exchange glances. He was young and he lacked experience. He would learn. "Never take anything for granted, Eystein. Let us assume they have reinforced and built strong defences. If they have not then it may be easier than we expect."

We began to move up the narrow gully to the track which I knew lay ahead of us. Here there were no Roman Roads. The paths that were here were either made by Saxons or Prince Butar. That was how I knew them. Suddenly Snorri appeared. He held his hand up for silence. He waved me forward. I signed for Erik Wolf Claw to command and then I led the Ulfheonar to follow Snorri. He led me down a short path to a dell. There I saw Beorn the Scout with his hand against the throat of a Dane.

Snorri spoke quietly, "I smelled something and followed my nose. It seems this Dane had eaten something which disagreed with him."

"Have you questioned him yet?"

"No, Jarl, I waited for you."

"What in the name of the Allfather is a Dane doing out on this desolate hillside?"

"That is what we thought."

Olaf pulled out a long narrow skinning knife he favoured, "I could make him talk."

Shaking my head I said, "Let us just ask him questions first and skin him if that fails." I saw from the Dane's face, that he had understood us. I smiled, "Who are you?"

"I am Einar the Slow."

"I am Jarl Dragonheart."

"I know."

That worried me, how did he know, "You know me?"

"I have heard of you and I saw you in Dyflin."

I knew then where he had come from. "You followed Hakon the Bald?"

"Aye and I like not the whelp you have placed there."

"So you and other Danes came to Man." He nodded. "To raid and plunder."

He laughed, "No, to trap you." His laughter stopped as he realised what he had said.

"Then there are others already here. And you knew we were coming."

"I will say nothing more. You can have the lump with the knife skin me but I will tell you nothing more." He shook his head, "I may be Slow in the head but even I know that Jarl Dragonheart has honour and he will not skin a man." He placed his hand on the hilt of his sword. "You will give me the warrior's death for my tongue has said all that I will allow."

I nodded to Olaf who slit his throat. Finni asked, "We could have made him talk, Jarl Dragonheart."

"If we had time and we do not have that luxury. Many Danes and Vikings fled Dyflin. I wondered where they went. Now we know. They are here. I know not how but Jarl Erik Eriksson knows of our raid and he is expecting us. We must hurry or Thorfinn Blue Scar will be slaughtered. He expects less than eighty warriors. There may be many hundreds!" I stood. "Snorri and Beorn take the Ulfheonar and find this war band. I will fetch the rest."

When I reached Eystein and Erik Wolf Claw alone they stared at me, "This is a trap. There is a war band of Danes heading for Balley Chashtal. We must hurry or the men of Ljoðhús will be massacred." I led them along the track.

The ground over which we ran was low lying and it was hard to see, in the dark, great distances ahead. The Norns had been busy. We were in the dark, quite literally. If Jarl Eriksson knew of our plans he would not be as weak as Raibeart had made out. Was Raibeart a spy for others? Had I been too trusting? Those judgements would have to wait until I returned to Úlfarrston. My men moved with more urgency now. Eystein looked worried as he ran next to me. Ahead I could see dawn breaking in the east. It was just a thin line but that would grow. Our questions had delayed us. We would arrive later than I had planned. And then I heard a clamour from ahead. Was it my Ulfheonar and the war band or had Thorfinn attacked early?

The undulating land rose ahead of us and when I reached the top I saw Balley Chashtal. There were flames. Thorfinn had attacked. Haaken appeared next to me and pointed ahead. I could see nothing. "The war band has split into two. They are heading to surround the men attacking the walls." I knew he was guessing what the band would do but it made sense.

"They go to the left and the right?"

"Aye Jarl."

"Take Erik Wolf Claw and my men attack the band to the right." I turned to Eystein. "Today I lead your men. There is a war band of Danes attacking your father. Your men must obey all of my orders."

"Aye Jarl."

We ran. We soon caught up with Ulf, Finni and Snorri who awaited us. They talked as they ran with us. "The rest of the Ulfheonar are with the band to the right. The Danes are less than half a mile ahead. See you can see their banners against the rising sun."

"Ready your weapons and spread out in a single line. We make them think there are more of us than there are. Keep silent until I shout." I drew Ragnar's Spirit and, as I did so I noticed that Hrolf had not gone with Erik Wolf Claw but followed me. "You stay close to either my Ulfheonar or me!"

"Aye Jarl."

I could not make out the Danes. They had formed a wedge; it was a mass of darkened warriors. Did they have mail? Ahead of them the rising sun illuminated Thorfinn and his men as they attacked the walls. The wedge would strike them hard and they would be driven back to the sea. We were helped by the noise of the fray and by the fact that the Danes were running in a wedge. It made them slow and there was a lot of noise within the wedge. In every wedge the best warriors are at the front. The ones with the mail are at the front. I saw the kyrtles and leather belts; I saw the helmets; I saw the banners but I saw neither faces nor mail. The trap had been reversed.

"Ragnar's Spirit!"

We hurled ourselves at the twenty men who made up the rear rank. This was an enormous wedge. I concentrated on my first blow. Our shout had made them turn. It made some stumble. I brought Ragnar's Spirit high over my head and brought it down across the helmet and face of the Dane before me. His face split like a ripe plum. Ulf, Finni and Snorri were next to me and we made our own wedge. We drove deep into the mass of Danes. I slashed to the man on my right. He raised his arm to block me and my sword sliced through his arm and into his side. I punched the warrior to my left. He fell back and I swept my sword around to tear open his side.

The four of us had driven deep into the wedge of Danes and now the ones at the front realised their danger. I heard a Danish voice shout, "Shield wall!"

We were in trouble. I had three warriors and some wild and reckless young men. "We charge through!"

I heard my Ulfheonar shout, "Aye Jarl!"

Then I heard Hrolf shout, "And I am with you, Jarl!"

I did not want the young warrior to die but I was proud that he would follow us. If you are to charge then you do not hold back. You throw yourself into the fray as though you do not expect to survive. You hope that the warrior who faces you has a family and does not relish Valhalla! At least we had stopped the attack on Thorfinn's flank. We had not let down our ally. We were lucky in that enough men without mail stood between us and the mailed Danes who wielded axes and waited for us.

I roared a shout which I brought from deep within me. The sun had now risen and I knew that it shone on my face. They faced red eyed wolves and the Danes who looked at us felt fear. I stabbed at the surprised Dane who left a gap between shield and sword. I flung his body aside as I punched the next warrior with my shield. His spear clattered off my helmet and as he staggered I brought my sword around to hack into the back of his knee. We could not stop. It was our momentum which carried us deeper and deeper into the heart of our foes. A huge Danish war axed swung at me. It was a frightening weapon... if you had not faced one before. Wielded two handed it meant my opponent had no shield. He had mail but no shield. I angled my shield and leaned my shoulder into it. The axe head slid and scraped down my shield and his middle was an inviting target. I pushed hard with Ragnar's Spirit and tore through his mail and his byrnie. I twisted as it entered his body and then pulled it sideways. It opened a long gash and he tried to shove his guts back into his body as he fell.

We had penetrated far further than I could possibly have hoped. We were facing the warriors who had been at the point of the wedge and these were the best Danes in the war band. What gave me heart and the strength to fight on was the fact that these had fled when Gunnstein had taken charge. These had been defeated by me once already.

I opened my arms and invited a strike, "I am Jarl Dragonheart! I wield the sword which was touched by the gods! You are faithless men who did not die with your lord. When I slay you then you will not go to Valhalla! You will writhe in Hel!"

I chose the largest warrior I could see. His arms were tattooed and ringed with armbands. He had a two handed axe and a mail byrnie down to his knees. I just ran at him. My legs were almost without strength and I knew I had one more attack left in me. My charge took him by surprise. His swing was slow and it was just the haft of the axe which struck me on the shoulder. I pushed my sword hard. It did not strike his middle but I tore the mail down one side of his byrnie. More than that my charge knocked him from his feet. I could not keep my feet and I fell on top of him. I raised my head and butted him hard. His nose erupted and spread across his face. As I tried to rise the warrior to his right swung his axe. I was dead! I had no chance of protecting myself. Suddenly Eystein Thorfinn darted forward with his sword and took the warrior in the neck. I rose to my knees and using both hands plunged Ragnar's Spirit into his throat.

A warrior swung his sword at Eystein who was celebrating his victory. A blade I recognised darted out and Hrolf sent Heart of Ice into the warrior's side. These were their best three warriors and they had been felled. My three Ulfheonar slew the four around them and we were alone!

Eystein turned and shouted, "Men of Ljoðhús! Will you let a boy do what you should! Slaughter them!"

Their honour impugned the young warriors threw themselves into the fray. It was too much for a wedge which had been gutted like a fish; a wedge who had seen their best warriors slain and now faced the Wolf Warriors and the sword which was touched by the gods. They fled!

The sun had now risen and we could see that we were almost at the walls of Balley Chashtal. The men of Ljoðhús were relentless they chased and charged at the fleeing Danes. Soon there were just seven of us left. I turned to Eystein. "I thank you, Eystein Thorfinn. I owe you a life."

He shook his head, "You owe me nothing! I am embarrassed that we did not follow as closely as we should. If it were not for this young warrior then I too would have been slain." He clasped Hrolf's arm, "I would that you would follow me for I wish to go A-Viking!"

Hrolf looked at me and his bloody sword. I nodded, "This is the Norns, Hrolf, this is *wyrd*!"

"Aye Jarl." He turned to Eystein Thorfinn and said, "I will follow you until my destiny calls me."

That moment changed all of our lives but we knew it not then.

"Come we must hurry, your father needs us."

"But my men have gone! There are but seven of us!"

"Seven men can change the world!"

We ran towards the battle at the wall. As we neared I saw Thorfinn Blue Scar standing on top of two shields as he battled the defenders. An arrow came from nowhere and struck him in the shoulder. He fell to the ground and his oathsworn gathered around with their shields. I heard his son, Gunnar, shout, "Fall back!"

We had failed. The attack, which should have been an easy victory, had ended in failure.

Chapter 18

This was where I regretted not bringing Aiden. Thorfinn Blue Scar had no healer. His men tended to his wound but he was, effectively, out of the attack. We gathered out of bow range after his men had bandaged him.

"What happened?" There was accusation in his tone.

"We were betrayed."

The silence showed how stunned they all were. Gunnar asked, "How do you know?"

"When we landed we found one of the Danes and he told us. He said they knew we were coming. We were lucky. They did not expect us to divide our forces. Their plan was to trap us against the walls."

Eystein said, "Had not Jarl Dragonheart charged great numbers of Danes they would have succeeded."

I could see that Thorfinn was weak. Gunnar asked, "Where are the rest of your men?"

I waved a hand, "This was but half of the Danes. They chased them. I fear for them."

Thorfinn opened his eyes and smiled, "This is my fault. I believed we would come here and teach this pup a lesson."

"His father was cunning and he has learned. We were betrayed and that is hard to bear but we deal with that when we get home. There is a spy either in my land or yours. First we destroy these Manxmen."

Gunnar said, "But they have thrown us back and there are more of them than we thought."

"That matters not." I looked him in the eyes. "Are they better warriors?"

"No, of course not!"

"Then we will beat them. First we get back the warriors who have chased the enemy. We complete the circle around the town and we eat and rest. They are going nowhere. When it is almost dark Gunnar and I will speak with this jarl and we will frighten him."

"How?"

Eystein was merely curious. He was not questioning my judgement. I smiled, "I have no idea but give me some food and some drink and I will come up with a plan."

Our men returned to us in small groups. Haaken led my men from the other side of the town. They had fought a hard battle against the Danes. My Ulfheonar had not lost any men but they showed that they had fought hard. Many homes in Cyninges-tūn would mourn their warriors but the Danes there had been destroyed. When this was over we would have much treasure to take home. Eystein's men had suffered far more. They had chased and followed when they should not. Out of a crew of thirty but five returned. Many of the Danes fled and they would have to be hunted, like wild animals, when this was over but for the moment we needed to consolidate and begin to plan how we would win.

Thorfinn was looking a little healthier after food and ale, "I should have brought more men. I thought this number would be enough."

"We can still take this place."

"But we have lost so many men."

" Jarl Erik now has no more reinforcements. He has no way of being supplied." I pointed to the harbour where the solitary Manx drekar stood, "and he is surrounded. We will speak with him just before dark."

"Why then?"

I had worked out how best to deal with Jarl Erik Eriksson; I would use his mind and his fear of his uncle, Dragonheart and his Ulfheonar. "For, Jarl Thorfinn, I want him and his men to wait all night for my Ulfheonar to attack. We will not, we will sleep. There are more ways to win a battle than just battering them with a sword. We have a mind and we should use it."

I took my Ulfheonar to one side and explained what I wished of them. "You know what to do, we have done this before. Keep moving and stay in pairs. I have no doubt that my nephew will know this tactic but this was our island. It is part of us and we belong here. Now rest while you can."

I went back to the camp we had made. We had brought food with us and we ate well; better than those inside the settlement. Gunnar took charge for his father, whilst lucid, would not be able to move and to fight. Gunnar and his younger brother Eystein would be the leaders. The men of Ljoðhús made up the bulk of our force. They would be the ones who would bear the brunt of the attack.

I was woken in the middle of the afternoon as I had requested. I walked with Gunnar to inspect the walls. "How did your attack go when you and your father came this morning?"

"They were ready for us, Jarl Dragonheart. They knew we were coming. The walls were manned and the gates barred."

"Aye the spy in our lands told them all. I wonder now how long he has been operating."

"There is just one?"

"There may be more but even one is enough to cause us harm. When this is over your father and I needed to scour our halls and rid them of rats." As we walked I saw that we were closely watched from their ramparts. "They have been standing too all day?"

"I think so. We changed sentries regularly and they told us that the walls were always manned."

"Good. I want every mailed warrior we have with us at dusk and I want them to bang their shields as soon as we began to walk back from the talk. I want my nephew to think we are stronger than we are. Tonight we build fires all around their town. Have our men divided into groups of six. Each six keep a fire burning all night. Two watch and four sleep. We will be rested." I smiled, "Tell them not to fear the wolves. I will summon them."

I could see that he was curious but he did not push me on the matter. He had only seen Jarl Dragonheart and his men fight as Vikings. When darkness fell he would see a different beast. I sat with Hrolf who watched my camp for me. He had emerged from the fray with scratches only.

"There are many enemies in the town, Jarl. I have counted the ones on the wall. They outnumber us and they are safe behind wood and stone. We will lose many men when we attack."

"Let me work out how we are to defeat the men who cower behind their walls. If they outnumber us why do they not attack?" I pointed to his sword. "You will need to put a fresh edge on your sword. Find whetstone and you can do mine too."

"You sharpen them when you have used them?" If he had been brought up in a Viking home he would have know that but he had been a slave in Neustria.

"Aye, Hrolf. Each time it comes from its scabbard and strikes something then it becomes a little duller. Your blade must be sharp enough to shave with every time you draw it. Erik Wolf Claw will have a stone. After this is over you should get your own." The sharpening of the blade kept his young mind occupied and stopped him worrying about what would happen later.

I returned the stone to Erik Wolf Claw. I had a task for him. He went, with a dozen men, to the harbour and the Manx drekar.

After I had rested I took Gunnar and Eystein down to the drekar and the waterfront. Erik Wolf Claw and my men had worked hard. They had cut the mast of the Manx drekar and the spare one into two. They had used the yard and spare yard to make carrying handles and then tied the improvised battering ram with ropes from the Manx drekar.

"Tomorrow morning, at dawn, when the sun peers from the east my men will take the ram to assault the gate. Gunnar, your mailed warriors will protect them with their shields. Eystein, you have few men left, you must use them as archers to stop the warriors of Balley Chashtal from attacking the ram."

They looked at me, "Where will you be, Jarl Dragonheart?"

"I will be the wolf warrior as will my men. Fear not, Ragnar's Spirit will be there when we breach this gate."

I did not don my red cochineal nor did I wear my helmet as dusk approached. My Ulfheonar had long since slipped away. No one had even seen them go. That was their skill. Eystein led the mailed warriors. There were forty of them. The rest were massed behind us. We made them into a solid block. It would disguise our paucity of numbers. It would not be a good way to attack but I did not intend that.

"Hrolf, stay with Eystein. The Norns have tied your threads together." He nodded and stood beside the young warrior. Gunnar and I had our shields behind our backs and our palms held before us as we walked towards the gates. We stopped beyond the range of their arrows.

"I would speak with my nephew, Jarl Erik Eriksson."

He must have been close by for a mailed warrior suddenly appeared. He looked like his father. His voice barely carried. "What do you want?"

"To speak."

"I cannot hear you; come closer."

I had a powerful voice, I always had had. My nephew's, by contrast, was weak and thin. When I spoke my voice carried to all of the warriors on the wall. "I do not trust you! If you swear, before all of your men that you will not break this truce we will advance and make the talk easier for you"

I could not see his face but I guessed that I had angered him by impugning his honour. His voice was a little louder as he spoke, "I swear you may talk and then retire. We will not harm you....yet!"

I began to walk. Gunnar said, "Do you trust him?"

"Not really but I trust the Norns. I cannot see them bringing us here to be killed by arrows. You may stay here. This needs just me anyway."

He chuckled, "No, Jarl Dragonheart. Let us cast the bones eh?" Each day he grew into a stronger leader.

As we approached I saw that few of the ones on the walls wore mail. The exception was my nephew and his oathsworn. He had grown into a powerfully built warrior. He had his helmet in his hand and I saw that he could have been his father's double. He also looked a little like my wife Erika. What would she have thought of this?

"What do you want, Jarl Dragonheart? Do you wish to surrender?" He laughed.

I waved a hand at his walls. I spoke loudly enough for everyone to hear. "I wonder why you hide behind your walls. Do you fear your uncle? You have more men than we do. We have killed your Danes but they have taken their toll of us. Why do you not attack? Are you afraid?" I had used the two words afraid and fear deliberately. I had no doubt that his warriors would begin to wonder. That wonder might turn to anxiety and doubt.

"You have invaded my land without provocation!"

Gunnar could not contain himself, "Without provocation? You attacked us when we closed with your coast. Is that not provocation?"

He said nothing. It mattered little what he said. I was merely buying time and worrying him. "We will leave if you pay us wergeld for the men you slew and if you swear not to attack either the men of Ljoðhús or the men of Cyninges-tūn." I saw Gunnar flash a look of disbelief at me. I gave a slight shake of the head. I knew he would not agree to this.

Jarl Erik laughed. "You grow senile, Dragonheart! Leave now for if I want a clown to amuse me I have my own within these walls."

"Think carefully, Erik. You are of my wife's blood which is why I give you this courtesy. You have one chance to walk from this alive. Take it and save the lives of your warriors." I could smell smoke. Erik Wolf Claw had done as I asked. Without turning I said, "Your last drekar is being burned. I lived on this island. Where will you get the wood for new ones? Where will you and your men get the materials to build a drekar?"

I could see the anger on his face. "Leave now. This is over. You say this was your land. Your body shall be sent to the four corners when I have done with you!"

"So be it!"

I turned and walked back to our men. The sun was setting in the west while in the harbour the last Manx drekar burned on the sand where my men had beached her. The warriors all began banging their shields in time. We walked back at the pace of their banging. By the time we reached them the sun was just setting in the west and we were silhouetted by the fire. It was the effect I had wanted. I wanted them to see me walk away into the firelight.

When we reached our men they all cheered and roared. I turned to Gunnar and Eystein and said, "You know what to do. Have the men disperse and begin the fires. Let my nephew begin to worry."

I went to my camp where Hrolf awaited me. He felt honoured to be helping me. I laid my shield down; I would not need that. I took off my wolf cloak. He helped me to paint the cochineal on my face. Then he tried to string my bow. He could not. I saw him looking embarrassed. "When you are a fully grown man and your forearms are like the branches of an oak then you will string a bow with ease." I strung it and handed it to him to hold for me. I slung the quiver over my shoulder and then donned my cloak. I needed to be as dark as the night. I put his shoulders between my arms. "You know what to do?"

He had blackened his face with charcoal and donned his cloak, "Aye Jarl. I go to the walls and I frighten the Manxmen."

"And?"

"And I do not close with the walls nor I do put my life in danger."

"Good. This will be good experience for you. I want you to live to have that experience and use it when you are a jarl like me."

It was now black night and the fires were springing up all around the walls of Balley Chashtal. The drekar had burned out but smoke still drifted across to remind Erik that he was trapped. Picking up the heavy sack I had prepared earlier I headed to the gate. I knew that my Ulfheonar would be at the rear gate. If there were an attempt to escape or send for help then that would be where they would try. The attack earlier on had cleared the few traps which the Manxmen had laid. I crept, like a shadow towards the gate. After dropping my sack I knocked an arrow and lined up on the warrior who peered out to sea. He was less than thirty paces from me. I waited. Suddenly, to my left, about a hundred paces away I heard the howl of a wolf. Hrolf had done as I asked. The sentry leaned forward to see and I released my arrow. I knocked another and as a second sentry looked in my direction I sent an arrow into his face. The two sentries fell. I then ran to my right.

I heard the commotion inside the town. I even heard someone shout, "To arms! They attack!"

I knocked another arrow and loosed it at another warrior who was foolish enough to show his face. I dived into the ditch as arrows down, blindly on the place I had stood. Then I heard the sound of cries and howls from the northern gate. My Ulfheonar attacked. Hrolf did as I had bid. He moved his position and howled again. I heard the men above me shouting orders. I took the opportunity to shift my position. I moved to the other side of the ditch, closer to our fires and howled. I was moving almost before I had finished and I returned to the main gate.

I was picturing the inside of the town. They had seen nothing. They had heard a circle of wolves around their town. Were we shape shifters? The arrows which had fallen into dead ground told me that they were loosing blindly. None had come close to hitting me. We had them rattled. We had to keep up the nervous tension and terror which would be racing like the plague in the town.

All went quiet as they sought us in the dark. I found the sack I had dropped and I took out two of the Danish heads. Rolf Horse Killer had fetched them for me from the battle field. There were eight of them. I laid down my bow and picking one up by the hair I hurled it over the walls. I did the same with the second. Then I picked up my sack and bow and ran to the south western corner of the town. I had not been there yet. I heard the cries and commotion as they found the heads. When I reached the corner I saw a tower. Four sentries stood there. I jammed an arrow in the soft earth, put a second in my teeth and knocked a third. Time was I could have released four arrows in a heartbeat. Now I would be lucky to send three. I loosed one and knocked a second before the first had hit the sentry in the head. My second caught his fellow and when I sent my third it struck a warrior in the shoulder. I took another head and hurled it over the wall, howling as I did so. Hrolf took up the howl further down the wall. I had not seen him and that was good. He was obeying my orders.

I picked up the sack, much lighter now and moved all the way along the wall to the south eastern tower. Stones and arrows were being wasted on an attack which never materialised. They were loosing them blind. There was no way for them to replenish their supplies.

I waited in the dark. I could hear howls from the northern side and occasional cries as my Ulfheonar struck sentries. I waited while Hrolf continued to move and to howl. Once I heard him less than thirty paces from me but I could not see him. The gods had given us the blackest of nights. I took a head from the sack and my bow and closed with the tower. They were wary now. I stood in the ditch and I threw the head to land on the walkway above me. It landed with a thud.

"What was that?"

"Go and check it Sven. We will have an arrow ready in case one of these shape shifters has climbed up."

I had my arrow already aimed as Sven found the head and peered over the palisade. My arrow hit him in the face and threw him backwards. I howled and I ran. This time they were luckier. I felt an arrow ping off my helmet. I picked up my sack and I moved out of arrow range. Hrolf's howls and those of my Ulfheonar occupied them for some time. I got my breath back. I had a swig from my water skin. I estimated that we were halfway through the night. I hoped that our men had taken advantage of our distraction to sleep. We needed them alert and the Manxmen in a state of tired confusion.

I had four heads left. I moved towards the gate, the place I had first attacked. There were two small towers and I guessed that there would be up to ten men there. I crept as close to the gate as I could get. Hrolf's howls distracted them enough to allow me to do so. Then I hurled two heads as far as I could throw them and, finally my last two heads to land on the gate. My bow had an arrow knocked and when a head appeared I loosed one. It struck him. I had a second ready for the second man and he died.

A voice from above me, to the right shouted, "There is just one of him! Let us rid ourselves of this Ulfheonar!"

I moved across the ditch and waited. I had an arrow in my teeth and another held with the bow. The gate opened and my arrow struck the first warrior in the shoulder as they came to get me. The gates opened wider and six men raced towards me. I sent my next arrow into the neck of one and my last into the chest of a second. I dropped my bow and taking out my seax and sword I howled. Instead of fleeing I ran at them.

I ducked beneath the spear and gutted one with my seax as a second ran into my sword.

"I am Jarl Dragonheart! I wield the sword which was touched by the gods! You are dead men you just do not know it yet!"

The last two turned and ran back into the safety of the town. I hacked a head from one of the bodies and threw it over the closing gate. Then I turned my back and headed into the dark. I had four arrows left and I spent the rest of the night howling like Hrolf and loosing my arrows when a target appeared.

I saw false dawn and headed back to our camp fires, still burning brightly. I caught up with Hrolf who was moving to a new position. "You have done well, Hrolf. There are many warriors who will survive this day and they will owe that to you."

"But I killed no one! I howled!"

"And you terrified them."

I saw that Eystein and Gunnar had the men ready to assault. Gunnar was grinning. "You terrified me and I knew what you were about."

Eystein said, "Were you not afraid when they came from the gate for you?"

"I have a name which strikes fear into men. They came out to kill one man; when they found out my identity they became afraid. Never fear another man, Eystein. If you do then you have lost the combat. Always believe that you can win."

I saw Thorfinn limping towards us. "I cannot fight but I can watch!" He chuckled, "I would not have believed that ten men and a boy could cause so much terror. I have much to learn from you Jarl Dragonheart."

"It is time, Gunnar!"

Hrolf brought me my shield and took my bow. The assault party gathered and began to move, like a metal snake, towards the gates. Eystein led his handful of men with their bows to follow his brother. I raised my sword and the rest of the warriors moved forward. There were not many of us but we were rested and we were in good spirits.

I heard the alarm from inside Balley Chashtal. The wall filled with men. This time Gunnar and the men he led would have to endure the full force of the defenders. Eystein and his men darted like insects to release their arrows and then move to a new position. Men fell from the walls. The shields which protected the ram did their job but when they drew close then the stones and spears thrown from above would begin to take their toll. I heard Gunnar shout a command and they ran the last twenty paces. I saw two men fall but, by that time, the ram had the speed and the momentum. It smashed into the gate and I could hear, from fifty paces away the creak and crack. When it had opened in the night I knew they had not nailed it shut. It was not like the one we had attacked in Frankia. Erik Wolf Claw and my men pulled the ram back and ran again. Another two warriors fell but this time there was an audible crack when the ram struck the gates.

The next time it would break. I raised my sword, "Charge!"

Even as we ran to the rear of the ram the gate was cracked wide open and the metal snake burst into the settlement. The warriors dropped the ram and raced in. They had lost warriors in the attack and now they would wreak their vengeance!

Gunnar quickly organised his men so that the mailed warriors were at the fore. As I passed through the gate I saw that Jarl Erik had organised a shield wall. Gunnar placed himself at the front of the wedge and they moved forward. I saw Rolf Horse Killer with his axe. "Come with me and you two as well." Sven Finehair and Einar Bluetooth were with him and they too had axes.

I did not run towards the shield wall but up a path between huts. Two warriors raced towards us, having descended from the walls. I contemptuously fended off the blow from the spear with my shield and ran him through with my sword. The other fared no better. Rolf smashed his skull in two with a single blow. I turned left and headed along the wall to the northern gate. There were eight men bracing themselves against it. I could hear my Ulfheonar as they tried to break in. Snorri and Beorn were using their bows for a warrior fell from the ramparts with an arrow in his chest.

Two of them had their backs to the gate and they faced us. I saw terror as they beheld the four of us. We did not stop and I needed to issue no orders. I slashed my sword across the top of the thighs of the warrior who faced me. Three others had their heads staved in by three long war axes. I smashed my shield into the face of another. They had stopped holding the gate to face us. I took a blow from one sword on my shield and blocked a second with my sword. Then the gates sprang open. Olaf Leather Neck stood there, his face infused and red. He was almost a berserker. Even as I watched he bit the edge of his shield. He was now lost to us. I stood aside and he ran towards the sounds of combat close to the hall of Jarl Erik.

I pointed to the gate. "Rolf Horse Killer, you and the others guard this gate. No one leaves but I say so."

"Aye Jarl!"

"Ulfheonar, let us end this!"

With drawn weapons we headed for the warriors gathered around my nephew. Everyone knew that there would be no prisoners. This was a fight to the death. The shield wall had disintegrated, on both sides, and it was a free for all with warriors fighting each other or in groups of friends. Olaf Leather Neck did go berserk. It was a frightening sight. I yelled, "Out of Olaf's way he does not know friend from enemy!"

He tore into the mailed oathsworn of Jarl Erik. We hurried after our brother. He would not stop until either they were dead or he was. His sword smashed into the mail of two warriors laying their sides open to the bone. He seemed oblivious to wounds. Haaken, Ulf, Finni and I ran to protect his back. I saw that my nephew had surrounded himself by the last of his warriors. It was foolish; it would mean he was the last to die, that was all. Olaf made for him. His sword, blunted now, broke the thigh bone of a warrior. He began to smash the man's skull with the edge of his shield. His berserk rage ended when a war hammer caught him on the side of his helmet and he fell unconscious. Haaken leapt across his body and made himself a human spear as he threw himself at the hammer wielding warrior. He impaled hum with his sword.

Snorri and Beorn threw themselves across Olaf's body and the rest of us carried on Olaf's charge towards my nephew and the eight oathsworn who remained. He should have fought but I think he was terrified. He stood as my red eyed wolf warriors hacked, slashed and chopped in cold anger. Jarl Erik's oathsworn were brave but they were rusty. It had been many years since they had fought. Their arms tired and their reactions were slow. My men were at the peak of their powers and keen to avenge Olaf. It was a one sided fight.

As his oathsworn fell I made for my nephew. He threw down his sword, "Spare me uncle! For the sake of your wife, my father's sister!"

Until he opened his mouth I might have spared him but it was a cowardly comment. His father had tried to kill my wife and my children. He had allowed good men to die for him and now he pleaded for his life. He was not worthy to live.

All else had fallen and there was just the sound of the dying being sent to Valhalla. A circle formed around us. I threw my shield down. "Pick up your sword and fight me. If you do not I will kill you and you will not go to Valhalla."

"I beg you to spare my life. I will tell you who the traitor is in Cyninges-tūn!"

That made it even worse. Haaken shouted, "Let us use Olaf's skinning knife. He will tell us when the skin is peeled from his face!"

It was then that Erik realised his words and offers were futile. He was going to die. He picked up his sword and lunged at me in one movement. I barely managed to deflect his strike and it gave him heart. He tried to punch me with his shield as he drew his sword back. I spun around and his shield hit air. I continued my turn and brought Ragnar's Spirit into the back of Erik Eriksson, Jarl of Balley Chashtal and the last child of a faithless warrior. The blow cut through his mail and his backbone. He died quickly as his spine was severed and he crumpled to his death.

Every warrior cheered but I was too concerned with Olaf for the cheers and approbation of my men. Snorri grinned as he shook his head, "I know not how, Jarl, but he lives. He breathes and shows signs of waking. He must have a harder head than Haaken!"

Haaken smiled. "And if he lives then I am happy."

We were all too tired to celebrate. We spent the rest of the day burning the bodies of our enemies and building a barrow for our own. We slept in Balley Chashtal and ate the few supplies they had. The women, it seems, had been sent away some days earlier.

We discovered this from the one wounded warrior whose life we spared. Bjorn Bloodaxe had been a boy when I had lived on the island and when we discovered him I was sick of the killing. He told us all. "We have known what you were up to for some time. A ship would land secretly and Jarl Erik would discover where you were sailing. He planned to attack your ships each time they returned laden. A week ago he told us to prepare for an attack in the early hours of the morning. He had the Danes prepare to come to our aid. He had the time confirmed just two days ago and sent for the Danes to ambush you. I told him he would not fool Jarl Dragonheart but he would not listen."

"Do you know who the spy is?"

He shook his head, "I was not important enough to be told."

"And the ship he sailed?"

"Only Jarl Erik met the captain. I am sorry Jarl."

"What will you do now Bjorn Bloodaxe? Would you come with us to my home?"

He shook his head. "I have a family here now. They went to Hrams-a for safety. I will return there. I was happy there when I grew up. I will farm."

As he limped off I said, "May the Allfather be with you."

I was glad that I had saved at least one. As we prepared to leave Hrolf came to me, "Jarl Dragonheart I would beg to leave your service."

"You were never bound to me but I will miss you." I waved a hand around my men, "We will all miss you."

"And I will miss you but you have taught me that destiny is important. Eystein Thorfinnson has offered me a bench on his drekar and he intends to go a-Viking. He would be like Jarl Dragonheart."

"Then I wish you well. The sword I gave you shall be a reminder that you will always be welcome in my home." I clasped his arm, "May the Allfather be with you."

My men all took their leave of him and I saw that he was so filled with emotion that he could barely speak. He had been in our lives but a short time and yet he had made a great impression. The Weird Sisters had other plans for him. We headed across the island to Erik and our ship. We were going home. We had wrought our vengeance and our enemies were punished.

Epilogue

As we headed across the seas to Úlfarrston we used just the wind. There were many empty benches. Only twenty warriors returned from Man. There was no hurry and we would get home when the wind allowed. I sat at the stern with my Ulfheonar. Haaken shook his head, "I shall miss Hrolf, Jarl. He was courageous and he never complained."

"Our threads are still bound. There will come a time when we cross paths again. I feel it. Perhaps when we get home Aiden can explain it."

Haaken pointed to Olaf who lay sleeping, bathed in bandages. "He will need to examine Olaf. How he is not dead I do not know."

"Aye and we have a more difficult problem of our own."

"What is that Jarl?"

We must discover the viper in our nest. We must seek out the traitor and find the enemy who spies." I shook my head. "Putting a plate in a head will be child's play compared with uncovering this."

I could see that they had not thought through Bjorn Bloodaxe's words. "Perhaps he was wrong Jarl."

"No Ulf. Many things which have gone awry are now explained. Somewhere in our land there is an enemy. We have to unmask the Viking Traitor. I will not sleep easy until we have done so.

The End

Glossary

Afon Hafron- River Severn in Welsh
Alpín mac Echdach – the father of Kenneth MacAlpin, reputedly the first king of the Scots
Alt Clut- Dumbarton Castle on the Clyde
Balley Chashtal -Castleton (Isle of Man)
Bardanes Tourkos- Rebel Byzantine General
Bebbanburgh- Bamburgh Castle, Northumbria Also know as Din Guardi in the ancient tongue
Beck- a stream
Blót – a blood sacrifice made by a jarl
Blue Sea- The Mediterranean
Bondi- Viking farmers who fight
Bourde- Bordeaux
Bjarnarøy –Great Bernera (Bear island)
Byrnie- a mail or leather shirt reaching down to the knees
Caerlleon- Welsh for Chester
Caestir - Chester (old English)
Casnewydd –Newport, Wales
Cephas- Greek for Simon Peter (St. Peter)
Chape- the tip of a scabbard
Charlemagne- Holy Roman Emperor at the end of the 8th and beginning of the 9th centuries
Celchyth- Chelsea
Cherestanc- Garstang (Lancashire)
Corn Walum or Om Walum- Cornwall
Cymri- Welsh
Cymru- Wales
Cyninges-tūn – Coniston. It means the estate of the king (Cumbria)
Dùn Èideann –Edinburgh (Gaelic)
Din Guardi- Bamburgh castle
Drekar- a Dragon ship (a Viking warship)
Duboglassio –Douglas, Isle of Man
Dyrøy –Jura (Inner Hebrides)
Dyflin- Old Norse for Dublin
Ein-mánuðr- middle of March to the middle of April
Eoforwic- Saxon for York
Faro Bregancio- Corunna (Spain)
Ferneberga -Farnborough (Hampshire)
Fey- having second sight
Firkin- a barrel containing eight gallons (usually beer)
Fret-a sea mist
Frankia- France and part of Germany

Fyrd-the Saxon levy
Garth- Dragon Heart
Gaill- Irish for foreigners
Galdramenn- wizard
Glaesum –amber
Gleawecastre- Gloucester
Gói- the end of February to the middle of March
Grenewic- Greenwich
Hamwic -Southampton
Haughs- small hills in Norse (As in Tarn Hows)
Heels- when a ship leans to one side under the pressure of the wind
Hel - Queen of Niflheim, the Norse underworld.
Here Wic- Harwich
Hetaereiarch – Byzantine general
Hí- Iona (Gaelic)
Hjáp - Shap- Cumbria (Norse for stone circle)
Hoggs or Hogging- when the pressure of the wind causes the stern or the bow to droop
Hrams-a – Ramsey, Isle of Man
Hywel ap Rhodri Molwynog- King of Gwynedd 814-825
Icaunis- British river god
Itouna- River Eden Cumbria
Jarl- Norse earl or lord
Joro-goddess of the earth
kjerringa - Old Woman- the solid block in which the mast rested
Knarr- a merchant ship or a coastal vessel
Kyrtle-woven top
Leathes Water- Thirlmere
Ljoðhús- Lewis
Legacaestir- Anglo Saxon for Chester
Lochlannach – Irish for Northerners (Vikings)
Lothuwistoft- Lowestoft
Louis the Pious- King of the Franks and son of Charlemagne
Lundenwic - London
Maeresea- River Mersey
Mammceaster- Manchester
Manau/Mann – The Isle of Man(n) (Saxon)
Marcia Hispanic- Spanish Marches (the land around Barcelona)
Mast fish- two large racks on a ship for the mast
Melita- Malta
Midden- a place where they dumped human waste
Miklagård - Constantinople
Nikephoros- Emperor of Byzantium 802-811
Njoror- God of the sea
Nithing- A man without honour (Saxon)

Odin - The "All Father" God of war, also associated with wisdom, poetry, and magic (The Portesmūða -Portsmouth Ruler of the gods).
Olissipo- Lisbon
Orkneyjar-Orkney
Penrhudd – Penrith Cumbria
Pillars of Hercules- Straits of Gibraltar
Ran- Goddess of the sea
Roof rock- slate
Rinaz –The Rhine
Sabrina- Latin and Celtic for the River Severn. Also the name of a female Celtic deity
Saami- the people who live in what is now Northern Norway/Sweden
St. Cybi- Holyhead
Syllingar Insula- Scilly Isles
Scree- loose rocks in a glacial valley
Seax – short sword
Sheerstrake- the uppermost strake in the hull
Sheet- a rope fastened to the lower corner of a sail
Shroud- a rope from the masthead to the hull amidships
Skeggox – an axe with a shorter beard on one side of the blade
South Folk- Suffolk
Stad- Norse settlement
Stays- ropes running from the mast-head to the bow
Strake- the wood on the side of a drekar
Suthriganaworc - Southwark (London)
Syllingar- Scilly Isles
Tarn- small lake (Norse)
Temese- River Thames (also called the Tamese)
The Norns- The three sisters who weave webs of intrigue for men
Thing-Norse for a parliament or a debate (Tynwald)
Thor's day- Thursday
Threttanessa- a drekar with 13 oars on each side.
Thrall- slave
Tinea- Tyne
Trenail- a round wooden peg used to secure strakes
Tynwald- the Parliament on the Isle of Man
Úlfarrberg- Helvellyn
Úlfarrland- Cumbria
Úlfarr- Wolf Warrior
Úlfarrston- Ulverston
Ullr-Norse God of Hunting
Ulfheonar-an elite Norse warrior who wore a wolf skin over his armour
Vectis- The Isle of Wight
Volva- a witch or healing woman in Norse culture

Waeclinga Straet- Watling Street (A5) Windlesore-Windsor
Waite- a Viking word for farm
Werham -Wareham (Dorset)
Wintan-ceastre -Winchester
Withy- the mechanism connecting the steering board to the ship
Woden's day- Wednesday
Wulfhere-Old English for Wolf Army
Wyddfa-Snowdon
Wyrd- Fate
Yard- a timber from which the sail is suspended
Ynys Môn-Anglesey

Historical note

The Viking raids began, according to records left by the monks, in the 790s when Lindisfarne was pillaged. However there were many small settlements along the east coast and most were undefended. I have chosen a fictitious village on the Tees as the home of Garth who is enslaved and then, when he gains his freedom, becomes Dragon Heart. As buildings were all made of wood then any evidence of their existence would have rotted long ago, save for a few post holes. The Norse began to raid well before 790. There was a rise in the populations of Norway and Denmark and Britain was not well prepared for defence against such random attacks.

My raiders represent the Norse warriors who wanted the plunder of the soft Saxon kingdom. There is a myth that the Vikings raided in large numbers but this is not so. It was only in the tenth and eleventh centuries that the numbers grew. They also did not have allegiances to kings. The Norse settlements were often isolated family groups. The term Viking was not used in what we now term the Viking Age beyond the lands of Norway and Denmark. Warriors went a-Viking which meant that they sailed for adventure or pirating. Their lives were hard. Slavery was commonplace. The Norse for slave is thrall and I have used both terms.

The ship, '**The Heart of the Dragon**' is based on the Gokstad ship which was found in 1880 in Norway. It is 23.24 metres long and 5.25 metres wide at its widest point. It was made entirely of oak except for the pine decking. There are 16 strakes on each side and from the base to the gunwale is 2.02 metres giving it a high freeboard. The keel is cut from a piece of oak 17.6 metres long. There are 19 ribs. The pine mast was 13 metres high. The ship could carry 70 men although there were just sixteen oars on each side. This meant that half the crew could rest while the other half rowed. Sea battles could be brutal.

The Vikings raided far and wide. They raided and subsequently conquered much of Western France and made serious inroads into Spain. They even travelled up the Rhone River as well as raiding North Africa. The sailors and warriors we call Vikings were very adaptable and could, indeed, carry their long ships over hills to travel from one river to the next. The Viking ships are quite remarkable. Replicas of the smaller ones have managed speeds of 8-10 knots. The sea going ferries, which ply the Bay of Biscay, travel at 14-16 knots. The journey the 'Heart of the Dragon' makes from Santander to the Isles of Scilly in a day and a half would have been possible with the oars and a favourable wind and, of course, the cooperation of the Goddess of the sea, Ran! The journey from the Rhine to Istanbul is 1188 nautical miles. If the 'Heart of the Dragon' had had favourable winds and travelled nonstop she might have made the journey in 6 days! Sailing during the day only and with some adverse winds means that 18 or 20 days would be more realistic.

Seguin I Lupo was Duke of Vasconia and he briefly rebelled against the Holy Roman Emperor. This was around the time my novel was set. After a few years he was deposed, killed and the Dukedom absorbed back into the Empire. The wine trade at his capital, Bourde (Bordeaux) had been established by the Romans and would continue to draw trade to this region. The Asturias Kingdom was expanding west at this time too and gradually absorbed Galicia.

Nikephoros was Emperor from 802-811. Bardanes Tourkos did revolt although he did not attempt a coup in the palace as I used in my book. He was later defeated, blinded, and sent to a monastery. Nikephoros did well until he went to war with Krum, the Khan of Bulgaria. He died in battle and Krum made a drinking vessel from his skull!

I have recently used the British Museum book and research about the Vikings. Apparently, rather like punks and Goths, the men did wear eye makeup. It would make them appear more frightening. There is also evidence that they filed their teeth. The leaders of warriors built up a large retinue by paying them and giving them gifts such as the wolf pendant. This was seen as a sort of bond between leader and warrior. It also marked them out in battle as oathsworn. There was no national identity. They operated in small bands of free booters loyal to their leader. The idea of sword killing was to render a weapon unusable by anyone else. On a simplistic level this could just be a bend but I have seen examples which are tightly curled like a spring. Viking kings were rare it was not until the end of the ninth century that national identity began to emerge.

The length of the swords in this period was not the same as in the later medieval period. By the year 850 they were only 76 cm long and in the eighth century they were shorter still. The first sword Dragon Heart used, Ragnar's, was a new design, and was 75 cm long. This would only have been slightly longer than a Roman gladius. At this time the sword, not the axe was the main weapon. The best swords came from Frankia, and were probably German in origin. A sword was considered a special weapon and a good one would be handed from father to son. A warrior with a famous blade would be sought out on the battlefield. There was little mail around at the time and warriors learned to be agile to avoid being struck. A skeggox was an axe with a shorter edge on one side. The use of an aventail (a chain mail extension of a helmet) began at about this time. The highly decorated scabbard also began at this time.

A wedge was formed by having a warrior at the front and then two and so on. Sometimes it would have a double point, boar's snout. A wedge with twenty men at the rear might have over a hundred and fifty men. It would be hard to stop. The blood eagle was performed by cutting the skin of the victim by the spine, breaking the ribs so they resembled blood-stained wings, and pulling the lungs out through the wounds in the victim's back.

I have used the word saga, even though it is generally only used for Icelandic stories. It is just to make it easier for my readers. If you are an Icelandic expert then I apologise. I have plenty of foreign words which, I know, taxes some of my readers. As I keep saying it is about the characters and the stories.

It was more dangerous to drink the water in those times and so most people, including children drank beer or ale. The process killed the bacteria which could hurt them. It might sound as though they were on a permanent pub crawl but in reality they were drinking the healthiest drink that was available to them. Honey was used as an antiseptic in both ancient and modern times. Yarrow was a widely used herb. It had a variety of uses in ancient times. It was frequently mixed with other herbs as well as being used with honey to treat wounds. Its Latin name is Achillea millefolium. Achilles was reported to have carried the herb with him in battle to treat wounds. Its traditional names include arrowroot, bad man's plaything, bloodwort, carpenter's weed, death flower, devil's nettle, eerie, field hops, gearwe, hundred leaved grass, knight's milefoil, knyghten, milefolium, milfoil, millefoil, noble yarrow, nosebleed, old man's mustard, old man's pepper, sanguinary, seven year's love, snake's grass, soldier, soldier's woundwort, stanchweed, thousand seal, woundwort, yarroway, yew. I suspect Tolkien used it in the Lord of the Rings books as Kingsfoil, another ubiquitous and often overlooked herb in Middle Earth.

    The Vikings were not sentimental about their children. A son would expect nothing from his father once he became a man. He had more chance of reward from his jarl than his father. Leaders gave gifts to their followers. It was expected. Therefore the more successful you were as a leader the more loyal followers you might have.

    The word lake is a French/Norman word. The Norse called lakes either waters or meres. They sometimes used the old English term, tarn. The Irish and the Scots call them Lough/lochs. There is only one actual lake in the Lake District. All the rest are waters, meres, or tarns.

    The Bangor I refer to (there were many) was called Bangor is-y-coed by the Welsh but I assumed that the Vikings would just use the first part of the place name. From the seventeenth century the place was known as Bangor of the Monks (Bangor Monachorum). Dolgellau was mined for gold by people as far back as the Romans and deposits have been discovered as late as the twenty first century. Having found gold in a stream at Mungrisedale in the Lake District I know how exciting it is to see the golden flecks in the black sand. The siege of the fort is not in itself remarkable. When Harlech was besieged in the middle ages two knights and fifteen men at arms held off a large army.

    Anglesey was considered the bread basket of Wales even as far back as the Roman Invasion; the combination of the Gulf Stream and the soil meant that it could provide grain for many people. In the eighth to tenth centuries, grain was more valuable than gold. The Viking raids began in the early ninth century and plagued the inhabitants thereafter.

    When writing about the raids I have tried to recreate those early days of the Viking raider. The Saxons had driven the native inhabitants to the extremes of Wales, Cornwall, and Scotland. The Irish were always too busy fighting amongst themselves. It must have come as a real shock to be attacked in their own settlements. By the time of King Alfred almost sixty years later they were better prepared. This was also about the time that Saxon England converted completely to Christianity. The last place to do so was the Isle of Wight. There is no reason to believe that the Vikings would have had any sympathy for their religion and would, in fact, have taken advantage of their ceremonies and rituals not to mention their riches.

There was a warrior called Ragnar Hairy-Breeches. Although he lived a little later than my book is set I could not resist using the name of such an interesting sounding character. Most of the names such as Silkbeard, Hairy-Breeches etc are genuine Viking names. I have merely transported them all into one book. I also amended some of my names- I used Eric in the earlier books and it should have been Erik. I have now changed the later editions of the first two books in the series.

Eardwulf was king of Northumbria twice: first from 796-806 and from 808-810. The king who deposed him was Elfwald II. This period was a turbulent one for the kings of Northumbria and marked a decline in their fortunes until it was taken over by the Danes in 867. This was the time of power for Mercia and East Anglia. Coenwulf ruled East Anglia and his son Cynhelm, Mercia. Wessex had yet to rise.

Bothvar Bjarki was a famous berserker and the Klak brothers did exist. I did not make either name up! Guthrum was also a Dane who lived in East Anglia. Seguin I Lupo was Duke of Vasconia which broke away from the Empire briefly at the start of the ninth century.

Slavery was far more common in the ancient world. When the Normans finally made England their own they showed that they understood the power of words and propaganda by making the slaves into serfs. This was a brilliant strategy as it forced their former slaves to provide their own food whilst still working for their lords and masters for nothing. Manumission was possible as Garth showed in the first book in this series. Scanlan's training is also a sign that not all of the slaves suffered. It was a hard and cruel time- it was ruled by the strong.

The word 'testify' comes from Anglo-Saxon. A man would clutch his testicles and swear that the evidence he was giving was the truth. If it was not then he would lose his testicles. There was more truth in the Anglo Saxon courts than there is these days!

The Vikings did use trickery when besieging their enemies and would use any means possible. They did not have siege weapons and had to rely on guile and courage to prevail. The siege of Paris in 845 A.D. was one such example.

The Isle of Man(n) is reputed to have the earliest surviving Parliament, the Tynwald although there is evidence that there were others amongst the Viking colonies on Orkney and in Iceland. I have used this idea for Prince Butar's meetings of Jarls.

The blue stone they treasure is aquamarine or beryl. It is found in granite. The rocks around the Mawddach are largely granite and although I have no evidence of beryl being found there, I have used the idea of a small deposit being found to tie the story together.

There was a famous witch who lived on one of the islands of Scilly. According to Norse legend Olaf Tryggvasson, who became King Olaf 1 of Norway, visited her. She told him that if he converted to Christianity then he would become king of Norway.

The early ninth century saw Britain converted to Christianity and there were many monasteries which flourished. These were often mixed. These were not the huge stone edifices such as Whitby and Fountain's Abbey; these were wooden structures. As such their remains have disappeared, along with the bones of those early Christian priests. Hexham was a major monastery in the early Saxon period. I do not know it they had warriors to protect the priests but having given them a treasure to watch over I thought that some warriors might be useful too.

I use Roman forts in all of my books. Although we now see ruins when they were abandoned the only things which would have been damaged would have been the gates. Anything of value would have been buried in case they wished to return. By 'of value' I do not mean coins but things such as nails and weapons. Many of these objects have been discovered. A large number of the forts were abandoned in a hurry. Hardknott fort, for example, was built in the 120s but abandoned twenty or so years later. When the Antonine Wall was abandoned in the 180s Hardknott was reoccupied until Roman soldiers finally withdrew from northern Britain. I think that, until the late Saxon period and early Norman period, there would have been many forts which would have looked habitable. The Vikings and the Saxons did not build in stone. It was only when the castle builders, the Normans, arrived that stone would be robbed from Roman forts and those defences destroyed by an invader who was in the minority. The Vikings also liked to move their homes every few years; this was, perhaps, only a few miles, but it explains how difficult it is to find the remains of early Viking settlements.

The Isle of Man(n) was one of the first places settled by Norsemen. The names on the island reflect their long Viking history. The world's first parliament, the Tynewald was held there. The Calf of Man is a small island off the south western coast. The three legs of Man which makes up their flag still came from an early Jarl on the island. I have used Jarl Erik as that warrior. It is, of course, fiction of my own creation.

The place names are accurate and the mountain above Coniston is called the Old Man. The river is not navigable up to Windermere but I have allowed my warriors to carry their drekar as the Vikings did in the land of the Rus when travelling to Miklagård. The ninth century saw the beginning of the reign of the Viking. They raided Spain, the Rhone, Africa, and even Constantinople. They believed they could beat anyone!

There was a King Egbert who did indeed triumph over King Coenwulf. He founded the power base upon which Alfred the Great built. It was also at this time that the Danes came to take over East Anglia and Yorkshire. The land became, over the next 50 years, Danelaw. Its expansion was only halted by Alfred and was finally destroyed when King Harold defeated his brother and King Harald Hadrada at Stamford Bridge in 1066. Until Alfred the Danes were used as hired swords. They fought for gold.

I have made up Elfrida and Egbert's marriage to her but the kings of that time had many liaisons with many women. Some kings sired up to twenty illegitimate children and many legitimate ones. The practice continued into the late middle ages. Wives were frequently taken for political reasons. The inspiration for the abduction comes from the story of the Welsh Princess Nest (Nesta) who, in the

12th century had two children by King Henry 1st and was then married to one of his friends. She was abducted by a Welsh knight who lived with her until her husband recaptured her and killed her abductor. Harald Klak became King of Denmark in 826 but I made up his brother.

The Danish raids on the east coast began in the late 700s. However the west coast and Hibernian were raided by Norse and Rus warriors who also went on to settle Iceland. There is less recorded evidence of their raids, attacks and settlements. The records we have are the Anglo Saxon Chronicles and they tend to focus on the south and east of what was England. The land that is now the lake District was disputed land between Northumbria and Strathclyde however the Norse influence on the language and its proximity to the Isle of man and Dublin make me think that the Norse there would not have been part of what would become Danelaw.

I used the following books for research

    British Museum - 'Vikings- Life and Legends'
    'Saxon, Norman and Viking' by Terence Wise (Osprey)
    Ian Heath - 'The Vikings'. (Osprey)
    Ian Heath- 'Byzantine Armies 668-1118 (Osprey)
    David Nicholle- 'Romano-Byzantine Armies 4th-9th Century (Osprey)
    Stephen Turnbull- 'The Walls of Constantinople AD 324-1453' (Osprey)
    Keith Durham- 'Viking Longship' (Osprey)
    Anglo-Danish Project- 'The Vikings in England'

Griff Hosker November 2015

Other books by Griff Hosker

If you enjoyed reading this book, then why not read another one by the author?

Ancient History
The Sword of Cartimandua Series (Germania and Britannia 50A.D. – 128 A.D.)
Ulpius Felix- Roman Warrior (prequel)
Book 1 The Sword of Cartimandua
Book 2 The Horse Warriors
Book 3 Invasion Caledonia
Book 4 Roman Retreat
Book 5 Revolt of the Red Witch
Book 6 Druid's Gold
Book 7 Trajan's Hunters
Book 8 The Last Frontier
Book 9 Hero of Rome
Book 10 Roman Hawk
Book 11 Roman Treachery
Book 12 Roman Wall
Book 13 Roman Courage

The Aelfraed Series (Britain and Byzantium 1050 A.D. - 1085 A.D.
Book 1 Housecarl
Book 2 Outlaw
Book 3 Varangian

The Wolf Warrior series (Britain in the 6th-7th Centuries)
Book 1 Saxon Dawn
Book 2 Saxon Revenge
Book 3 Saxon England
Book 4 Saxon Blood
Book 5 Saxon Slayer
Book 6 Saxon Slaughter
Book 7 Saxon Bane
Book 8 Saxon Fall: Rise of the Warlord
Book 9 Saxon Throne
Book 10 Saxon Sword

The Dragon Heart Series
Book 1 Viking Slave
Book 2 Viking Warrior
Book 3 Viking Jarl

Book 4 Viking Kingdom
Book 5 Viking Wolf
Book 6 Viking War
Book 7 Viking Sword
Book 8 Viking Wrath
Book 9 Viking Raid
Book 10 Viking Legend
Book 11 Viking Vengeance
Book 12 Viking Dragon
Book 13 Viking Treasure
Book 14 Viking Enemy
Book 15 Viking Witch
Book 16 Viking Blood
Book 17 Viking Weregeld
Book 18 Viking Storm
Book 19 Viking Warband
Book 20 Viking Shadow

The Norman Genesis Series
Hrolf the Viking
Horseman
The Battle for a Home
Revenge of the Franks
The Land of the Northmen
Ragnvald Hrolfsson
Brothers in Blood
Lord of Rouen
Drekar in the Seine

The Anarchy Series England 1120-1180
English Knight
Knight of the Empress
Northern Knight
Baron of the North
Earl
King Henry's Champion
The King is Dead
Warlord of the North
Enemy at the Gate
Warlord's War
Kingmaker
Henry II
Crusader
The Welsh Marches
Irish War

Poisonous Plots
The Princes' Revolt

Border Knight 1182-1300
Sword for Hire
Return of the Knight
Baron's War
Magna Carta

Modern History
The Napoleonic Horseman Series
Book 1 Chasseur a Cheval
Book 2 Napoleon's Guard
Book 3 British Light Dragoon
Book 4 Soldier Spy
Book 5 1808: The Road to Corunna
Waterloo

The Lucky Jack American Civil War series
Rebel Raiders
Confederate Rangers
The Road to Gettysburg

The British Ace Series
1914
1915 Fokker Scourge
1916 Angels over the Somme
1917 Eagles Fall
1918 We will remember them
From Arctic Snow to Desert Sand
Wings over Persia

Combined Operations series 1940-1945
Commando
Raider
Behind Enemy Lines
Dieppe
Toehold in Europe
Sword Beach
Breakout
The Battle for Antwerp
King Tiger
Beyond the Rhine

Other Books

Carnage at Cannes (a thriller)
Great Granny's Ghost (Aimed at 9-14-year-old young people)
Adventure at 63-Backpacking to Istanbul

For more information on all of the books then please visit the author's web site at http://www.griffhosker.com where there is a link to contact him or you can Tweet him @HoskerGriff

Printed in Great Britain
by Amazon